MY BUDDY GAVE ME A
STARSHIP

MY BUDDY'S STARSHIP
BOOK 1

MY BUDDY GAVE ME A STARSHIP

MYLES CHRISTENSEN

MOON ZOOM PRESS

Copyright © 2024 by Myles Christensen

All rights reserved.

No portion of this book may be reproduced in any form without written permission from the publisher or author, except as permitted by U.S. copyright law.

For my wife:
All the stories are for you, though you might not like them all equally. ;)

Chapter One

I wasn't even at work half an hour before my world came crashing down.

Walking along the factory floor—trying to get back to my assembly station before anyone noticed—I happened to run into my boss, Tim, the plant manager at Armada Avionics.

"Mitch, let's go visit in my office," Tim said.

"Sure," I said with a nod. I thought it was strange that he didn't say something brusk or end the request with the word "pronto" like he usually did.

I walked at his side through the rows and rows of machinery laid out in perfect lines in the sprawling factory. Without meaning to, I ticked off the products as we passed—that one made butterfly valves for the F-22 engine, that one was set up for the pressure regulator on the pilot's suit for the F-35, and the group of machines against the wall churned out the housings for the heads-up-display projector that the Air Force used on several different aircraft.

Everywhere I looked, there were pieces of airplanes—or what would become airplanes.

As we passed through the doors into the office suite attached to the factory, the aircraft theme continued. Walls and doors in almost every room were plastered with posters of fighter jets, helicopters, and stunt planes. Pretty much everyone who worked at Armada Avionics was passionate about airplanes and flight, and I had to admit that I could have been the poster boy.

Once inside Tim's office, he walked around his industrial-looking desk and collapsed into his chair, letting out a long breath. "Close the door and have a seat, will you?" he said.

Now I knew something was up.

I settled awkwardly into the chair across the desk from him. It wasn't like I hadn't sat in this chair dozens—even hundreds—of times before. Tim had been my boss for the last three years, and I frequently came to his office when I had questions. He'd helped me move from intern to technician to, most recently, machine operator.

"What's going on, Tim?" I asked warily.

He let out another long sigh, making his ample gut heave up and down. He ran a hand through what was left of the hair on top of his head then looked me straight in the eye. "Mitch, I don't know how to say this, but I have to let you go."

I felt like a two-ton metal press had just been dropped on my chest. "What?! Why?"

Tim scrubbed his hand across his face. "I've tried to give you a chance in this new position, but it's just not going to work."

"But I've been getting better," I said.

Tim nodded. "That's true. You've improved. But the higher-ups just don't think it's enough. You've fallen short on all your performance metrics for the last three months."

"I thought you said I would have six months to hit those," I complained.

"They might have given you six months except for the mistakes."

"Those were accidents, Tim." I paused. "You said they wouldn't be held against me."

Tim shrugged his meaty shoulders. "I guess when an accident costs the company a 9.3 million dollar contract..."

I sat back in my chair as the reality sunk in. After a few moments, I asked, "Can I have a second chance? Now that I know what I did wrong, can I try and make it right?"

The sadness in Tim's eyes told me the answer even before he opened his mouth. "Sorry, Mitch, I did already ask them that. Bottom line is, they've just run out of patience."

I gazed through the window at the cars parked outside. The walk out to my car at the end of the day always represented freedom in my mind.

The prospect of walking out there right now felt less like freedom and more like sky-diving without a parachute.

I turned my attention back to my boss—no, former boss. "So that's it then?"

"I can have Shannon give you some paperwork for filing unemployment, if you want to go that route." Tim looked genuinely sad about the situation. "I'm sorry, Mitch. I wish there was more that I could do."

I took a deep breath and stood. "It's okay, Tim. Thanks for trying." I stuck out my hand to him.

Tim took my hand, nodding his acknowledgement to my words. "Maybe I'll see you around."

I let out a short laugh as I turned to leave his office. "Maybe."

Five minutes later, I peeled out the tires of my Dodge Charger as I rocketed from the parking lot. I realized it was childish, but I didn't care. After a few turns, I was back on the main road of our small central-Oklahoma town. At the speed I was going, I'd be through the town in forty-eight seconds—assuming I hit all three lights green. Either that, or I'd be sitting on the shoulder of the road explaining to Ross, the town deputy, why I was in such a hurry.

I lifted my foot off the gas. No need to add to my problems.

I'm not sure how many times I drove up and down the main drag, but I eventually decided that without a steady job anymore, I couldn't afford to waste money on gas.

I pulled into my regular parking spot at Bob's Burgers about thirty minutes before I normally would have. It was convenient that I'd gotten fired on a Thursday because that meant I wouldn't have to wait long to tell Gabe. Thursday was the weekly lunch and vent session with my best friend.

When I walked into the burger joint, Sissy was there, just like she always was on Thursdays at lunch. She didn't even bother showing me to my table. Gabe and I were such regulars that she never had to show us to our booth. We knew where to go. One of Sissy's brows went up when she saw me there so early.

She came straight over to my table. "How y'all doing today, Mitch?" She said it in a way that made it sound like she was expecting me to not be doing well.

Well, she was right on that one.

"I'm just a little early today, Sis. I'm sure Gabe'll get here soon."

"Okay, you just wanna hang out until he gets here?" Her gum chewing pace was a little faster than normal. Maybe my abnormal behavior was making her nervous.

"Sure," I said morosely. "Actually, on second thought, bring me an apple pie a la mode, hold the apple pie."

Sissy sighed. "Large bowl of ice cream. Got it," she said with an empathetic tone. Then she turned and walked back to the kitchen. She may have paused and looked back at me, but I wasn't really paying attention.

By the time Gabe finally got there and made his way back to our table, I had already finished two large bowls of ice cream, and my mood was only marginally better.

"Hey, Mitch. What's up?" Gabe asked as he slid into the booth across from me.

I looked across the table at my best friend since kindergarten, not surprised that he would sense something was wrong. He would have known even if I didn't have my third, half-empty bowl of ice cream in front of me.

Growing up, we had been inseparable to the point that people had started getting us confused. We never understood why. Our names—Mitch and Gabe—didn't sound anything alike. And we didn't look like each other, either. We were about the same height—a little over six feet—but I was stout while Gabe was lean. My hair was more on the blond side, his was more on the brown side. My eyes were green, his were blue.

"You know, I'm not sure my life is going the way I thought it would. It might be time to mix things up a little," I said to my buddy as I motioned Sissy back to our table.

Gabe nodded slowly, scrutinizing me with a look of suspicion. "You want to go on a trip to the Bahamas or something?"

I laughed. "Not a bad idea. But I'm going to start with changing my regular order." I turned to Sissy. "Hey Sis, today I think I'll try the double onion cheeseburger with extra onion."

"I thought you hated onions," she replied.

"Maybe I'm ready for something different," I said proudly as I handed the menu back to her.

Gabe eyed me. "That's probably an easier way to mix things up than a trip." He turned to Sissy. "I'll just have my usual, thanks Sissy."

Sissy smiled, chewing on her gum all the while. "I'll have those out for y'all in a jif."

A few moments of awkward silence passed after she left. Gabe continued to stare me down while I pretended nothing was out of the ordinary—except a new burger choice and a bowl of ice cream. I knew I'd eventually have to tell him what happened with my job—I could never keep a secret like that from my best friend. But I wasn't quite ready.

"Now that you mention it," I began, "maybe a trip to the Bahamas or Hawaii or Italy is just the thing I need to get things back on track."

"I didn't know things were off track," Gabe said dryly.

I shrugged. "I might need to think about where my life is going. Maybe a fancy trip somewhere will help me get some perspective."

Gabe nodded. "Yeah, that's a great idea. I'm sure you've saved up enough vacation days at Armada. Don't they let you carry those over from year to year?"

At the mention of my job, I scowled. "I'm not sure that job at Armada was right for me. I never felt like it was taking me in the right direction."

Gabe's brows knit as he stared across the table at me. "You said 'was'." He glanced down at the empty bowl, suddenly piecing together why I had arrived early and been eating ice cream. "Did something happen at work?"

"I made one little mistake, and they decided to fire me."

"Was it the time you were learning to run the new milling machine, and you cut a gouge in the mounting vice?"

I frowned. "No."

"Was it the time you accidentally knocked the fire extinguisher off the wall and made a huge mess in the break room?" Gabe's sense of humor was coming through now.

"Funny," I said. "So two—I guess three—little mistakes and they kick me to the curb?"

"Oh, I have more," Gabe quipped.

I gave him a look that said I wasn't in the mood.

He held his hands out in surrender. We stared at the table in silence for a moment. "I'm sorry, man," Gabe said finally.

"Whatever," I said, waving away his condolences. "You know what? I'm glad they fired me. This is just the thing I need to get me heading in the right direction." I pounded my fist on the table.

Gabe chuckled at my enthusiasm. I leaned against the high-back bench and considered my friend. I could feel some of my indignation easing.

"You remember when we were in junior high and high school, and we wanted to grow up to be fighter pilots or astronauts?" I said.

Gabe laughed. "Don't remind me. It cost five hundred bucks to sign up for that online flight training, and we didn't even get our pilot's licenses."

I smiled at the memory of Gabe begging the flight school to refund us the money after being assigned to an eccentric eighty-year-old flight instructor with bad eyesight.

"What about that trip to Huntsville for Space Camp?" Gabe said. "That wasn't cheap either."

"Hey, I used the inheritance money for that one," I shot back.

Gabe shrugged. "It was still expensive."

We fell silent as we usually did when talking about either of our parents. I found the years had dulled the pain of their passing, at least for me. "Money well spent, I say."

"Don't forget the week-long boot camp you roped me into," Gabe said with a grin.

"Oh yeah. That was when we thought we wanted to be Green Berets or Navy SEALs."

"*You* wanted to," Gabe corrected. "I was just trying to be supportive."

I laughed. "Oh, come on, I'm sure you enjoyed the survival training." I knew it was the part he had hated the most.

Gabe just shook his head. "I'm an insurance agent, Mitch. When am I ever going to need to survive for a week in the forest with only a sharp stick?" He grinned. "Now, the hand-to-hand combat might come in handy. You know how my clients can get sometimes."

I leaned forward and lowered my voice. "That's just it, don't you see? We had such high hopes for what we would do when we grew up."

"Yeah," Gabe agreed with a wry smile. "And then we grew up and became responsible adults."

Sissy brought our food over and we both dug into our meals. The onion burger wasn't half bad, but I knew I would regret it later.

After a few minutes, I set my half-eaten burger down and looked up at Gabe. "I'm just not sure where my life is going anymore. I mean, is this where you thought we'd be in our thirties?" I held my arms wide to indicate the table, the diner, pretty much everything. "Still here in this small town, not doing what we hoped. Working dead-end jobs."

"Hey," Gabe objected.

"Or not working a job at all, dead-end or otherwise." I pointed at myself, trying to ease the sting of my rant. "I thought I would have started a new business, or moved up the corporate ladder, or won the lottery, or something." My brow furrowed as I thought about it. Maybe I hadn't set very good goals for my life, after all.

We sat in silence, staring at each other for several moments. Gabe nodded knowingly. "Believe me, Mitch, my life definitely didn't go the direction I thought it would." His gaze drifted to the back wall where Bob, the owner, cook, and chief bottle-washer, let some of his favorite, most loyal customers hang pictures of themselves and sign them like they were celebrities.

Immediately, I knew which picture he was looking at, and my stomach felt like a brick.

In the middle of that wall hung a picture of three incredibly loyal customers, huddled close together, arms around each other, smiling and waving to the camera. A younger version of me, a younger version of

Gabe. And right next to Gabe—a few inches shorter, with long red hair, brown eyes, and in all of her youth and vitality—Gabe's wife, Tera.

Gabe and Tera were high school sweethearts, and they had married just a few years after we all graduated. That picture on the wall of the three of us had been taken when they were newlyweds, while they still thought they had their whole lives ahead of them.

Before the cancer.

Before the months of painful treatments.

Less than a year later, she was gone.

I let out a long breath. "Dude, I'm sorry for rambling like this. Losing my job is nothing compared to losing Tera."

Gabe tore his attention from the picture on the wall to look back at me. Even though it had been over ten years, he was usually pretty sad when talk of Tera came up. I couldn't blame him. He grows up with the love of his life, finally convinces her to marry him, and bam, he loses it all.

He shrugged off my apology. "No problem, man. I understand. Besides, it's not like I get the corner on the market for grief just because I lost my wife." His voice sounded tight at the end.

"Yeah, but I was still being a jerk."

We both looked away, staring at nothing in particular for several moments.

"It does get a little easier with time," Gabe said quietly,

I watched him as he spoke. The sadness was still there, but I could see something else there, too. There was something in his eyes that looked hopeful.

Almost like a spark.

I was about to ask him—as tactfully as possible—if he had started thinking about dating other women.

But before I could ask, Gabe said, "Why don't you come over to my place tomorrow?" There was definitely a gleam in Gabe's eye now. Something mischievous. "I have something I want to show you."

I raised a brow. "Something I'll like?"

Gabe nodded slowly and deliberately. "Oh yeah. You'll like it."

I shrugged. "Sure. Why not? I'm obviously not doing anything tomorrow." I cast him a sidelong glance. "Except planning a trip to the Bahamas."

Gabe grinned back at me. "Hold off on that plan for now."

I wasn't in any rush to get over to Gabe's house the next afternoon. After all, I was unemployed and suddenly had no reason to wake up at the crack of dawn. Well, except for the normal reasons that a person wakes up each day—food and a bathroom. I jumped in my Charger and drove out of town, along the small country highway, until I reached the dirt road to Gabe's farm.

I had once made fun of Gabe that he was just a hobby farmer. He had inherited the place when his parents passed away a few years ago. Gabe's grandfather had grown alfalfa and hay, but Gabe wasn't really interested in the regular crops. He happily let his neighbor take over the management of those fields when he asked. Instead, Gabe was completely obsessed with his watermelons. He tiptoed through the patch of vines every day, measuring sizes, tapping the melons, checking the coloring. It was quite comical, actually.

Fortunately, Gabe's insurance agency was well managed, and it gave him the freedom to have a flexible Friday here and there. I pulled up into the long drive of his farm and parked the Charger next to his SUV.

Gabe opened the front door before I even had a chance to knock. "Let's head out back," he said immediately.

I could tell there was a bounce in his step as we walked around the modest rancher through his backyard and over toward the large red barn.

"It's an interesting coincidence that you've been remembering our dreams of being astronauts or test pilots because I've been thinking about that lately, too," Gabe said. "And I've got something I've been meaning to show you." He motioned with a hand toward the barn.

I laughed. "What did you do? Steal a top-secret fighter jet?"

Gabe forced a laugh. "It doesn't count as stealing if it landed on my property, does it?"

That was a weird question to ask, unless he really did have a fighter jet inside his barn.

Instead of grabbing the barn door, Gabe stopped and put a hand on my shoulder. He stared straight at me, deadly serious. "You have to promise not to freak out."

I tilted my head. "You're sorta freaking me out just by asking me not to freak out," I said. "Gabe, what could you possibly have in the barn that would freak me out? You're the most law-abiding citizen I know. Besides, I'm your best friend. If you needed me to get rid of a body, I'd help you get rid of a body."

Gabe's eyes flitted toward his pecan grove, but he seemed to relax after that. "Okay, but don't say I didn't warn you."

He grabbed the handle of the huge barn door, gave me one more mischievous look over his shoulder, then threw it open wide.

I stood there looking up at something that had no right to even exist.

Crammed into the cavernous space of Gabe's giant barn was a metal monstrosity that my brain just refused to process. "Is that . . ."

Gabe chuckled. "Yeah."

"But how in the world?" I took a tentative step forward then glanced at Gabe.

"It's safe," he said. "I've been working on it for a few weeks now."

I released a long breath. I'd seen some pretty cool aircraft in museums, but nothing this advanced or up close. I stepped past Gabe and began circling the giant craft. At first glance, it looked like a cross between the old space shuttle design and some advanced attack helicopter. The body was twice as long as it was wide, and all the edges were round and smooth, almost tear-drop-like, with no flat surfaces anywhere. And there weren't any real wings, just a pair of wing stubs with weapons pylons on the ends.

It had to be one of the next generation attack jets that I had heard rumors about. But it was closer in size to a bomber than a fighter jet. It had three massive landing struts that crouched low on the dirt floor like they were ready to pounce. Most of the craft was a grayish-silver, like a brushed nickel but with a sheen that sort of reflected other colors.

I came around to the front of the ship and stared up at the gleaming cockpit looming ten feet over my head. Just below the leading edge of the nose, a broad section of the hull with a slightly different surface texture caught my attention. I stepped up and touched the discolored area. No seams or weld lines, just a slight difference in the reflectivity.

"You like my patch job?" Gabe called out.

"You did this?" I pointed to the spot. "It's amazing."

Gabe smiled. "That's where it crash-landed."

I stepped back and surveyed the plane. "I can't believe an attack jet crashed on your farm."

He scowled at me. "Attack jet?"

The expression on his face made me think I might have missed something.

"This is a spaceship!" he declared.

"A spaceship?!"

"Yes. It's certainly not some little attack jet."

"This is a spaceship?" I repeated.

Gabe nodded solemnly.

I gaped at Gabe. "Is this some sort of trick?" I asked, searching around the walls of the barn for hidden cameras. "You're not trying to get famous on one of those prank shows, are you?"

Gabe smiled and shook his head.

I stared at the giant ship filling his oversized barn. I had to admit that his explanation would make much more sense. It did sort of look like a spaceship, after all. And I had heard about the government's research in hypersonic orbital vehicles. This was even cooler than an attack jet.

I held my hand up. "Hang on. You're telling me a spaceship crash-landed on your farm?"

Gabe nodded.

"Where?"

He pointed toward the back corner of his property.

"When?" I asked.

"Last month."

My eyes went wide. "A month?! A spaceship crashed on your property a month ago and you didn't tell me?"

Gabe scratched his head, looking apologetic. "I was going to."

"When? Next year?" I asked sarcastically. I couldn't help being a little hurt.

Gabe didn't reply, but I could tell he felt bad. My annoyance only lasted a few seconds.

"Wait a minute. If it crashed a month ago, how do you not have government agents swarming all over this place?"

"I'm sure this thing has advanced stealth technology," he said with a shrug. "Plus, it crashed in the middle of the night, and you know how far out in the country we are."

I frowned. "Yeah, but wouldn't the government be missing it by now? I'm sure they're scouring the area where it went down."

A smirk spread across Gabe's face. "I never said it was a government spaceship."

I scowled at him. "What do you mean? Is it Chinese? Russian?"

Gabe shook his head and pointed his finger straight up.

"From God?" I asked, a little afraid of what the answer might be.

Gabe laughed. "No. From outer space."

I looked at the ship then at Gabe then back at the ship again. "No way."

"I promise you, this spaceship is not from our planet," he said confidently.

You're telling me an alien spaceship crash-landed in your alfalfa field? Then what happened? You checked out a book from the library on how to repair flying saucers and you just got to work?"

Gabe laughed. "It's okay that you don't believe me. I barely believe it myself, and I've seen more than you have."

I gave him a skeptical look. "Like what?"

"The alien pilot," Gabe said bluntly. My eyes must have bugged out of my skull at this point. "He was already dead when I found him," he quickly added.

"You saw an alien?!" I shook my head emphatically. "No. No, there's no way. This is nuts."

Gabe shrugged. "I can show you where I buried him."

I stared at Gabe. We had known each other since we were five years old. We had gotten into and out of a lot of scrapes together. We'd bent the truth a few times to get out of groundings and whoopins.

But through all that, Gabe had never lied to me. Ever.

"Wow," was all I could manage.

Gabe nodded in agreement.

We stood staring at each other for several seconds.

Finally, Gabe said, "D'you want to see inside?"

I smiled broadly. "Uh, yeah."

He waved for me to follow. We walked around the bulky, low-slung hull toward the rear of the ship. The back end was much broader than the nose. It looked almost like the tail of a cargo plane. Gabe stepped up and touched a small recessed spot next to a seam in the metal. It must have been some sort of biometric reader because immediately a tall ramp lowered down in front of us.

As it settled onto the dusty floor with a reverberating thud, I stared up into a large cargo hold. Shelves and cabinets lined the walls of the wide bay with dozens of crates stacked in rows in the space between. Several of the containers stood open, their lids lying to the side.

"Go ahead," Gabe nodded, urging me forward.

I stepped onto the ramp and moved inside what Gabe had assured me was an alien spaceship. The items around me looked completely normal and yet completely foreign at the same time. Several tools lay scattered on the metal floor of the cargo bay. I easily recognized the earthly tools—probably from Gabe's garage—but the other implements didn't even look remotely like the stuff I could get at the local hardware store. I couldn't even begin to guess what the two-handled implement with the long snout was for. It could have been a ray gun as far as I knew.

I turned a circle inside the ample cargo area—easily as large as a comfortable living room—and gaped at everything as the reality sunk in.

"This is a real spaceship?" I asked.

"Yep," Gabe replied with a grin. "But if you get this excited about the boring part, you're going to lose your mind when we get to the good stuff."

"There's more?!" I gestured for him to lead the way. We walked to the other end of the cargo bay and through a large door that opened into a short hall running perpendicular to the main body of the ship. Gabe pointed at several doors on the opposite side of the hall. "Those are just more storage and a few of the ship's systems." He pointed at a round hatch at the far end of the hall. "And I think that's an airlock in case you need to leave the ship while you're in space."

I nodded mutely, still not completely sure this could be real. Space? That was the stuff of sci-fi movies.

Gabe indicated a set of rungs built into the hull on the end of the hall opposite the airlock. "These lead up to the upper deck."

"Ooh, a two-story spaceship? Aren't you uppity?"

Gabe laughed as he climbed the ladder to the top deck. I stepped off the ladder and found myself in a very clean-looking open kitchen and living area. Metal deck plating covered the floors, and light-gray walls with storage compartments mounted every few feet surrounded what looked like a little kitchenette—assuming such a thing existed on spaceships. In the middle of the kitchen, there was a table with attached benches. And opposite the kitchen there was a set of furniture that I could have sworn looked like a sofa and loveseat.

"Are you telling me aliens nap, too?" I quipped. Gabe must have dragged these into the ship as a joke. How universal could the afternoon nap really be?

With a glance at the couches, Gabe smiled. "Actually, I'd say they're masters."

I walked over to the sofa and stared down at it. The surface looked like polished metal or maybe plastic; it was hard to say.

"Try it out," Gabe said.

I eyed him, but he clearly wasn't worried about my safety, so I turned my attention back to the couch. As I sat down in the middle, I was struck by the feel of the surface. I had expected something cold, like a metal park bench. But it was slightly warm, more like a heated blanket. And the material had a slight give to it. I swung my feet up on one end and leaned my head back against the other. The warmth remained, and the material's pliancy increased. I sunk at least three inches into it, which would have been a scary experience if it hadn't felt so incredibly comfortable. The material molded to the shape of my body all the way from my head to my feet. It felt like being cradled in a cloud.

"I don't have to see anything else. I'm sold," I said.

"Don't get too comfortable. I've saved the best for last," Gabe replied.

I opened one eye and squinted at him. I could tell from his excitement that there really was something better to see. Reluctantly, I stood and walked back toward him. His attention was on the single door that seemed like it would connect to the cockpit of the ship.

Gabe walked forward, gesturing for me to follow, and touched a panel next to the door.

The door slid open sideways to reveal what looked like a control room with a wide, curved canopy spanning three sides. I could see the rafters of the barn just feet from the top of the ship's hull.

"This is the flight deck," Gabe said, a wry grin on his face.

Suddenly, something in the corner of the room moved. I jumped and so did my heart—into my throat.

A woman walked toward us.

I blinked several times to make sure I wasn't seeing things.

It was Tera.

Gabe's dead wife.

"Tera?" I said softly.

"Hi, Mitch," she replied with her characteristic, reluctant wave.

My mouth must have been hanging open.

"Pretty realistic, isn't she?" Gabe said.

As my brain recovered from the hiccup—and I got a better look at her—something seemed off. She had the same tall, slim frame and long red hair—much longer than she had during her cancer treatments. This wasn't the twenty-something newlywed Tera. She looked way younger than when I had last seen her, more like the Tera I knew from high school. And I noticed a shimmering texture to her fair skin. In fact, she didn't seem to be entirely there because I could still sort of see the controls of the flight deck behind her.

Maybe the spaceship could communicate with spirits. The absurdity of that thought snapped me out of my initial shock. "What's going on here?" I asked, turning to Gabe.

He chuckled, clearly amused at my reaction. "This is Tera." he said, sweeping a hand toward the shimmery figure in front of us.

"Right. Ghost-Tera," I deadpanned.

Gabe scratched his head. "Actually, she's more like AI-Tera."

"What. She's the computer?" I asked.

"Excuse me." She cocked her head in exactly the same way as Gabe's wife always did when she was annoyed. "I'm not the *computer*." She said the last word as if she had a bad taste in her mouth. "I'm the artificial intelligence matrix built into the Mark 7 Advanced Long-Range Tactical Strike Craft."

"Hoo, boy." Gabe shook his head. "She does *not* like to be confused with the computer. I made that mistake a few weeks ago."

I shook my head, trying to clear the confusion. "A spaceship—pre-programmed with your wife's appearance and personality—just happened to crash land on your little farm. Doesn't that seem a little suspicious to you?"

"The *Starfire* didn't come with Tera's personality. I did that part while I was working on it," he replied.

"*Starfire*?" I repeated.

"This particular model of the Mark 7 is called the *Infinite Supernova Starfire*, roughly translated," AI-Tera explained. "But my sweetie, Gabe, likes to call it the *Starfire*."

"The whole name's too much of a mouthful," Gabe said.

"And why does she look and act like a teenage version of your wife?" I asked.

AI-Tera put a hand on her hip and cocked her head to the side. "I'm standing right here, Mitch. I know your mama taught you better manners than to talk about someone right in front of them."

"Sorry," I said.

She nodded in satisfaction.

Gabe took a breath and glanced at AI-Tera. "Let's start at the beginning, and we'll try to explain everything. Right pumpkin?" He used his pet name for Tera, and she beamed.

It was uncanny seeing Gabe interact with his wife, who had been dead for over ten years. It would have been even more strange watching a guy in his mid thirties acting cute with a teenager, except that I had seen them act like this when they were both teenagers, and it didn't seem weird to me at all. They had always been sappy; they still were.

I tried to shake that idea loose. They were still sappy because Tera was standing right in front of me. Sort of.

Gabe must have seen my struggle, because he jumped straight into the explanation.

"About a month ago, I was out in the alfalfa fields early one morning when I saw smoke coming from the edge of the woods. When I got there, I found the ship"—he held his arms wide—"at the end of a quarter-mile, still-burning, gouge in the dirt. The nose section was completely beat up from the impact, but amazingly, the ship was still intact."

I shook my head in disbelief. "A spaceship crashed in your field. That's unbelievable."

"Yeah," Gabe replied. "Some mornings I would wake up and wonder if I'd dreamed it all, but then I'd see the ship still here in the barn." He held a hand up. "But I'm getting ahead of myself. It took me a while to figure out how to get inside the ship, particularly with the damage to the hull. After a few hours of prying and pulling, I finally got the cargo door open. As I was exploring the ship, I found the pilot here." He pointed at the seat in front of me.

"Dead?" I asked.

Gabe nodded. "Probably from the crash."

"What did he look like?" I scowled as I considered my next question. "And what did you do with the body?"

"Except for a slightly different skin tone and an odd color to his hair, he looked almost human. I buried him near the ravine out past the pecan grove." He thumbed over his shoulder.

I looked over at AI-Tera, wondering if she had anything to add to the story.

"I don't remember any of this. My systems were offline."

"But how did your wife end up in the computer?" I asked.

AI-Tera leaned forward, glaring at me. "Artificial. Intelligence. Matrix." She said each word slowly, as if I was a small child.

"Be patient. I'm gettin' to that part," Gabe said. "So, I dug the ship out and tried to drag it back to the barn with my tractor. I couldn't get it to budge an inch until I reactivated the ship's systems."

"This is the part I remember. When Gabe turned everything on, my matrix had been reset to the very basic interface with no personality." AI-Tera gave a slight shudder.

"The hologram was a generic guy in a black jumpsuit called Dack. He had stiff manners and no sense of humor," Gabe added.

"Don't remind me," AI-Tera said.

"But he was glitchy. Apparently, the computer and the AI matrix had both been damaged so badly that nothing was really functioning right. The AI was forced to initiate a full rebuild of the system. When the interface came back online, it asked me to enter the customization parameters for the AI's appearance and personality." At this point, Gabe gave me a guilty smile. "Sort of as a joke, I gave it Tera's description."

I glanced at the hologram of Tera. "That's amazingly true-to-life for just a description."

"We didn't get it right on the first try," AI-Tera said with a giggling laugh.

"But even our first try was better than the default." Gabe smiled at her, a look of nostalgia in his eyes. He turned back to me to continue his explanation. "After we got the hover emitters operational, I hooked up the tractor and dragged the ship to the barn."

I guess Gabe's oversized barn had finally come in handy. I looked around at the advanced technology evident on the walls and control panels of the flight deck, and I didn't doubt that there was some pretty amazing stuff that the ship could do.

"After that, Tera and I worked on getting the ship fixed up," Gabe said as if that were the end of the story.

"I helped Gabe figure out how to use the ship's repair systems, and he helped me get a real personality." AI-Tera looked at Gabe with loving adoration.

"Which brings us back to my original question," I said. "How do you have the personality of teenage-Tera?"

She shrugged. "That's just what Gabe put in my matrix."

I turned to Gabe, hoping for a better explanation.

Gabe rubbed the back of his neck. "I know it was probably a silly idea, sorta like going back through old photo albums of someone you've lost, but I thought it would be nice to have a familiar face around while I was working on the ship."

"I don't mean programming her to be Tera; I think that's great." My best friend had lost his wife. I wasn't about to judge him for it. "I mean, why is she the teenage version of Tera?"

Gabe grinned. "Oh, that's because my first attempt to customize the AI's appearance gave me a woman who might fit Tera's description on a police APB, but didn't really look like her. I had to give the matrix examples of what she actually looked and behaved like in real life. So I fed hours of video from Tera's social media channel into the AI system, and this is what the matrix created." He held out a hand to Tera. She tilted her head coyly to the side, one hand under her chin.

"I wonder why the AI matrix chose to portray Tera in her teens, though. Shouldn't it have shown her the way she was before she . . ." I trailed off. I still wasn't good at saying she had died. Especially not in front of Gabe.

"She made fewer videos as she got older. There were only a handful from after we got married," he said.

"Maybe she was busy doing other things," I observed airily, giving Gabe a small smirk.

"Right," Gabe said, grinning back. "The matrix must have averaged the inputs and settled on the teenage version of Tera." Gabe looked lovingly at AI-Tera. "I haven't figured out how to force the matrix to render the older version of her yet."

AI-Tera absently twirled a lock of her long, red hair. "Gabe tried to explain age to me, and it didn't make any sense. He said it happens to a person over time, but I told him that time and space are perceptual constructs based on his body's physical experience of gravitational forces."

Gabe and I shared a look. As far as I knew, teenage-Tera didn't have any background in the theories of space-time or gravitational constructs or whatever she had just said. The AI's appearance must just be an overlay on the underlying matrix.

"Anyway, I just haven't had the time, or the heart, to try and fix it." Gabe held out a hand toward the Tera hologram. "After all, this is the Tera I fell in love with."

AI-Tera smiled lovingly back at him as she put her forefingers and thumbs together in the shape of a heart.

I decided we'd better steer the conversation in a different direction before things got too mushy. "Have you flown it yet?"

A broad smile spread across Gabe's face. "Not yet. We just brought the ion reactor online yesterday, and I was going to test out the main drive system today. It's a good thing you lost your job so you could be here for it."

I nodded, thinking the same thing. Then something occurred to me. "Wait. What would you have done if I hadn't lost my job?"

Gabe adopted an innocent expression. "Oh, I would have brought you over, anyway. Probably. Eventually."

"Sure," I said, shaking my head.

"No, really. In fact, I'm officially making you First Officer of the *Starfire*."

"Huh. And what does that mean?"

Gabe shrugged. "You know, if we're out in space on one of our adventures, and the aliens do some mind-infiltration on me, then you take over the ship and save the day."

I smiled. "I can do that."

Gabe stood and turned to AI-Tera. "Pumpkin, can you make a note in the log that Mitch is the *Starfire's* First Officer, with all the privileges commensurate with the rank."

"Sure thing, sweetie."

This was the most unprofessional starship I'd ever been on. Of course, it was the only one I'd ever been on. They smiled at each other again for several seconds, until I loudly cleared my throat.

"Right," Gabe said, looking a little embarrassed. "Is everything ready for our engine test?"

"Ready when you are," she said.

"Then let's see if we can impress Mitch with a demonstration," he replied.

I thought it was funny that they planned to impress me with an engine test. As if seeing an alien spaceship and meeting its incredibly realistic AI representation of a dead high school friend wasn't enough. But I was game. "What should I do?"

Gabe motioned me forward to the co-pilot's seat. "Sit up here with me. Tera technically doesn't need a seat."

"I can still be annoyed that he's replacing me," AI-Tera said with a pout.

"It's okay, pumpkin," Gabe cooed. "He'll be gone soon enough."

That made Tera smile.

I followed Gabe's lead and buckled myself into the co-pilot's chair. Tera settled in a seated position in the gap between us.

"Are we gonna take it to space?" I asked in giddy excitement.

"Not today," Gabe said as he punched buttons on the control panel. "We're just gonna float out into the field and singe some grass." He gave me a side-long glance. "And hopefully not catch half the county on fire."

When he tapped another button, Tera announced, "Engaging hover emitters."

"Landing struts coming up," Gabe said. The ship shuddered slightly, and I suddenly felt like we were on a boat on the lake.

"Did you close the cargo bay door?" I asked, trying to be helpful.

Tera and Gabe simultaneously turned and gave me nearly the exact, are-you-serious expression.

I held up my hands. "Sorry. Just thought I'd ask."

Gabe reached out and took hold of the control sticks. They didn't look like any flight controls we'd ever trained on—or even learned about. A moment later, the barn rafters began sliding forward as the ship glided backwards out of the large doors. Bright afternoon sunlight streamed in through the large flight deck windows.

Gabe's farm was so far away from town and neighbors that I didn't worry too much about anyone noticing the large spaceship emerging from a barn. But it did make me wonder if the engine test might show up on a government satellite. Hopefully, they weren't looking at our tiny section of Oklahoma at the moment.

The nose of the craft swung gently around, and Gabe maneuvered the ship across his large backyard until he reached the hayfield that marked the center of his property.

"If we're not going for a ride, why didn't you just do the engine test from the barn?" I asked.

"These fields have built-in fire suppression." He pointed to the long pipes and large rugged wheels of the farm's irrigation system. "Plus, I'm not one hundred percent sure I fixed everything. If the ship blows up, I don't want it to destroy my barn."

"Gabe, if the ship blows up with you in it, what difference does it make what happens to your precious barn?"

His only answer was a small shrug.

I tightened my safety harness and gripped the armrests until my knuckles turned white.

Gabe tapped an icon that I now recognized as the landing struts. "Struts down." He tapped another button. "Hover off."

"Ion engines coming on line," Tera announced in a level voice.

"We'll test them at fifty percent and go from there." Gabe watched the status indicator on the panel in front of him.

I searched my own panel for the power indicator. Despite what I'd seen in sci-fi shows, I didn't think this ship had a display showing how soon the ship would blow up.

The status indicator showed that the ion engines were online. Gabe's hand hovered over the engine activation control. "Should I do a countdown? I feel like we should do a countdown," he said.

I nodded enthusiastically. "Definitely do a countdown." My heart continued to pound, but I realized it was more from excitement than dread.

"Five . . . Four," Gabe began.

I joined in. "Three . . . Two . . . One."

He pushed the engine control lever forward, and the ship began to rumble. I really wished I could look out a window to see if the engines were setting the hay on fire. I turned to Gabe. "Don't we have a rearview mirror or something?"

He smiled at me and tapped another control. A video feed of the field behind us flashed onto the wall panels on both sides of the main canopy windows. The ship actually did have rearview mirrors—albeit very high-tech ones.

The field of hay behind the ship shook and pulsed violently. There was no flame coming out of the engines—just a long blue stream.

I watched the rear-view feed as Gabe slowly pushed the throttle from half to ninety percent. Nothing caught fire, which was both a relief and a disappointment.

Then it hit me—I was sitting in an actual spaceship. It was exactly what we had dreamed of when we were kids, and now, somehow, it had come true.

After a minute, Gabe eased all the way back on the engine throttle, and the ship stopped shaking. My best friend and I gaped at each other like giddy schoolboys.

"That. Was. Awesome!" I screamed.

Gabe grinned back. "We are the luckiest guys in the world right now!"

"Let's take it up for a quick spin," I said.

Gabe shook his head. "I still don't trust that everything is fixed right. I want to look the ship over again before we do a real flight."

"That's what an old person would say," I teased. "How can you be responsible at a time like this?

"Besides, shouldn't we make sure I don't get any visits from government agents this evening?"

I clasped my hands in front of me. "Please," I begged.

Gabe laughed. "See, this is why I couldn't tell you earlier. You're as bad as a kid on Christmas."

"With a present like this, who wouldn't be?" I shot back with a grin.

"You didn't even know about this ship until an hour ago; I'm sure you can wait one more day." He reached through Tera and patted me patronizingly on the arm.

With a huff, AI-Tera stood and moved away from the flight seats. "Y'all are acting like a bunch of nerdy teenagers. The *Starfire* is an inter-system starship meant for transportation and defense. Once installed, the Quake Drive will make travel between neighboring stars instantaneous."

Gabe and I both gaped at her.

Tera cocked her head to the side. "I think my matrix just gained access to a previously damaged portion of the ship's memory."

Gabe nodded. "The auto-repair routine we started yesterday must be doing its job."

"Did she say Quake Drive?" I asked.

"I think so," Gabe replied. "And I'm pretty sure there was something about instantaneous travel."

We shared a knowing look.

"We've got a lot to do tomorrow," I said.

Gabe nodded. "Yep."

Chapter Two

The next morning, I woke up way before dawn. In fact, it would be hard to say that I really woke up considering the fact that I barely slept for more than an hour at a time. Gabe was right; I really was like a kid on Christmas morning.

The idea of taking a ride on a real spaceship had drifted in and out of my dreams all night. During my more lucid moments, I was sure that it couldn't be real. How could my best friend have found and repaired a spaceship? But it had to be real; I'd actually been on it, touched it with my own hands.

I scarfed down a quick breakfast and hit the road in my Charger while there was still some morning dew on the fields. I flipped my visor down to shield my eyes from the morning sun, doing my best not to go more than ten over the speed limit. The last thing I needed was for Ross to pull me over and chat my ear off. Or worse, he might want to know where I was going in such a hurry. He'd know from the look on my face that it was something exciting, and he'd probably want to join in. I wasn't ready to share this with anyone else yet. Besides, it technically wasn't my secret to share.

After what seemed like an abnormally long drive to my friend's house, I finally turned onto Gabe's long drive. I parked the Charger in front of the garage and nearly skipped to the front door. I knocked and did my best to wait patiently. When he didn't answer after the second knock, I was tempted to simply let myself in. That had been a pretty common occurrence in our teens and early twenties. But when Gabe and Tera got married, I decided I'd better start knocking again. Just in case.

I shook my head and smiled to myself.

Tera.

Gabe's attitude had been lighter yesterday than I'd seen in a while. Probably because he'd found a way to spend time with his wife again—sort of.

As I reached for the doorknob, I heard a clanging sound from the back of the house. I don't know why I was knocking on the front door, anyway. Gabe was probably already out in the barn getting things ready for the test flight.

I walked along the front of the house toward the barn.

A moment before I reached the corner, a man in a black tactical combat outfit came around the corner. He wore wraparound sunglasses and a black skullcap.

I was so shocked to see anyone but Gabe that it took me half a second to process what was happening. Fortunately, that week of pseudo-boot-camp kicked in as the guy reached for his gun and raised it toward me.

I lunged forward and grabbed his elbow. Using my momentum—and one of the disarming moves they'd taught us—I swung the intruder around, smashing him against the solid brick wall of Gabe's house. The guy grunted in surprise. Though he appeared slightly dazed, I didn't like my chances in a fair fight, so I smashed my elbow into his nose, slamming his head back against the brick again.

That was the knockout punch, and the guy slid down the wall into a heap on the ground. I still had a grip on his forearm, so I grabbed his weapon before I let him drop.

I stared down at the unconscious soldier, adrenaline coursing through me. What was going on? I glanced around the front yard. Everything suddenly felt so surreal. I had no idea where this guy had come from or if there were more soldiers waiting for me in the back. I inched toward the corner and peeked around the edge until I could see the large red barn and part of the backyard.

About half a dozen figures—dressed in the same black combat gear—trudged across the lawn lugging something between them. A tall, stocky man with jet-black hair blocked my view. He yelled something unintelligible as he walked past them.

I caught a glimpse of what they were carrying. It looked like a jet engine from a museum display or maybe a mad scientist's time travel device—all metal conduits and electrical wiring. This group seemed busy enough that they wouldn't notice me, but I scanned the area for others, just in case. I glanced at the barn to see if the ship was still there.

The large doors hung wide open, and a body lay on the ground between them.

My breath caught in my throat, and it felt as if all the air was being pressed from my lungs.

It was Gabe.

And he wasn't moving.

I immediately dashed from the corner of the house toward the side of the barn. Halfway there, I glanced toward the group of soldiers carrying the crate, just to make sure they hadn't seen me. My brain refused to process what I saw in the field behind them.

A starship—about the size of Gabe's—stood on the edge between the hayfield and the backyard. But unlike the smooth curves and chrome surface of Gabe's ship, this one looked menacing. It had an angular, pock-marked hull, with guns and cannons bristling from all sides.

I might have slowed as I gaped at this new ship, but only momentarily. Putting on a burst of speed, I reached the side of the barn undetected. My breathing came short and fast as I tried to comprehend what I had just seen. I looked down at the gun in my hand—the one I'd taken from my first attacker. It was lighter than it should have been, made of some exotic alloy that caught the sunlight in strange ways. Most of it was a dark, gun-metal gray with various buttons I'd never seen on a gun. Plus, there were some weird words in a foreign language.

Not a foreign language, I now realized. This was alien writing on an alien hand gun.

How could this be happening?

My brain snapped back to Gabe. I needed to get him—and myself—out of there. I had no idea what type of damage an alien gun could do, but I hoped it wasn't beyond the ability of a regular Earth doctor to fix. What kind of world—or universe—was I now living in that I referred to our town physician as an "Earth doctor?"

Inching to the edge of the barn, I checked the group of aliens moving toward their spaceship. I figured they were far enough across the lawn that I could get to Gabe and drag him to safety before they had a chance to see me.

I shoved the weapon in my waistband, took a deep breath, and ran out from behind the barn toward Gabe. A strangled cry threatened to burst from my throat when I reached him. More than half of his chest was scorched and blackened. His face was a peaceful mask, but I couldn't see any indication of breathing.

"C'mon, Gabe," I pleaded as I leaned closer to him. "Please don't be dead."

Even with my cheek next to his face, I couldn't feel any breath. I put a finger against his neck, searching desperately for a pulse.

I tried to force my brain to remember what to do in an emergency like this, but I had never even dreamed I'd have to rescue my injured best friend from invading aliens.

Before I had a chance to figure out if Gabe was still alive, I heard a shout from behind me, back in the direction of the house. I glanced over my shoulder and saw a single soldier standing guard by Gabe's back door. He had a rifle raised and pointed in my direction.

The muzzle flashed just as I ducked. Wood from the barn door splintered above my head, showering Gabe and me with dust and ash. I grabbed my buddy under the arms and heaved him to the side just as another hole appeared in the door where I had been standing.

More unintelligible shouts came from the direction of the large starship on the edge of the yard.

There was no way Gabe and I could get away now.

The lowered ramp of Gabe's starship caught my eye. We couldn't get away, but we might stand a chance of not dying if I could get us inside the ship. I dragged Gabe further inside the barn and onto the cargo ramp. The last thing I saw were the alien soldiers rushing across the backyard toward me.

Near the top of the ramp, I yelled over my shoulder. "Tera! Tera! Help! Close the bay door! Hurry!"

AI-Tera must have heard me because the ramp started rising, almost pushing us into the cargo hold as its angle increased. Tera's holographic form appeared immediately next to me. She took one look at Gabe's limp body and screamed bloody murder.

That was not the reaction I was expecting from an alien computer matrix.

"What happened?!" she yelled, watching helplessly as I pulled Gabe's body across the cargo bay.

"Does that door lock?"

Either she didn't hear me or she was ignoring me. "He's been shot! Is he okay?!" AI-Tera screamed.

I wished I could grab the re-creation of my teenage friend and shake her back to rationality, but her only being a holographic projection made that impossible. Instead, I was forced to yell back at her. "Tera!" Her eyes snapped up to mine. "There are aliens outside the barn that want to kill us. Can you lock the cargo door?"

She nodded, and I heard an immediate scraping of metal against the door frame.

"Oh, Gabe," she said sadly as her projection dropped to her knees next to him. Holographic tears slid down her cheeks. Then suddenly, she shot back to her feet. "We need to save him! Hurry! Get him to the med-pod!"

"What's a med-pod?" I asked.

Her shimmery body rushed to the front of the cargo bay as the hatch automatically swung open. She led me across the hall to a room that Gabe had said was only storage.

As I dragged Gabe into the room, I heard several pings against the outside hull. I looked up at AI-Tera. "What was that?"

She only had eyes for Gabe. "Small arms fire," she answered absently. "Hurry. We need to turn on the med-pod!" She pointed toward a long bed with various instruments and wires running out of it.

Momentarily leaving Gabe on the deck, I rushed to the med-pod and slammed my palm into what must have been the control panel. Then I pushed several small boxes and other junk out of the way. Once the bed was clear, I dragged Gabe over and hefted him onto the top. "Now what?" I asked her. I heard several new impacts outside.

She gazed intently at the control panel on the side of the pod. "It's not connected to the computer systems. You'll need to operate it manually." She gestured frantically to it.

I glanced at the strange menu. "I can't read this."

"Touch here" She pointed, and I tapped the screen. "Now touch this." She pointed again, and I obeyed. Then Tera said something unintelligible. "There. I've switched the interface to English."

I frowned. "How could it possibly—"

"Stop asking stupid questions!" she yelled, then pointed at the console.

I tapped a button labeled *Emergency Triage*. The various accessories and sensors on the pod suddenly came to life, rotating into position above Gabe's body.

A few seconds later, the med-pod flashed the results.

Respiratory System: Breathing — None
Circulatory System: Heartbeat — None
Nervous System: Brain Activity — Minimal

My heart sank when I saw how bad it was. I tapped the blinking icon for the circulatory system and saw an expanded status.

Heart Muscle: 38% Tissue Intact
Circulatory Integrity: 72% Vessels Intact
Cardiac Conduction System: Electrical Signal Absent — Intervention Inadvisable

I touched the flashing words *Intervention Inadvisable*, and a warning message filled the screen.

Cardiac Conduction System Intervention is Unlikely to Revive Patient Due to Missing Heart Tissue. Would You Like to Override Standard Procedure?

I mashed *Override*, and almost immediately, an arm with a long, spindly probe swung into position above Gabe's chest. The arm lowered until the probe pressed through Gabe's charred shirt. I felt another round of impacts from the soldiers outside firing at us. After a few seconds, the familiar heartbeat traces appeared on a status screen above Gabe's head.

"His heart is beating!" AI-Tera cried.

I navigated back to the menu showing the respiratory system. That screen showed a status alert as well.

Right Lung: 47% Tissue Intact
Left Lung: 22% Tissue Intact
Diaphragm Muscle: 96% Tissue Intact
Respiration Not Occurring — Intervention Possible

Just as I had with the heart, I instructed the med-pod to force Gabe's lungs to work. Two arms with suction-cup-looking ends moved into position against Gabe's chest and began pulsating regularly.

We both watched for a moment, mesmerized by the life-saving movement of his chest and diaphragm.

I glanced back at Tera. "What's going on outside?"

Tera shook her head dismissively.

"Tera, listen to me. The soldiers were taking shots at the ship, but now they've stopped. We need to know what they're doing," I insisted.

AI-Tera waved a hand. "The soldiers are going back to their ship. They couldn't do any damage to us with their small guns, so they're probably planning to attack with the ship's cannons."

"What?! Why didn't you say anything about this earlier?" I nearly yelled.

"I don't know!" she yelled back. "Gabe's situation seems to have short-circuited my standard subroutines."

At the moment, I didn't have time to troubleshoot an alien computer—or AI matrix or whatever. "Can we get away from them? You know, fly out of here or something?" I asked.

"The auto-pilot subroutines can follow basic command inputs," Tera said morosely, never taking her eyes off Gabe.

"Then do that!" I said. "Please," I added.

The ship shuddered as the systems engaged to initiate liftoff. A sudden shift of the room told me we were moving, and a slight jolt indicated that we had either cleared the too-small barn doors or we had taken a portion of the barn with us on our way up.

I stared down at the med-pod's display, wondering if the machine could do anything else for my friend. I panned through several other menus of the various subsystems of Gabe's body. The readouts painted a grim picture. And none of them had any other recommended interventions. I leaned against a nearby support column.

After several seconds, AI-Tera asked, "Will he live?"

I blew out a long breath. "I don't know," I said. "But I think we've done everything we can."

We both looked back at Gabe's body, moving very unnaturally with the external intervention of the med-pod.

I turned my attention to the holographic figure at my side. "You really feel an attachment to Gabe, don't you?" I asked.

She nodded, several tears dropping from her virtual cheeks and disappearing halfway to the deck plates. "While we were working together repairing the ship and reprogramming my personality matrix, Gabe helped create several non-standard subroutines for emotional responses. So, yes, I do feel very attached to him. I love him."

An impact rocked the ship, throwing me against a pile of storage boxes and onto the floor. Fortunately, Gabe was belted into the med-pod. And of course, AI-Tera didn't have any mass, so she wasn't affected by regular physics.

"What was that?" I asked.

"The enemy ship has begun firing low-yield explosive slugs at us," she said with a sigh. "And the auto-pilot doesn't evade enemy fire very well."

"Shouldn't you be flying the ship instead of the autopilot?"

"I'm a little better at flight maneuvers than the auto-pilot, but not as good as a human pilot." Tera said, still not turning her attention from Gabe. "Besides, with the havoc those new emotional-attachment subroutines are causing to my matrix, I wouldn't trust myself at the helm right now."

I stood and moved back to the med-pod controls. Everything was still functioning, as far as I could tell. "Do you have the ability to deactivate the distracting subroutines?" I asked.

"Gabe gave those to me." AI-Tera sounded hurt, like I had just insulted her parentage, if she'd had any. "Why would I turn them off?"

"So that we don't get killed by the enemy ship." I held an arm out in the direction that I thought was the rear of the ship.

"My algorithms must be stuck in a recursive loop. I don't think I can shut them off, even if I wanted to," she said, turning back to Gabe.

"Tera, having emotions doesn't mean you just stop living. Humans have to push through them. That's why I asked if—" Another impact rocked the ship. I turned toward the hatch. "Nevermind."

"Where are you going?" AI-Tera called after me.

"Somebody has to save our skins," I answered over my shoulder. It may not have been the most appropriate time for a Star Wars quote, but I hardly cared. My best friend was lying on an alien medical bed, his systems only working because of some advanced technology that I didn't understand, while other advanced technology outside the ship was trying to blow me to smithereens.

I reached the flight deck several seconds later after only a few collisions with bulkheads due to the auto-pilot's apparently sub-par evasive actions. I jumped over the pilot's chair and landed squarely in front of the controls. We were flying a few hundred feet above the farmland below, weaving slowly back and forth.

I stared at the flight controls. One time observing Gabe maneuver the ship on the ground wasn't enough to make me an expert. But maybe I could figure out how to keep us from dying. I grabbed the sticks lightly and tried to feel what was happening as the auto-pilot moved us through the atmosphere. As I exerted more control on the sticks, the ship began responding more to my movement. A notification popped up on the control display.

Pilot Input Detected. Disengage Auto-Pilot?

I wasn't sure that was a good idea yet, so I ignored the question. I continued pulling and pushing on the control sticks to get a feel for the way the ship handled. I glanced up at the rear video feeds. The enemy ship shifted side to side, attempting to follow us. I saw a bright flash near the front of their ship and a blinking red triangle appeared on the screen, superimposed on a small black object that grew larger and larger. I could tell that it would hit our right wing, so I pulled sharply on the control sticks to veer away from the impact. The auto-pilot resisted my effort slightly—like a lane-assist feature on a car—but I fought through the haptic feedback and pulled the ship away just in time.

Through the right window, I caught a glimpse of the black slug before it disappeared in a blinding explosion. The ship shook but stayed in one piece.

I looked down at the control panel in front of me, eyeing the auto-pilot disengage option, wondering if this was really a good idea. Finally, I decided that I'd rather try my luck at dying on my own rather than having the auto-pilot do it for me.

As soon as I disengaged the auto-pilot, the ship began to lurch wildly up and down. I tightened my grip on the control sticks, attempting to fight the oscillation. Another black slug expanded on the rear view monitor. Fortunately, the enemy hadn't anticipated a crazy person with zero experience attempting to fly the ship, so the slug missed by even more this time.

Take that, auto-pilot.

AI-Tera's holographic form suddenly materialized in the co-pilot seat. I jumped, causing the ship to lurch upward.

"Isn't there a more subtle way for you to arrive on the flight deck?" I asked as I tried to bring the ship back under control.

"I've been doing some thinking, and I feel like I really need to do better at being present with my grief without lashing out at you," she began.

"It's fine. Don't worry about it." I would have waved a hand, but I needed both of them on the sticks at the moment. I banked the ship and pulled hard to avoid another incoming projectile. Then I decided that maybe I should figure out a way to hide. I flew the ship into a nearby cloud bank. That should make it harder for them to shoot us out of the sky.

"No, Mitch. We need to talk this out," AI-Tera insisted. "My emotional subroutines tell me that if we let a disagreement fester, it will only get worse."

I chuckled. "Wow, Gabe really went all out on those emotions of yours."

"He had hoped to make me as real as possible. Apparently, he and the real Tera had a very deep relationship."

"Well, I'm not looking for that depth of relationship right now, so I accept your apology. Now, let's figure out a way that we—or at least I—can avoid getting killed."

Tera stared at me. "I'm trying to repair my emotional-attachment subroutine, but every time it loops back to Gabe's location, my logic gets blocked, and I can't process any additional input. Is this what feeling distraught is like for a human?"

"Actually, most humans aren't that great at feeling their feelings." I pushed lightly on the stick to keep from flying out of the clouds. "Especially the unpleasant ones."

"Why even have them, then?" she asked. "Especially if they make it difficult to function logically."

I shook my head. "Can we have this discussion later? I need to focus."

"That's another thing. Human's inability to focus on more than one thing at a time seems—"

"Tera!"

The AI matrix must have been programmed with enough of my real friend to know that she needed to drop it. "Got it. Later," she said. She glanced out the flight deck windows as if barely realizing what was going on. "We're still under attack."

A nearby explosion lit the thick fog around us. Despite being a great place to hide, apparently the cloud bank wouldn't protect us from being blown up. "We need to get out of this cloud," I announced.

"We need to get out of this atmosphere," Tera replied.

I frowned. "What?"

"The *Starfire's* stealth technology has kept it hidden from your planet's military, but even primitive Earth radar systems can detect explosions like that."

"How long do you think we have before they'll scramble fighter jets to intercept us?" I asked.

"Oh, that happened a few minutes ago while I was working through my distress. Two F-35s with the Air National Guard took off from the airfield in Tulsa. They should be within visual range in just a few minutes."

My eyes bugged out at her. "If I survive this, we need to have a conversation about what you share and when," I said as I banked the ship away from Tulsa.

A few seconds later, we pulled through the top of the cloud. My breath caught in my chest at the view. Through the scattered cloud cover, I could see the sprawling center of Oklahoma City to my right and ahead of me, nothing but farms and fields dotted by the occasional small town. My eyes went back to the rear display. The alien ship popped out of the clouds and fired a salvo from its side cannons. I took evasive action, trying to gain altitude.

"Good idea to head southwest," Tera said. "It'll take them a little longer to catch us that way."

"The enemy ship?"

"No. The F-35s." She gave me a skeptical look. "Pay attention, Mitch. We were just talking about the F-35s."

I blew out an exasperated breath. "I'm way more worried about the alien ship than the F-35s right now."

Tera folded her virtual arms, looking annoyed. She glanced at the control readouts. "You're still flying at the auto-pilot default velocity," she observed. "Why don't you speed up and outrun them?"

I did a barrel roll as another pair of slugs nearly took off our wings. "I've been a little too busy not dying to figure out how to change the speed."

"It's right there." Tera pointed. "And if you need them, those are the controls for the vectored thrusters. Or the gravity capacitors might help if you're desperate." Her holographic finger was a blur as she indicated different buttons on the panel.

After narrowly dodging an incoming slug, I grabbed the handle Tera had pointed to and jammed it forward.

The nearly instantaneous thrust pressed me back into my seat. "Wow! That's what I'm talking about!"

"The enemy ship is increasing speed to match," Tera announced.

"Can they keep up with us?"

She shrugged her holographic shoulders. "In the atmosphere, yes. The computer says that their drive-system is nearly as powerful as ours. But they're not as—" Tera stopped speaking, and her head jerked to the side. "Another pair of jets just scrambled."

"More from Tulsa?" I asked.

"No. These are from Fort Worth."

"Oh, that's more than an hour away," I said, focusing on the alien ship behind me.

"Not at the speed we're going. We'll be in range of their weapons in less than six minutes."

My eyes went wide. "That's bad," I said. "How are we gonna get out of this one?"

"You could take the ship out of the atmosphere."

I gaped at her. "You want me to fly into space?"

She shrugged. "All the local Earth-based scanning systems have detected us. As long as we're in your country's airspace, they will continue to launch fighter aircraft to intercept us." She paused for a moment as a small smirk crept across her face. "The F-35s can't follow us into space, though."

I shook my head. "This is crazy." As much as the kid inside me really wanted to go to space, I somehow knew this was a big decision.

"Mitch, this ship is designed to engage in both atmospheric and extra-planetary maneuvers," she said with a note of exasperation. "It's the obvious answer to our situation. You need to fly straight up."

Gripping the control sticks, I gazed out at the sky. "I can't believe I'm contemplating flying an alien ship into space."

"Can you believe you're talking to an alien AI?" Tera asked.

"Fair point," I replied.

After another moment of contemplation, I pushed the throttle to maximum as I pulled back on the sticks. G-forces pinned me against the pilot's seat as our nose pointed skyward. While the rear display still showed the brown and green of the Oklahoma countryside, the view in front of us had already changed to deep blue, almost black.

That took care of the F-35s.

"The alien ship has matched our climb," Tera said. "And they're firing again."

As a pair of slugs from the alien ship closed in on us, I jammed the control sticks to the left.

The ship hardly moved.

"What happened?!" I cried.

"We've left the atmosphere. You need to switch to zero-G thrusters." Tera pointed to a button on the panel.

I pressed the toggle and tried to make the ship turn. Instead, we immediately began a slow spin to the side. "What's going on now?"

Both slugs missed the ship, but just barely. One exploded within a few feet of the tail fin.

Tera watched with a look of half annoyance, half amusement. "There's no air out here. You have to point the ship where you want to go and then apply the thrust."

Despite the name, spaceships apparently don't actually fly in space.

I tried to reorient my brain, but I only ended up rotating the ship too far. Now we were looking straight back at the oncoming enemy ship but still traveling away from it. More incoming slugs forced me to lay into the throttle as soon as we were pointed sideways again. But instead of moving straight in the direction we were pointing, we just lazily drifted that direction.

"According to the computer, that other ship is a Vezor-class runabout. It's bulkier and less maneuverable than we are. You should be able to fly circles around it," Tera said.

I gritted my teeth as our ship began rotating in a completely different direction. "Flying circles is about the only thing I *can* do at this point."

"Plus, its shields and armaments are much worse than ours. You could probably destroy it anytime you want."

"Clearly not anytime I want." I found myself leaning the direction I wanted the ship to go, but it didn't respond to my body language.

"And the sensors say it's running without a transponder signal, if that helps," AI-Tera said.

"It really doesn't."

I got the ship to twist more or less in the way I had meant to. Two more slugs passed within feet of the ship. The explosions didn't rattle the ship like they had before, but there was an eerie pinging sound as shrapnel hit the hull.

I vectored our ship away from the enemy runabout, but it just turned slowly to follow.

"This isn't working," I said.

"I agree. The probability of the other ship—despite its inferiority to the *Starfire*—landing a lucky shot at some point in the next two hours is above ninety-nine percent."

"Great. Just great."

AI-Tera continued. "At which point, you'll get sucked out into the vacuum of space and suffer a short but painful death."

"What about my chances of learning how to shoot back and destroy them before we get killed?"

AI-Tera gave me a dead-pan look that I remembered well from high school.

The runabout fired a spread of six shots—five slugs in a star formation with a single one in the middle.

There was no way I could outmaneuver this one.

I slammed the thrust forward. Maybe if I could outrun the shots long enough, I could slip between them.

"This is not good," I said as my body pressed backward into my chair with the increased thrust. "We have to get out of here somehow."

AI-Tera—completely unaffected by the thrust forces—cocked her head to the side. "We could try an intra-space jump," she said.

"Is that like warp drive or something?" I asked.

"Not really. It's more like hyper space. It drops the ship into an alternate dimension—just temporarily—so that the distance to another place is much shorter."

"Can the alien ship follow us there?" I asked, struggling to even move my head against the increasing Gs.

"They can monitor our heading when we jump, which would give them a guess as to where we're going. But they can't follow us into intra-space. Each jump happens on a unique, and randomized, dimensional plane."

"Do it," I said as I watched the star-spread slugs draw closer and closer.

"Where should we go?" Tera asked.

The slugs were within a hundred feet now. We only had a few seconds left. "Anywhere but here," I ground out.

The muscles in my body tensed as I waited for death.

Chapter Three

I had no idea where AI-Tera had taken us. One minute the view outside the flight deck windows was black, speckled with stars, the next minute everything melted into a grayish-brown. And the force pinning me back against the pilot seat suddenly eased away to nothing. If this was what she meant by a jump, it wasn't the epic, stars-flying-by moment or intergalactic tube I would have imagined. It was just a mild nothingness.

But at the moment, I didn't really care. We weren't dead, and I had to get back down to Gabe. As the adrenaline slowly faded, I stumbled out of the flight deck. I somehow made it down to the makeshift infirmary. The med-pod's display showing the status of Gabe's internal systems had changed. His body continued to pulsate in an unnatural way as the various instruments forced his heart and lungs to continue working. But now, instead of displaying the amount of muscle tissue remaining in his vital organs, the pod showed the amount of atrophy occurring in the systems throughout his body.

No matter which menus I chose or what instructions I put in, the med-pod still insisted that there was no brain activity, no electrical impulses, nothing.

Basically, my best friend was dead.

The only real option the med-pod gave me was *Body Preservation*.

I was pretty sure I knew what that meant, and I wasn't ready to accept it yet.

I collapsed against the bulkhead across from the med-pod and glared at the infernal piece of alien technology that refused to bring my friend back to life.

A few minutes later—or possibly hours, it was hard to tell—AI-Tera shimmered into view across the room from the med-pod and hurried over to look down at Gabe's broken body. She didn't say anything; she didn't need to. Her sensors, or matrix, or however she perceived her surroundings, could see as well as I could that Gabe wasn't coming back.

She glided over and sat next to me. Or rather, her holographic projection hovered at floor level with her legs crossed. She looked small already, being a fifteen or sixteen-year-old representation of my high school friend, but in this moment, she appeared even more fragile. We couldn't hug or touch each other—no physical manifestations of mutual grieving—not that I was sure that she really could grieve.

I sat slumped against the bulkhead for what felt like several days, but might have only been hours, alternating between crying, yelling, and gazing absently at nothing.

When I started nodding off, AI-Tera finally said, "Mitch, you need to find a bed to sleep in."

I shook my head emphatically and continued staring at the med-pod.

She must have let me doze because I remember drifting in and out of consciousness for several more hours until her voice jolted me awake from a particularly vivid dream of falling through the blackness of space.

"Mitch, as a biological lifeform, you need regular intervals of REM sleep to be fully functional. I'll watch Gabe and let you know if anything changes."

Her voice was so soothing and compassionate. And in the back corner of my brain, I knew she was right. She could watch Gabe while I got some sleep. It just made sense.

I staggered to my feet and wandered away, looking for a place to collapse. Behind the kitchen and living area on the upper deck—on the opposite end of the ship from the flight deck—there was a short hall with two private bedrooms, one on each side. I stumbled into one and crashed onto the surprisingly comfortable, extra-terrestrial bed. The last thing I remember was being grateful that aliens cared about soft sheets.

When I woke up, the heavy weight of Gabe's condition came quickly back, crushing down on me. Slowly, I began to realize that I'd have to come to terms with losing him, and even let him go.

Eventually.

But first, there was something I absolutely had to do.

I climbed down to the lower deck and stood at the entrance to the cluttered storage room that held the med-pod. I had asked myself a million times how we had ended up here, but there were no good answers.

I stepped over and looked down at Gabe—or his body, anyway. I took a deep breath. "I'm sorry buddy," I began. "For a lot of things."

I wasn't sure I would make it through this, but I felt like I had to. It might be the last chance I'd have to tell him everything.

"I'm sorry I picked Jimmy Francom instead of you for my football team that time I was trying to impress Tiffany Miller in sixth grade." I couldn't help a small smirk at that memory. "I'm sorry I told you Tera wasn't right for you that time you two broke up our sophomore year." Gabe had probably forgiven me for that one a long time ago, but it still felt good to say it. "And I'm sorry I dragged you on that one tough mudder race when you had the flu."

I told him everything I had always felt bad about. Everything I wish I had done differently. And I told him some of the things I loved about our friendship, and how grateful I was that he had always been there for me, always had my back.

Once I had finished unburdening myself about the past and telling him how important he was to me, I stopped and looked around the small storage room.

"I'm sorry you lost Tera so early in your life together." I sighed as I remembered that painful time. "And just when you get a chance to sort of get her back—and maybe have the adventure of a lifetime—a bunch of lowlife aliens come along and . . ."

I still couldn't bring myself to say it.

Swallowing hard, I checked the med-pod display one more time, not that I had much hope of what it would say. In fact, the numbers were worse than the day before. The large *Body Preservation* button caught my attention again.

I shook my head.

I may have been ready to get all those regrets off my chest, but I wasn't ready for that yet.

I glanced down at my friend's body again. "I couldn't have asked for a better friend," I said softly. "Love ya, Gabe."

I couldn't think of anything else to say, and I couldn't just stand there watching his body being kept alive, so I decided it was time to go.

When I turned to leave the room, AI-Tera materialized in the doorway.

She glanced at me and then over my shoulder at Gabe. "Is it really time to say goodbye?"

Not trusting myself to speak at the moment, I shrugged then nodded sadly.

AI-Tera stepped up to the med-pod, holographic hands floating near Gabe's body, unable to actually make contact. She leaned over him, and her shimmery red hair cascaded over her shoulders. "Goodbye, my love," she whispered.

As I watched holographic tears fall down her cheeks and disappear on their way to the floor, I considered her. "You really do seem to feel his loss."

She glanced over at me. "We both know I'm just a collection of complex circuits and algorithms meant to simulate humanoid behavior." She turned back to Gabe. "But, yes, all of my programming tells me that I'm in pain right now."

"Can you really feel loss, though?" I asked, not sure if I believed that a computer simulation could actually feel emotions.

She turned her attention to me. "What does losing someone feel like?"

I took a breath. "Well, I guess it's an ache right here." I banged lightly on my chest. "And a sinking feeling in the pit of your stomach." I tapped my gut. "And your whole body just hurts."

"Since I don't have a body, those aren't very good explanations, Mitch. Can you describe it with something besides physical symptoms?"

I stared up at the wall, trying to figure out how I could explain mourning and loss in terms that didn't involve actual, physical feelings. "Well, when you lose someone, it's hard to think about anything else but them. You find yourself reminiscing about your times together. And it's hard to focus on things. Normal activities become dull. Desires for things like food or entertainment are completely gone." I turned back to look at AI-Tera, knowing how impossible it would be for her to feel any of those things.

She considered me for several seconds. "A composite recording of my experiences with Gabe has been repeating in my secondary processors for the last forty-seven hours. The feedback loop in my emotional-attachment subroutine has caused me to miss several important sensor inputs, as you probably noticed. And the waypoint reminders buried in my primary databanks have nearly taken us off-course about a dozen times." She stared at me, timid defiance burning in her holographic eyes. "I think those match pretty well what feeling loss would be like for an artificial intelligence."

I had to admit, she made a convincing argument. "Who am I to tell you you're not feeling sad? You're as close to the real Tera as there is, and she certainly would be grieving." I shrugged. "I just wish you had an actual shoulder I could cry on." I hadn't been sure I could ever crack a joke again, but that one had almost come naturally.

We both stared down at Gabe's body for a while. Finally Tera said, "Do we have to disconnect him from the med-pod yet?"

I took a deep breath, wondering if I had the courage to do what had to be done.

I didn't.

"No," I said, shaking my head. "I'm not ready."

She nodded. "Good."

When I turned away from the med-pod, Tera followed me, casting a small wave over her shoulder at Gabe.

If the situation wasn't so sad, her behavior would have been adorable.

Back on the upper deck, I glanced around the kitchen area. I didn't feel like eating. But I didn't feel like sitting around either.

I turned to Tera. "I need a distraction."

She nodded. "You could familiarize yourself with the ship's systems. That might come in handy."

"If by familiarize myself with the ship's systems, you mean figure out a way to get us back home, then I'm all in favor." I started toward the flight deck, knowing that was where the ship-flying happened. "How long will it take us to get back to Earth, anyway?" I asked Tera over my shoulder.

"An intra-space jump back to your planet would take approximately the same amount of time as the jump here took—forty-seven hours."

I slowed. Had it really been forty-seven hours since the battle with the alien ship back on Earth?

"It will also take the same amount of fuel to make the return trip." Tera paused, waiting for something.

I turned around and lifted my brow. "And?"

"And we don't have that much fuel," Tera finished.

"We don't have enough gas to make the trip back to Earth?" I probably sounded like an idiot repeating what she had just said, but no one besides my holographic friend was around, so I didn't care.

"No."

"So, where do we get more fuel?" I asked.

"Most settled planets in the cluster would have fuel processing facilities."

I put a hand to my forehead, squeezing my temples. "Wait. Did you say 'settled planet'?" I had a sinking feeling. "We're not in the solar system anymore, are we?"

Tera put a hand on her hip. "You know, there are lots of star systems that could be called the 'solar system' by their inhabitants. But, no, we're not in Earth's solar system anymore. We're not even in a nearby star system."

"Where are we then?"

"We are in the Bonara Star Cluster—your Earth scientists would know it as Messier 44. It's about six hundred light-years from Earth."

My eyes went wide. "We traveled six hundred light-years in two days?"

My holographic assistant nodded. "Intra-space jumps average about ten to fifteen light-years per hour, depending on the tuning of the drive and the specific dimensional plane chosen."

"But what are we doing hundreds of light-years away from Earth?" I asked in exasperation.

"Well, our jump to the Talprean system ended about thirty minutes ago, so right now, we're just floating in non-planetary orbit until we—"

I held up a hand. "I mean, why are we in the Bonanza—what did you call it?"

"Talprean system, Bonara Star Cluster." Tera enunciated each word slowly, like she was speaking to a child.

"Right. Why are we—"

A loud bang echoed through the living area, interrupting my interrogation of the ship's uncooperative AI.

It sounded like we'd hit something.

I rushed to the flight deck and jumped into the pilot's seat. I nearly fell right back out of it when I saw the view through the sweeping window. A giant purple and orange nebula spread out in front of me, like something from an AI rendering or a sci-fi movie.

Tera—who apparently was unaffected by the view—said, "There's a small scavenger vessel behind us. It seems to have launched a tow anchor at us."

I shook myself, attempting to tear my focus away from the mesmerizing, intergalactic kaleidoscope. "Can we get it off?"

"Someone—which means you—would have to go outside the ship and remove it."

Fiddling with cameras for the rear display, I brought up a view of the scavenger. It was slightly smaller than our ship, but looked like it was being held together by baling wire and chewing gum. "Can we break free of the tether somehow?"

"We could fire at the scavenger to warn it off," Tera said.

"We have weapons?"

"You didn't know that?" Tera asked incredulously. "The *Starfire* wouldn't be much of an advanced tactical attack ship if it didn't have weapons."

"Then let's use them!"

"Tap that panel to activate the weapons system." She pointed to the controls at my right.

I activated the system and gazed at the projection of a star field floating in front of me. It was like a jet's heads-up-display, only holographic.

"Your control sticks can also command the weapons system after you switch them over," Tera said.

"Can't you fire the weapons?" I asked.

"The safeguards in the AI matrix would only allow me to fire the plasma cannons in self-defense. And even then, I would be limited to non-lethal use of those weapons."

I frowned. "Fine. I'll use the weapons. But how do I fly while I'm controlling the weapons system?" My hands hovered over the control sticks, which suddenly felt foreign now that I had weapons at my fingertips.

"You don't," Tera said curtly. "You have to toggle between flight controls and weapons controls." She pointed at a large button between the somewhat-familiar flight display and the newly activated weapons display.

"Wish I had a co-pilot," I muttered under my breath. I tapped the button, and the hovering star field rushed toward me. I leaned back instinctively. "Whoa. What did I do?"

Tera laughed. "You've got the long-range rail gun selected, so your targeting display shows a zoomed-in view."

I looked at the heads-up-display and noticed a small crosshair in the center. I pushed the sticks to the right, and the view panned slightly to the right. I pushed forward, and the view panned slightly down. But all I could see in the holographic display were stars.

A sudden jolt—definitely the feeling of the ship starting to move backward—brought me back to the task at hand. I needed to target the scavenger trying to steal my ship. "How do I shoot the other ship?"

"Switch to the plasma cannons." Tera pointed to the small picture of the ship on the weapons console. "Those are the ones mounted on the winglets."

I glanced down and saw a diagram of the ship from top and side views. I tapped one of the cannons hidden inside the wing stubs, and the icons lit up. The hovering heads-up-display in front of me zoomed out to show a much wider view, a large red crosshair floating in the center.

"Wow. Now what do I do?" I asked.

"Aim and shoot," she replied dryly. "Isn't that how guns work?"

Using the control sticks, I swung the under-wing cannons around until I could see the small scavenger vessel and squeezed the trigger. What looked like tracer rounds streamed out from under the wings.

Fortunately for my would-be kidnapper, most of the shots missed. The one round that did hit caused an explosion near its underbelly. The scavenger immediately released the towing cable and thrusted away from us.

"Wow. That was effective," I said.

"You won't meet many ships that are equal in power to the *Starfire*," Tera stated matter-of-factly.

I frowned. "How do you know that?"

Her brow furrowed, and she tilted her head. "I'm not sure. That's just the information that the computer is feeding me."

I gazed out of the canopy at the broad expanse of a completely foreign-looking star system. Eventually, my attention turned back to the console in front of me. I scanned the ship diagram for information on other weapons.

"What's this one?" I pointed to the icon of a large gun mounted under the fuselage.

"That's the rail gun. It's mounted in a bay under the belly and fires remotely explodable slugs—like the ones the enemy runabout was firing at us, only better. The rail gun has the longest range, but the most limited aim. It can only shoot within ten degrees of the direction the ship is facing."

Next, she pointed to the wing stubs. "You've seen how the plasma cannons work. They're short-range defensive weapons, but they have the highest range of motion and the most immediate effectiveness."

I nodded, doing my best not to get distracted by the sheer impossibility of what she was saying.

"And here we have the laser batteries." She pointed at several locations on the top of the ship behind the flight deck and two spots in the rear on either side of the tail. "The lasers have a full range of motion, covering virtually every direction of approach to the ship. Their effect is cumulative. If several of them can stay locked on a target for long enough, they can neutralize an enemy ship if it has thin armor. They can also be used defensively against incoming slugs or missiles."

I glanced sideways at her. "That might have been nice to know."

Tera continued as if I hadn't spoken, but I could see a shimmery flush in her cheeks, almost as if she was embarrassed by not having told me about the lasers during our earlier battle. "And the ship still has a few more empty bays if we can get our hands on other weapons."

I scowled. "We don't really need more weapons as much as we need more fuel. Why did we jump to this system, anyway?"

"You said to go anywhere but Earth, and this was the closest system in the computer's databanks, so that's where we jumped."

"Are you from this star system, I mean, your matrix?" I asked.

Tera's eyes went slightly out of focus for a moment. "I don't know. The information about the ship's origin must be in the part of the computer's databanks that is still being repaired."

"But this system is familiar, right? What about other nearby systems?"

She nodded. "The computer has star charts and planet maps of most of the Bonara Cluster. In fact, those are the only systems I have detailed charts for, so the *Starfire* probably did come from somewhere in the Bonara Cluster."

I gazed absently out the front glass. "Do we know anything else about this area?"

"There are nearly a thousand stars in the Bonara Cluster, but according to the computer, less than half of those have habitable planets or moons. These include: the Atarania System, the Auridoliff System, the Brapulia System, the Brooxika System, the Caridya System, the—"

I closed my eyes, pinching the bridge of my nose. "Tera, how long is this list?"

"Four hundred sixty-three. Unless you want me to list the individual planets and moons."

"No." I held up a hand. "That's okay. I'm just glad we've got that information in the computer somewhere." A thought occurred to me. "When we were fighting the aliens on Earth, you said something about their ship."

"Yes. It was a runabout attack vessel, Vezor-class."

"Do the databanks have anything about where that ship comes from?"

Tera's eyes scanned back and forth. "No. That information is corrupted."

"But the computer made a positive ID on the ship, so it must come from this cluster."

"I don't know for sure, but it would make sense," Tera agreed.

"So now all we need to do is find a police station to report what happened and they can track down the aliens who attacked Gabe and tried to steal his ship," I said.

"That could work," Tera said begrudgingly. "Assuming the Bonara Cluster has the equivalent of a police station."

"Well, let's go find out."

Tera and I watched the surface of the planet for at least an hour. To her, it looked vaguely familiar. Something about the bits and pieces from the computer's databanks.

To me, it was completely alien.

We sat high enough in orbit to not be a nuisance or threat to anyone, but low enough that we weren't geosynchronous. There wasn't much point in examining a planet if you could only see one part of it.

It took me a while to get used to having the nose of the ship pointed straight at the surface of the planet. All the sci-fi movies I'd ever seen showed the ship with the bottom toward the planet. That's the way our brains like it, apparently. Because when we tried to point the nose toward the planet, I felt like I was going to fall out of my seat and careen down toward the surface.

Tera turned off the gravity capacitors temporarily to see if that would help. It did a little bit, but only because it took my mind off falling. It was hard to feel like I was falling when I kept floating out of my seat.

She turned the capacitors back on and after a while, the vertigo sensation passed.

"So, that's the biggest city?" I asked, pointing straight in front of us as we floated over a large metropolis for the fifth time.

"Yeah. That's what the map in the computer says," Tera replied. "Plus, the majority of the radio broadcasts I'm picking up are coming from there."

"I suppose we could start with a smaller city, or maybe a town." I watched more of the planet slide by underneath us. "But I don't want to risk being the first alien that some backwater guy has ever seen." I turned to Tera. "Do they have shotguns on this planet?"

She rolled her eyes at me then tried to recover by acting serious. "Uh, let me check." Her holographic eyes roamed the inside of the flight deck for a few seconds. "Nope. That's just an Earth thing. They do have plasma rifles, though."

I chuckled and shook my head. I had forgotten how sarcastic teenage Tera had been. If we were going to spend more than a few days together, I might need a break. Either that, or the sarcasm subroutine might need a tweak.

"What's the name of this place, again?"

"The planet is called New Talpreus. The city is just called the Big City."

"Very imaginative of them," I replied. I gripped the control sticks. "I guess we have to start somewhere, so Big City it is."

The ship jetted forward as I applied thrust. I had run a few zero-G, extra-planetary training exercises, so I felt marginally competent at maneuvering the ship outside of the atmosphere. As long as we didn't get into another space dogfight.

The outline of Big City filled the viewscreen, and I could feel the atmosphere begin to buffet the ship. I was about to ask Tera if the ship had any kind of thermal shielding—I assumed it did, given the crash landing on Earth—when a holographic alert message flashed in the air in front of me.

Incoming Communication

I pressed the button to open the channel. My heads-up-display morphed into a mid-air video screen. A bored-looking woman sitting at a gray desk stared back at me. At least, I thought she looked bored. She might have been happy. She might have been angry. I'd never seen an alien before, besides the ones I fought at Gabe's house.

Her eyes were large and wide-set, but they looked half-closed. Her skin was pinkish red, like she had just spent a few hours on the beach with no sunscreen. She stared at me for a moment, almost as if I was meant to be the one to speak first.

Soon, the silence became too awkward to bear. "Hi," I said.

"This is Big City traffic control. Are you operating as an authorized Bonara Defense Force vessel?" The woman spoke indifferently, as if reciting from a script.

"Bonara Defense Force..." I repeated, glancing over at Tera, who almost imperceptibly shook her head. I turned back to the woman on the viewer. "Uh, no. I don't think so."

The controller nodded. "Please state your name and destination," she said.

"Mitch, er, Mitchell." I turned to Tera to ask if we knew what part of Big City we wanted to visit, but before I could say anything, the woman continued.

"Mitcher Mitchell, do you have a destination?" She spoke even more slowly now.

"Uh, I'm not sure. We just wanted to visit the city," I replied brightly.

"Do you have a berth reservation?"

"A what?"

"Have you reserved a place to land your ship?" she answered. Her voice sounded so bored that I wouldn't have been surprised if she slid right out of her chair. I was surprised at how clearly I understood her. I'd have to ask Tera later how this woman knew English so well.

"Uh, no. Sorry. Did we need a reservation?"

"What form of payment would you like to use to secure a berth?"

I looked at Tera. "We don't have any forms of payment, do we?" I asked.

My normally talkative AI co-pilot simply shook her head.

The traffic control woman must have seen Tera's reply. "If you do not have a form of payment on file with Landing Authority, I'll need to direct you to public parking."

"Actually, I really just wanted to find out some information. If you could tell me—"

She continued speaking like I hadn't said anything. "Maximum parking time at a public berth is one standard day."

"If I could just ask you a quick question."

"With a public berth, you'll be required to pass through advertising zones as you disembark."

"Advertising zones?"

"Your assigned public berth is 11739." A small green pin marking our designated landing spot flashed on my display. "Is there anything else I can help you with?" she asked.

"Yes. I would like to know if—"

"Have a nice stay in Big City," the controller said dryly. The connection terminated, and I was left staring out the windows.

I turned to Tera. "That was weird," I said.

"Yeah. She was not very helpful."

"Speaking of not being very helpful. You didn't say much," I told her.

Tera shrugged. "People don't like AIs butting into conversations."

"Well, in the future, I wouldn't mind some whispered answers here and there."

"We'll see," Tera replied.

We sailed over the main hub of the spaceport toward the public berth area. I could see large cruisers and yachts in a portion of the port that must have been reserved for those with money. As we flew farther from the center of the port, the berths began to look less opulent, more utilitarian. And the docked ships looked more and more plain.

We reached a point where there was only a single, tube-like building extending from the central port. Far in the distance, I could see berths sprouting from the end of this branch of the spaceport complex. In fact, the closer I got to our designated parking spot, the more it looked like the branch of a tree. Rather than an organized collection of berths laid out with plenty of space between each, these landing pads looked like they had been built one at a time by seventy different contractors, all trying to prove they could fit their berth in the smallest space possible.

Our assigned berth was actually quite small, and I knew I didn't have the skills to maneuver the ship in those tight quarters, so I gladly turned over control to the auto-pilot. The ship hovered down to the ground level, rotated, and smoothly slid forward into the appropriate spot. I stared at the markings above our landing pad, but I couldn't make heads or tails of them.

"Are we sure this is Berth 11739?" I asked as we settled into place.

Tera's brow went up. "Why wouldn't it be?"

I shrugged. She seemed confident, so I'd go with that.

I sat on the flight deck and looked out over the open-air concourse in front of the spaceport entrance doors. Hundreds of people of all hues and sizes criss-crossed the area. Hair and skin of every color in the rainbow—and some that I don't think I'd ever seen before—were in the crowd. I watched for several minutes, feeling completely overwhelmed in this alien place. I wanted justice for Gabe, but I had no idea where to even begin.

I turned to Tera, who sat—more or less—in the co-pilot's seat. "Is there a link that you can establish with the Internet on New Talpreus? Actually, I have no idea what they call the Internet here. But you know what I mean."

Tera's face scrunched in concentration. After a few seconds, her expression relaxed. "What would you like to know?"

"How are we going to figure out what those aliens were doing on Earth—on Gabe's farm, of all places?" I was mostly thinking out loud.

Tera's expression changed focus again.

I held out a hand toward her. "Wait. That wasn't meant to be the search query. I mean, unless you think their Internet has the answer. That would be amazing." I thought for a moment. "What we really need to find out is where we can go to ask questions."

"A library?" Tera offered.

I frowned. "Would a library have a book on 'who killed your best-friend and why'?"

"No. That sounds more like the headlines coming up in my Big City network search. 'Top Ten Extreme Sports that Might Kill You. Number Eight Will Blow Your Mind.'"

I laughed. "I guess humanoids are more or less the same throughout the galaxy."

I continued watching out the window as Tera searched the Big City archive. There were some hilarious interactions to be seen. Like the couple with the long, flowing green braids who regularly stopped walking and started dancing in the middle of the plaza. Or the family with at least a dozen little children in tow—literally—as each successively smaller child held tightly to the hand of the one in front. The last one in line got whipped around like a kite as the mother changed directions in the crowd.

I decided if I ever got bored in the Bonara Cluster, I should just come to New Talpreus and park in a free berth at the Big City spaceport. It was incredibly entertaining.

"What about a local government office?" Tera suggested.

I turned to her, still smiling from my people-watching. "Yeah, maybe I could ask them to open an investigation or something."

Tera's eyes scanned back and forth. This was clearly an intentional feature built into the AI matrix so that the biological crew could understand when the AI was accessing information. I found it fascinating.

"There's no fee for reporting a crime, but requesting an investigation costs twenty Bonmarks."

"What are Bonmarks?" I asked.

"It's the standardized currency in the Bonara star cluster." Tera considered me. "And you don't have any."

That was stating the obvious.

I leaned back in my seat. "I wonder if this ship has anything we can barter with. Did Gabe ever search the storage containers downstairs?"

"He opened a few when he first came on-board. But I think he got distracted once he started reprogramming my matrix." Tera smiled.

"Okay." I stood up and headed for the flight deck door. "I guess I'll see if there's anything of value on the ship. Transfer down to the cargo bay, and I'll meet you there."

I slid down the ladder rails on my way to the lower deck. The gravity felt slightly off from normal. A little weaker than Earth. Not enough for me to start doing double backflips, but enough that I had to watch myself as I bounded down the hall.

Tera was waiting for me when I walked through the hatch into the cargo bay. Several of the storage containers had spilled their contents on the floor. I frowned as I looked around. "I don't remember the cargo bay being such a mess." Then I remember that I hadn't been in this room since I'd dragged Gabe away from the alien killers in his backyard on

Earth. And we'd done some pretty crazy flying since then. The realization of how far away I was from home—and how much I'd lost—hit me like a ton of bricks.

I shook my head, not wanting to spiral into that same grief again. I crouched down next to an overturned bin. Dozens of silvery plastic pouches lay scattered around it. I picked one up and scrutinized the label. It was just gibberish scribbling, as far as I could tell. "Tera, can you read this?"

She glanced over at it. "It's a medical kit—gauze, antiseptic—that sort of thing."

I looked at Tera as she moved around the cargo bay, inspecting various items. "Tera, your hologram doesn't actually have eyes, right?"

Her head jerked toward me, and she immediately put her hands up to her eyes. "What's wrong with my eyes?!"

I held up my hands in a calming gesture. "No, no. Your eyes look fine." I had forgotten how touchy teenage Tera had been about her appearance. "I meant that your hologram is just a projection of light. You don't actually have any visual organs receiving and processing information."

"Oh. Yeah, that's true," she said.

"Then why did you—or your hologram—just look at the package in my hands?" I asked.

"My matrix mimics humanoid behavior. That's what humanoids do; they look at things with their eyes." She was very matter-of-fact about it.

"No, I guess I should say, how did you actually read the package?"

"Uh, the cameras." She waved a lazy hand at the ceiling and upper corners of the walls.

I looked closer and noticed—for the first time—that there were dozens of cameras spaced evenly around the cargo bay, most of them high enough to command a full view of the area. "Can you see with the cameras in other parts of the ship—like when you're not being projected there?"

"Uh, yeah. If I need to," she said as she walked around the cargo area, her matrix still intent on portraying human searching behavior despite the fact that she could sit in the corner and still see everything. Of course, the fact that the alien programmers—and Gabe—had designed her to act like a biological humanoid certainly made my interactions with her more natural.

"What about these?" Tera said from across the bay.

I walked over to join her and looked down into a large bin full of rectangular metal containers. Again, the packaging looked more or less like scribbles to my untrained eye, but this time there were pictures as well. Of course, the pictures didn't help much either. "What are they?"

"Food packs," Tera replied. "These are Otani pickled sprigs—sort of like asparagus on Earth. These are meat pies from Varus Prime. And those are Caridyan tarts." She pointed to each group of food packs.

"At least we know we won't go hungry." I glanced awkwardly at my holographic companion. "Sorry."

Tera shrugged. "I'd probably think these were gross, anyway. They're just space rations. Vacuum packed sawdust and cardboard, if you ask me."

I thought she might be overdoing the description a little, probably because of my comment about eating, but I let it slide. I picked up a tin of the one she said was a tart—though the picture looked like something from a sci-fi horror flick. The shape was an amorphous blob of yellow and brown, with green slime oozing from the top. I forced myself to imagine how I would feel if the green was close to a color I would expect from a dessert, like a purple or red fruit syrup. It still didn't look appetizing, but I'd eat it rather than starve.

"I wonder if we could sell any of these things." I held up the ration pack and pointed back toward the pile of med kits. "Would we be able to get enough money to pay for an investigation?"

Tera looked off into the distance in front of her, eyes scanning back and forth. "Our entire collection of food might be worth a few hundred Bonmarks. So it would be enough to pay for an investigation, but I'm not sure I'd recommend it."

"Why not?"

"Because the investigation would be limited to the efforts of the police force here on New Talpreus. You need an agency that can investigate things throughout the star cluster."

I frowned. She was probably right.

"Besides, if you sold all this," Tera spread her holographic arms wide, "then you wouldn't have any food." She said the last part with a heavy dose of false compassion.

I chuckled at her theatricality. "Well, we're going to need money at some point. Maybe I'll try a few of each." I tucked the ration tin under one arm and grabbed an errant med-kit from the ground as I walked toward the cargo ramp.

"Wait, are you actually going outside?" Tera asked.

"Yeah. Why? Is the atmosphere poisonous or something?" I asked, only half joking.

"No. Humanoids in the Bonara Cluster have a tolerance for atmospheric pollution that's pretty close to humans," Tera explained. "I just wasn't sure if you'd want to risk first contact with so many alien races at once."

Normally, I might agree with her. Visiting an alien world would have seemed daunting just a few days ago. Now, especially after watching the people outside the ship, it didn't seem so scary. "We're here, so I might as well do something," I said. "Besides, it's hard to find a buyer for these"—I held up the packets—"from inside the ship." I walked over and pressed the button to open the loading ramp.

"Okaaay," my holographic friend said in true teenage-Tera style. "Just don't go get yourself killed."

I smiled to myself. She sounded indifferent, but I could tell she was a little concerned for my safety.

I bounded down the ramp then came to a sudden, screeching halt at the bottom.

Was I about to be the first person from Earth to set foot on an alien planet? Should I say something momentous?

I looked around at the menagerie of people passing by our landing pad. None of them seemed to be paying any attention, so it probably didn't matter what I said.

"I come in peace," I announced as I stepped off the ramp. It wasn't the most original statement. In fact, no one even turned to look at me.

Standing on the edge of the landing pad, ready to dive into this alien experience, I took a deep breath, savoring the fresh air. It had smells that I had never experienced before, sort of a fishy pine tree mixed with something I had smelled coming from an alley in Oklahoma City.

I took another deep breath and started to feel dizzy. Maybe that was enough deep breathing for the moment. I'd have to ask Tera if New Talpreus had the same oxygen mix as Earth.

I set off through the concourse, following a flow of other visitors toward the nearest door to the spaceport. Having seen the layout of the facility from above, I knew I had a long walk ahead of me. The invigorating feeling of extra oxygen in the air made me relish the idea of a brisk stroll.

The doors to the spaceport slid open, and a new smell suddenly reached my nose. It was the most delicious aroma I had ever experienced. Like an entire holiday meal had somehow been condensed into a single whiff. My stomach growled urgently. I felt an overwhelming desire to find the source of that smell.

I glanced at the people around me. None of them seemed as intent on the smell as I did. Were they not able to smell it, or had they simply become immune to it?

As I followed the flow of the crowd into the spaceport, the din increased, dozens of sounds at once. There were at least four different songs playing at full volume—unless that was the style of music in this part of the galaxy. And the yelling was intolerable. I passed a man with a long black beard and purple-tinged skin sitting on the ground. He wore very little clothing, and as I walked by, he flexed the muscles in his arms and chest and screamed something unintelligible at me.

Right behind the muscle-man was another alien—dressed in several poofy layers of what looked like foam or maybe sponges—who bounced up to me and bumped into my shoulder with the sponges. She rattled off a phrase or two in a way that made me feel like I was being accused of killing her beloved pets. I held up my hands defensively, hoping that was a universal sign that I meant no harm.

After those two first-contact experiences, I realized what was going on. I stopped in the middle of the wide corridor and looked over the heads of the people in front of me. Booths and stalls lined the hall as far as I could see. This was what the traffic controller meant when she said that

I would have to pass through the advertising zone if I used a free landing berth.

As I remembered the traffic controller and how easily I understood her, I realized that communicating was going to be more difficult than I expected. How had she spoken such perfect English? How many people were there on this planet who spoke English? And how would I find them?

What if she was the only one—like an interpreter at a visitor's center? I felt suddenly deflated at my daunting task.

I glanced down at the med-kit and ration pack in my hands. No one in this part of the spaceport was going to buy what I wanted to sell, not when they had hundreds of vendors hawking their wares on all sides.

Another vendor approached me, speaking loudly and pointing at the products in his booth. I assumed it was some sort of gadget for hair, because he gestured at the top of my head then to the flamboyant green and pink hairdo he was sporting.

"I have no idea what you're saying," I said to him.

He cocked his head to the side, considering me. After a second, he spoke again. Still gibberish. The vendor next to Hairdo-Guy grabbed my arm and pulled me toward her booth. She apparently was trying to sell some poisonous drink cocktails because her table looked like a mad scientist's lab.

"No, I don't want any of your stuff, either," I said loudly.

The Hairdo-Guy started yelling at Cocktail-Lady like he was arguing over my attention, but he kept pointing at me and then pointing at his own ear. The Cocktail-Lady's brows went up, and she began to chuckle, pointing at me and then her own ear.

Maybe this was some sort of ritual or inside joke on New Talpreus.

"Is something wrong with my ear?" I asked.

Both vendors immediately reacted, almost as if they had understood me. Hairdo-Guy laughed loudly, but Cocktail-Lady waved her hands back and forth. I wasn't sure, but that seemed like the universal sign for no.

A third vendor, who had been watching the exchange from his booth of exotic shoes, walked over to me. He patted my arm in a consoling way then began to mime out a message.

He pointed at my mouth then made several wavy, loopy lines in the air and then pointed at the Hairdo-Guy, who smiled and smacked the back of his head. I had no idea what the hand to the head meant, but the mouth and waving in the air seemed to indicate my speaking.

Mr. Scary-Shoes then pointed at Hairdo-Guy's mouth and made the same loopy lines through the air before pointing at me. That was the communication back to me. Was I supposed to slap the back of my head like Hairdo-Guy had done?

Before I could contemplate this oddity of non-verbal communication, the shoe salesman grabbed me by the head and turned my ear toward him. He held two fingers, pointing toward the spot directly behind my ear. He touched the skin with his fingers and made a loud "bam" sound.

I immediately stumbled backward, to the amusement and glee of Hairdo-Guy and Cocktail-Lady. I was unsure if Mr. Scary-Shoes was threatening me or initiating me into some brotherhood. Either way, I realized that, without the ability to communicate, I was on a fool's errand.

I quickly backed away from the three vendors, not immediately willing to take my eyes off them. The first two continued to laugh and point at me, but the shoe salesman simply shook his head in resignation.

The crowd jostled me around as I fought my way back to the ship. I wasn't sure what I had expected, plunging myself into an alien spaceport like that, but I certainly hadn't expected utter failure. Of course, it could have been worse. I could have been mugged and left for dead in a back alley.

The cargo ramp lowered as I approached, thanks to Tera's keen observation skills, no doubt. Her holographic form shimmered into view at the top of the ramp.

"You didn't die," she said dryly, but I did detect a slight note of relief under the sarcasm.

I hit the button to close the ramp behind me. "I don't know what I thought was going to happen out there, but it was not what I expected. I didn't come across anyone I could understand. Not even a little bit."

"I'm sure most of them understood you. But why would you think you'd be able to understand anyone on New Talpreus?" Tera asked.

Now that she mentioned it, I had wondered if some of the vendors could understand me. I shrugged. "I don't know. The traffic controller woman obviously spoke English," I replied defensively.

"She didn't speak English," Tera shot back.

"Yes, she definitely did. And pretty well."

"No. She was speaking modified Bonarish. The computer's linguistic processors translated it into English for you."

"What? No way. I thought for sure her mouth moved with the words." Now that I thought back to the exchange, her mouth really hadn't moved much during the conversation. I had chalked it up to boredom, but maybe it had been something else.

"The computer tweaks the lips on the video feed, too," Tera said.

I stopped and leaned against a storage container—probably full of rocks or dirt or some other useless commodity. "You're telling me I won't be able to understand anyone"—I waved toward the concourse and the spaceport—"on this entire planet?"

She shook her head. "Not without a translator."

I stared at her for several seconds before letting out a long breath. "Okay, so I can only talk to people using the ship's comm system." I moved around the cargo bay, absently glancing at the storage bins as I thought. "Can we call anyone else on the planet? Besides the traffic controller, I mean."

"Nobody is going to answer some random call from a ship docked at the spaceport," Tera said.

That gave me an idea. "What about the other ships docked here? Would we be able to contact any of them?"

She shrugged. "Sure. But why would they be willing to help you?"

"Hmm." I continued wandering around the cargo bay, thinking out loud. "There has to be something we could use to entice someone to help us." I had already given up on the idea of using the med-kits or the food-packs. Then I remembered the living quarters that I had crashed in. Had that room been empty?

I hustled through the bay door and up the ladder to the top deck. Past the kitchen, I turned toward the rear of the ship.

Tera reappeared in the living area as I passed. "What are you doing?" she asked.

"I'm going to see if there's anything in these rooms that might be valuable to trade," I called over my shoulder.

I stepped through the door into the small room and looked around. I hadn't really paid much attention to it before; I'd been in too much of a daze. I checked the closet and drawers built into the wall next to the desk. Those were all empty. A few small bins sat against the far wall. I opened one of them. Inside was a stack of clothing—shirts, pants, jackets—all in navy blue with gray highlights. I lifted a jacket out of the bin to examine it. The fabric was smooth to the touch, and the texture of it was extremely comfortable. If this was how they made clothes in this part of the galaxy, I might need to pick up a few things before I headed back to Earth.

I wasn't sure if these would be worth anything in a barter arrangement. Plus, I was hesitant to part with them because I only had the clothes on my back, and it was probably time to see if the ship had a laundromat. I tossed the jacket aside. I'd come back for it later.

Crossing the hall to the other crew quarters, I saw that I had apparently chosen the unoccupied one to crash in. This room had a variety of items strewn about, though the bed was made up tight, as if housekeeping had just been through.

Like the first room, this one had a pair of bins against the wall, but they were already opened and partially empty. In the desk drawers, I found several other items. A tablet with a perfectly smooth display that lit up before my fingers even touched it. I had no idea what the symbols on the surface said, so I left it alone. It must not have been linked with the ship's computer, because it wasn't set to display English. I also found a worn paper book with similar alien markings as the tablet. In the corner of the shelf, there was a carved sculpture of a bright gold star cradled by an open hand.

Before I had the chance to examine anything in more depth, a view screen on the wall turned on. A video of Tera appeared. "What are you doing?" she asked.

I frowned at her. "I'm looking for something valuable to barter," I replied. "And why are you on a wall screen instead of standing next to me?"

"I can only go where there are holographic projectors," she huffed. "And apparently the designers of the *Starfire* didn't think the crew would want me popping up in their room."

That made sense. Though it seemed like the screen suddenly turning on would be equally disconcerting.

"I found these." I placed the star back on the shelf and held the tablet and the book up toward the screen. "Do you know what they are?"

Tera shook her head. "Bring them out where I can see them better."

"You don't have cameras scattered around the crew quarters?" I asked as I scanned the room.

"Earth humans aren't the only ones who value their privacy, you know."

I chuckled and walked back to the kitchen where Tera stood waiting for me. I held out the book and tablet for her to inspect.

"This is an electronic logbook." She pointed to the tablet. "And this is a novel about a great warrior princess who is forced to ride into battle against her potential suitors."

"Sounds riveting," I said.

"Don't get snooty just because it's not what you're used to. It's a pretty epic story, especially when she finally meets the one she loves and she's forced to decide whether—"

I held up a hand. "Don't spoil the ending. What if I decide to read it one day?"

Tera cocked her head to the side. "You can't. It's not translated into English."

"You could read it to me as a bedtime story." I couldn't help a small smirk.

Tera rolled her eyes. "Anyway, these are both written in modern Otanian."

"I don't know what that means," I said. It was sort of a common refrain at this point.

"It means they most likely came from the planet Otania Sancterum," Tera explained.

"But who did they belong to?" I asked, looking closer at the tablet.

"Well, there's only one other person who's been on this ship besides you and Gabe."

"The original pilot?" I asked.

"Yeah. But we don't know who he was because the computer's databanks are still corrupted."

I glanced at the book and tablet in my hand. "Hmm. That's not really much to go on. But I guess it's better than nothing. I didn't get much out there in the Big City." I pointed out a nearby portal. I hadn't even made it past the advertising concourse. How were we going to make a difference in tracking down Gabe's attackers?

A wave of exhaustion washed over me. Maybe I'd be able to think better after some rest.

I wandered back to the room I'd used before and collapsed on the bed.

Thanks to the alien bed technology, I was only awake for a few more seconds.

Chapter Four

The next morning, I sat at the kitchen's small table staring at my reconstituted breakfast. Actually, I had no idea if it was breakfast or not. I had simply grabbed the first meal-pack I could see—besides the green slime one—and put it into the reconstitution machine to heat and steam it back to life. Tera had assured me that all of the meal packs were safe for human consumption. But I wasn't sure if safe necessarily meant tasty.

It wasn't half bad. It was sort of like a meat pie with vegetables except that the meat was slightly on the orange side, and the vegetables were various shades of purple. Plus, the crust had a hint of what tasted like anise and caramel.

Strange but satisfying.

As I ate, a plan started forming in my mind. We had lifted off from the Big City dock that morning—free berths only lasted so long—and were floating somewhere in the Talprean system. But I knew we couldn't stay there forever.

When Tera appeared standing across the table from me, I was just about ready to make things happen.

"You're sure these are written in Otanian, right?" I tapped the book and tablet on the table next to me.

"Yeah," Tera replied.

"And the only place they speak Otanian is . . . what did you call it?"

"Otania Sancterum," she said.

"Easy for you to say," I quipped.

Tera rolled her eyes. "According to the information I looked up on New Talpreus, the answer is yes, Otania Sancterum is the only planet that speaks or writes in Otanian. Well, there are some weird conspiracy theories about where the language came from, but they sounded pretty dumb."

I nodded, not quite sure what that all meant. "Okay, then let's go there and start asking some questions." I looked at Tera to see what she thought of that idea.

Her face scrunched as she considered. "Yeah. We might as well. Either that, or we follow the waypoint reminder that keeps popping up in the navigation system."

"Was that waypoint for the pilot's original destination?" I asked.

Tera shrugged. "Maybe."

I frowned and glanced absently toward the nearest portal. "I'd rather not blindly follow some questionable hidden message in the partially corrupt databanks, so let's go to the pilot's homeworld."

"The intra-space jump is ready," Tera said. "Just tell me when."

"Wait," I said, suddenly remembering something. "If we make another intra-space jump, aren't we going to run out of fuel?"

"The distance across the inner core of the Bonara Cluster is about twenty light years. Our fuel reserves would allow for dozens of jumps within the cluster before we would need to worry. Earth, on the other hand, is over six-hundred light years away. We would run out of fuel about three quarters of the way there."

"Oh. In that case, go ahead."

Tera nodded, and the view of blackness outside the portal shifted to a gray-brown.

I turned back to my holographic assistant. "I just thought of something," I said as I took another bite of alien breakfast pie.

"You want to trade the ship for a homestead on Kalera Five and learn how to farm feego root?"

I laughed. "That is a weirdly specific plan. Should I be considering it?"

Tera shrugged. "Another section of the computer's databanks just got recovered."

I shook my head. "No, I was thinking that I'm going to have the same problem on Otania that I had on New Talpreus. I won't be able to understand anyone."

"You need a translator implant," she said bluntly.

"An implant?"

"You think all those people on New Talpreus were from the same race? Or even the same planet?" Tera asked.

"I guess I hadn't really thought about it," I said.

"They understand each other because they all have an implant behind their ear that connects directly to the auditory cortex. It feeds in the electrical impulses that correspond to each person's language. It can actually override the sound they hear through their ears." Tera spoke as if reciting a paragraph from the computer's databanks.

I thought back to the interaction with the vendors in the spaceport. "So when the guy at the spaceport acted like he was shooting me behind the ear . . . he wasn't really pretending to shoot me?"

"Probably trying to tell you that you needed to get an implant," Tera said.

I held up my hands. "I don't think I'm quite ready to have some alien microchip inserted into my body." It all sounded a little too much like a UFO abduction. "All I need is a way to put that translation technology into an earpiece or something."

"I guess you could build one," Tera replied.

I frowned at her. "I'm not some futuristic inventor. I can barely build the F-22 landing gear—or at least I could back when I had a job."

"Just use the design lab," Tera countered.

"What design lab?" I said.

"It's down on the lower deck in the room next to the infirmary. I'm surprised you haven't looked in there yet," Tera said.

"Gabe said it was storage."

I hustled down the ladder to the first deck and walked to the middle of the short hall. Sure enough, there was another room, symmetrically matching the one with the med-pod. I pushed open the door, and the lights came on. There were a pair of empty workbenches in the middle of the room and several machines lining the walls.

I was already peering into the first machine when Tera appeared next to me.

"You wouldn't want to do that when the machine's on," she observed dryly.

I pulled my head away from the opening. "Why not? What is this?"

"That's a material fabricator. It has a magnetic plasma field that can form molten metal or plastic into whatever shape you want."

"Wow," I said. "What about this one?" I pointed to the next machine in the row.

"That's a circuitry grower. You program it with an electronic design, and it seeds the metallic slurry with bio-mimetic alloys that grow into the circuitry that you want."

"And this?" I pointed to a setup that looked sort of like a photo booth.

"That's the scanner. The parts you create will fit much better if you use that."

I glanced around the newly discovered high-tech factory. "Let's make a translator, then." I approached one of the workbenches and activated the control screen. It showed several design options that I could browse. I tapped the button that said *Custom Input*.

"*Specify product,*" the automated voice said.

"I need a translator device that can fit in my ear."

I looked over at Tera to see if she thought my description was a good one. She gave a noncommittal shrug.

A few seconds later, the interface replied, "*Optimal design calculated.*" A small device that looked very much like a modern hearing aid appeared on the screen in front of me. "*Five thousand two hundred languages loaded. Anatomical matching to custom humanoid specimen required. Short-range, single-duplex transmission only. Proceed with fabrication?*"

The design looked and sounded amazing. "Yes," I replied.

"*Please present appropriate humanoid orifice in scanner,*" the machine directed.

I chuckled when I imagined what alien ears might look like if the machine used the word *orifice* then stepped into the box. The light inside grew even brighter after I entered.

A disembodied voice said, "*Please hold still.*"

I did my best.

A moment later, the light dimmed, and the voice instructed me to step out. I looked over at the two fabrication machines, already working on the custom design. "Now what?" I asked Tera.

"It'll take about an hour to finish building it. Maybe you should shower or something." Tera scowled at me like I stank—which might have been true, but a hologram wouldn't know that.

I glanced down at the dirty jeans and grimy T-shirt I'd been wearing for the past two and a half days. When I'd thrown these clothes on, I hadn't planned on traveling several hundred light-years across the galaxy and meeting aliens.

If I had known, I might have worn a collar shirt.

Until I had the chance to find a second-hand clothing store on one of the inhabited planets we visited, I'd need to make do with what I had.

Then I remembered the flight suit I'd seen in the bin in my room. That might be better than some hand-me-down alien clothes. I popped up to the crew quarters, grabbed the flight suit from the open bin, and headed to the shower.

It probably wouldn't be accurate to call it a shower when it was more like a high-pressure steam bath. I'm not sure how the ship made steam that didn't scald my body, but it floated around me in a cloud until I was completely clean.

On the way out of the bathroom, I stopped in front of a tall mirror. I wasn't sure if the flight suit was designed to make the wearer look amazing, but I thought it did on me. My still-damp blondish hair hadn't changed, but the muscles in my shoulders and arms looked more defined. Maybe it was the fit of the flight suit. Hopefully, they were meant to be worn a little snug.

Tera met me at the spot where the hall from the crew quarters met the kitchen. "You look good in that."

"Thanks," I replied as I made my way to the flight deck. The planet below was awash in greens and blues. Lakes and rivers crisscrossed giant continents. "You better bring me up to speed on things here," I said as I settled into the pilot's seat.

Tera re-materialized next to me. "Otania Sancterum is home to the Otanian people. As a general rule, they reject violent confrontation and war of any kind. They do have advanced technology, but they use it primarily for personal conveniences rather than monetary gain. They allow visitors to their planet, but they don't really trust outsiders."

"Will they allow me to contact the pilot's family?"

Tera shrugged. "I've never met them personally. I'm just reading from the encyclopedia entry I downloaded on New Talpreus."

I stared back at the beautiful planet in front of us and took a deep breath. I would find out soon enough.

With the newly finished translator earpiece firmly in place, I stepped off the cargo ramp onto our assigned pad. Ours was the farthest of a cluster of low stone platforms in a large, circular landing zone. I stood in a deeply recessed space, like an artificial glen surrounded by tall stone walls covered with an ivy-looking plant. It felt like I'd stepped into an archaeological expedition or a fantasy painting except for the obvious evidences of modern technology—the gleaming glass doors built into the stone on the opposite side of the glen—and the fact that nothing was crumbling. Unlike New Talpreus, this docking facility did not have any other visitors. As I surveyed the empty, cavernous space, I began to wonder if we were even in the right place.

Given that there was only one way out of the glen—besides flying away—I walked toward the glass doors. But before I had even made it halfway, the doors slid open to reveal a slender woman dressed in a long cream robe. Her skin was medium brown, and she had long silver hair that sparkled in the light as she moved toward me.

She touched her fingertips together and bowed her head. When she spoke, her voice was soft and melodic. A moment later, a fair approximation of her voice sounded in my ear. "Welcome, esteemed visitor."

I stopped and turned to see if someone else had landed behind me. I couldn't imagine she meant me. When I realized that I was the only one in the landing zone, I turned back around. Maybe she'd been fooled by the fancy flight suit.

I watched my host for any change in her demeanor, but she didn't falter in the least. Her expression was serene and slightly proud.

"Thanks. I mean, thank you very much." I tried to imitate the hand gesture and the nod.

A small smirk touched the corner of her lips.

So much for first contact.

She spoke again, and the earpiece translated. "What service may we offer during your brief stay on our planet?"

That was a subtle but efficient way to keep visitors at a minimum.

"I am looking for a family of—" How should I explain who I was in relation to the dead pilot? "—a colleague of mine."

"What is the name of your colleague?" she asked.

I rubbed the back of my neck and glanced up at the orange sun setting behind the tall stone wall. I should have known that would be her next question. "Well, you see, I never caught his name. I just know he is from Otania, and—"

"Otania Sancterum." The full name of her planet didn't require a translation. Nor did the coolness in her correction.

"Sorry, Otania Sancterum. So this colleague was the former pilot of my ship." I gestured behind me. "But unfortunately, I can't." This part needed to be delicate and not a complete lie, just in case these people could read minds, which was a disturbing possibility. "He's not available for me to contact at the moment. I was hoping to find his family or friends here that might be able to help me."

My beautiful attendant scrutinized me for several excruciating seconds. Finally, she nodded deeply and turned toward the door, beckoning me to follow. I hurried to catch up to her as we walked into an opulently adorned atrium. Everything was bathed in the bright orange light spilling from windows high above our heads. The space was almost entirely empty—one attendant, similarly dressed to my own, stood at a door at the far end of the enormous room.

My attendant escorted me to an ornately decorated marble table that stood to the side. She tapped the surface, and the marble morphed into a series of jumbled scribbles that I was now able to recognize as the Otanian language. Maybe I would need to have the fabricator lab on the ship create a pair of glasses that could translate written words for me.

She touched a set of words near the center of the table. "What is the name of the family?" my earpiece translated.

"I don't know," I replied. I was sure she was going to become frustrated with my lack of understanding, so I pulled out the book and the flight log. "This is all I have from the previous pilot. I was hoping to visit his family to return these items to them."

My escort glanced at the tablet, but didn't take it. Instead, she took the book in her hands as if cradling a precious object. "I remember the first time I read this book." Her voice sounded wistful and nostalgic, but that might have just been the translation. She opened the front flap and pointed to another collection of scribbles.

"I can't read it," I said apologetically.

She smiled patiently before speaking. The translation followed a second later. "The name of your colleague is Fosso Shonara. We will search for the Shonara family name."

She touched more letters on the surface of the marble. Everything morphed and shifted until a map appeared. Next to it there was a picture of a bright red door set into a milky-colored wall. I leaned forward to scrutinize the image.

"The ancestral home of the Shonara clan is located in the Nashielle settlement. It is about"—the translator stuttered on the translation of the distance—"three hundred miles northeast from this city. You may land your craft in this zone only." She pointed to an open area on the map, and I tried to memorize it.

I thanked my kind host and exited the reception atrium, heading back toward the ship. I shook my head as I considered the contrast between New Talpreus and Otania Sancterum. On New Talpreus, I barely had room to breathe for the crush of people. Here, I had only seen two Otanians, and the entire time I felt like I had to whisper.

Back on the ship, I explained the exchange to Tera.

"Do we know where this Nashielle settlement is?" I asked.

Tera nodded and pointed to my heads-up-display. "The Otanian reception center was kind enough to transmit a map when we landed. It was actually to inform us of all the places we aren't allowed to land the ship, but it works for navigating to Nashielle, too."

I powered up the engines, and we lifted off from the pristine stone-walled landing zone. As I guided the ship over the country-side of Otania Sancterum, I could see why the Otanians worked so hard to protect their planet. It was strikingly beautiful. We flew over lush meadows and dense forests, followed by jagged cliffs dotted with lakes and streams. It was almost as if a gift shop display had been knocked over and all the postcards of beautiful vistas had spilled into a collage next to each other.

If the Otanians weren't so cold to outsiders, I might've considered living here. Maybe I could open a bed and breakfast. I'd make a killing.

After a brief, atmospheric flight, we found Nashielle, and I set the ship down in the designated landing zone on the outskirts. I closed the cargo bay door and started the short walk into town, aiming in the general direction that I thought would lead to the Shonara home. The streets of Nashielle reminded me of pictures I'd seen of quaint little European villages. The roads looked like cobblestone and the homes lined the road in one continuous wall of doors and windows. Residents walked up and down the streets, greeting each other and making pleasant conversation. They were all tall and thin, with various shades of dark skin and silvery hair. And I couldn't help but notice they were strikingly beautiful, even the older ones. Most of the people wore more sensible clothing than my host in the capital city—various shades of green, brown, and beige.

The looks that I got as I passed weren't openly hostile, but they weren't necessarily welcoming either. I wandered from street to street toward the part of the town that I thought the attendant had shown me. Most of the doors to the homes were brown or gray, but a few were red, like the picture I'd seen.

I stopped at a corner near two older-looking men and asked if they could tell me where to find the Shonara home. One of the men just gaped at me like I was speaking gibberish—which to him, I probably was. The other man pointed down the road. "Two streets and then right," his translated voice said.

I thanked them and continued down the street until I found the right door. I stared at the red surface and wondered if this culture had doorbells or if I was supposed to knock. Maybe they used some sort of sensing technology, like an advanced doorbell camera. Without anything else to go off, I decided to knock lightly and take my chances.

I had just raised my hand to the door when it swung wide.

A young woman—possibly a teenager or early twenties, if Earth years had any meaning on this planet—opened the door. She was lean, almost athletic-looking, with medium brown skin and long purplish-silver hair. Her bright green eyes considered me curiously.

"I'm looking for Fosso Shonara's family," I said politely.

She held a stiff palm out to me. "Shh!" she hissed. "You speak the Unspoken."

I frowned. What did that mean? Had I mispronounced the name? I was fairly certain that's the way my attendant had said it. "Fosso Shonara?" I repeated slowly.

The girl's eyes went wide with annoyance and something that looked almost like fear. She scrutinized my flight suit then glanced up and down the street. Finally, she reached out and grabbed me by the arm. "If anyone sees you in that outfit or hears you speaking the unspoken, they won't stop talking about it for three months." She yanked me inside, slamming the door quickly behind her.

I stumbled a few steps until I caught my balance. She stood staring back at me, brows raised. I finally realized that she might be waiting for me to offer some explanation.

I opened my mouth, ready to explain, or at least try, when an austere woman with short silver hair and a flowing lilac robe entered the room. It would have been more correct to say that she stormed in.

"What is going on here?" she asked coldly. "Rachia, why have you admitted a stranger to our abode?" She was lithe and tall and looked to be in her fifties. The expression on her face reminded me of Ms. Patterson, my junior high librarian, when she would catch me talking too loudly.

"He was standing at the entrance wearing that." The girl—Rachia—pointed at my clothes. "And he was speaking the Unspoken. What was I supposed to do?"

The tall woman turned a piercing stare on me. "What do you want?" I was impressed that my translator had so perfectly captured the icy tone in her voice.

I had no idea what was going on. But maybe if I explained who I was, I might be able to diffuse the situation. "I think we might have a common acquaintance." I stuck with a generic word since I'd never met the guy. "He's a pilot on a starship. Fosso Shonara?" I hadn't meant for it to come out like a question, but I couldn't help it. This woman made me feel like I was in trouble.

A look of dawning comprehension crossed her face. The loathing in her eyes that followed spoke volumes. "You have already taken my only son. What more could you possibly steal from us?" the translation screamed in my ear. It was like being yelled at twice. "Are you going to take my daughter now?!" She held out a hand toward Rachia.

The girl moved toward the woman. "Mother, please calm down. We do not want the neighbors to hear."

The woman took a deep breath that calmed her expression, but her eyes still held fury. "If you are with the Resistance, you must leave right now." She pointed toward the door. "We want nothing to do with you or your crusade."

I stared from the girl to her mother. "I think there's been a slight misunderstanding," I began. "I've never heard of the Resistance. My friend found an alien ship and fixed it up. Later, when we were attacked and I tried to get away, I accidentally flew here." I took a breath. "I really only came to talk to the family of whoever owned these." I produced the book and the tablet and held them out to the woman.

Rachia rushed forward and grabbed the book with both hands. "This is Fosso's," she cried, clutching it tightly. She moved to a wide couch against the wall and sat down with the book in her lap, ignoring a reproving look from her mother.

I offered the tablet to the woman. She eyed me suspiciously but finally took it. After examining the device, she returned her attention to me. "You say you do not know anything about the Resistance, and yet, you bring the flight log of a Resistance pilot." She held up the tablet.

I raised my hands in what I hoped looked like a calming gesture. "I can't read the tablet or the book."

I must have appeared sincere or trustworthy or whatever, because the woman's expression softened. "Tell me your name, young man."

"My name is Mitchell," I replied. "But you can call me Mitch."

"Come sit down, Mitchell." She waved toward a sofa-looking seat on the opposite side of the room from her daughter, who was still enthralled with the book I'd brought. "Your responses seem delayed to me." She caught a glimpse of the translator earpiece as we sat down. "Just as I suspected, you are using inferior technology for communication. You need an implant." She suddenly seemed almost motherly.

I smiled apologetically. "I just found out about translator implants yesterday, and I'm not sure if I want to get one."

"You should," Rachia called from across the room. "It would make conversations much faster."

I hadn't realized that my responses were that slow. I was just happy to be understanding them at all.

"My name is Anan Shonara." The woman pointed to herself. "This is my daughter, Rachia." She gestured to the teenage girl. "We are of the Third House of Nivee Shara." Anan leaned forward. "Fosso was my son," she whispered gravely.

I was surprised that she already spoke of her son in the past tense. "Was?" I asked without thinking.

"I should be ashamed to even speak the name of an Unspoken. But to refer to him in the now, rather than the past, would be unthinkable," Anan said.

I was momentarily caught off-guard by this explanation, but I decided to press ahead with what I needed to tell her. "I'm sorry that I don't know all the details of what happened to your son. I wasn't actually there, so I can't tell you exactly—"

Anan held up a hand. "We would not receive such details, even if you could share them." She paused a moment before speaking again. "You see, when my son left our planet to join the Resistance, he forsook our ancestral ways. He became an Unspoken. As such, we are required to turn our backs toward him until he makes amends. That includes not receiving any messages or other news from him until he returns to touch our backs and turn us to him again."

I wasn't completely familiar with the turning and returning phrases—probably literal translations of Otanian idioms—but I got the general gist. If they weren't willing to hear anything about Fosso, that could complicate my efforts to find out more. Plus, I felt like they needed to know the truth. "He's not coming back," I said bluntly.

"He is not . . . coming . . ." Anan's impassive mask slipped ever so slightly, and I caught a glimpse of a mother's pain at finding out what she probably already knew.

"What's happened to Fosso?" Rachia cried out, sorrow choking her voice. "He's not dead, is he?"

"Rachia, please temper your emotions," Anan demanded.

I looked at Rachia sympathetically and gave a small nod.

Rachia shook her head, her wails only intensifying. She stood and fled from the room, leaving the book behind on the couch.

"I apologize for my daughter's outburst," Anan said calmly.

"That's okay. I completely understand," I replied.

"What you may not understand is that in our culture, it is inappropriate to mourn publicly or in front of strangers. We only grieve privately." She glanced in the direction Rachia had gone and sighed. Then she looked back at me and straightened her posture. "Given that Fosso will not have the opportunity to perform the returning ritual during this life, you are now free to share what details you have."

I nodded, feeling the weight of what I was about to tell her. Hopefully, she would manage it better than Rachia. "I'm from a system several hundred light-years away from here. Apparently, your son was piloting a ship that crashed on my planet. My best friend, Gabe, found the ship and your son's body. He hadn't survived the crash." I couldn't remember if Gabe had specifically mentioned that, but it was a small fib I was willing to risk for a mother's sake.

Anan nodded, prompting me to continue.

"Gabe buried your son's body near the crash site."

At this information, Anan let out a short sob, her hand flying to her mouth. She immediately schooled her features, and after a moment, nodded for me to continue. I was surprised that she would react so strongly to details of her son's burial but not to the news that he had died in the crash.

I decided to press on with what I could tell her. "Gabe worked on the ship, trying to get it to fly again. Then, on the day he and I were going to test it out, a ship of aliens arrived. Gabe was shot, and I barely escaped by jumping here to the Bonara Cluster." I stopped and took a breath, trying to gather my thoughts. "I'm just trying to find out who killed my friend and why," I finished quietly.

Anan stared at me for several seconds. Long enough that I started to wonder if the translation delay was getting worse. Finally, she shook her head. "I am sorry to tell you, young Mitchell, that I do not know anything about my son's enemies. Nor do I care to know. I never understood why this resistance movement even began. The Bonara Defense Force has always protected the citizens of the Bonara cluster. We have no reason to doubt that they will continue to do so."

"The controller on New Talpreus mentioned the Bonara Defense Force. What is it?" I asked. Now that I had a sympathetic listener—someone who might be willing to explain things to me—I planned to take advantage of it.

Anan's brow lifted slightly. "It is the administrative organization that coordinates all of the militaries of the various friendly systems when there is a need for defense or other action. The Otanian security contingent participates in Bonara Defense Force operations when required by law or treaty, but no more."

That sounded similar to military alliances on Earth. "Do you think they would help me figure out who killed my friend?"

Anan shrugged. "I do not care to concern myself with the Bonara Defense Force or its machinations. I trust that it serves its purpose, but I do not rely on it for anything more. Our people can take care of ourselves, and young people should not bring shame to their families by pursuing anything beyond our own interests."

Clearly, there were some deep-rooted feelings among Otanian people—and certainly this particular mother—about how they should deal with the outside world.

We sat in silence for a while. I didn't know what I could say to make things better, and I wasn't sure I should press for any more information.

I glanced over at her and saw a single tear course down her cheek. She quickly swiped it away.

"Perhaps this is all my fault," she said with emotion in her voice. "My husband died when Fosso and Rachia were very young. Not knowing how else to connect my son with his father's clan, I encouraged him to develop a relationship with his father's father. Little did I know that as a result of their interactions, Fosso's mind would become poisoned with thoughts of the Resistance."

I didn't know what else to say, so I simply nodded.

Anan glanced out the front window, as if seeing something in the distance. "Now, because he has died far from this world, the circle of our bodies will be forever broken."

I waited for her to explain more, unsure whether I had understood correctly. When she didn't, I asked, "What does 'circle of bodies' mean?"

She smiled patiently at me. "In our culture, each family has a garden where they are buried, arranged in an ever-growing circle with the rest of their family. The garden of our clan is vast, filled with hundreds of family members who have journeyed beyond us." She glanced out the window again. "There is a place for me to lie next to my husband when my time comes. And plots were created for Fosso and Rachia when they were both born." Another tear ran down her cheek, but she made no attempt to stop it. "Now that space will be forever empty. Fosso has left a gap in our circle that can never be repaired." Anan's voice choked with emotion as she finished.

"I'm trying to figure out a way to get back to my planet. Maybe when I'm there, I can get Fosso's body and bring it back to you." I had no idea when I would be able to make the trip to Earth, to say nothing of another round-trip to bring Fosso's body back. But I wanted to offer her something.

"Dear young Mitchell, that is a very kind offer. However, the only thing worse than a broken circle of bodies is to remove a body from the ground once it has been laid there." She shook her head. "He will need to remain on your distant planet, and our circle will remain broken. It is only fitting, considering what he put this family through."

An idea suddenly occurred to me. "Does your culture permit having another—someone from outside the family—buried in the empty space to complete the circle?"

Anan looked at me with sad eyes. "It is considered the greatest act of selflessness, but you have too much of your life ahead to make such a serious commitment now."

"No, not me. I mean, I suppose I might consider it someday. But I meant my friend Gabe. It would be fitting, after all. Fosso should be here in your circle of bodies, but instead, he's buried back on Earth. Gabe should be laid next to his wife in our town cemetery, but instead he's being kept alive by a med-pod on a spaceship in some distant star cluster." Now it was my turn to get a little choked up. "He could take your son's place."

At Anan's sharp intake of breath, I thought perhaps I had offended her. But when she reached out and took my hand, I realized she was simply overcome with surprise. "Would you really do that for us?"

I nodded, glancing out the window in the direction of the ship.

It was time to accept that Gabe was dead. And with no family back on Earth to visit his grave, I couldn't think of anything better than for him to be the first person from Earth to be buried on another world. Besides, it's just the type of thing my kind friend would have done for a friend—or even a stranger—in need.

I turned back to Anan. "I think Gabe would have been honored to join your circle."

Chapter Five

The arrangements for the burial on Otania Sancterum took a day—which I discovered was four hours longer than a day on Earth. That might have explained why I was so tired when it was over. Or it could have been the emotional exhaustion.

The service was strange and lovely at the same time. Hundreds of members of Anan and Rachia's extended family were there. My earpiece did a fair job of translating the burial ceremony except for the parts about turning a circle and returning to a circle. I was completely lost for that, so I just followed the lead of Rachia and Anan. When they turned, I turned.

Before the guests departed the garden at the end of the ceremony, the entire group linked arms and created an enormous circle. Then they broke the chain next to Anan, and each one walked by Anan, Rachia, and me—because apparently I was now included in their family—to bid farewell with a traditional touch of the hands. They would face us directly, and we touched one hand to the other person's hand at chest level. Sort of like an incredibly soft high-five. Several of Rachia's older female cousins stood particularly close to me and lingered longer than the others as they performed the farewell.

I tried not to read too much into it.

The whole ceremony was quite cathartic. I had already come to terms with Gabe's passing, but to have an entire clan join in that final goodbye brought me such calm and consolation. I still wanted justice for Gabe, of course, but knowing that his final resting place was on a planet of such beauty brought a measure of peace.

My farewells with Anan and Rachia were similarly touching. Anan held my face in her hands as if I were her own son departing. She told me to be careful and wise and my journey would be blessed. Rachia grabbed me around the waist in a huge bear-hug and told me to come back to visit if I could.

When I finally returned to the ship, I staggered to my quarters and collapsed unceremoniously on my bed. I told Tera to take care of lift off and orbiting, and that I would wake up in a few hours to figure out what we should do next.

I awoke—what felt like minutes later—to the vague feeling of nothing. Despite not having more than a few days' experience with space travel, I was beginning to notice the difference between regular space and intra-space. I glanced out the portal of my quarters to see the gray and brown-tinted nowhere of intra-space.

Why had Tera not stayed in orbit of Otania Sancterum until I woke up?

Groggily, I rolled off the firm, yet incredibly enveloping, alien mattress and stumbled out into the hall. When I reached the flight deck, I looked around for Tera. She wasn't in her normal spot. I glanced down at the flight controls. We were mid-jump. The coordinates for our location and heading were numbers I could read, but they still didn't make any sense to me. I would need to have Tera explain that again—probably four or five more times.

I stepped back out into the living area. "Tera?" I called.

"Yes," a voice answered a few seconds later.

I spun around to see her standing in the doorway of the flight deck. "What's going on? Are you playing hide-and-seek or something? I was just in there and I didn't see you."

Tera gazed at the wall behind me, her eyes scanning back and forth. "I was momentarily off-line," she said finally.

I moved around her and sat down in the pilot's seat. "That's not good. Why would you take yourself offline right when we made a jump into intra-space?"

"I would never do that," she replied, sounding a little hurt. "One of the computer's subroutines deactivated me an hour ago. It must also have engaged the intra-space jump."

I jerked my head in her direction. "That's *really* not good. If you're not controlling our course, then where are we going?"

"If it's the same subroutine that's been trying to take over the ship since we arrived in the Bonara Cluster, then we're probably heading to the Thetis system. I've been fighting with that algorithm for days, but it's relentless."

I nearly fell out of my seat. "Part of the computer has been trying to take over the ship? When were you planning to tell me?"

Tera fixed me with an icy glare. "I *have* mentioned that waypoint reminder several times. But I had it under control, so it was fine."

I took a deep breath. "Next time, tell me. You don't have to explain everything that's going on with the ship, but losing navigational command functions is something I'd want to know about, even if you do have it under control."

She lifted a holographic shoulder to acknowledge that I'd spoken, which was exactly the way my teenage friend would have reacted to a snub. I waited for a few moments to let the sting to her pride subside.

"So, why would the computer want to take us to the Thetis system? Does the computer have anything in its databanks about it?"

"The rendezvous point," she answered.

"What rendezvous point?"

"For the original mission."

I sighed. She was clearly taking my earlier comments a little too personally—if that was possible for an AI matrix. "Tera, I'm sorry if I was harsh earlier. I'm still trying to figure out how to run the ship and keep us safe, okay?"

She nodded.

"So the computer has an algorithm that's taken over the ship?" I prodded.

"That's *temporarily* taken over the ship," Tera interjected. "We can stop our intra-space jump at any time and head back where we came from."

"Great. See, that's good to know." I figured positive reinforcement might be helpful. "And you're guessing that the algorithm is trying to take the ship to its original destination?"

"It must be," she replied. "Who else would have entered a location in the navigation system?"

I leaned back in my seat, contemplating the situation. We had no idea what Fosso had been doing when he crash-landed on Earth. And without the information in the damaged parts of the computer databanks, we might never know. At least going to the ship's original destination might give us some answers. I turned back to Tera. "You said we could change course at any time. Does that mean we can get rid of the subroutine that took control of the ship?"

"Not without some serious hacking of the ship's navigational programming," she said. "The security protocols protecting it are not easy to crack."

"So we're stuck with a rogue ship that will always try to fly us to the Thetis system?"

"There's a prompt for an override code," Tera added. "But that information probably died with Fosso. Unless someone else in the Resistance knows the code."

I put my hands behind my head and stretched. "Well, we hit a dead end with Fosso's family. Maybe continuing to his original destination is the next thing to try. Hopefully, the subroutine will terminate once we get there. If not, maybe we can track down someone who has the override code."

I looked over at Tera, and she nodded once to show her agreement.

"How long until we get there?" I asked.

"A little over an hour," she said.

I jumped up from the pilot's seat. "Great. Just enough time for a shower and a bite to eat."

It turned out to be more than enough time for a shower and a meal, so I did some exploring around the ship while I waited to arrive in the Thetis system. I found a few more crates of food and medical supplies in the cargo bay. Eventually, I would probably need to catalog and label those things, but I wasn't really interested at the moment.

The infirmary didn't have much beyond the empty med-pod and a few other medical devices that I didn't understand. I didn't stay in there long.

In the room with the design lab, there were several bins and crates stacked against the wall. I had originally thought they would be filled with raw materials for the fabricators, and some of them were. But one particularly large bin actually had a robot in it.

A robot that looked vaguely like an animal.

I reached into the crate and pulled the robot out. It was surprisingly light for its size.

"Tera?" I called, hoping she would hear me on one of the dozens of microphones I was sure were in the room.

She materialized in the design lab a few seconds later.

"Oh, you found our companion bot," she said happily.

I set the robot animal on the deck. "Is this one of those things you should have mentioned to me before?"

Tera waved airily. "I'm sure that list will just keep on growing." She crouched down next to the small, motionless robot. "Can you turn it on? The power switch is on the chest, right where the sternum would be." Tera pointed for me to look.

I tilted the bot slightly sideways and pressed the power switch. The robotic animal immediately sprang into a crouch, its head swiveling side to side.

Tera clapped her holographic hands with glee. "Let's call her Skeeter."

"Skeeter? I'm sure we can think of something cooler than that." I examined the bot and its amazingly realistic movements. When Tera didn't respond, I glanced up at her.

The frown on her holographic face bordered on a childish pout. "Skeeter was my grandpa's pet name for me—er, the real Tera."

Leave it to me to offend an AI matrix.

"Okay. We can call her Skeeter." I said, hoping to appease my friend. "As long as I get to name our next pet," I added with a smirk.

"Sure," she said with a shrug before turning her attention back to the bot. "Hopefully, I can connect to her systems." She stared intently at Skeeter, who, at the moment, was stepping cautiously around the small fabrication room. "There. Now I can see and hear everything Skeeter does. So if she goes with you off the ship, I'll be able to know what's going on."

As I watched Skeeter move around the room, I decided she acted more like a cat than a dog. Although she was the size of a labrador, her movements were sly and stealthy—very catlike. Perhaps the Bonara Cluster had domesticated larger felines that Earth had. I couldn't imagine having a cat that size clawing at my couch or jumping from the top of the blinds onto my head.

For the next half hour, Tera and I played with Skeeter on the lower deck. It was closer to the truth to say we were testing out the various commands that she would respond to—she did everything Tera asked and about half of what I asked. I had a suspicion that Tera was cheating with her digital link to the bot, but I decided not to complain. My holographic companion was acting happier than I'd seen her since this adventure had started.

"We're almost to the Thetis system," Tera announced suddenly. "I'll be on the flight deck." She disappeared.

Skeeter immediately walked out of the design lab. I followed, curious to see what the bot would do when faced with the ladder to the upper deck. I guess I wasn't surprised when she crouched, leaped halfway up the ladder, and clambered somewhat gracefully up the last rungs to the upper deck.

Definitely a cat.

I followed our new pet up the ladder and over to the flight deck. Skeeter had settled into the jumpseat behind Tera, whether by instruction or choice I didn't know.

When I looked out the front windows and saw the planet in front of us, I froze in my tracks. "What is that?" I asked Tera.

"That's Thetis Max, the largest moon of Thetis Four," she replied.

"Wow. It looks nothing like Otania Sancterum." I climbed over the back of the pilot's seat and slid into my spot, all the while unable to take my eyes off the orb in front of me.

Where Otania Sancterum was green and blue, this world was black and gray striped with orange and red. Even on the side exposed to the light of the Thetis sun, the rocky surface was almost as black as the starfield behind it.

"Thetis Max is a cooling lava planet. There are still a few lava flows, but most of the surface is black pumice and obsidian," Tera explained.

"Why does this feel like a bad idea?" I asked.

"Are you worried about it being a trap?" Tera shot back.

"If it is a trap, and someone steals the ship, leaving me stranded hundreds of light-years from my homeworld, is it too much to ask that it happen on a resort planet?" I glanced back at the dead lava moon. "Just my luck, I get stranded somewhere like this," I muttered.

The auto-pilot brought us into low orbit, where I could get a close-up look at the galactic equivalent of a desert island.

"Does your rogue algorithm say where we're supposed to land?" I asked after half an orbit.

"Yeah," Tera said with an impish grin. "But I don't think you're going to like it."

"There's no way there could be anything on this moon worse than we've already seen," I said emphatically.

I was wrong.

As we floated over a solidified lava ocean, Tera pointed at a sinkhole, rimmed with orange molten rock, a round, black island in the center. It was difficult to judge size from so high up, but the island must have been as big as Oklahoma City.

I looked back at Tera. "What exactly are you pointing at?"

She pointed again, straight into the gaping crater in front of us. "See that facility down there, on the island . . ."

I squinted and could just make out a collection of gray, man-made buildings. "You've got to be kidding me."

She shook her head, almost gleeful at my dismay.

"What exactly is it?" I asked as the island from the underworld grew larger in the window.

"It has to be a mining facility of some kind, but it's not registered. It was either abandoned so long ago that nobody bothered to include it on the map. Or . . ."

The way she drew out the end of the phrase didn't bode well. "Or what?" I asked.

"Or it's an illegal operation run by space pirates. You know, the kind that will be super unhappy if we show up on their doorstep." Tera grinned.

I scowled at her obvious enjoyment. "You do know that if we get boarded by pirates, they'll probably wipe your matrix and start over with someone more agreeable."

She stuck her holographic tongue out at me.

The atmosphere on Thetis Max was thin, but still maneuverable. I knew because I wasn't spinning out of control as I steered the ship toward what I thought looked like the landing pad next to the largest building.

The ship settled onto the cracked and crumbling surface of the moon with an ominous thud. I checked the screen for external status. The ship appeared to be stable. The gravity of this moon was only about half of Earth's. The thin atmosphere did have oxygen, but the display showed a bunch of other gasses that I didn't recognize.

"You might want to wear a breather unit," she said, "but the pressure should be enough to keep your organs on the inside just wearing your flight suit."

"We're going to need to talk about your sense of humor when I get back." I got up and walked toward the stairs. This would be my first chance using the airlock. There was no way I wanted to risk letting the lava moon's atmosphere into the ship.

"Take Skeeter with you," Tera called. A second later, I heard the sound of the robot's feet padding along the deck toward me.

Down on the lower deck, I pulled open the airlock hatch. It was by far the heaviest door on the ship, except for the cargo ramp. Skeeter hopped through the door and I pulled the hatch closed behind me. The breathing mask resembled a modern scuba facemask. When I pulled it over my face, I had to fight off a brief wave of claustrophobia. I touched the airlock control panel to activate the cycle. Once the pressure had equalized, the outer hatch opened, and I stepped out into a hellscape.

Heat eddies warped my vision as the wind whipped hot and cold air around me. This was much more what I had imagined my first step onto an alien planet would be like.

Skeeter leaped forward toward the nearest building, apparently unaffected by the strange atmosphere. I followed after her, bounding in double-long strides as I adjusted to the lower gravity.

When we reached the nearest door of the building, I gripped the handle then paused, looking down at Skeeter. "Tera, are we sure this is the right place?"

Her voice crackled on the bot's external speakers. "That building is the waypoint."

"And the rogue program hasn't reset now that we're here?" I asked hopefully.

"Nope. Either you find some override code in there, or I'll need to hack the guidance system subroutines." She paused. "Or we could just stay in this vacation paradise."

"Or maybe you could tell me what this writing says." I pointed to the harsh lines on the door. Skeeter's head turned upward.

"It says 'Authorized Personnel Only.' And below that it says 'Airlock 529.'"

I guess that would be good enough. At least I wasn't trying to open the emergency lava flow release door. I pulled hard on the handle crank and the locking mechanism squealed in protest. I held the door open for Skeeter to scamper inside before closing and cycling the system. I was glad to have the breather in place, just in case this rickety-looking air-lock decided to start spewing toxic gas at me.

A minute later, the dusty control panel lights switched from purple to yellow. I assumed that meant the cycle was done, so I unlocked the inner door and pushed it open. The interior of the mining operation was a confused floorplan of conveyors, carts, and excavator machines. We must have stumbled into a storage warehouse of some kind. It certainly didn't appear to have been operational for some time. A thin layer of volcanic ash coated the floor.

The high windows of the warehouse glowed a pale orange from the lava outside, casting a dim, otherworldly color on everything I saw.

"Skeeter's sensors are reading breathable air in there," Tera said. "You can take off the breather now."

"I think I'll keep it on for a few more minutes, just in case," I said as I stared around the dim warehouse. "But I wish I'd brought a flashlight."

"Skeeter has a removable light source that you can use," Tera said.

That was handy. I looked down at my robotic companion and saw a small, rectangular object rise up from her back. I grabbed it and switched the light on.

The giant face of a robotic digging machine loomed in front of me in the new light. I jumped back several feet, my heart racing.

"What happened?" Tera asked as Skeeter's cameras twisted to look at me.

I shook my head. "Nothing. It's just a little spooky in here."

I took a deep breath to calm my nerves and started along the edge of the room until I reached a doorway leading to a long hall. Lacking any windows, it was completely black. The illumination from my small flashlight didn't even reach the end. Skeeter padded forward into the hall, completely unfazed by the darkness. I decided to follow her.

About halfway down the hall, I heard a faint clang in the distance.

"Did you hear that?" I asked.

"Skeeter's sensors are registering dozens of inputs, including the shifting of the tectonic plates under this island. What sound are you talking about?"

"I thought I heard something down this hall. Do you think someone could still be living here?"

"That's much more likely than alien zombies," Tera said dryly.

"Thanks, Tera. I hadn't even been worried about zombies until now."

I hustled to keep up with Skeeter. A moment later, I had the distinct feeling that someone was watching me. I glanced over my shoulder, flashing the light down the long hall we had just traveled. Nothing but dusty footprints and an eerie sunset-glow from the warehouse at the end.

We reached an intersecting corridor, and I thought I could see a faint light coming from deeper inside the facility.

I looked down at Skeeter. "In for a penny, right?" I said to the bot.

"If you're speaking to me, I have no idea what you're talking about," Tera said.

"No. I was just talking to Skeeter." I replied.

"Skeeter can't talk back," Tera said.

I waited a moment before replying. "Exactly."

I heard a "hmph" from my AI friend.

I walked down the new hallway with my trusty robopet for company. The corridor grew brighter the further we went. Coming around a corner, I found light spilling from an open door. I slowed and peeked around the corner. It was a small lounge with an eating area and some ancient-looking appliances. I might not have known they were appliances at all except that one of them had a pot with some type of stew in it.

And the stew was steaming.

I glanced around the room, trying to discover any other clues about who its recent resident might have been. A blanket lay crumpled on the end of a couch, and several food containers were scattered around the space.

When I turned to face the door I'd entered through, a woman stood in the middle of the doorway. I nearly dropped my flashlight in surprise. There may or may not have been a small yelp, too.

She spoke in quick, harsh tones and my communicator earpiece started translating a second later. "Took you long enough to get here," she said. "Did you decide to take a vacation on the sands of Invathea?"

I stared at her through the now-fogging visor of my breather. She stood half a head shorter than me, wearing a flight suit similar to mine. She had long blond hair with frosty-blue highlights that shimmered when she moved. Her skin was pale, and her cheeks were tinted blue instead of pink. She looked like a water-nymph who had gone to space.

"You're not Otanian. Your skin's too fair," the water-nymph said.

I shook my head.

"And why are you wearing a breather? The air in here is fine." She spoke with commanding authority, like she was used to getting things done her way. "Didn't you check the readings about the atmosphere?"

My heart rate had nearly returned to a level that I trusted myself to speak again. "I didn't quite believe it," I said as I cautiously took off my breather.

She cocked her head, scrutinizing me. "Why didn't someone notify me that Fosso wouldn't be making the drop?"

I opened my mouth, preparing to explain everything that had happened, but not really knowing where to start.

But before I could say anything, she said, "I know, I know, secrecy for the mission." She shrugged, a wry grin on her face. "But it's just my luck. I've been waiting on this rock for you for five weeks, and you get here when I'm in the bathroom." She shook her head ruefully.

I laughed politely, not sure exactly how to respond to that.

"Just let me grab my stuff and we can get going. I obviously haven't had any communications from headquarters while I've been here, but I'm sure they're anxious to get the Mark 7 into action."

Before I had a chance to say anything, she turned and dashed down the hall into the deep darkness. Skeeter sidestepped next to me. "She seems to think you're delivering the ship to her," Tera's voice said quietly.

"I know," I whispered in reply. "But we need her to give us the unlock code, and I'd rather not make her upset before that happens. She seems kinda high-strung."

Half a minute later, the woman was back in the doorway, a bag slung under her arm. "Let's go." She didn't even wait for me to follow; she simply turned on her heel and started down the corridor back the way I had come.

I looked down at Skeeter and imagined she understood my confusion. I wasn't excited about being left behind in the spooky mining facility, so I hustled after my new alien companion.

I waited until I was next to her before I attempted to start my explanation.

Before I could begin, she said, "I don't know if they told you, but my name's Vrynn." She touched her palm to her chest.

"Mitch," I said, mimicking her motion. I figured I should say something now, while there was a small lull. "I'm probably not who you think I am."

"Yeah, like I said, I was surprised when you weren't Fosso." She spoke slowly, eyeing me as if I was coming late to the conversation. "It was his mission to get the ship and bring it to the drop-off." She shrugged. "But one thing I've learned with the Resistance is not to ask too many questions. You know what they say, the knowing know and the unknowing don't."

I'd obviously never heard that saying, but I didn't want to confuse the issue. "I'm actually not—"

"Besides, I definitely don't want the responsibility of command." She pulled a face as if she smelled something rotten. "Too much planning and headaches. Just give me a mission, and I'll get it done." Vrynn added a small salute for good measure.

I couldn't help but smile at her enthusiasm.

We reached the airlock, and Vrynn tapped the control panel to begin the cycle. "So how does the Mark 7 fly? Do the gyros keep the attitude stable when you engage the Quake Drive?"

My head snapped toward her. Tera had said something about a Quake Drive that day Gabe had first shown me the ship. I was about to ask her what she knew about it when she tapped the facemask of the breather she had just put on and pointed at the one in my hand.

I quickly pulled the breather over my head, trying not to hyperventilate and nearly being poisoned by noxious moon gasses.

"It doesn't really matter," Vrynn continued. "Just having the Quake Drive at all will be a huge help, even if the ride is a little bumpy on the way."

I pondered that comment as we walked out onto the dusty, black surface of the landing pad.

She turned to look at me as we walked. "I do hope you'll explain why you're late. I mean, if something came up, and you couldn't make it in time, I understand. But it would have been nice if you could have sent a message." She laughed. "Actually, that's a crazy thing to say. The rendezvous was supposed to happen here so no one could make contact with me or track the exchange."

As we approached the ship, her chatter abated, and I understood why. It was an impressive sight, crouched on the landing pad. It exuded a sense of speed and power. We walked around the long, broad nose, the flight deck windows partially visible high above our heads. Vrynn craned her neck to catch a glimpse.

I bent our path around the winglets, and Vrynn gaped at the weapons mounted underneath.

"Impressive," was all she said.

When we reached the low-slung tail of the ship, I tapped the outer panel and the large cargo ramp slowly lowered to the ground.

"Wow," Vrynn said as she walked up into the cargo hold. "So this is the Mark 7." She gazed around the cluttered space, seemingly oblivious to the mess I'd already made.

"Actually, we call it the *Starfire*," I said, even though I hadn't really ever called it that. "And hopefully, when we get to the flight deck, you can fix the navigation system."

"Let's go take a look," Vrynn said as she bounded out of the room.

I finally caught up to her in the living area. Vrynn stood across from Tera, staring at her. "What happened to the AI Matrix?" she asked without taking an eye off Tera.

"Oh, uh, this is how she was when I got the ship." That was a bit of a fib, though it was technically true.

"I saw the video report that Fosso sent. He was interacting with a male AI matrix that looked like a middle-aged technician, not a teenage girl." Vrynn gazed at Tera and started a slow walk around her.

Tera stood still as Vrynn circled her, but not without a fair amount of eye-rolling.

Vrynn finished her review of Tera's holographic projection and faced me again.

"So, did I pass the inspection?" Tera said, her tone dripping with sarcasm.

Vrynn's head whipped toward Tera then back at me. "And it has an annoying personality? That's completely unacceptable."

"I could say the same about you," Tera muttered.

Vrynn's eyes narrowed at me. "Have you made modifications to the Mark 7?"

I didn't answer for a moment, partially because of the delay of my translator earpiece, and partially because I wasn't sure how to answer. "I didn't make—"

"What did you say happened to Fosso?" Vrynn pressed, not letting me finish my lame explanation.

I took a deep breath. There was no sense putting this off any longer. "Unfortunately, he didn't survive when the ship—"

Suddenly, Vrynn drew a blaster from her hip holster.

"Whoa, whoa." I held my hands up to show that I wasn't any threat to her. "Why are you pointing a weapon at me?"

"You just admitted that you stole this ship and brought it here to find out the location of the Resistance's secret base," she replied.

I'm sure my eyes nearly bulged out of my skull. "I absolutely did not say that. Is your translator malfunctioning? Maybe mine isn't working." I brought a hand up and tapped my earpiece. "Say something again. Less crazy this time."

She took a menacing step forward and brandished the gun at me again. "Tell me who you're working for! How did you get the ship? Did you kill the pilot?"

"Nope, still crazy," I muttered.

"You need to start explaining right now," Vrynn said.

I held my hands up even higher. "I promise I didn't steal this ship. It crashed on my planet, and my buddy got it flying again."

"What planet?" Vrynn didn't look like she believed me yet.

"It's called Earth," I replied.

"Dirt? That's not the name of a planet."

"No. Not dirt. Earth."

Vrynn cocked her head at me. "You just said dirt twice."

I glanced at Tera for help.

She exhaled a long, annoyed sigh. "Vrynn is from a planet called Mareesh that's covered almost entirely with water. In her language, they only have one word for dirt."

I looked back at Vrynn, scowling that she still had the weapon pointed at me.

"It doesn't matter." Vrynn said, shaking her head. "You're going to get off this ship, and I'm going to complete my mission."

"You can't abandon me on this moon," I protested.

"Why not?"

"That would be cruel and heartless."

"You left me here for weeks," she replied.

"That clearly wasn't my fault. I had no idea you even existed until ten minutes ago."

"You know what?" Tera said in a bored voice. "It doesn't matter, anyway. The navigation algorithm that brought us here won't let us leave."

Vrynn scowled. With her weapon still trained on me, she moved toward the flight deck door. It refused to open for her. She tapped on the override controls, but still nothing. "That's absurd. The algorithm was meant to bring the ship here if something went wrong with the mission. It wasn't meant to lock out the ship." She turned back to Tera. "Hologram, transfer your matrix onto the flight deck and open this door."

I saw a flash of annoyance in Tera's eyes before she nodded at Vrynn. Tera turned her gaze to the sealed flight deck door and clamped her eyes shut, her virtual fists clenched in front of her. She looked like a little girl trying to will a pony into existence. After a few seconds, her hands and face relaxed. "Sorry," she said to Vrynn, "Still locked out."

Now I was as puzzled as Vrynn. Aside from a slight annoyance, the rogue navigation sub-routine hadn't really caused any problems with controlling the ship, and it definitely hadn't locked us out of any of the systems. When I looked back at Tera, I saw the slightest flutter of her eye. Was that a wink? Did my AI friend understand the subtleties of subterfuge?

"Yeah, there's nothing I can do without the override code," Tera said to Vrynn.

Vrynn let out a frustrated sound. "Find the homing algorithm and enter the code 5299 Bizon Shoren Drell."

A moment went by, then Tera announced, "Code accepted."

Had Tera just tricked this Resistance operative into giving her the override code? I couldn't believe it. Now we just had to get rid of Vrynn and we were free.

"Now, take the ship into orbit and set a course for Dreporox," Vrynn instructed.

For several long seconds, Tera didn't reply. She simply stared at Vrynn. Then she turned lazily and looked at me. "By the way, Mitch, I think we have full control of the ship now."

I smiled broadly. "Great," I said, lowering my hands.

"Why are you talking to him?" Vrynn brandished the gun in my direction. My hands shot back up immediately. "I'm the one in command of the ship now."

Tera's holographic brow went up. "Uh, I don't think so."

"This Mark 7 is property of the Resistance," Vrynn said, her voice rising. "And it's a vital part of our strategic plan. I am taking control of this ship right now."

She stared from Tera to me and back again.

I turned to Tera. "Who's in command of the ship?"

"You are," Tera replied. "I'm not trusting Gabe's hard work to some crazy woman."

Vrynn fumed. She turned her attention back to me. "What did you do to the ship's AI matrix? The last thing I need for this mission is to have to fight with a moody hologram the entire time."

I knew how she felt, but at the moment, I couldn't bring myself to feel guilty about it.

I heard a soft voice in my ear. "Should I use Skeeter to incapacitate her?" It was Tera.

I glanced over at her. She hadn't moved her lips, but she gave me a meaningful look. Somehow, she must have figured out a way to send a transmission to my translator earpiece.

I glanced down at the robot animal sitting next to my feet. Skeeter seemed to be crouched, ready to pounce. I wasn't excited about the prospect of Skeeter attacking when Vrynn had her gun pointed right at me.

Fortunately for me, Vrynn made a big mistake.

She suddenly turned the gun toward Tera. If Vrynn had been hoping to threaten the AI into giving her control of the ship, she got way more than she bargained for.

Tera threw her hands in front of her face and shrieked—a completely irrational response for a holographic projection, but a normal one for a teenage girl.

At that exact same moment, Skeeter leaped from my side and clamped her robotic jaw down on Vrynn's wrist—the one holding the gun.

Vrynn yelped in pain, and the gun clattered to the floor. I scampered around Skeeter and grabbed the gun, quickly pointing it at Vrynn. "Skeeter, down," I called.

Vrynn rubbed her wrist as she glared at me.

"Sorry about that," I said, using the gun in my hand to indicate her injured wrist.

Vrynn eyed the gun warily, a confused look on her face. "Who are you really working for? Nexus mercenaries don't usually apologize."

"I'm not working for anyone. I told you, the ship—wait. Who's Nexus?"

"Nexus is the organization the Resistance is sworn to oppose."

I nodded. "Okay, I've heard of the Resistance. Would these Nexus people have tried to steal this ship?"

"Certainly," Vrynn said grudgingly. "But it would have been an impossibility for them to even know about the Mark 7. Unless they somehow have an operative on Otania Sancterum."

"Otania Sancterum. I just came from there." It was nice to feel like I had a small clue of what was going on. I must have been brandishing the weapon a little too casually, because Vrynn's posture stiffened, and she took a small step back. "Sorry." I lowered the gun, and she seemed to relax a bit.

I stared at her awkwardly. I was the one in charge again, but I didn't know what I should say. I'd never taken a hostage or prisoner before, so I wasn't quite sure what came next. Plus, being around beautiful women tended to cross the wires in my brain. And this one was an alien on top of that.

I decided I'd better steer the conversation back on topic. "You say Nexus would have tried to steal the *Starfire* if they could?"

Vrynn nodded mutely.

"Would they have a . . ." I turned to Tera. "What was that ship called?"

"Vezor-class runabout," Tera supplied.

"Right. Could they have a Vezor-class runabout?" I asked Vrynn.

Vrynn raised an eyebrow. "Sure. They could have a runabout like that, or even dozens. Nexus is a faction within the Bonara Defense Force." She made that declaration as if no more explanation was necessary.

I waited for her to elaborate, but she didn't. "So . . . they're part of the military," I said, turning to Tera. "That sorta fits with the group that attacked us."

"They're more than just part of the military," Vrynn said, frustration evident in her tone. "They're a ruthless, power-hungry disease that's growing inside the BDF. And no one besides the Resistance seems prepared to stop them."

"And what would they want with the *Starfire*?" I asked.

"Obviously, to stop the Resistance," Vrynn replied.

"So, you were going to take on the Nexus with just one ship?" I said. "Must not be much of an adversary."

"Nexus isn't like a traditional army or navy that you can attack with a comparable military force. They're insidious. They hide in plain sight as part of the BDF's hierarchy. But then, without warning, fleet detachments will attack former allies, or random ships will raid vulnerable outposts. It's all a power grab, and you can't fight it with brute force. You have to be strategic."

I watched her take a deep breath after finishing her rant. "And that's where the *Starfire* comes in?" I asked.

Vrynn opened her mouth like she wanted to give me another verbal lashing but then thought better of it. "I'm not telling you anything about our plans," she said.

I shrugged. "Fine. Then tell me more about the Nexus. Where are they located?"

"They're not located anywhere. They're everywhere."

That might have been a mistranslation, but I shrugged it off. "Is there a leader? Some sort of hierarchy? Who can be brought up on charges?" I was more and more certain they were responsible for Gabe's death, and I planned to see that they faced justice for it.

Vrynn barked a short laugh. "Gralik is the leader. But you'll never bring charges against him. You'll never even get close to him. Besides, he's a senior commander in the Bonara Defense Forces. He's untouchable."

"No one's untouchable. I'm sure he's responsible to someone or something. We just have to talk to the right people." If this part of the galaxy was so much more advanced than Earth, surely they'd figured out how to deal with corruption and abuses of power.

Vrynn's mouth slowly spread in a wry grin. "If you ever find out how wrong you are, I hope I'm there to see it."

I laughed. "Not much chance of that happening." I didn't plan to spend any more time with this crazy—albeit attractive—alien woman than I had to.

We stared at each other for several more seconds. I was hoping she would continue giving me information about Gralik. She probably hoped I would give her the ship. After a while, her brow furrowed. "You really don't know anything about Nexus or Gralik or anything?"

"No. I'm only here because some goons attacked my friend and as we were trying to get away, we accidentally jumped to the Bonara Cluster. And I'd really love to see the thugs brought to justice before I go back home."

A calculating look crossed her flawless face. "If you give me control of the Mark 7, I'll take you home, and I promise I'll do everything I can to destroy Gralik." She held her hands wide. "You get what you want, and I get what I want."

That did sound like an enticing offer. She certainly seemed intent on using the *Starfire* to fight Nexus and Gralik—whoever he was—but I wasn't completely certain Nexus had been responsible for Gabe's death. Plus, I had no idea if Vrynn was a freedom fighter or a terrorist, though that distinction probably depended on a person's point of view, so I didn't really want to just hand the ship over to her.

"Not much of an offer," Tera said. "Once we get more fuel, Mitch can jump back to Earth whenever he wants."

"The Resistance has plenty of fuel," Vrynn replied, obviously implying that was part of the offer.

I looked at Tera, getting the impression that she felt the same as I did about Vrynn's proposal. Tera met my gaze with a frown and shook her head.

That was enough for me. Returning my attention to our unwanted—but formerly useful—passenger, I said, "Unless you have more that you want to tell us about Nexus or the Resistance, then you'll need to get off now."

"Get off the ship?" She looked incredulous. "You can't leave me here."

"Why not?" I shot back. "You threatened me with the same thing just a few minutes ago."

"And you said yourself that it would be cruel and heartless."

I stared at her for several seconds, wishing that she was wrong. Finally, I let out a long sigh. "Fine. If you tell us where we can talk to someone about investigating Gabe's death, we'll drop you at the nearest inhabited planet."

Vrynn shrugged. "Probably the External Affairs Office at the Bonara Defense Force headquarters on Varus Prime. In the capital city, Vasielle."

I smiled appreciatively. "See, I knew we could help each other."

Vrynn scowled at me.

I turned to Tera. "How far to the closest inhabited planet?"

"Rulioa IV is in the next star system. We could be there in fifteen minutes," Tera replied.

"Perfect. Let's give Vrynn a ride to Rulioa IV," I said. "Then, assuming she didn't just lie to us, we'll swing by Varus Prime."

Vrynn looked extremely unhappy with our plan, but since I had the weapon, there wasn't much she could do about it.

Twenty minutes later—after a brief chat with Rulioa IV's spaceport controller—we touched down on a small landing pad on the outskirts of the planet's only settlement. The port only had about a dozen pads, most of which were in disrepair. But at least the spaceport wasn't completely abandoned; there were a handful of other ships docked. The one next to us looked like it had been at the spaceport for several months, possibly even years. Maybe Rulioa IV offered long-term rentals.

"Let's go," I said to Vrynn, waving the weapon toward the ladder down to the lower deck.

As she walked to the ladder, I considered the gun in my hand. It probably wasn't a good look to walk down the cargo ramp holding a woman at gunpoint. I went back and placed the gun on the pilot's seat and locked the flight deck door behind me.

I looked at Tera. "Keep that locked until I get back, will you?"

She nodded.

Down in the cargo bay, I opened the loading ramp and waved a hand toward the buildings of the nearby spaceport. "This is your stop. Thank you for choosing *Starfire* Space Travel."

Vrynn folded her arms across her chest. "I'm not getting off this ship."

"You can't come with us," I said.

"I'm not leaving," she replied. "You'll have to shoot me and drag me off the ship." She looked down at my empty hands. "Oh look, you can't even do that because you don't have a gun."

I could feel my temperature rising. I had tried to be civil and humane with this woman, but she was going to drive me to do something I would regret. She had to go. And if that involved manhandling, then so be it.

In one quick motion, I bent forward, wrapped my arms around Vrynn's legs, and hefted her onto my shoulder. She let out a surprised squeal and then began beating my back with her fists while flailing her legs. I leaned my head away from her heavy boots, not wanting to be on the receiving end of one of those. The punches to my back were annoying, but not incredibly painful.

I lugged her across the cargo bay and down the ramp. As I reached the bottom, she scored a direct hit on one of my kidneys, and I faltered for a moment. Vrynn must have realized that she'd hit a tender spot in my anatomy because she doubled down on her strikes to my lower back.

When she hit a tender spot again, I unceremoniously dropped her onto the ground at the bottom of the ramp.

Vrynn scrambled to her feet and struck a defiant pose. "I'm not letting you leave this planet without me."

I let out a frustrated grunt. "Like I've already said, you can't come with us." I held out a hand toward the spaceport. "Go annoy someone in the spaceport until the next transport comes along."

Vrynn opened her mouth to reply when we both heard the sound of chuckling nearby. I followed her gaze to a small space skiff on the next pad over. A grizzled old pilot with long gray hair and light brown skin sat on the end of a wing strut watching us.

He laughed again, shaking his head. "I've had plenty of arguments like this with my wife, and I can save you the trouble by telling you how it ends."

Vrynn and I both began speaking simultaneously.

"Oh, we're not married," I said.

"I wouldn't want to be stuck with this pile of treckla dung."

I turned back to Vrynn. "I have no idea what a treckla is, but now you're just being mean."

Her demeanor suddenly lost all of its proud defiance. She held her hands together. "Please, Mitch, you don't understand what's at stake here. How could you? You probably never heard of the Bonara Cluster or Nexus while living your little life on your dirt planet."

She wasn't winning any points with her speech so far.

"But I really need the Mark 7 for my mission to fight Nexus. You can't possibly understand how important it is. People—entire civilizations—are counting on me."

Even I knew that she was laying it on a little too thick. "I feel bad that it has to be this way, but you're not coming with us, and I'm certainly not giving you the *Starfire*. You'll just have to figure out how to do your mission without it." I gave her a long glare before turning and heading back up the ramp.

"If you had wanted to leave me here, you shouldn't have told me where you're going," she called up after me.

I paused for a moment. What did she mean by that? I turned back and saw a smug look on her face.

She casually glanced away as she spoke. "It should only take me a few minutes to hire a ship to fly to Varus Prime. And since I know exactly where the Bonara Defense Force headquarters building is, I might even beat you there." Her gaze drifted back to me, triumph evident in her eyes.

This woman was going to be a thorn in my side if I left her here. Of course, she'd probably be a thorn in my side if I brought her along.

I exhaled loudly and walked back down the ramp. I lowered my voice so that our port neighbor couldn't hear. "Fine. Keeping an eye on you is probably a better idea, anyway. But know this." I pointed a finger at her. "You try to sabotage my ship, even a little, and I'll push you out the airlock." I held her gaze, happy to see that she apparently believed me.

Finally, she nodded her acceptance.

As we walked back up the cargo ramp, I heard the old pilot on the next ship call out to us, "Yep. That's how most of my arguments ended, too."

Chapter Six

The star-speckled black of regular space out the flight deck windows slowly shifted to the gray-brown swirls as Tera engaged the *Starfire's* standard intra-space drive.

"The jump to Varus system should take about fifteen minutes," Tera explained after giving me a short rundown on the role of Varus Prime as the origin of life in the Bonara Cluster and, therefore, home to the central government. This came as no surprise, given that we were heading there to visit the headquarters of the Bonara Defense Force.

"Now, what are we going to do with her?" Tera tilted her head toward the living area just outside the flight deck, where Vrynn waited.

"Lock the door behind me," I said under my breath as I stood from the pilot's seat and left the flight deck. I crossed the living area and situated myself in my favorite loveseat, right next to the large viewing portal. I could have stayed safely locked on the flight deck and not interacted with Vrynn, but I needed her to know that this was my chair.

Vrynn sat on a nearby sofa, glaring at me. It was a little unnerving. To say that she was unhappy would have been an understatement.

I wasn't excited about the situation either. It's not like I'd chosen to get flung to a distant star cluster and lose my best friend in the process. And I couldn't help the fact that I was the only one who cared about my friend's murderers facing justice. And I certainly didn't ask to have a crazy malcontent hitch a ride with us along the way.

But I wasn't going to get into a staring contest over it.

I finally turned my attention from the boring grayish brown out the window to the aggravatingly beautiful stowaway sitting across the room from me. "So what's your story?" I asked in what I hoped was a marginally civil tone. I was going to be stuck with her for the foreseeable future, after all.

"What do you mean?" she asked.

"I mean, why'd you join the Resistance? What made you want to fight Nexus?"

"It's personal," she said, turning to look away.

"Huh." That was vaguely non-specific. But it had gotten her to stop glaring at me, so I was happy.

"Let's just say that Gralik destroyed my life and leave it at that," Vrynn said.

I shrugged and turned back to the portal.

Several minutes passed before she spoke again.

"I've been dying to ask you," Vrynn said, pulling my attention back. "Why did you choose to change the ship's hologram to a moody, teenage girl?"

I glanced around at the various cameras and microphones in the kitchen and living area. Tera would be able to hear anything I said. But at this point, I felt defensive on her behalf, so I wouldn't have said anything disparaging, anyway. "My buddy, Gabe, found this ship crashed on his farm. The pilot was dead, and the ship was badly damaged. So he buried the pilot and—"

Vrynn sucked in a breath. "The pilot was Otanian. He's not supposed to be buried anywhere but his homeworld."

I nodded. "I visited his family a few days ago and smoothed it over."

One of Vrynn's eyebrows rose, as if she didn't quite believe me.

I pressed forward, attempting to answer her original question. "Anyway, Gabe's wife died about ten years ago, so when the ship asked how he wanted the AI customized—after it was damaged in the crash—he chose his wife's appearance and personality."

"How young do your people get married on dirt?" Vrynn asked.

I chuckled. It was a fair question, considering how young my holographic friend looked. "Tera was the same age as Gabe and me. The hologram is a teenager because that's the video material Gabe fed the matrix."

"Hmm. I guess that makes sense." Vrynn glanced toward the flight deck. "Still, it's an unfortunate situation."

I shrugged. "It's working out pretty well so far."

A second or two passed in silence before Tera's voice sounded on the ship's speakers. "We'll finish the jump to Varus Prime in three minutes."

The fact that she'd waited until a lull in the conversation told me that Tera had indeed been eavesdropping. I smiled as I stood and walked through the door to the flight deck.

"Thanks, Mitch," Tera whispered as I sat in the pilot's chair.

I nodded, happy to have stuck up for my friend. Or the AI version of her, anyway.

After a minute, a voice called from behind me. "Am I allowed in?"

I looked over my shoulder. Vrynn stood in the doorway, peering into the flight deck.

I turned to Tera. "I'm still the one running the ship, right?"

"Yeah. Besides me," she said with a bored grin.

"Good." I turned back to Vrynn. "Sure. You can come in. As long as you behave yourself." I indicated the jumpseat behind the copilot's chair.

Instead, Vrynn came and settled herself into the co-pilot's seat.

Tera gave me a look that said it wasn't good that Vrynn was making herself this comfortable.

Vrynn gazed at the readouts and controls around her, but fortunately, was smart enough not to touch anything.

A few moments later, Tera announced, "Intra-space jump terminating in three . . . two . . . one."

In a flash of light, the gray-brown swirl dissolved into the familiar black void, dappled with stars and nebulae. A blue and brown planet loomed in front of us. I could make out dozens—probably even hundreds—of cities dotting the hemisphere facing me. The few bodies of water I could make out were far too circular and symmetrical to be natural.

This was the fourth, or perhaps fifth, planet that I'd visited since arriving in the Bonara Cluster. I shook my head in disbelief that not only was I getting used to looking out the flight deck window at a new and completely foreign planet every time we made an intra-space jump, but that this had all happened in less than a week. At least, I think it had only been a week since I lost my job. On the other hand, I wasn't even sure what day it was, so maybe my perception of time was off.

This particular planet was different than the others, though. As we got closer, I could see that most of the surface was covered in man-made buildings, roads, and structures. Almost none of its surface was untouched by the civilization living there. On one medium-sized peninsula, I counted at least twenty metropolis-sized cities.

"Where's Vasielle?" I asked. I didn't care if Vrynn or Tera answered. I just needed to know where to steer the ship.

Before either of them could say anything, the incoming message icon flashed on my console. I accepted the transmission and the holographic image of a very beautiful flight control agent appeared in the air in front of me.

She smiled more broadly than a normal person should. "Welcome to Varus Prime," she said in a happy, sing-song voice. "Tell me where you're planning to visit today."

"We'd like to land in Vasielle," I said.

"Excellent. The beautiful metropolis is waiting for you. What brings you to Vasielle on this excellent occasion?"

"Just say 'business,'" Vrynn whispered out of the side of her mouth.

"I have a business meeting," I replied to the controller.

Her fake-looking smile broadened. "With the favorable exchange rate and low tariffs, Vasielle is a terrific place for established firms and fledgling companies alike."

The controller was sounding more and more like a travel brochure. And I wasn't even sure if she was a real person. Regular customer service agents didn't tend to be this perky.

"If you'd like to tell me who you have a meeting with, I'd be happy to route your ship to the nearest landing pad," the controller said.

Even before Vrynn could whisper her advice, I knew I would decline the controller's offer. "No thanks. If you could transmit a few of the options around Vasielle, we'll take whatever works best for our plans."

The controller's expression didn't falter in the least. "Great idea. Transmitting vacant pad information. Have a wonderful stay with us on Varus Prime."

The transmission terminated.

I let out a low whistle. "Wow. That lady sure was chipper." I glanced over at Vrynn and Tera to see their reactions.

"That was obviously a recorded matrix of an actress," Vrynn said confidently.

"Please deactivate me if I ever start sounding that stupid," Tera said dryly.

Vrynn perked up. "Just tell me where the switch is," she said brightly.

Tera's scowl deepened.

My new self-appointed co-pilot was already getting along great with my AI-assistant.

I followed the flight path down through the atmosphere toward the city of Vasielle. "Where is the BDF headquarters?" I asked Vrynn.

She pointed toward the central cluster of buildings in front of us. "It's that tall, silver one on the right."

"That looks like an office tower," I said.

Vrynn glanced at me. "It is. What were you expecting?"

"I don't know. Maybe something like an army camp out in the forest with guards posted at the gate. Or some abandoned warehouse turned into a training facility where you have to give a password to get in."

She laughed. "No. The BDF is mostly run by bureaucrats here on Varus Prime. The actual work is done by the defensive forces who operate throughout the cluster."

I glanced at the map of landing pads available and tried to match up that building with what I recognized on the map. I couldn't see any available spots within a reasonable distance, and I wasn't excited about walking halfway across an alien city that I wasn't familiar with, not unless we could arm Skeeter with plasma cannons.

"What about there?" Vrynn pointed to the top of what looked like a parking garage but for spaceships.

"That's not one of the empty spots listed on the map," I said, indicating the dots on the console in front of me as we zoomed past the parking garage.

"There's a spot." Vrynn held out a hand toward a wide, squat building that looked like the roof had caved in. "Just land on the part that's still intact."

"I'm not going to land the *Starfire* on a collapsing building. I don't need suggestions unless they're safe and legal."

We floated closer to a single dot on the map that corresponded to a small landing pad tucked between two large buildings. It reminded me of the shady lots they had in downtown Dallas, the ones where you never knew if the guy actually worked for the lot owner or if he just happened to be standing around taking people's money.

"Yeah, that's a good spot," Vrynn said as she leaned forward to look out the viewing windows at the lot below us.

"I don't think we can fit in that spot. The ship's too big," I said.

"Oh, try it. I'm sure we'll fit," Vrynn replied.

I pulled the ship into a hover, attempting to judge how large the landing pad was. The ship had fit inside Gabe's oversized barn, after all. Surely, this spot was about as big as a barn.

I must have considered the situation for too long, though, because another ship zipped underneath us and landed neatly on the pad. I shook my head. "We wouldn't have fit, anyway."

Vrynn folded her arms. "Maybe you need to start listening to my advice."

After a few more minutes of searching, I finally settled on an open spot in a landing zone much farther from the BDF building. I could tell Vrynn thought it was a dumb idea.

I stood from the pilot's seat and grabbed the handgun I'd taken from the soldier at Gabe's farm. "Okay, let's get going."

Vrynn simply stared at me. "I'm not going anywhere."

"What? Why not?"

Her brow went up. "First off, I've told you that this is a stupid idea. You're not going to find anyone in the BDF who's willing to investigate an attack that might have involved Gralik." As I opened my mouth to say that I had to try anyway, she held up a hand. "Second, I'm a Resistance fighter. I don't think it'd be a good idea for me to waltz into a building crawling with Nexus collaborators."

That left my mouth hanging open. "So what am I supposed to do? Just walk in and ask to speak to the person in charge of alien attacks?" I asked.

Vrynn lifted a shoulder. "Whatever it was you were planning to do before you met me." Her lips spread in a grin. "Storm the guard post, or something like that."

Unhelpful jokes aside, she did have a point. I glanced down at my flight suit, realizing that I should probably look a little more inconspicuous. The Resistance might not have an official uniform, but I didn't want to draw any unnecessary attention to myself.

"Can the fabricator build me a new set of clothes?" I asked Tera.

Her eyes scanned back and forth, reading the empty air in front of her, then her brow drew down. "I guess it technically could, but you might not like the results."

"Why not?" I asked.

"It would take about three days to make an outfit that would feel natural," Tera said.

"Can't it make something in an hour or two?" I didn't want to spend the next three days sitting in a public parking spot in Vasielle's questionable part of town.

"Sure, but it would be a little stiff, like wearing a plastic pair of pants."

Vrynn stifled a laugh.

I scowled at her then turned back to Tera. "I guess I'll put my old clothes back on." I trudged from the living area down the hall to my quarters and pulled on my clothes from Earth. Fortunately, I'd had Skeeter put them through the cleaning machine.

When I walked back into the living area, Vrynn laughed out loud. "You shouldn't have any trouble convincing them you're from another planet."

I ignored her and walked over to Tera. "Can you keep an eye on things here?"

"You mean, keep the vagabond stowaway from taking over the ship and stranding you here?" she asked.

"Uh, yeah. And don't let her fiddle with any of the systems, either. I don't want to come back to a boring AI matrix." I winked at her.

Tera actually smiled at that.

"I promise I won't steal the ship," Vrynn grudgingly announced.

I nodded and headed for the ladder.

"But if you get yourself killed, can I use the Mark 7 for my mission?" Vrynn called out.

"It's called the *Starfire*," I said over my shoulder. "And, sure, if I'm dead, you can have it."

From the look on Tera's face, she seemed to think I had just signed my own death warrant.

On my way through the cargo bay, I slipped the alien gun in a snug pocket just below my right hip. I hoped there weren't laws against carrying weapons on this planet.

I closed the cargo ramp behind me and set off through the alien city. It wasn't too different from the few big cities I'd been to. Despite the expectation that decades of sci-fi movies had created in my mind, Vasielle didn't have any floating sidewalks, or hoverboards, or bright, neon lights everywhere. The buildings were mostly glass and metal with transparent tubes on the outside, like the glass elevators at fancy hotels. The vehicles driving along the grid-like streets actually rolled on the ground. Apparently, despite having engines that could make spaceships hover, it was still the most efficient thing to use the old-fashioned wheel.

As I made my way closer to the BDF headquarters, I found there were more people walking along the streets. I tried not to stare at the different colors of hair and skin I saw. Not to mention the shapes of various facial features and appendages. I only saw bi-pedal humanoids, which made me wonder how they could look so similar to humans on Earth—not including the tints of greens, purples, and blues, which apparently were completely natural here.

No insectoids or furry monsters in sight.

Checking my surroundings, I realized that I was a few blocks off of my goal. I took a small side street to cross between city blocks. The alley smelled like most alleys on Earth would smell. Apparently, decay was universal.

As my enthusiasm for such a long walk began to wane, I finally reached the base of the spindly Bonara Defense Force headquarters tower. Giant glass doors slid open when I approached the entrance. Inside was a spacious lobby dotted with small round tables throughout. I glanced around to see if I could find a receptionist or some other attendant who could direct me to the right person.

Visitors around me bustled past, some heading toward banks of what must have been the Bonara cluster's version of elevators—giant tubes built into the walls that whisked people away with no platform visible anywhere, others heading back toward the doors I had just entered, and still others who stepped up to the various round tables and began speaking to no one in particular.

Rather than try my luck at the tube elevators, I stepped up to a table. As I approached, the top half of a holographic woman—the same one who contacted the *Starfire* to welcome us to Varus Prime—appeared floating above the table. "Hello. And welcome to Vasielle Tower, home of the Varus Prime police and Bonara Defense Force administrative offices." I could hear her actual words this time, just before the earpiece translated them. "Do you have an appointment?"

"Uh, no. I actually need to talk to someone in charge of incursions on planets outside the Bonara cluster." I decided to describe the situation in the broadest terms possible, hoping that whatever AI was behind this projection would be able to understand what I needed.

"The BDF does not conduct any military assaults or other campaigns against systems outside of the Bonara cluster," the perky holographic attendant replied. "Please restate your query."

I rolled my eyes. I must have made it sound like my planet had been attacked by BDF forces. "Can I talk to someone about an accidental death?"

"Active duty personnel or noncombatant?" The hologram asked.

"Noncombatant," I replied, trying not to make it sound like a question.

The attendant stared at me for a few seconds. Long enough that I was about to repeat myself. Finally, she said, "Please proceed to lift seven, bank two. The Department of Investigation and Arbitration is on level twenty three."

A large arrow flashed in front of her face, pointing toward the lift tubes against the wall. I walked over to the tube and hesitantly stepped in. As soon as I stepped through the opening, a burst of focused air pushed against me, shooting me up the tube.

After the initial surprise at being shot up a tube wore off, I glanced down at my feet. There was nothing under them, yet it felt as if I was standing on a soft platform. I looked up and saw the buildings around me growing smaller as I passed their roofs. About halfway up the tower, I slowed and stopped in front of an opening in the tube. I assumed this was my stop, so I stepped through the doorway into a narrow office hallway.

Illuminated arrows, similar to the one at the holographic kiosk in the lobby, pointed down the hall. Somehow, the building itself knew where I was supposed to be going. That probably cut down on the number of wandering visitors they received. Or salesmen, for that matter.

The customized path led me past a variety of offices—staffed by a variety of military-looking aliens—to a door with what looked like flashing scribbles on it. I double-checked that the arrows didn't continue beyond this door before stepping through into a small office. A pudgy, middle-aged man in a light-gray military uniform sat behind a broad—somewhat messy—desk.

Looking mildly amused at my sudden appearance, he rose and came out from behind the desk to greet me. "I don't get many walk-in consultations, but welcome anyway. I'm Chief Sergeant Zondy Ruver."

"Mitch Foster," I replied. "Thanks for meeting with me, Chief Sergeant Ruver."

The man scowled and waved a hand down. "No need to be that formal. Everyone calls me Sergeant Zondy."

I nodded my acknowledgement. Sergeant Zondy stood a head shorter than me, but what I had initially thought was pudginess, apparently, was his natural build. He was broad from his feet to his shoulders, but none of it appeared flabby or extra. He seemed to perspire a great deal because his pinkish skin glistened in the light. And his smile looked slightly unnatural, but perhaps, like the rest of him, it was just wider than I was used to.

"Have a seat. How can I help you today?" Sergeant Zondy moved back around the desk and settled into his chair, staring at me intently.

"My friend was killed by alien—" I caught myself. No need to get started on the wrong foot. "—by soldiers that were trying to steal his starship." I wasn't sure if regular citizens in the Bonara cluster owned starships, but it seemed like a fair bet.

Sergeant Zondy didn't have any problem with that explanation. "Can you provide me with the security footage of the event?" he asked.

"Uh, no. I don't have any recordings of the event."

"Were the recordings damaged?" the sergeant asked quickly.

"No."

"Were the cameras somehow disabled prior to the assault?"

"No."

"Were there—"

I cut him off. "There weren't any recordings because my friend doesn't have security cameras at his property."

Sergeant Zondy cocked his broad head with an expression that clearly said he didn't quite believe me. "What system did you say you're from?"

"Well, I've only ever called it the solar system. But my planet is called Earth." Hopefully, this guy's language had more than one word for dirt.

"Earth. Earth," he repeated absently. "You mean, the Earth Protectorate?"

"Uh, I've never heard it called that before."

"Let's see." He began tapping on symbols on the edge of his desk, glancing at a holographic display. "Ah, yes, here it is." He pointed at the display. It showed a scrolling series of scribbles and then what looked like a satellite image of Earth, complete with all the familiar continents—though the view was up-side-down.

"Yeah, that's Earth," I said.

"Pretty far from home, aren't you?" he asked, eyeing me up and down, probably noticing my clothes.

I nodded. He had no idea how far it felt sometimes.

"Your planet—in fact, your entire system—is part of the Earth Protectorate. Actually, it's more of a nature preserve than a protectorate, given that we don't have any formal relations with your planet's government."

Did he think the entire planet had a single government?

The sergeant continued, "So Earth is completely off-limits to any travelers—or any contact at all, really—from the Bonara Cluster." He glanced at his display, apparently checking some information there. "That law was passed several thousand cycles ago, during the age of the galactic king."

"The galactic king?" I repeated.

Sergeant Zondy smiled. "It was the empire of power in the Bonara Cluster four ages ago." He looked back at his display. "His forces of exploration stumbled upon a planet called Earth that had a thriving—though still primitive—civilization. Apparently, the exploration team made the mistake of assisting them in constructing some monuments." He waved his hands. "Anyway, it was a whole debacle when they returned and the great galactic king found out. But it did finally solve an ancient cold case that had investigators stumped for an age."

"Cold case?" My head spun with the news that travelers from the Bonara Cluster had visited Earth several millennia ago.

The sergeant sat back in his chair and scratched his chin. "Yes, this would have been about sixteen thousand cycles ago. Apparently, a rich newlywed couple on their honeymoon had set off from Varus Prime in a small, jump-capable ship. Neither of them knew anything about spaceflight or navigation—this was before ships had auto-pilot to help fly. Well, they never came back."

Sergeant Zondy apparently had a penchant for the dramatic because he let that bit hang in the air for several seconds.

"After they had been missing for a cycle, the families mounted a huge search effort, but they were never found. Everyone presumed they had run out of fuel or been smashed by an asteroid or something like that."

I nodded, wondering what this story had to do with Earth.

"Come to find out, they had crash-landed on your planet—and actually survived. By all accounts, a starship of that era should not have been able to travel so far." Zondy laughed loudly. "So when the explorers found the thriving civilization, the galactic king decreed that there would be no interaction with your planet. Not like anyone cared; it's so far away that only the most curious paleontologists even risk an illegal trip to your world."

I held up a hand. "Hang on. Are you telling me my planet was populated by shipwrecked newlyweds from the Bonara Cluster?"

"Sure. I mean, if intelligent life on your planet had developed independently, you might have ten eyes or six arms, right?" He grinned at me, clearly thinking it was a funny joke.

I sat dumbfounded.

"Welcome back, cousin." Zondy boomed.

My head was in a daze. Of course, I'd barely met this guy. Maybe he was pulling my leg.

Zondy continued his earlier explanation. "So, you see, it wouldn't be possible for any BDF personnel to be involved in the unfortunate death of your friend. There are no approved flights or any operations at all in your system."

"Listen, I saw these soldiers with my own eyes. They were definitely not from Earth," I insisted. "They chased me into space." That sounded like an air-tight reason to me, but maybe this guy had heard that excuse a hundred times.

The sergeant's brows furrowed. "Tell me about the ship that chased you."

"It was about the same size as our ship." I realized that didn't help because he hadn't even seen my ship. I was about to compare it to the width of a basketball court, but that probably wouldn't translate. "It was about fifty feet long." Hopefully, the broadcasts they had received from Earth included both systems of measurement.

"No, I mean, what type of ship was it?" Zondy said.

"Uh, it was a runabout." I scrunched my eyes closed, trying to remember what else Tera had said about it. "Veezle-class?"

"Do you mean Vezor-class?"

"Yes, that was it. And it was running without a transponder signal."

Zondy leaned back in his seat, folding his arms across his broad frame. "That's actually not possible. The transponders are built into the drive system. If the ship is moving, the identification signal has to be transmitting."

"Well, my AI thinks it could be—"

"You enabled the thinking feature on your ship?" Sergeant Zondy interjected. "I hate to tell you, my friend, that's mostly just hype from salesmen trying to earn a quick Bonmark. These autopilot computers can't really think."

I frowned at his easy dismissal of Tera's intelligence. Of course, I hadn't ever been on anyone else's starship. Maybe their AIs weren't as smart as mine.

Sergeant Zondy sighed and leaned forward again, tapping the input on his desk surface. The display showed more lines of indecipherable text. "Listen, even though I doubt it would yield any results, I can initiate an investigation into the event." He paused and looked up at me. "Assuming you can pay the administrative fee."

I sagged slightly in my chair. The police on New Talpreus had listed a fee, so it shouldn't have surprised me that the BDF had a fee, too.

The sergeant must have read my body language. "If you can't afford the fee, the best I can do is file a report of the incident."

I pulled the alien blaster from my thigh pocket—causing Sergeant Zondy to stiffen for a moment—and placed it on the desk. "This is the weapon I took from one of the alien soldiers. I guarantee it is not from my world."

Zondy pulled the gun across the desk. "Hmm. I don't recognize this specific type of blaster," he said. "But then I'm not really an expert in this area."

He scrutinized the weapon for several moments then looked up at me. I wasn't sure, but it almost seemed like he felt sorry for me.

"Look, I can't really open an official investigation, but let's see if we can get some answers for you." He touched a spot on his desk and spoke toward it. "Corporal Kyuli, report to my office."

A few seconds later, the office door opened, and a tall man in a matching light-gray uniform stepped inside. His features were all very long and narrow to my eyes, almost the opposite of Sergeant Zondy's. His skin was yellow-tinged, and his hair—both on his head and on his arms—was slightly purple.

"Yes, sergeant," he said with a crisp salute.

"As you were, Kyuli." Sergeant Zondy held out the alien weapon. "Take a look at this. Do you recognize its origin?"

The corporal reached across the room—almost without taking a step—and took the blaster. I watched his expression as he examined the weapon. It might have been my own inability to read alien races—something that I had not thought was a shortcoming until recently—but it almost looked like he recognized it but was taking extra precautions to make it look like he didn't recognize it. He was extremely thorough in his inspection.

Sergeant Zondy must have thought so, too, because he appeared to grow impatient. "Well?"

Corporal Kyuli cleared his throat—at least, that's sort of what it sounded like—and said, "It looks almost like a Caridyan pulse phaser..."

"And..." Sergeant Zondy prodded.

"And I know the Vanguard Dragoons used this weapon in the past, but not for the last ten cycles."

"The Vanguard Dragoons," Zondy said reverentially. "Isn't that Gralik's fast-attack platoon?"

Kyuli nodded.

"That's an impressive unit," Zondy said. "One of the best records in the Force."

Kyuli nodded again.

This discussion was quickly losing focus, and I wasn't sure these two military men even remembered that I was still in the room with them. "Oh, I also wanted to ask you about Gralik," I said, pulling their attention back to the problem at hand. "I've heard that he's part of a group called Nexus that's working to undermine the efforts of the BDF." I couldn't remember if that's the way Vrynn described Nexus, but I figured it was close enough.

The men stared at me like I was a naive child. Zondy chuckled. Kyuli just shook his head sadly.

"Nexus is a fictitious group that's often brought up by insurrectionists who are unwilling to recognize the authority of the Bonara Cluster central government," Corporal Kyuli said in a condescending tone. "They try to convince others that some shadowy organization called Nexus is pulling the strings behind the scenes. It's fear mongering and subversion at its worst."

"You're still new to the Bonara Cluster, Mr. Mitch," Zondy joined in. "So I'm sure no one would accuse you of being a political agitator." He spared Kyuli a reproachful look. "Just be careful who you spend time with. They might be filling your head with nonsense. Commander Gralik is one of our most highly decorated leaders."

I suddenly got the feeling that I was way out of my league here. I had no way to know if these men were telling me the truth and Vrynn had lied to me or the other way around.

"Huh." Sergeant Zondy looked at me for a moment, either collecting his thoughts or hoping I would take his suggestion to heart if he stared me down long enough. Finally, he held a hand out to Kyuli who returned the pulse phaser to him. "And have you heard anything about a recent incursion into the Earth Protectorate?" he asked the corporal.

"The Earth Protectorate?" Kyuli repeated, staring sidelong at me. It wasn't a benevolent look, either. More like something meant for a slug or a creepy insect. He shook his head once. "No, sergeant, most of the illegal paleontology flights stopped about twenty cycles ago."

Maybe members of Corporal Kyuli's race, or species or whatever, tended to speak slowly and emphatically when they were sure of something, but my translator earpiece made him sound like a troublemaking teenager who was lying to his teacher about throwing spitballs.

"Fine, you're dismissed, corporal." Sergeant Zondy waved a thick hand toward the door.

The lanky corporal spared me one last, lingering glance before exiting Zondy's office.

It gave me the creeps.

Sergeant Zondy glumly held out his hands. "You see, Mr. Mitch. Without opening a formal investigation—which I should add would be complicated by the need to gather evidence within the Earth Protectorate zone—there isn't much else I can do at this point. I am very sorry about your friend's death, and if any other opportunity arises for me to help find the guilty party—within the bounds of what I'm allowed to do—you can rest assured that I will do my best."

Despite his attempt to encourage me, I felt all the wind go out of my sails. I didn't know who had killed Gabe, and even if I could somehow find the person, it would be next to impossible—unless they suddenly decided to confess—to get enough evidence to hold them accountable.

Sergeant Zondy stood and walked around his desk to me. He put a hand on my shoulder. "I know it must be hard, but maybe the best thing you can do for your friend is to head back home and live your best life."

I stood and numbly took the blaster back from him. It wasn't really his fault that I was in this position. And maybe he was right. Nothing I did here in the Bonara cluster would bring Gabe back. Maybe it was time to focus on getting myself home somehow.

I wasn't sure how I made it back down to the lobby and out on the streets of Vasielle—it most likely involved those fancy guidance arrows watching me everywhere I went and pointing me where to go.

I gazed at the alien city surrounding me, momentarily unsure what I should do next. I'd taken my complaint to the very top—at least, as far up as I could go—and I'd come up empty. What's worse, I had the distinct impression that Sergeant Zondy didn't believe Nexus was real. Of course, I didn't know if they were real either, but if they were, Zondy wouldn't be the person to ask for help. Maybe I needed to find out what proof the Resistance had that Nexus was a threat—or even a reality at all.

Finally, I shoved the weapon back into my pocket holster and set off toward where we'd parked the *Starfire*. I didn't know if Vrynn's native language had an equivalent for 'I told you so,' but if so, I probably deserved it.

I crossed one of the larger roads and turned down the back alley I'd used on the way there. At least, I was fairly certain it was the same one. All the streets in Vasielle were starting to look the same. As I walked past a pile of bins that held some sort of decaying goo, I heard a sound behind me. I glanced over my shoulder and saw a guy walk into the narrow lane behind me.

I doubled my speed, focusing on the end of the alley in front of me. If I could make it out into the open, maybe I could keep from getting mugged by some alien street thug. I didn't know if the regular, everyday citizens of Varus Prime would stop to help someone getting attacked, but I figured I'd take my chances out in the open.

Leaning forward, I broke into a full run. The alley exit was just a few feet away.

Suddenly, two more very rough-looking guys stepped around the corner, blocking my way. They had blotchy purple and blue skin and closely shaved heads, a few tufts of purple and black here and there. The one on the right had a bright yellow scar down his cheek, the other had one purple eye and one silver eye—the entire eyeball.

The one with the scar leered at me. "In a hurry?" The translator relayed his question as more of a grunt.

I reached into my pocket and pulled out the handgun. Scar and Silver-Eye tensed as I raised it toward them, and the steps behind me slowed. I spared a glance over my shoulder. The thug who had followed me into the alley was still at least fifty feet from me. I turned my attention back to Scar and Silver-Eye. "I just want to get back to my ship," I announced to my would-be assailants, trying my best to keep the tremor out of my voice.

"Oh, you'll make it back to your ship," Silver-Eye sneered. "In fact, you're going to take us there right now."

They wanted the *Starfire*. Were these some of the same goons who killed Gabe? Their clothes were nothing like the group that had invaded Gabe's farm. But maybe there was a street-hobo version of their uniform.

I wasn't about to take them anywhere near the ship.

Silver-Eye may have reached behind his back for a weapon, or he might have just had a sudden itch. Either way, I pulled the trigger. And I continued firing as I dove for cover. My first shot caught Silver-Eye in the knee, another in the neck. He fell backward, screaming. Hopefully, he was out of the fight.

Scar dove behind a stack of crates and started firing for my hiding spot. I loosed a few rounds back at him.

I decided if I survived this fight, I'd need to do some weapons training. And maybe invest in a blaster-proof vest—if they made such a thing.

In a lull between our shots, a voice behind me yelled. "Stop shooting, you moron! Gralik wants him alive!"

The voice sounded familiar. I turned my attention to the slowly approaching form who had followed me into the alley in the first place.

It was Corporal Kyuli.

I knew there was a reason I didn't like that guy.

With those lanky limbs, he closed the distance much faster than I expected, rushing forward and punching me in the head just as I turned to take aim at him. I flew backward, and my gun clattered under a nearby pile of empty bins.

I lashed out with a boot and connected with Kyuli's groin. He doubled over, howling in pain.

At least some things were universal.

While I was on the ground, Scar scored a glancing blow to my head. I rolled away, clambering awkwardly to my feet, my back against the nearest wall.

They still had me trapped.

"You'll pay for that," Corporal Kyuli said through clenched teeth.

He seemed to be the weakest link at the moment, so I rushed him, hoping to fight my way through. But apparently, the corporal wasn't as injured as I had hoped. He straightened and swung a kick for my middle. It caught me so off guard that I didn't even dodge. All the wind left my lungs as I soared backward through the air. I landed on the hard ground with a jolt.

Scar was on me in a nano-second, aiming punches at my head. I dodged as best I could.

He said something that sounded like gibberish. When the translation from my earpiece never came, I suddenly realized that I could hear clearly from both ears. My translator must have gotten knocked out when Kyuli kicked me through the air.

When I didn't respond to his babbling, Scar leaned close to my face. His breath was putrid, and what teeth he had were rotted. He spoke some guttural nonsense that I obviously couldn't understand and punched me in the side of the head again.

I doubled over, attempting to shield my head with my hands. It wouldn't take much more punishment like this before I was dead—or at least unconscious—which was probably what they wanted.

Maybe it was better this way. If I was going to get pummeled into the dust, at least I didn't have to understand their final taunts. I could die in garbled peace.

A kick to my spine had me writhing in pain. I attempted to kick back, but was rewarded with another kick to the gut and evil laughter.

In my semi-delirious state, a low growl reached my ears. I wondered if maybe one of my attackers was part bear. Who knew what kind of species existed here in the Bonara Cluster?

Out of the corner of my eye, movement caught my attention. A large black shape slowly emerged from the shadows and growled menacingly at the goons standing over me.

Maybe I was seeing things. I blinked hard.

Nope. There was definitely what looked like a small bear or large dog padding lightly toward me. It had jet-black fur, a narrow head, and wide, intelligent eyes. The gibberish from my attackers changed pitch as their assault on me stopped. The beast-dog bared its knife-like teeth and roared at them. Corporal Kyuli reached behind his back for a weapon, but the beast was on him like lightning, sinking its fangs into his chest.

The corporal was dead before he even hit the ground.

The beast turned toward Scar, snarling, fangs dripping purplish blood. Scar turned and ran from the alley.

I looked up at the beast, wondering if this was how my life would come to an end, impotent on the ground, about to be the meal for a giant alien animal. The beast looked down at me, and its growl turned to a whine. It lumbered over and plopped down in front of me, leaning its huge hairy head against my leg.

Perhaps it wasn't my time to go quite yet. I lifted a hand hesitantly and touched the top of the beast's head. It almost sounded like the beast was purring. "Thanks, buddy." I rubbed its head affectionately, still eyeing the sharp fangs. "You saved my life."

I drifted in and out of consciousness as waves of pain washed over me.

The next thing I remember was a lithe figure entering the alley and hurrying toward me. In my half-delirious state, I thought that whoever this woman was, she had a very nice shape, especially silhouetted as it was against the light of the open street behind her. I struggled to keep my eyes open, not wanting to lose consciousness right as such a beautiful woman was coming to my rescue. As she drew closer, my eyes kept insisting that it was actually Vrynn, despite my brain knowing that Vrynn was far too annoying to be that beautiful.

But it was actually Vrynn.

I decided I would never trust my eyes again, despite how grateful I was that she had come to save me.

"Careful, Vrynn," I said weakly. "These thugs jumped me, and they could still be—Ow!" I flinched at the sudden pain in my side.

The beast in my lap growled when Vrynn tried to approach me, and she slowed. I patted its head. "It's okay. She's a friend."

Vrynn knelt down and moved cautiously toward me. She said something that sounded like "Breenok velop," but that might have been my brain having trouble keeping up with reality.

She repeated the phrase.

I shook my head, and my vision swam. Then I remembered that my earpiece had been knocked out during the fight. "Lost my translator," I croaked, pointing to my ear.

Vrynn searched the area around us. She said a few more things that were gibberish to my brain. She walked out of my view and then came back with what was left of my earpiece in her hand. It had been crushed to smithereens.

I started to chuckle, but it hurt too much.

Vrynn reached down and grabbed my shoulders, saying a different phrase this time, but the beast began to growl and bare its fangs, so she quickly pulled back.

"It's okay." I patted the over-protective monster. I looked back at Vrynn again, shaking my head slightly.

She said something that sounded similar, miming walking with her fingers.

I nodded slowly. "Yeah, I can try to walk."

I reached out and grabbed Vrynn's hand. She helped me into a sitting position.

The beast shifted until its head covered my thighs. It whined every time I tried to move. With some coaxing, I was able to get the animal to stand up. I wrapped an arm around its neck, which seemed to calm it slightly.

Vrynn positioned herself behind me and reached under my arms. Between her lifting and my grip on my animal protector, I was able to stumble to my feet. Pain shot through my back and down my left leg.

Maybe walking wouldn't be an option.

Vrynn put my arm over her shoulder and helped me hobble toward the end of the alley. It felt like we had run a marathon in just a few steps.

Holding a small device in front of her, Vrynn said something that I didn't understand. A voice that sounded just like Tera emanated from the device in a language I'm pretty sure the real Tera never knew.

Then the language shifted. "Vrynn says I should fly closer to her position, Mitch. She says that you've been hurt."

"Yeah. Please do," I groaned.

"I'll be there in two minutes," Tera replied. "Please don't die." Her voice sounded almost frantic, which reminded me that we never did look at dialing back her emotional subroutine.

Vrynn and I reached the end of the alley and turned down the street toward the ship, or at least, where the ship had been. The beast continued with us, staying close by my side. I wasn't completely aware of what was going on, but I could tell we were getting a fair amount of stares from passers-by.

The whoosh of thrusters roared above my head, and I looked up. The *Starfire* was descending onto the street in front of us, the cargo door already wide open. A cacophony of what probably passed for honking on this planet began as soon as the ship touched down. Between the stumbling and the swirling air and the blaring noise, I wasn't sure I was going to keep my lunch inside much longer.

The next thing I knew, I had collapsed on the cargo bay floor, the beast curled up against me once again.

Tera appeared and bent down next to me. "Mitch, speak to me! Mitch, please be okay."

I held up a hand toward her. "I'm fine, Tera. Thanks to Vrynn." I rolled my head to the side. "And this big fella." I patted the large animal in front of me.

Vrynn said something to Tera.

"She says we can't stay here in the middle of the street," Tera said.

I nodded, sort of, and it hurt. "Take us back into orbit."

Tera shimmered away, and I felt the ship rumble to life. I didn't really know how, but Vrynn was able to get me off the floor and across the lower deck into the med-pod. The automated medical devices worked their magic on me. The pain began to ease, and I felt my consciousness slipping away.

When I finally woke up, most of the pain in my ribs and head was gone, except for a slight throbbing behind my ear.

A few minutes later, Vrynn came into the room and pulled me from the pod. As she walked me to the ladder, I realized that the medicine from the med-pod must not have completely worn off because I felt light enough to drift away. When we reached the ladder, I stared at it, unsure of how I was going to manage to get up to the top deck. I was in no condition to climb anything.

"Go ahead, Tera," Vrynn called out.

"Go ahead and what?" I asked her.

Vrynn gave me a mischievous smile. "You'll see."

I heard a whine from somewhere at the front of the lower deck, then I started to feel weird. My arms rose in front of me, and my insides felt like I was on a free-fall rollercoaster ride. Vrynn's blonde hair floated away from her head, making her look like some sort of alien dandelion. As I chuckled and pointed at her, she grabbed me under the arms and heaved me into the air.

My eyes went wide, and I flailed my arms and legs. I floated through the opening to the top deck, and my foot connected with the wall, sending me drifting awkwardly in a slow cartwheel. My head still wasn't clear enough to know if this was reality or a hallucination from something the med-pod gave me.

Vrynn sailed gracefully up toward me and caught my ankle just before I smashed my head against the ceiling bulkhead. She pulled me back down toward the deck. "Pretty fun, huh?"

I grinned like a school-boy. I felt happy and light, and not just weight-wise. Though when I nodded, the room started to spin. Or it might have been the lack of gravity. "You turned off the gravity because you put it in a battery." I giggled at the little rhyme I'd made. I was definitely still a little loopy.

Vrynn gave me a patronizing smile as she hooked a foot under the edge of the couch. "Yeah, Mitch. That's what gravity capacitors do." She positioned me with my feet floating just a few inches above the floor then looked over her shoulder. "Bring it back up ten percent," she said.

Tera nodded, and I heard another whine from the lower deck. I felt like a thin kite string was pulling down on my body. My feet touched the deck as if I was a feather landing on a pillow. Without thinking, I flexed my legs and shot back off the deck again.

"Whoa there, bucko," Vrynn said as she grabbed my arm and pulled me down. "Tera, give us a slow ramp back up to fifty percent."

Within a few seconds, I was on the deck again, feeling a steadily increasing pull on my body.

"How are you feeling now?" Vrynn asked.

I nodded. "Pretty good." I stared at her for several seconds. She had lovely cobalt-blue eyes that I felt like I could dive into. And her skin looked soft enough to touch. I didn't know where that thought had come from, and I shook my head in an attempt to shake it loose. The med-pod must have given me something that messed with my thinking, too.

"Can you walk to your room?" she asked.

Standing so close, gazing at her face, I watched her lips move when she spoke, but there wasn't any delay in the sound. Was she speaking English?

"Say something again," I said as I stared at her lips.

"Lean any closer, and I'll knock you on your butt."

I realized that my face was only a few inches from hers, gaze locked on her lips. I took a half-step back, but my head began to spin.

Vrynn grabbed my arm again and walked me slowly across the kitchen to my room. I don't really remember whether I pulled the covers back or she did, but the next thing I knew, I was in the bed.

I was vaguely aware that she still stood next to my bed. When I glanced up, she had a puzzled look on her face that slowly morphed into warmth. "You're actually a pretty decent guy, Mitch," she said softly.

"Thanks," I mumbled, my head still incredibly foggy. "You have beautiful eyes."

I must have fallen asleep pretty quickly because when I opened my eyes again, the room was dark. I glanced out the portal and saw the familiar star-speckled blackness of normal space. As I slowly regained consciousness, my brain chugged on what had happened after my meeting with Sergeant Zondy.

I was fairly certain that before he died, Corporal Kyuli had said Gralik would want me alive. The only reason I could think that a complete stranger like Gralik would know about me—or care if I was dead or alive—was if he knew I had the *Starfire* and he wanted it. Maybe Nexus had been the group trying to steal the ship from Gabe, after all.

Speaking of Nexus, I had to admit that Vrynn was definitely right about the Bonara Defense Force being infected with Nexus sympathizers and outright operatives.

And apparently, I'd plunged myself right into the middle of the whole mess.

My sluggish gaze wandered to a nearby portal. The edge of a planet was just barely visible through the glass. I wondered which planet it was.

Had Vrynn tried to fly the ship to the Resistance base? Would Tera have let her?

A sudden thought occurred to me. What if Vrynn had hacked Tera's matrix and taken over the ship? Of course, if that had happened, I probably wouldn't have been lying comfortably in my bed. I would have been floating out an airlock. Or perhaps not. Maybe Vrynn had a soft spot for injured, hapless dirt-men.

I started testing out my muscles and decided it was time to get up. As soon as I sat up in bed, my ribs screamed in pain, and my head swam. I groaned and waited for the room to stop moving. "Room lights on," I said groggily. The lights came on, and I squinted against the sudden brightness.

As I shifted to the edge of the bed, preparing to stand up, the door to my room opened, and Vrynn walked in.

"Hey, I'm glad you're up," she said. "We can't orbit Varus Prime forever. We'll eventually need to resupply." She walked over to the bed and stood next to me. "How are you feeling today?"

"A little sore," I said as I checked the range of motion in my arms. "And I could really—wait. Did you say 'today'? How long have I been asleep?"

"Almost two days," she replied.

The sound of her voice was nearly in sync with her talking, though not quite. I touched my ear, but couldn't feel the translator earpiece. That wasn't surprising, given that it had been smashed during the alley fight. I leaned forward and squinted at Vrynn's lips.

"Oh no, don't start that again." She pushed against my shoulders, keeping me at arm's-length. "Your brain is still adjusting to the new translator. You'll get used to it soon enough."

"Translator? What are you talking about?" I asked.

Vrynn shrugged. "Tera and I discussed it, and we decided that for safety reasons you couldn't go around the Bonara Cluster with an earpiece that could get knocked out every time you get in a scuffle. So we had the med-pod install a subcutaneous translator node behind your ear." She leaned forward and tilted my head to the side. "It looks like the incision is healing nicely."

I put a hand up to my head and felt behind my right ear. There was a tiny bump—about the size of a dime—that felt tender to the touch. I glanced back at Vrynn. "That's why I can understand what you're saying without the delay I used to have."

She nodded.

"Wow." I touched the bump again. "I would have done this earlier, if I'd known it would be this amazing."

I paused for a moment, considering what this almost stranger had done for me. "Thanks for saving my life," I said quietly. "You could have just let me die and gotten your ship back."

"Don't think it didn't cross my mind," she said playfully. "But that would be cruel and heartless."

I chuckled at her repetition of the phrase.

"And despite how difficult you can be, you're actually a nice guy." She sat on the edge of a chair across from my bed and fell silent for a moment. "Besides, I've seen enough death already."

We stared at each other for several seconds. I was about to thank her again when Tera's voice came over the ship's speakers. "Not to interrupt this precious moment, but there's a giant Varusian Pantoboar making a nest in the back of the cargo bay."

Vrynn and I shared a concerned look. I stood and hurried out of my room and down to the cargo bay, only clumsily bumping into two bulkheads on the way. When we reached the cargo bay, there was the beast that had saved my life, wedged in the small alcove to one side of the cargo ramp, settled on a pile of packing material that had been discarded during my search of the food inventory.

I approached him warily, hoping that he remembered me as the nice guy he saved. "Hey there, big guy." I didn't know what else to call him at the moment. The beast purred at me, which I took as a good sign. I couldn't just keep calling him "buddy" or "big guy." He needed a name.

"How about we call you Rascal," I said to the large black animal. The purring deepened, so I figured he was okay with the name.

A moment later, Vrynn slowly approached and stood at my side. "Just so you know, keeping a giant beast like that on a starship is definitely not normal."

I looked down at her. "There isn't anything that's been normal about my life since I first saw this ship. So this seems par for the course." I held out my hands to indicate Rascal curled up in his nest. "Do you have any idea what I'd be doing right now if I was back on Earth? I'd probably just be getting off work and heading to Jenny's Cafe for dinner." The moment I said it, I realized it wasn't true. I didn't have a job anymore, so I wouldn't be getting off work at all.

Standing there in the cargo hold, I realized that I was floating in orbit around an alien planet circling a distant star. In an effort to distract myself from the sudden loneliness, I turned to Vrynn. "Where would you be right now, I mean, before you went to Thetis Max to wait for Fosso to bring the ship?"

"I don't really want to think about that. It wouldn't have been happy," Vrynn replied.

"Okay, then, let's think of something positive. If you could pick anywhere in the cluster, assuming you weren't fighting for the Resistance, where would you go?"

"The Colossal Falls on Kalera Five," Vrynn said almost immediately.

I couldn't help but chuckle at the speed of her response. "And what's it like there?"

Vrynn sighed deeply. "I don't know. I've only ever seen pictures. But I hear the view of the falls from the restaurant patio is amazing."

I nodded. "Sounds great. Count me in," I said.

Vrynn smiled, and I had to admit the effect was dazzling. But a few moments later, her expression fell as the reality of our situation came crashing back on us.

She looked up, those sea-blue eyes pleading with me. "Mitch, I really need this ship. Every day that passes is another day that The Resistance is without the protection it could provide. In fact, we left Thetis Max three days ago, and I haven't heard a thing from any of my contacts. Not even on emergency frequencies."

I grimaced. "I can't give you the *Starfire*."

Her expression fell.

"But..." I drew out the word and her eyes lifted to mine. "I get the feeling that Gabe's killers and Nexus and this ship are all intertwined somehow. If your friends can help me get justice for Gabe, I'll do what I can to help them in return."

A broad smile spread across Vrynn's face. "Really?"

I held up a hand, hoping to keep her exuberance in check. "I'm not saying I want to enlist in the Resistance." I stopped and considered the reason I was even willing to make this offer. "But I'd like to help."

Vrynn wasn't fazed by my stipulation. She took a step toward me. And for a moment, I wondered if she was going to hug me or tackle me. At the last second, she skidded to a stop. "Thanks, Mitch," she said with a shy smile. "I know this isn't really your fight—or at least it didn't used to be. But I appreciate the help."

I nodded and scratched the back of my neck. The look on her face told me she wasn't sure what else to say. "Maybe you could go give the coordinates of the Resistance base to Tera," I suggested.

She nodded once and bounded out of the cargo bay, heading for the flight deck.

And I was left alone with Rascal.

I turned to my hairy protector. "What have I gotten myself into, boy?"

Rascal lifted his head and stared at me, those intelligent eyes saying that he wished he could help, but I was on my own with this one.

At least, I like to think that's what he would have said.

Chapter Seven

After about an hour in intra-space, we arrived at our destination. The ship's autopilot settled us into orbit above a planet the computer identified as Dreporox, and we gazed down at a desolate-looking rocky world with a pinkish-red surface and almost no water visible. When I asked for the coordinates of where to land, Vrynn said that the location of the Resistance base was top secret.

"It's going to be a little difficult to land at the top-secret base if I don't know where it is."

Vrynn leaned close to the co-pilot's console, casting a last glance over her shoulder at me, and entered the coordinates manually.

"I have access to the navigation system," Tera said to Vrynn. "I can see exactly what you entered."

"Maybe you weren't the one I was keeping them a secret from," Vrynn replied before arching a brow theatrically in my direction.

Based on Vrynn's tone of voice and that look she just gave, I was fairly certain she was just teasing me. Besides, we were all about to see the location of the base. Unless, of course, she planned to blindfold me.

As I reached for the controls to start the maneuvers that I hoped would bring us out of our high orbit, Tera suddenly turned her head and focused at a point off to the right.

"I'm detecting another ship in orbit," she said.

"That's not unusual," Vrynn said. "I'm sure the Resistance would want to have a sentry ship to intercept any incoming enemy attacks."

Tera nodded. "I'll check the transponder signal."

I leaned forward and searched the planet below, but I couldn't see anything. "Can you magnify or zoom in or something?" I asked.

An enlarged view of the planet's horizon appeared in the air in front of me, a small red triangle floating over what looked like an empty spot. Then the sunlight glinted off of something shiny. I still couldn't tell from this high up in orbit, but I thought it looked like a small spaceship. I glanced over at Vrynn. She was leaning forward, too, scrutinizing the projected image.

After a few seconds, Vrynn shook her head. "That's not a Resistance ship. It's not from any of the systems that support the Resistance."

I frowned as I continued watching the ship grow on the display. "Could it be some sort of random ship that just happened to be orbiting Dreporox? Maybe looking to resupply?"

"Dreporox doesn't have any *known* settlements," Vrynn said. She obviously didn't count the Resistance's secret base. "Besides, if they were planning a resupply from natural resources, they wouldn't be heading up from the planet on an intercept course."

"I should be receiving its transponder by now, but I'm not getting anything." Tera tilted her head, staring at nothing in particular. "But I am getting a similar reading to the Vezor-Class runabout that attacked us at Gabe's farm. It's almost as if the true transponder is being perfectly canceled out, leaving what is essentially a blank transmission."

I watched the small blip on the screen, moving steadily higher as it rose to meet us. "But that would mean—"

"It must be a Nexus ship," Vrynn said.

I looked back at the floating image. "Are you sure?"

Vrynn nodded then turned to me. "What other explanation is there? It's not a Resistance ship. And its transponder is being actively blocked, just like the ship that attacked you on Dirt."

Despite being annoyed that she still couldn't seem to get the name of my planet right, I knew from the look in her eyes that she was certainly serious about the current situation.

"So what's the plan?" I asked. "Can we still get down to your base before the ship catches us?"

"No way. It's between us and the surface. It would catch us long before we made it," Vrynn said.

"Do we bug out and come back later?"

Vrynn furrowed her brow, deep in thought. "I can't understand why there's a Nexus sentry here at all. The Resistance wouldn't allow an enemy ship to remain in orbit like this. They would have eliminated it by now. Unless . . ."

I glanced at Vrynn. "Unless what?"

She stared at nothing in particular for several seconds before shaking her head. "Nothing." She refocused on the ship approaching us. "We need to get past the sentry. The most important thing is to deliver this ship to the Resistance."

". . . in one piece, right?" I added. As long as she agreed to the in-one-piece stipulation, I'd quibble with her later about whether the Resistance would be getting the ship or not.

"Obviously," Vrynn replied without missing a beat.

I let my gaze linger on my new co-pilot. She was so engrossed in preparing to take on the approaching ship that she didn't notice my attention. I certainly hadn't been excited when she had stubbornly refused to leave the ship, but watching her prepare to go into battle at my side, I found myself grateful to have her.

I took a deep breath and tightened my grip on the control sticks.

"Why don't I take over flying?" Vrynn asked. "I have more experience with facing off against Nexus attack ships."

Of course, she could still be a thorn in my side. I wouldn't have expected any less.

"Uh, I think I'll pilot the ship for now," I said, casting her a sidelong glance.

Vrynn raised a brow at me. I could tell she was confused by my insistence, particularly given what she had witnessed every time I tried to perform maneuvers outside the atmosphere.

Ignoring her obvious skepticism, I began moving us into position to attack the approaching sentry ship. True to form, I gave too much power to the rotational thrusters, and the ship veered too far past where I was aiming. I twisted the stick to correct, but that just overcompensated for the original problem.

Vrynn shook her head as she watched the enemy ship—and the planet behind it—drift back and forth as I tried to get lined up. "Do you want me to help now?" she asked innocently.

"I just can't seem to get the hang of zero-G flying," I said in frustration.

"Part of the problem is that it's not really zero-G flying at all. It's more like zero-G floating," Vrynn replied.

I stared at her, trying to figure out how much I trusted her to fly the ship and not just steal it from me. I decided we'd been through enough in the last few days that I trusted her to fight our way through the Nexus sentry and get to the surface. At this point, we definitely wanted the same thing.

Almost as if she read my mind, Vrynn said, "I'm not going anywhere with the ship. I want to land on the surface with minimal damage, just like you do."

Finally, I nodded and tapped a few buttons to transfer flight control to the co-pilot controls. I activated the weapons systems on my own controls, preparing to engage the other ship if it turned out to be hostile.

Vrynn leaned over and looked at my display. "Don't turn on the targeting system yet."

I disabled auto-targeting.

She tilted her head and considered the ship in front of us. "Actually, on second thought, turn them back on."

I gave her a confused look but went ahead and tapped the auto-targeting icon again.

"Now, turn them off and then on again," she said almost immediately.

"Are you just playing around with me now? Is it because suddenly you think you're in charge of the ship?" I asked.

Vrynn gave me a crooked grin. "It's part of my plan. Trust me."

"Whoever is on that ship probably thinks we're crazy," I said as I toggled the targeter.

"Good," Vrynn said as she grabbed the control sticks.

She began rotating us away from the oncoming sentry, pointing the nose of the ship out into space. It looked like we were preparing to leave orbit or jump away from the system entirely. I couldn't see the enemy ship through the windows anymore, but the heads up display continued to track it as we drifted the other direction.

Suddenly, we moved backwards.

I looked over at Vrynn, her brow knit in concentration. She pulled left and right, then up and down on the control stick. The ship veered around like a roller coaster as we continued to increase our reverse speed.

"You know, if you wanted someone who could fly this bad, why didn't you just leave me in control?" I asked sarcastically.

A small smirk spread across her face. "Just wait. This will work."

I turned my focus back to the floating picture of the enemy ship. "If your plan is to make them fall out of their seats with laughter, it definitely might work." I held my hand out to the ship on the display. "They probably don't know if we're worth shooting at."

The genius of Vrynn's plan hit me. They wouldn't fire until it was too late.

I looked over at my brilliant co-pilot. She gave me a brief, sidelong glance, her smile broad, as she continued to focus on her intentionally bad piloting. I checked the readout on the heads up display, watching the range meter tick down as our ships moved steadily closer together. Much longer, and they would have such an easy target that even a lazy marksman might take the shot just for fun.

"The computer just identified this ship's design as a light attack fighter from the Prentoro system," Tera said. "Its maneuverability is similar to ours, but we have it easily outgunned."

"Add the Prentoro system to the list with possible Nexus cells," I said.

Vrynn glanced at me. "Ready?" she asked.

I nodded, gripping the control sticks. My fingers hovered over the triggers that would unleash our plasma bursts from the turrets. We did have other weapons, but any move to open the weapons bays would obviously bring a response from the sentry ship.

Vrynn pulled hard on the stick and the ship swung around in a tight arc, still moving backward.

"The Prentorian ship is powering weapons," Tera announced.

Our ship had just angled into position, pointed straight at the sentry ship. "Now!" Vrynn yelled.

I squeezed hard on the triggers and twisted the controls back and forth. Streams of plasma balls shot from the twin cannons on the leading edges of the winglets. The space in front of us looked like a giant roman candle that some kid had decided to use on the neighborhood cat—not that I had ever witnessed that sort of thing.

Despite being caught off guard, the sentry ship fired several explosive slugs in retaliation.

"Tera, activate laser defenses," I said.

"Activated," she replied.

One of the slugs succumbed to the blanket of plasma fire before it got halfway to us. The other two were destroyed by our defensive lasers at the same time that my first dozen shots impacted the Nexus ship. It looked like the ship might survive—though disabled—until the next barrage impacted its hull, creating a fiery inferno.

Apparently, I had overdone it on the plasma cannons.

Fortunately, Vrynn had continued thrusting backward because when the Nexus ship's engine core breached, it exploded in a cloud of shrapnel.

"Well, that was exciting," Tera deadpanned.

I glanced over at Vrynn. She smiled back. Maybe we could end up helping each other after all.

Vrynn guided the ship out of high orbit until we were down in Dreporox's thin atmosphere. Her agitation seemed to increase the closer we got to the surface, causing her piloting to become more erratic. After a few more seconds, I announced that I was taking the flight controls back, partly for our safety and partly for the sake of her nerves.

When we reached the coordinates of the secret base, I understood what she had been worried about. The charred remains of half a dozen attack ships lay scattered near several cave-like openings in the pink and orange rock. Scorch marks peppered the cliff where weapons fire must have breached the walls.

I brought the ship down near the scene of the battle. Before the landing struts had even touched the dusty surface, Vrynn was out of the co-pilot seat and halfway to the ladder. As soon as the *Starfire* was safely on the ground, I jumped up and followed her.

Rascal perked up from his nest as I raced through the cargo bay. I motioned downward with both hands, hoping he knew that meant for him to stay.

Vrynn was nearly to the cave entrance by the time my boots were on the ground. "Vrynn! Wait!" I yelled.

She didn't even turn around before she disappeared through the opening to the hidden fortress. As I ran to catch up, a cold biting wind carrying dry sand stung my face. We hadn't even checked the breathability of the atmosphere before Vrynn opened the cargo bay door. Of course, she'd probably been here before, so maybe she wasn't worried about the air. I pressed through the wind and sand until I reached the protection of the cliffs and the entrance to the Resistance base.

As I cleared the breach in the main blast door, I was plunged into the semi-darkness of the interior of the cave. I slowed to a walk as I let my eyes adjust. The place was creepy.

I stepped up next to Vrynn. "You have your blaster, right?" I whispered to her.

Vrynn didn't reply. She simply stared straight ahead. I turned to see what she was looking at now that my eyes had adjusted better to the dim interior.

What I saw turned my stomach.

The floor of the large cavern-turned-headquarters was littered with dead bodies. They wore uniforms similar to Vrynn's flight suit. From the positions of the bodies, it looked like they had all gone down fighting, though not in any organized sort of way. Their attackers—assuming it was Nexus—must have caught them completely by surprise.

We stepped over the dead as we began sifting through the chaos. From the initial evidence, it appeared to have been an overwhelming win for Nexus—the only bodies we saw were Resistance soldiers. But then I saw weapons lying discarded next to long streaks of blood across the floor. Streaks that led back the way we came.

The Nexus attackers must have retrieved their dead and wounded but left the Resistance casualties where they fell.

I crouched down to look at one of the fallen Resistance defenders—a young man probably in his early twenties, or whatever the equivalent age was on his planet. He had died from a plasma shot to the chest, quite quickly if the size of the scorch mark was any indicator. I was immediately transported back to that moment a few weeks ago when I had found Gabe lying in the entrance to his barn with a similar wound. I pushed the feelings of grief and anger aside to keep them from overwhelming me.

As I scrutinized the young soldier's face, I noticed that his skin had a leathery appearance to it, dried out, almost like a mummy. The lack of decomposition in the bodies explained why the cavern didn't reek of death.

I stood and glanced at the streaks of blood I'd seen earlier. On closer inspection, they had clearly been dried for some time.

"I should have been here," Vrynn said as she stared at the tragic scene. "If they'd had the *Starfire*, maybe they would have won."

I walked over to stand beside her. "Look at the bodies," I said, pointing to a nearby casualty of the fight. "They died weeks ago, maybe even before the *Starfire* crashed on Earth." I placed a hand on her arm. "Besides, if you had been here, you'd just be one more dead body on the ground."

A single tear slipped down her cheek and fell to the ground. She swiped at her face. "Let's keep moving," she said as she strode through the large vehicle hanger toward the hallway leading deeper into the caverns.

Suddenly, an explosion rocked the small fighter pod next to me. I dove to the ground next to Vrynn. Looking up, I saw a bright plasma round streak above our heads.

"Grab a better weapon," Vrynn said as she pocketed her blaster and reached for a discarded plasma rifle.

I looked around the floor near me. There weren't any other weapons nearby except the ones still being held by dead bodies. I inched over to a fallen Resistance soldier and apologized softly as I pulled the gun from her stiff grasp. Plasma rifle in hand, I inched back to Vrynn's side. She was kneeling behind a stack of cargo containers, periodically firing wild shots over the makeshift battlement.

"Can you see who's shooting at us?" I asked when I reached her.

"No, but I'm betting it's a Nexus soldier left behind to guard the base in case someone like us comes along."

"Should we just leave?" I asked. In my mind, there was no shame in running away from someone who wanted to kill you.

Vrynn shook her head. "We're pinned down here. We'd never make it out the blast doors without getting shot in the back." She took a peek over the edge of the container. A second later, another plasma round hit the ship behind us. "Besides, I won't let them get away with this," she said, an icy edge to her voice.

I glanced around at the fallen Resistance fighters and understood why she felt that way.

"You head over there." She nodded toward the right side of our protective stack. "I'll go the other way. Let's see if we can flank them."

I nodded and got low to the floor. Between overturned crates, vehicles, and random equipment scattered around the hanger, there was enough clutter to give me cover. I crept along the ground, ducking as plasma rounds occasionally exploded near me, until I had nearly reached the far wall. I hid behind a small treaded vehicle. Vrynn tried to keep the heat off me by firing every time I moved to the next bit of cover.

Safely hidden behind my large metal barricade, I stole a glance over the top of the alien tank. The Nexus soldiers were firing at us from a small tunnel opening that must have led deeper into the caverns of the base.

Several rounds exploded just in front of the spot where Vrynn had taken cover, sending a stack of cargo containers toppling onto her. Vrynn's scream reverberated off the walls of the cavernous hangar.

A moment later, laughter echoed from the entrance to the tunnel. A soldier tromped out, heading straight for Vrynn. It took all I had to stay put and not run straight for her. Or the soldier.

I waited until I had a clear shot and lined up the plasma rifle. I knew if I didn't take this guy out, Vrynn was a goner.

Just as I was about to fire, I heard a voice call out from the tunnel opening. "If she's still alive, Gralik will want her."

There was a second soldier. And they were definitely Nexus soldiers.

"Gralik can wait his turn. She's mine first," the first soldier yelled back.

Not if I had anything to say about it.

I gripped my rifle tighter, staring down the sights at my target, unwilling to allow this piece of scum to get anywhere near Vrynn.

At the rate they were walking, though, the first soldier would reach her before I had a clear shot at the second soldier. I would have liked to take them both down at once, but I absolutely couldn't let the first one find Vrynn.

I watched the first soldier inch carefully closer to the pile of bins pinning my co-pilot, keeping my sights lined up on him even as I glanced back to the tunnel opening, waiting for the second soldier to emerge.

As the first soldier reached out to dismantle the pile of crate, I knew my time had run out. Out of the corner of my eye, I caught a glimpse of movement in the tunnel entrance—the second soldier stepped partially into view. I squeezed the trigger, quickly firing three rounds at the first guy. One shot went wide, but two caught him in the torso, launching him backward as they exploded.

Once I knew he had gone down, I turned quickly to take aim at the second soldier. I squeezed off a couple more rounds as he dove for cover. He raised his weapon and fired back from behind a generator box. I ducked, barely avoiding the plasma bursts as they exploded behind me. I brought my rifle up and fired a few wild shots in his direction. His return fire exploded through the openings in the treads in front of me.

I couldn't just trade shots with this guy all day. Eventually, he'd get the upper hand, given the fact that he was already trained as a soldier.

Plus, I needed to get to Vrynn. I didn't know how hurt she was.

I fired another volley and immediately jumped from behind the tug tractor, ducking low next to a crate of supplies. When my enemy's shots hit the treaded vehicle again, I let out a long, unmanly scream, hoping that the hangar was echoey enough that he wouldn't know where I was.

After a few more shots at my former hiding spot, the guy grunted and sauntered toward me. If I had planned right, I'd get a clear shot at him at the last second, just before he discovered me. If I hadn't planned right, I'd be dead.

I held my breath as his footsteps moved closer and closer.

A long shadow, cast by the hangar's emergency lights, fell across the ground in front of me. I could nearly hear the wheeze of his labored breathing.

That was close enough.

I lunged from my new hiding place, rifle pointed at the spot where I expected my enemy to be.

Fortunately, my guess was better than his. I fired several shots as I fell in slow-motion to the ground. At least, it felt like slow motion. He swung his weapon toward me and fired as well, but he only got two wild shots off before he took several plasma rounds to the chest.

The impact knocked him backward into a stack of bins as his weapon clattered harmlessly away.

I scrambled to my feet and ran back to Vrynn's hiding spot. "Vrynn," I called. "Are you okay?" When I heard groaning, I started pulling storage containers off the pile.

"I'm here," a soft voice said

I lifted one more container and found her underneath.

She smiled up at me. "I knew that would work," she said weakly. Even injured, her confidence showed through.

I dropped to my knees next to her. "Are you hurt?" I wasn't sure where to even start looking for injuries.

She shook her head. "I'm sure I'll have a few bruises, but nothing's broken." She stared up at me for a few moments. "Thanks," she said softly.

I nodded and helped her up to a sitting position. "What happened?"

"I wanted to draw their attention to me so that you would get a good shot."

I chuckled. "Well, it worked. You certainly got their attention."

"A little more than I wanted," she added.

When she was ready, I helped her stand. We walked by the new casualties on our way to the tunnel opening, this time with weapons at the ready.

A short distance down the tunnel, we found several branching hallways cut into the rock. The passages led to various rooms—planning rooms, quarters, an armory. We didn't find any more Nexus soldiers lurking around, but there weren't any Resistance personnel either—at least none that were still alive.

At the entrance to the command room, Vrynn paused and turned to me. "I'll see if I can find out what the plan for the ship was. Why don't you check if any of the equipment or supplies are salvageable." She nodded her head toward a nearby supply area.

I guess it didn't matter who did which job, but I got the distinct impression that she didn't trust me with the Resistance's secret plans quite yet. I nodded and headed deeper into the caverns.

In the supply room, I found some bins of food. None of it was fresh food, but it looked better than the rations we had on board our ship. I wandered farther down the main tunnel until I found another large staging area. Crates lined the walls and various weapons were scattered haphazardly, as if they had been grabbed from well-organized piles in a hurry.

I decided we could definitely use the food, and some of the weapons would come in handy, too. The only problem was that I wasn't too excited about lugging the crates back to the ship.

I needed a cart.

As I wandered back toward the hangar, looking for a cart, I came across something better.

Tucked in the corner of one of the larger storage rooms were half a dozen rover-style bots the size of ice chests. They had four wheels on each side and a wide, flat top. I tapped the top of the closest one to see if it was sturdy enough to hold the bins I needed to move. It seemed fairly robust, so I tried to roll it away from the wall.

Multiple lights flashed on the side, and the cart-bot suddenly started moving toward me on its own. In a very happy voice that reminded me of a 1950s product announcer, it said, "How can this unit be of service?"

I was so surprised to have a mechanized cart, much less one that talked to me, that at first, I wasn't quite sure how to respond. "Uh, I need to move some stuff."

"Please direct this unit to the objects that need to be moved," the bot said happily.

I stood up and walked back toward the staging area, all the while checking over my shoulder that the cart was following me. When I arrived at the containers of food, the cart stopped next to me. It didn't do anything, so I pointed to the stack of bins. "I need to move these to my ship."

The cart turned toward the stack and scanned it with some sort of laser. "This collection of objects exceeds the rated capacity of this unit. Can the stack be divided into smaller subsets?"

"Sure," I replied. I was glad I'd found a smart cart.

"Other units can be summoned to complete the task faster," the cart said.

"Yeah, that would be great. Let's call the others."

The cart repositioned itself right next to the stack, and two arms that resembled miniature lifting cranes extended from hatches on both sides of the body. The arms reached the crate on the top of the stack and lifted it carefully down until it rested on top of the cart.

"Please direct this unit to the appropriate location to deposit this item," the cart said.

"Smart cart," I said to myself as I walked back toward the hangar blast doors.

On the way, the rest of the cart-bots passed us, heading toward the storage area. This was going to be the easiest moving job I'd ever done.

After lowering the ship's ramp and explaining to my overly defensive AI friend what was happening in her cargo bay, I directed the first cart to set the food bins against one of the walls.

"The stack of items has been collected by the other units," the first cart announced proudly. "Would you like more items transferred to this location?"

"Definitely. Let's bring all the food crates that will fit in the cargo bay." I didn't know if the cart was smart enough to understand that type of instruction, but I figured the smart device I had at home could turn off the lamps in my living room when I asked it, so this cart ought to be able to figure out which bins had food in them. At least, I hoped it could.

I followed one of the smart carts on its return journey back into the base. I wanted to make sure it was grabbing the right stuff.

I never made it back to the storage area. As I passed one of the control rooms, Vrynn called out, "Hey, Mitch. Come look at this."

I stepped into the control room and joined her at one of the computer consoles. I tried not to notice the bodies of two Resistance fighters as I walked across the room.

Vrynn had a video cued up on the screen, showing the room we were in. There were two people—a man and a woman—dressed in Resistance uniforms, sitting at the computer console. I glanced briefly over my shoulder. The bodies on the ground were a man and woman of the approximate build as the officers in the video feed.

Unfortunately, I already knew how this was going to end.

"The Nexus soldiers were looking for something specific," Vrynn said. "Watch this."

The video started playing, and a few seconds later, I could see multiple alarms flashing on the console. Even if there hadn't been sound on the video, I would have been able to tell by their reactions and the shaking of the cameras that the battle was going on.

The Resistance fighters grabbed their weapons and moved out of the video. I looked at Vrynn to see if anything was going to happen while the screen was empty. She tapped the screen to advance the video. The recorded sounds of the battle were much closer to the control room now. A minute later, the woman rushed back into the room and began working on the computer. She made a frantic call on the comms, but her voice was low so that I couldn't understand what she said.

A moment later, the man backed into the room, his weapon at the ready.

"I have you trapped," a nonchalant voice off camera said. "If you don't surrender, you'll be killed."

The man didn't appear to consider the offer long. His plasma rifle roared to life, aiming at the doorway, but the exchange was brief as multiple rounds struck him in the chest and face. The impact threw him across the room and his weapon went silent. The woman at the computer reached for the gun lying on the desk beside her, but a single plasma round caught her outstretched hand and knocked the weapon away.

"I hope you're not as foolish as he was," the off-camera voice said.

The woman stood from her chair and shifted to block what she had been doing on the computer. A tall soldier moved into view, a handgun held casually at his side. He had jet black hair with faint grayish stripes running down the middle, almost like a skunk had sat on his head.

I sucked in a breath. "That's the leader of the group of soldiers that killed Gabe," I said.

Vrynn glanced at me, a look of compassion in her eyes, before turning back to the screen. "That's Gralik."

My eyes narrowed as I focused my hatred on the figure on the screen.

"If you give me what I need, I might let you live," Gralik said in the recording.

The woman didn't answer. She didn't even twitch.

The soldier lifted his weapon, leveling it at the woman. "Give me the Quake Drive ship," he said.

"Quake Drive. You and Tera have both mentioned that before. What is it?" I asked Vrynn.

She shook her head but didn't answer.

The woman on the video laughed. "Not a chance. That's the ship we're going to use to end your pitiful little power grab."

The man took another threatening step forward. "I know it was meant to be delivered to you already," he said.

The woman's expression faltered. "You couldn't possibly know that."

The soldier's smirk grew. "I have my sources." He casually glanced around the control room at nothing in particular. "It doesn't matter how I know," Gralik said. "What matters is that you're going to tell me where the ship is, or I'm going to kill you. Very slowly."

"I think you're going to kill me anyway," the woman replied. For the first time, I noticed that the woman in the video was using her body to block something from view. As she shifted, the surveillance camera caught a glimpse of a small weapon in her hand. Gralik hadn't noticed it yet.

"Probably," Gralik replied flippantly. "I've killed hundreds of people already. And I'll kill hundreds more if it gets me what I want."

I found myself rooting for the woman, hoping she would be able to pull the gun out fast enough to kill the Nexus leader and save herself. One glance at her lifeless body just a few feet away told me that hadn't happened.

In a flash, she aimed the weapon at the computer console next to her and fired multiple rounds.

"No!!" Gralik screamed as he fired a barrage of plasma rounds at the woman.

I glanced over at the other computer and saw the evidence of her efforts. It had been completely destroyed.

"That computer must have held the information about the *Starfire*," I said to Vrynn, nodding toward the destroyed equipment. "Why else would she be so intent on destroying it?"

Vrynn nodded. "She sacrificed herself to make sure Nexus didn't get it."

Vrynn shut off the video, and we stood in silence, contemplating what had happened here. I glanced at Vrynn and noticed a change in her expression. The sadness it had held when we first entered the base and discovered her fallen comrades was now replaced with steely determination.

"At least they never got the *Starfire* or its Quake Drive," she said.

I grimaced. "Actually..."

Her eyes went wide. "What?"

I rubbed the back of my neck. "The day they killed Gabe, I saw Gralik leading a group of soldiers carrying a large piece of equipment from the *Starfire* to their ship."

"You lost the Quake Drive, the most important part of the ship?" Vrynn said, her voice rising.

"Hey, I didn't lose it. They stole it."

She opened her mouth to retort when Skeeter trotted into the room.

"Tell her, Tera. Tell Vrynn whether I could have stopped the Quake Drive from being stolen."

Tera's voice emanated from the bot's speakers. "Mitch wasn't there when it happened. Gabe wasn't even there." Her voice carried a note of sadness.

"And what kept them from stealing the *Starfire* itself, then?" Vrynn asked.

"I did," Tera replied curtly.

Vrynn and I shared a puzzled look.

"What do you mean?" I asked.

"When the Nexus soldiers boarded the ship, they demanded that I give them control of the *Starfire*. I refused. They threatened to disable my matrix and then take the ship. I told them to go stomp needles—it's an expression that makes more sense in their language. I immediately wrote a command subroutine that would lock all flight control systems if they tried to terminate my matrix. That's how they didn't get the ship," Tera declared with finality.

"And how did they figure out how to remove the Quake Drive?" Vrynn asked. Her tone had shifted from accusatory to curious.

"I have no idea." I could imagine my AI friend shrugging. "They made the mistake of shutting down my matrix, so they were stuck with a brick of a ship. I don't have any record of what happened until Mitch reactivated me."

Vrynn turned to me. "I guess it wasn't really your fault," she said in a conciliatory tone.

I nodded. "I wish I could have stopped them."

A few moments passed in silence, broken only by Tera's voice. "This is all very sweet, and I'm sure I'll want to talk about it later, but we have a problem."

"What's going on?" I asked.

"Scanners just picked up three ships in orbit. They match the Prentorian ships that intercepted us earlier."

"What about their transponder signals?" I asked.

"Masked. Same as before," Tera replied.

I frowned. "Why didn't you say something earlier?"

"You didn't really give me a chance. But in the interest of full disclosure, we have ten minutes before they reach us."

"Let's get out of here," I said as I raced for the door. Vrynn was hot on my heels.

We raced through the hangar, jumping over crates and winding our way around various vehicles. As we ran through the main blast doors, we passed a pair of empty cart-bots coming back from the *Starfire*. I wondered what they would do when they came back with their next load to find the ship was gone. Thinking of the little bots reminded me that Skeeter had been in the base with us, too. I glanced over my shoulder to see our robotic feline companion scampering along behind us. Halfway across the cold, sandy landing pad, we even caught up to another cart-bot laden with a stack of supplies.

Vrynn, Skeeter, and I hustled up the ramp into the cargo bay.

"Get us in the air, Tera," I called out as I ran for the ladder.

We were airborne, moving away from the Resistance's base by the time I made it to the flight deck. I slid down into the pilot's chair, and Vrynn jumped into the co-pilot's seat a second later.

Grabbing the controls, I checked the heads up display. "Three small fighters?" I asked Tera.

"Yep. They must have been in orbit on the other side of the planet when we arrived," Tera replied.

"Any idea on their armament?" I asked.

"Same as the earlier ship—plasma cannons and atmospheric missiles," Tera said. "No match for the *Starfire*."

I pushed the sticks forward, keeping the *Starfire* low to the planet's surface, heading directly away from the approaching ships. They still had orbital velocity, so I knew we couldn't technically outrun them. But they were high above the stratosphere, which meant they had to decide when to drop out of orbit to engage us.

I planned to use that to my advantage.

"Have they entered the atmosphere yet?" I asked Tera.

"They had started their reentry, but now that we're running away, they boosted back above the stratosphere to catch you faster," Tera said.

I nodded, watching the zoomed-in view of the ships on the display. Once the distance had closed to five hundred miles, I pulled back hard on the stick. The *Starfire* shifted steeply upward in a half loop, the bulkheads complaining under the strain. At the top of the half loop, I twisted the ship right-side-up. Having completely reversed course, I pushed the ship as fast as it would go, not bothering to stay close to the surface. If my trick didn't work, I would have some dogfighting to do, and I needed space to maneuver.

"All three ships just entered the atmosphere," Tera announced.

Obviously, if they had continued in orbit, they would have overflown us, and I could easily come up behind them. The enemy ships hadn't really had any other choice.

Heading straight at each other, our range was closing fast now. The first two interceptors dove at a steeper angle, either trying to come right at me or trying to bleed off speed faster by biting into more of the atmosphere.

I smiled. That was exactly what I had hoped they would do.

The third ship didn't dive as sharply, which forced it to overfly us. But I had no doubt it would eventually slow down enough to turn around and join the fight. I'd have to take care of that one later.

My display showed the external hull temperature of the two reentering ships rising to critical levels. Their sensors would be momentarily blinded by the intense heat.

Now was the time to strike.

"Fire the rail gun," I said to Vrynn.

Vrynn lined up the shot and fired twice.

With no advanced warning of an incoming projectile, the first shot plowed right through the middle of the nearest interceptor, shattering it into hundreds of burning metal shards.

The second interceptor must have seen the explosion because it veered to the side at the last moment, causing the rail gun round to miss.

The second ship was now reaching atmospheric maneuvering speeds, and it was bearing down on us.

I pushed the controls forward, forcing the *Starfire* into a dive. The Nexus ship matched my maneuver—or at least the beginning of it. I quickly reversed my dive, pulling up to face the enemy ship head on. Fortunately, the *Starfire's* gravity capacitors were able to slough off much of the G-forces that otherwise would have flattened us into puddles.

I mashed the throttle full-forward as we climbed straight up. "Get ready with the weapons," I said to Vrynn.

My heads up display painted a red triangle over the oncoming ship. I waited until it filled the targeting indicator, and I pulled hard on the stick again, sending the *Starfire* inverted momentarily.

"Now!" I yelled at Vrynn.

With most of our weapons mounted on the underside of the hull, my upside-down maneuver gave Vrynn full range of motion with anything she wanted to use—except the rail gun. She immediately let loose a barrage of plasma rounds—spraying the area all around the enemy—followed by a pair of fin-controlled target-seeking rockets.

I flipped the ship back upright and sped away. As Vrynn continued firing at the interceptor behind us—bursts from the plasma turrets and more rockets—I started searching for the third interceptor. My scanners found it still at high altitude, turning slowly to meet us. I pulled up and increased our speed, zeroing in the crosshairs on the first ship.

"Woo hoo," Vrynn yelled.

I glanced over and saw the remnants of the second ship on her display. She must have scored at least one direct hit. Or perhaps multiple, given how she had been using the cannons.

The final enemy interceptor suddenly dove toward the ground. I glanced at Vrynn, confused. Was this some sort of fighting tactic to get me to make a mistake?

Vrynn tilted her head toward the ship, the invitation to pursue clear in her expression. I nodded and put the ship into a shallow dive, tracking the interceptor's course toward the surface.

As the enemy ship approached the ground, I half expected to see a fireball erupt from the orange hills below us, but it cleared the dusty surface with a few feet to spare. I cut the throttle and let the *Starfire* drop. If that ship wanted a low-level dogfight, I was going to give it to them.

The interceptor flew over rolling hills toward a series of nearby canyons. At this point, our only choice was to follow him in, or leave the planet entirely. We certainly couldn't stick around here with it lurking nearby.

I kicked the throttle to maximum once more and sped after the interceptor. Initially, I stayed high above the canyons, but they were so deep, I lost sight of the interceptor multiple times. If I wanted to catch the other ship, I'd need to be down there with it. I dove after the enemy ship, matching its zigs and zags as we entered the steep-walled canyon.

As I steered the *Starfire* into a particularly tight turn, we flew close enough to the canyon walls to see the red flakes of rock rolling down.

Alarms went off on my console, and I felt like the controls were resisting my efforts.

"Why are the control sticks fighting me?" I yelled.

"The flight systems have safety protocols to keep you from smashing into things," Tera said.

"Can you turn them off?" I asked, as I flipped the ship for a turn in the opposite direction.

"I *can* turn them off, but I don't think it's a good idea," Tera said. "You look like you're trying to smash us into those mountains."

"If we lose track of this guy, will the safety protocols keep us from getting blown up by his missiles?" I asked through gritted teeth.

Tera didn't immediately reply. Finally, she said, "Flight safety protocols disengaged."

I pulled hard against the controls, and the ship responded immediately. In fact, it responded so well that I had to ease off.

"Please don't smash us into the cliff right after asking her to disengage the safeties," Vrynn said.

I nodded absently as I focused on the enemy interceptor weaving back and forth through the canyons in front of us.

Then an idea occurred to me. "Tera, the atmospheric missiles have remote steering capabilities, don't they?"

"Yes, but the missiles are designed to be guided automatically to their target," she replied haughtily.

"But can they navigate a canyon like this and hit that ship?" I nodded to indicate the Nexus interceptor weaving back and forth in and out of view.

"The probability of achieving a direct hit in a situation like this is only ten percent."

I glanced at Vrynn. "Do you think you can manually steer the missile?"

Vrynn nodded and tapped a few buttons on her console, readying an atmospheric missile.

I pulled another tight turn as the enemy ship swerved off into another canyon. "Any time you're ready."

Vrynn squeezed the trigger, and a rocket flew forward ahead of our ship, only barely outpacing us. Watching the video feed on her screen,

Vrynn deftly maneuvered the missile through the tight canyon. Despite its higher speed, the missile's smaller size made avoiding the canyon walls much easier.

I let up on our speed, just in case. If she did smash the missile into the side of the canyon in front of us, I didn't want to get caught up in the explosion.

The rocket had closed half the distance between our ships when Tera announced, "Two more interceptors have just entered the atmosphere."

My head jerked toward her. "What? Where did they come from?" I had to look back at the terrain a second later to keep from smashing into the canyon walls.

"I have no idea," she replied. "I'm just telling you as soon as I see stuff. Do you want me to stop doing that?"

"No," I said, pulling the ship sharply to the right. "How long before they reach us?"

"About two minutes," Tera said.

"That's fine," I said. "Vrynn has enough time to hit this last fighter before we make a run for it."

Tera added, "But they'll be in weapons range in about thirty seconds."

I spared a quick glance over at Vrynn. She shook her head. "I need more than that."

We could just bug out now, or we could risk another confrontation, still outnumbered.

"Twenty seconds now," Tera announced.

"I'm almost there," Vrynn said as she steered the rocket closer to its weaving target.

I squeezed the control sticks harder as I waffled between our options.

"Ten seconds," Tera said. "Should I count down by seconds now? Just to make it harder for you to think?"

I jerked on the stick, pulling the *Starfire* up out of the canyon. "Stay with them as long as you can, Vrynn," I said as I steered the ship away from the oncoming interceptors. Hopefully, the control range on the guided missile would last long enough for her to find her target.

My tactical display showed incoming plasma rounds. I rolled the ship and turned sharply to avoid the bulk of the shots. I slammed the throttle forward and pulled up into a steep climb. We needed to get out of the atmosphere as soon as possible.

"Vrynn, can you return fire on the two new interceptors?" I asked.

"I'm still . . . trying . . . to get this other one," she muttered, her eyes focused on the video feed from the guided rocket.

I glanced at Tera. "Can you take some shots at them? Just to keep them busy?"

"Safety protocols built into my matrix prevent me from using any offensive weapons. Didn't I already tell you that?"

"Well, can you fly the ship straight up?" I asked in frustration.

"Sure," Tera replied.

I switched my display from flight to weapons control and selected our under-belly plasma turrets. Aiming at the pair of incoming interceptors, I fired a wild spread with the plasma cannons. They would have no problem dodging without any damage, but that wasn't the point. I needed to buy us some time.

"Yes!" Vrynn yelled. "Got him!"

I looked down at my aft video feed and saw a giant fireball erupt from one of the small slot canyons below us.

"Nice!" I took a few more shots at the incoming ships. "Take over weapons for me."

She nodded and switched to weapons control. Once she was firing the cannons, I switched back to flight controls.

I didn't really need to do much more maneuvering, as my whole goal was to get off the planet and escape the Nexus ships. We reached the edge of the atmosphere a few seconds later, and the ship suddenly felt awkward and sluggish again.

"Should I take over flight controls now that we're out of the atmosphere?" Vrynn asked.

I shook my head. "Nah. We're not sticking around." I turned to Tera. "Just jump us out of this system."

"To where?" Tera asked.

"Anywhere but here."

She raised a holographic brow. "Are you sure? Last time you told me that, you ended up stranded in the Bonara Cluster."

"Good point," I said, trying to think of where we could go now to get away from the Nexus ships. "We can't go back to Varus Prime; they'll find us there. Let's jump to the Otania system. Anan made it sound like they only support the BDF out of obligation. I doubt they have any Nexus factions in their security forces." I stopped to think for a second. "But just to be on the safe side, make a double-jump, stopping at some highly populated system on the way there. That way, the Nexus ships can't track us."

"How about Ludros Binary?" Tera asked. "There are five inhabited planets orbiting the two stars."

"Perfect," I declared.

A few seconds later, everything outside turned gray and brown.

Chapter Eight

Vrynn wandered out of the flight deck as soon as we made the jump to intra-space. I jumped up and followed her.

"Vrynn?" I called across the living area, but she rushed through the kitchen and down the hall to her quarters.

I decided to give her some time, not knowing what I would have said anyway that could make anything better after everything we'd just seen at the Resistance base.

Instead, I headed down the ladder to the lower deck and made my way to the cargo bay and Rascal's nest in the back. I wasn't initially sure if he would let me get close to him, but as I approached the giant black animal, he shifted to the side of his nest and whined. I took that as invitation enough to make myself comfortable next to him. Once I was settled, Rascal shifted and rested his large head against my leg.

"That was rough," I said quietly, talking as much to myself as to Rascal. "So much death." I sat in silence for a few moments. "Oh, and I finally found Gabe's murderer."

Rascal waited patiently, finally whining a little as I stopped rubbing his head.

"Of course, it doesn't do me any good because the guy responsible for killing my best friend just happens to be extremely high up in the BDF. No one will believe me if I accuse him of murder, and I doubt I'll have a chance to get close to him, even if I decided to take justice in my own hands."

Though I didn't admit it to Rascal, I'd already considered how complicated it might be to sneak into BDF headquarters on Varus Prime and deliver swift justice to Gralik personally.

Of course, I'd never make it out alive.

Besides, Gabe would never have wanted me to become an assassin, consumed by hatred and living with cold-blooded murder on my conscience.

I realized in that moment that I had a choice to make. Either continue down this path of revenge, or let go of the unfairness of what had happened to Gabe and rely alone on what justice could do.

It was both the easiest and most difficult decision I'd ever had to make.

"We're going to fight Nexus now, Rascal." I looked down at my furry companion, rubbing his head affectionately. "I just thought I'd tell you that now, in case you object and want to part company at the next spaceport."

I smiled at the idea that Rascal, beast that he was, would have any moral objections to joining the struggle against Gralik and Nexus. Of course, maybe he'd understood everything I'd said, and he agreed because it was the right thing to do. There were those intelligent eyes of his, after all.

Having declared my new resolution aloud, I felt even more sure than ever. There was nothing more I could do to bring justice to Gabe's killer. He was beyond the reach of justice in his current position. But maybe the efforts of the Resistance could make a difference. Maybe they could expose Gralik for what he really was—a bully and a thug. Or maybe it really wouldn't make a difference in the end.

Either way, my only choice at the moment was between scraping together enough fuel to make the round trip intra-space jump back to Earth, thus abandoning Vrynn to continue her fight against Nexus alone, or staying in the Bonara Cluster and doing my small part with the *Starfire* to see that Nexus was destroyed. Going back to Earth now seemed like giving up. Besides, what did I have to go back to? My best friend was gone, and I didn't have any other close family. Not to mention losing my job—that one still stung. But I had a job here, one that really mattered.

I patted Rascal on his side. "Thanks, boy. This has been a big help."

Rascal's purring stopped when I moved to stand. Hopefully, he wasn't angry that I had only used him as a sounding board for my ideas—and a fair bit of comfort that I was doing the right thing.

When I went back up to the flight deck, there was still no sign of Vrynn anywhere. I sat in the pilot's seat, and Tera shimmered into view next to me.

"So . . ." she said slowly, "what do you think of Vrynn?"

"Uh, she's been helpful," I offered. "I'm glad we didn't abandon her back on that other planet."

"And?"

"And I'm glad she hasn't tried to kill me and take over the ship yet," I said with a laugh.

"Actually, that's a possibility we can't rule out yet," Tera replied, straight-faced.

I chuckled. It seemed much less likely than it had a few days ago.

"But I mean, you're a man." She paused for dramatic effect. "She's a woman." Another pause. "Do you think . . . maybe . . ."

When I realized what she was asking, I turned to look directly at her. "Didn't you just say there was still a chance she might try to kill me? Now you're asking if there might be something romantic between us?"

"Love is complicated sometimes," she said, sounding like a teen magazine article. "The computer has calculated that there's only a three percent chance she'll try to kill you. But there's a seven percent chance that she'll end up being romantically interested in you."

"Love is complicated," I muttered under my breath.

"And the probability increases two and a half percent each day you spend together, plus an additional four percent if a life-threatening—"

I held up my hand. "For now, let's not worry about the percentages and just see what happens."

My holographic friend gave me a deadpan look. "You're a guy, Mitch. Things aren't just going to happen."

I thought that was overly stereotypical and more than a little pessimistic, especially considering that humanity in general—and men, specifically—had been getting along quite well for millennia. "Okay, how about this? You keep an eye on her for romantic behavior, and we'll figure it out later."

That seemed to satisfy Tera, and she nodded and fell silent for the rest of the intra-space jump.

When we reached the Otanian system, I did a little more practicing with my zero-G piloting. I brought us into high orbit over Otania Sancterum, staying far enough away to not be a danger to anyone, just in case I messed up.

Once we were parked in a safe orbit, I left the flight deck. Though I hadn't expected to see Vrynn, I found her in the kitchen, sitting at the table, staring into a bowl of some sort of rations. I couldn't blame her. If I'd gone through what she just had, I'd probably be on my fifth carton of ice cream, at least.

I swung a chair out from the table and sat down across from her. "I've decided what I want to do next."

She absently picked at her food. "Fine. Do whatever you want."

"What. You're not going to beg me to join the Resistance?"

She lifted a shoulder. "What difference does it make? They're all gone."

"They would want you to keep going, right? To continue the fight?"

She sagged in her seat. "The fight's over. Nexus won," she said bitterly.

"So that's it? There's nothing else we can do?" I said.

Vrynn looked up from her bowl, her eyes mostly out of focus. "Like you said before, you're in command of the ship. Do whatever you want."

I stared at her, not really knowing what I could say to help her get past this tragedy. I held my hands wide to indicate the ship. "Look, we still have the *Starfire*. We can still make a difference in the fight."

Her eyes came a little more into focus. "Just us? With one ship?" She sounded like she wanted to believe me but wasn't sure.

"Why not? From what I've seen, the *Starfire* is more powerful than any we've come up against."

Vrynn's posture lifted a little. "That's true. But we could never take on Nexus alone."

"Maybe not head on, but if we're strategic about where we engage—like just now back on Dreporox—we could still make a difference."

She nodded, her mouth set in a firm line. It would take time for her confidence to return, but at least the spark was still there.

"So where do we go now?" she asked.

"Actually, I was going to ask you that."

Her brow furrowed in thought.

"But, while we're in the Otania system," I continued. "We could stop by Fosso's family. It would be nice to have a break from the ship for a day or two. Plus, we could take the opportunity to get restocked."

Vrynn frowned. "The Otanians tend to be rather standoffish. Are you sure you want to show up and ask for help?"

I nodded. "They wanted me to come back as soon as I could."

Her expression turned pensive. "If we're visiting Fosso's family, maybe we could also find out about what he was meant to do with the *Starfire*. Or how he found it to begin with."

"Uh, I'm not sure that's such a good idea," I replied. "They seemed very opposed to the Resistance and its efforts."

"Maybe," Vrynn said with a shrug. "But we might find out something."

Tera shimmered into view next to us.

"Oh, good timing," I said. "Can you make contact with Otania—"

"We have a stowaway," Tera said abruptly.

"What?" I jumped to my feet.

"In the cargo bay," Tera added.

Vrynn and I hurried down to the lower level. I had just been in the cargo bay, and hadn't noticed anyone but our last stowaway, Rascal.

Our last stop had been the Resistance base on Dreporox. We hadn't seen anyone there but Nexus soldiers, and we hadn't left anyone alive. If we had an intruder on the ship, bent on commandeering the *Starfire*, that could be a problem.

When we reached the cargo bay, I touched the control panel, and the door slid open.

Tera materialized in front of us. Fortunately, I was more accustomed to her appearing at random, so I didn't scream. I was about to tell her to get out of sight when she pointed to a nearby corner of the bay.

I leaned my head inside and saw one of the cart-bots from Dreporox pushing against the wall, apparently trying to roll through it.

"Oh yeah. We took off from the base so quickly that we must not have let it get back off."

Vrynn walked over and tapped a button on the cart's small control panel.

The little cargo bot turned and rolled toward us. "Please, return this unit to its station," the overly friendly announcer-voice said.

"Sorry, little guy. We're not planning to go back to that planet for a while." I glanced at Vrynn and added, "if ever."

The perky voice didn't flag or show any emotion in the least. "This unit operates at peak efficiency when connected to its control station and linked with the other units."

I shook my head. "I don't know what to tell you. We're not—"

Tera held up a hand. "Let me try something." She focused intently on the small utility robot, probably creating some wireless connection. After a moment, she relaxed and held out a hand.

"Would you like this unit to be reassigned to the current location?" the bot asked.

I glanced at Vrynn. She looked happy with the idea.

"Sure," Vrynn said.

I turned back to the bot. "Yes, please reassign the unit accordingly."

"Reassignment complete. This unit can perform any variety of tasks you might need in the current location."

I glanced around the cargo bay. "Uh, we'll let you know when we need something."

"I can take care of that, too." Tera volunteered.

"What should we call him?" Vrynn asked as she knelt next to the wheeled robot.

"Call him?" I asked. "It's just a self-guided utility cart with a sound system."

"He needs a name," Vrynn insisted. "How else will we ask him to help around here?"

I sighed. Hopefully, Vrynn wouldn't make a habit of adopting every stray robot we found. I glanced toward Rascal's nest in the back of the cargo bay. Of course, I didn't have much room to talk. "If he's going to be helpful around here, let's call him HelperBot."

"I like that," Vrynn replied. She turned to the cart-bot. "Would you like your name to be HelperBot?"

"This unit can respond to any designation you choose," HelperBot announced happily.

"Great. As long as you don't make a mess down here or annoy the large animal in the corner, I think we'll be fine." I clapped my hands. "I'll be up on the flight deck getting some more flying practice on our way to Anan and Rachia's house."

A few minutes later—after making contact with Otania Sancterum's orbital control and convincing them that we did actually have an invitation to come back and visit the Shonara family—we were flying on our way to Nashielle again.

As we floated over the beautiful landscape below, I leaned forward to get a better view. I caught sight of a large lake pouring its contents over an enormous waterfall. I pointed. "Are those anything like the falls on Kalera whatever?"

"The Colossal Falls of Kalera Five," Vrynn said patiently as she leaned forward to get a better look. "No," she declared. "They're definitely beautiful, though."

I craned my neck a little further as the falls passed under our right wing. It was then that I noticed another ship on our right side, trailing slightly behind us. "What's with that other ship?" I asked Tera.

"That's the Otanian escort ship," she replied.

"Escort ship? Do they think we're suddenly going to be dangerous on this trip?" I said.

Tera shrugged. "Or our last trip."

I frowned. "What do you mean last trip? We didn't have an escort ship on our last trip."

"Actually, we had two escort ships," Tera said.

"No way," I said, shaking my head. "Don't you think I would have noticed that we had escort ships?"

Tera gave me a dead-pan look. "Seriously, Mitch? You could barely steer the ship at that point. Do you think you would have noticed whether we had escort ships nearby?"

I shook my head and pulled my focus back to flying—something I felt like I was getting quite good at, despite my snarky AI friend.

We landed at the town's small, and infrequently used, spaceport and made our way through the village to the Shonara house.

The front door swung open and Rachia jumped out, wrapping her arms around my neck. "We didn't know you were coming for a visit!" she squealed.

As we spun around, I caught a glimpse of Vrynn. She eyed Rachia with something akin to suspicion, like a recent friend might regard the entrance of an old friend. She almost looked annoyed at Rachia's youthful antics.

Rachia seemed unaware, though. She quickly ushered us into the house.

As I walked into the small living area, Anan crossed the room and pulled me into an embrace. "Mitchell, it's so good to see you again." She waved to Rachia. "Go and notify the family that Mitchell has returned for a visit." She turned back to me. "On such short notice, we may only be able to gather half of the clan."

Anan's gaze trailed toward Vrynn, and I made the introductions, intentionally omitting the part about Vrynn being with the Resistance.

"As a friend of Mitchell's, you are certainly welcome at our gathering," Anan said.

It wasn't what I would call a warm welcome, but it wasn't bad.

Within only a few minutes, extended family members began to arrive. Anan guided us to an open courtyard behind their house and sat Vrynn and me at the head of the table.

As Anan and Rachia continued with their last-minute preparations, Vrynn leaned over to me. "I can't believe that an Otanian family is this welcoming to an outsider. Particularly one who isn't even from the Bonara cluster." She shook her head in good humor. "Even my eyes can't believe it."

"Is it really that rare?" I asked. The Otanians did seem a little formal and withdrawn, but the Shonara family had been incredibly kind to me, once they knew I wasn't really part of the Resistance. Of course, my feelings about actively fighting the Nexus takeover had changed considerably since I had last been on Otania Sancterum. I decided not to volunteer that information yet.

"Extraordinarily rare." A smirk slowly spread across her face. "Maybe they just felt sorry for a poor dirt boy lost so far from home."

I smiled at her joke.

"Or more likely," Vrynn lowered her voice, "it was the grief of losing their son."

"Probably our mutual grief since I had just lost Gabe, too. He's buried here, you know." I added, casually waving in the direction that I thought might be the family's burial circle.

Vrynn gaped at me, her eyes wide in surprise. "Your friend is buried with their clan?"

I nodded.

"Well, no wonder they consider you part of the family," she said, looking around at the bustle of the small gathering. She turned back to me as if really considering me. "That was a very selfless thing, putting your friend in their son's place."

I shrugged. "It seemed like the right thing to do, considering what had happened to Fosso."

Vrynn didn't say anything else about it, but I caught her glancing at me throughout the evening. I didn't want to make too much of it, but maybe she was starting to think I was an okay guy.

The celebration was amazing, particularly the food. The Otanians don't bother with things that don't taste exquisite. Of course, most of the fruits were completely unfamiliar, but they were delicious. My particular favorite was a round, orange fruit about the size of a grapefruit with the bumpy skin of an avocado. When it was cracked open, a slushy reddish yellow mixture oozed out. It looked sort of like a citrus smoothie, but it tasted like holiday-flavored cotton candy. Definitely a strange combination.

After we had finished the meal, Vrynn looked across the narrow table at Anan. "I'm so sorry for the loss of your son," she said.

Anan nodded curtly.

"It's unfortunate that his assignment didn't go as planned," Vrynn said. "The ship he was delivering might have really changed the—"

"Mitchell, would you like me to pass you another janara nut?" Anan asked, speaking over Vrynn's question.

"Uh, sure," I said.

Vrynn tilted her head, considering Anan. "Do you know how he found the Mark 7? If there was any possibility that more of—"

"What about another strasa root?" Anan offered me a food-laden tray, completely ignoring Vrynn's questions.

I glanced from Vrynn to Anan. "No thanks," I finally said. "I'm getting full."

Vrynn leaned toward me and whispered. "Why don't you ask her about the ship? She likes you."

"Yeah, and I don't want to ruin that," I whispered back.

Rachia was sitting across from me—an awkward arrangement because she had been accidentally bumping my feet the entire meal. She looked at Vrynn and me and said, "One time, Fosso told me that there was a special place where he could—"

Anan cleared her throat, shooting a withering glare at her daughter before turning her attention back to me. "Mitchell, do you think it wise to be keeping company with those"—she cast a haughty glance at Vrynn—"who would cause trouble in our peaceful system?"

Vrynn turned back to Anan and opened her mouth. But before she could say something that would get us kicked out, I spoke first. "Anan, I appreciate your sage advice. I *might* need to reconsider who I associate with." The last part had enough emphasis that I hoped Vrynn would understand that she needed to keep quiet.

Vrynn scowled at me. "Thanks for tossing a stone at my head," she muttered. A moment later, her voice repeated, "for throwing me under the bus." I tilted my head. My implant chip must have translated the actual words then found a more appropriate phrase in English to capture Vrynn's meaning.

The rest of the luncheon passed in awkward conversation with Anan and continued exuberance from Rachia.

When we finally stood to leave, Rachia jumped up and said that she would walk with us back to the spaceport.

Anan nodded and rose to give me a hug. Her attitude toward me was somewhat colder than before, but that was nothing compared to the snub she gave Vrynn a moment later when she completely ignored her and walked back into the house.

"Come," Rachia said, motioning to a gate in the side wall of the courtyard.

We followed her out into the streets and back toward the spaceport. We passed a few of Rachia's neighbors as we zigzagged through the town. They nodded or spoke brief greetings to her. After a few more turns, it became obvious to me that we weren't heading back the way we had come.

"Rachia, I don't think we're going the right way," I said.

"Shh," she hissed quietly before smiling at a passing neighbor.

I watched her expression change from friendly to cautious as soon as the friend went by. "We're not going back to the spaceport yet," she whispered.

I shared a puzzled look with Vrynn. She shrugged, tilting her head that we should follow. Clearly, she wasn't concerned that Rachia posed any sort of threat.

Several seconds later, Rachia glanced up and down the empty lane before turning quickly down a small side street. Vrynn and I followed, eager to keep up with her increased pace.

"I'm sorry that my mother was rude to you at the party," Rachia said to Vrynn as we continued down the dark alley. "Our culture disapproves of violence and dissent. So what Fosso did—leaving our world to fight—brought extreme censure from the clan. Only my mother's standing within the family—and her promise that Fosso would never be spoken of or honored—has kept the clan from disavowing my brother's memory entirely. I think they felt sorry for her after . . ."

I felt certain that what Rachia had been about to say was connected to her out-of-the-ordinary behavior. I waited a moment and asked, "After what, Rachia?"

Rachia stayed silent as she led us out of the alley, across another street, and to some stairs leading down another narrow road. Finally, as we reached a less populated part of town, she said, "Why do you think my father is never spoken of?"

"I have no idea," I said.

"Did he go against the family?" Vrynn asked.

Rachia nodded. "Sort of. He was a historian. One of the first in our culture in two centuries. My people do not wish to dwell on what happened in our past. But my father thought there was something to be gained by learning of our ancestors, by finding out everything he could."

We turned onto a dusty, neglected road, and even I could tell we had entered a part of the town that wasn't as well off as where Rachia and her mother lived.

"My father discovered that the original settlers of Otania Sancterum were not what is always portrayed in the ancient traditions. They weren't a noble-minded, enlightened group of colonists seeking a higher, more fulfilling life." At this point, Rachia pulled up short and turned to face us. "They were refugees. The lucky ones. They had fled a planet-wide civil war with nothing but what they could carry onto the last few transports leaving their world."

I tried to imagine what it must have been like for Rachia's father—or Rachia herself—to find out that what they had always known about their people wasn't true. "And what did he do?" I asked.

Rachia sighed. "He tried to tell others what he had found. But between contradicting our people's traditions, plus spinning tales of advanced computer intelligences and traveling through portals, no one believed him. When he refused to be silent, he was put on trial for sedition. The decision to convict was swift."

"And the punishment?" Vrynn asked.

Rachia blinked back tears and shook her head.

I remembered part of my first conversation with Anan, when she mentioned her husband. "He was condemned to death, wasn't he?" I asked quietly.

Rachia nodded.

We stood looking at each other as Rachia struggled to regain her composure. Finally, she turned and continued down the lane. "Despite being forced to publicly renounce my father's beliefs, my mother was unwilling to sever ties with his family. Though, after Fosso left, I wasn't allowed to interact with my father's family unsupervised. She blamed my father's father for putting dangerous ideas into his head." A mischievous grin spread across Rachia's face. "I'm not even supposed to come down this way unaccompanied. But many summer afternoons, when my mother thought I was visiting friends, I would walk here."

Eyeing the rundown street, I asked, "What's down this way?"

"My grandfather," Rachia said happily.

Vrynn and I shared a look. I wasn't sure exactly what she was thinking, but I wondered whether we were going to meet a crazy old man or someone who could actually help us.

"Here we are." Rachia pointed to a small hut near the edge of a cliff overlooking a broad ravine.

Vrynn and I stepped up to the door behind Rachia. She rapped three times in quick succession before turning and walking away.

"Where are you going?" I asked her.

"I have to get back before mother suspects where I've taken you," Rachia called over her shoulder.

"You think she could have at least introduced us," Vrynn muttered under her breath.

The door creaked open and a very elderly-looking man stood staring at us. His eyes flitted over my shoulder, up the road behind us, and he nodded curtly. "Come in," he said in a gruff voice.

Vrynn and I shared a look of resignation. We could have simply turned and left, but part of me wanted to find out what Rachia's grandfather knew. Once inside the small house, Rachia's grandfather pointed to an old sofa across from a well-worn armchair. "Sit," he commanded.

Vrynn and I dutifully obeyed, and the old man settled himself into the chair across from us. He scrutinized our clothes, then our faces.

"Rachia doesn't bring many friends to see me," he stated matter-of-factly.

I leaned forward in my seat. "Sir, we were hoping you could tell us about your grandson, Fosso. We are part of a group called—"

The old man held up his hand. "Shh. You don't need to say it," he whispered. Then he leaned in, a knowing look on his face. "Who do you think told Fosso about it to begin with?" Then his expression clouded over. "But Rachia tells me that he was killed."

I nodded, a flood of memories coming fresh to my mind. "Yes, sir. When my friend found his ship, he was already dead."

Rachia's grandpa leaned back in his chair, arms folded. "So you're the one who completed the circle of my daughter-in-law's family. Or rather, your friend did."

"It seemed like the right thing to do," I offered.

He considered me for a moment before leaning forward. "Why did my granddaughter risk her standing in the clan to bring you here?"

"She said you could tell us why Fosso joined the Resist—er, why he joined this fight," I said.

The old man nodded and scratched his graying beard. "Fosso learned the same stories about the ancient ones as my son, his father, did. I mean the true stories. Much of who they really were has been lost. But there are those who still remember." He tapped a finger to his temple. "They learn the stories, imprint them in their minds, and pass them down to future generations."

"What stories can you tell us?" Vrynn asked in a friendly tone.

The man sat back in his chair and gazed out a nearby window overlooking the ravine. "Long ago, at least ten generations, my people lived in a system on the edge of the star cluster. It was a beautiful world, plentiful resources, temperate climate, everything anyone could want to live and prosper. The ancient ones developed technology that allowed them to extract more, produce more, do more."

I leaned forward, knowing that his story didn't begin and end with an enviable paradise.

"But instead of creating ease and prosperity, their abundance engendered greed and bitterness. They divided into clans in an ever-growing race to possess more. As generations passed, distrust and animosity grew. Whispered rumors became accusations. Exclusion became violence.

"And when war finally broke out, my ancestors had the technology to destroy themselves so efficiently that entire cities were wiped out in a matter of hours. In the chaos, people fled the planet with whatever they could. Some went as clans, some in broken families. Others were fortunate to simply be alive. Hordes of refugees, with no planet to call their home, flooded into neighboring systems.

"One of the caravans found this planet and began the arduous task of conquering the wilderness and bending it to their will." The man spread his arms wide. "Our ancestors turned this planet into a paradise, but at a terrible cost. As our people began to rediscover the technology they'd lost, strict limitations were put in place by the clans, supposedly to avoid repeating the catastrophe that had destroyed our homeworld."

His history lesson didn't really help us much, but I did my best to be patient.

"Though they did eventually rebuild a society with advanced technology," the old man continued, "the truth of who we were and what had happened to us was lost or intentionally forgotten. Erased from our collective memories."

"Your people were nearly wiped out," Vrynn said gently. "It's understandable that they wouldn't want to repeat the past."

Rachia's grandfather nodded. "But over the generations, those limitations have morphed into fear of anything outside our world. Our clan leaders reject everything that would increase our contact with the wider society of the Bonara Cluster. Visitors may come to our planet—but only temporarily. And no Otanians ever leave. At least, if they do, they aren't welcome back."

At this final pronouncement, he fell silent. I stared at Rachia's grandfather then looked over at Vrynn then back at the old man. "That can't be all. There must have been more to the story," I said.

He chuckled softly. "Fosso had nearly the same reaction when I told him what I just told you."

I leaned forward in my seat. "And is there more?"

The man nodded solemnly.

This could be the information Rachia wanted us to hear. "What was it? What else did you tell him?" I asked urgently.

He scrutinized me with shrewd eyes, probably trying to judge my character and whether I deserved to be told. His voice dropped low. "This is the secret we've passed down for generations—that our home world still exists. That the knowledge and freedom we once had can be reclaimed. Technology beyond anything we can imagine is waiting, if we have the courage to seek it." He held an arm up, pointing toward the sky.

"Wait, are you saying that your home planet still exists out there somewhere, and no one has gone looking for it?" I said.

He frowned and let his arm drop. "Of course, the world still exists."

"There's no technology that can destroy the actual planet, Mitch," Vrynn said in a tone that sounded like she was explaining something to a little child. "Just the people on it."

I scowled at their replies. It wasn't my fault that the only thing I knew about alien civilizations before two weeks ago was that they could blow up planets. "But wouldn't all that technology have been destroyed in the war?" I asked.

Before he could answer, Vrynn jumped in. "Obviously it wasn't." She turned to Rachia's grandfather. "You told Fosso about this, didn't you? And he went looking for the ancient homeworld."

The old man nodded, and his gaze drifted to the window. "Yes. But I never saw him again."

Vrynn looked at me. "He must have found it," she said excitedly.

"The *Starfire*," I whispered.

Vrynn nodded. "It all makes sense." She paused. "Except how it ended up on Dirt."

"Earth," I corrected. Then a thought occurred to me. I turned to Fosso's grandfather. "How did Fosso find your homeworld? Have you been there?"

He shook his head slowly. "I've never visited my people's homeworld. But my mother taught me where to find it in the night sky. And I taught my grandson." The man looked out the window again.

Vrynn leaned forward and touched him gently on the knee. "Tell us what you told him," she prodded.

He stood from his chair and walked across the small room. On the wall hung a picture of a rocky landscape at twilight. The old man pointed to a collection of stars above the horizon. They looked like a half circle but surrounded by bright clouds. "This star, in the middle of the crescent nebula, is the sun of our homeworld."

I moved in for a closer look. It was certainly a distinct shape. I glanced at Vrynn, who also looked closely at the picture.

Fosso's grandfather looked visibly tired, so we thanked him for his help and let ourselves out.

Back on the road from his home, Vrynn turned to me. "This could be the break we're looking for. We don't have to face the Nexus forces with just one ship; we can build a fleet of ships first."

Vrynn's optimism tended to bring out my pessimism. "A forgotten planet with ships and technology for the taking? Seems like an old man's delusion."

Vrynn was undaunted by my skepticism. "The *Starfire* is real, isn't it?"

I shrugged, unable to deny that fact.

"The rest of it is real, too. I'm sure of it. And I can't wait to find this forgotten planet so I can prove you wrong."

"I'd love nothing more," I replied.

Chapter Nine

A few hours later, we were back on the *Starfire*, jetting into orbit. As soon as I handed control back to the autopilot—begrudgingly this time, because I swear I was about to get us out of that uncontrolled flatspin—I glanced down at my navigational control panel and started tapping through the menus.

"What are you doing, Mitch?" Tera asked with a sigh. "Was nearly crashing the ship not enough? Now you want to snarl the computer, too?"

"We weren't in any danger of crashing; we were heading away from the planet. Besides, I think I'm getting better." I stopped my search of the navigation system to turn to my AI friend. I lifted a brow, daring her to contradict me.

Vrynn walked into the flight deck at that moment. "He's definitely getting better," she said.

Tera gave me a knowing look when Vrynn came to my defense. I'm not sure why she thought anything was going on between us, though. Even a friend would say something like that.

Vrynn plopped into the co-pilot seat. "By the way, there are a few crates down in the cargo bay that I don't recognize. Did you—"

"What were you working on there, Mitch?" Tera asked, talking over Vrynn.

I frowned at the interruption but decided that a slightly inconsiderate AI matrix was the least of my worries. I returned to my display panel. "I'm trying to find the star system Rachia's grandfather told us about." A few more swipes told me I had no idea how the system was organized. I started paging through more and more menus, trying to figure out a way to bring up a view of space. I sat back in frustration.

Vrynn reached across the small gap between our seats and grabbed my arm. "Let me help," she said. "Tera, can you show the star field that's visible from Nashielle? We're looking for a crescent-shaped nebula with a single star in the middle."

Tera shot a conspiratorial look my way—clearly thinking that a simple touch from my co-pilot meant something monumental. A moment later, a holographic representation of the stars appeared in the air in front of us. "This is the view that's visible right now, assuming it wasn't daylight."

Vrynn and I scrutinized the holographic view, looking for the telltale shape of the system that Rachia's grandfather had pointed out.

"There it is!" Vrynn exclaimed, pointing at a bright star with a nebula background.

"What is that star supposed to be?" Tera asked.

"Fosso's grandfather said that it's the ancestral home of the Otanian people," I said.

Tera frowned. "That can't be true."

"Why not?" Vrynn asked.

"That's the Mezok star," Tera said. "It's a quarantined system. The computer says the entire population of the only habitable planet was destroyed by biological weapons."

I glanced over at Vrynn. "That sounds like it could match up with what Rachia's grandfather told us. He said their ancestors fled a war as refugees when they came to Otania Sancterum."

"Should we check it out?" Vrynn asked.

I nodded.

"You want to visit a quarantined system?" Tera asked.

Vrynn and I looked at each other. "Yeah," I said.

"Maybe having a biological brain isn't all it's cracked up to be," Tera muttered.

Vrynn and I laughed at that.

Tera set our course, and we jumped to intra-space.

With nothing else to do, I wandered into the kitchen area to grab a bite to eat. Vrynn sat down on the nearby sofa.

"So, why did you join the Resistance?" I asked as I prepared myself an alien snack.

"It's a long story," Vrynn replied in a curt tone.

This wasn't the first time she'd been evasive about her life before joining the Resistance. Maybe it was time to see if she would be willing to share more. I figured that's what a friend would do.

With my greenish pastry in hand, I walked over and sat on the chair next to her. "I've got plenty of time," I said, trying to gauge how much I could press her on the subject. "But it doesn't have to be right now. You can tell me whenever you're ready. We're going to be spending lots of time together."

She considered me for a moment then heaved a theatrical sigh. "My system has two habitable worlds. My home planet, Mareesh, was the second to be colonized by the people from Barchee, the other habitable planet. Our two worlds lived in harmony for hundreds of years, mostly because Barchee considered us primitive and backward and pretty much left us alone."

I remembered something that Tera had mentioned about Mareesh when we first met Vrynn. "And your planet is all water, right?"

Vrynn's brow furrowed. "Not *all* water. But there are only three main islands in the southern hemisphere that are habitable."

I nodded my understanding.

"When our deep-sea scientists made a discovery of rare natural resources on the ocean floor, Barchee suddenly became very interested in our planet. Shortly after, Barchee ships arrived with an invasion force. Our military set up defensive positions to protect the larger cities, allowing them to hold the invaders at bay temporarily while our government appealed to the Bonara Defense Force. A BDF detachment arrived, led by Gralik. We believed that the BDF would intervene and send the Barchee back to their planet."

I could guess where this story would end. She didn't end up sworn to fight against Gralik for no reason.

"But rather than remove the Barchee, Gralik struck a deal with them to betray Mareesh. Under cover of night, Gralik and several of his trusted lieutenants each led groups of Barchee soldiers disguised as BDF members through the defensive checkpoints into the heart of the capital city. The slaughter that followed . . ."

Vrynn trailed off, her eyes filling with tears. I reached out and placed a hand on hers, hoping to offer some comfort. She offered me a watery smile.

Taking a breath, she continued. "By the time news of what had happened reached the authorities on Varus Prime, the Barchee's control of my world was so firmly established that it would have been nearly impossible to free us without catastrophic loss of life. So my people were reduced to nothing more than a vassal state."

"Wasn't Gralik punished for betraying you?" I asked.

"He and his lieutenants made up the lie that it was Mareesh traitors who had let the Barchee force enter the city. And that those traitors had conveniently been killed in the battle. Of course, the Barchee didn't contradict him, and there were no Mareesh witnesses left to prove him wrong."

I shook my head sadly. "I'm so sorry."

She wiped a tear from her cheek. "I was the only one of my family to survive the invasion. Gralik took everything from me."

"And that's when you decided to join the Resistance?" I asked.

Vrynn nodded. "I had nothing left on Mareesh, so I jumped on the first off-world transport I could. A few months later, I made contact with a Resistance agent, and I've been fighting ever since."

Now I understood why Vrynn hated Nexus so much. It represented everything that she had lost.

We continued to visit about her planet and what it was like to grow up with so little land underneath her city. And we talked about Earth and what it was like to grow up with so little water around.

It wasn't long before we had been talking for over an hour. When Tera appeared and announced that we were approaching the Mezok system, I could hardly believe it. Vrynn and I walked back into the flight deck and took our places.

We came out of our intra-space jump just outside the orbit of its single, orange and green moon.

Immediately, the flight deck filled with a loud alarm and a blaring robotic voice. "Warning. Warning. This planet is quarantined for atmospheric biological agents. Do not approach. Do not approach. Warning. Warning. This planet—"

"Can we turn that off?" I asked over the repeating loop.

"It's a safety alert, Mitch. It's not meant to be turned off," Tera said haughtily.

"Fine," I replied with a scowl. "Can you at least turn down the volume so I can think straight?"

Tera shrugged and the alert message went silent.

My shoulders relaxed. "Thank you."

I stared out the windows at the mysterious orb below us. The planet looked similar to Earth—mostly blue with green and brown land masses—but the continents looked obviously alien to my eyes. As we drew closer to standard orbit, I began to notice strange lines crisscrossing the surface, connecting large circular shapes.

"Tera, can you project an enlarged view of those shapes right there?" I asked, pointing to the geometric patterns.

A magnified view of the dusty, brown surface appeared in the air above the control consoles. Immediately, I could see that they weren't geometric designs, but human-made structures. The large circular shapes were actually giant cities, and the lines were roads or transit connectors of some kind.

"Can you zoom in even closer?" I asked as I leaned forward.

The view grew, and I could make out individual buildings. Some were still standing, others were fallen and broken. It looked like an archeological dig—everything was either partially covered in dirt or overgrown with foliage.

"Definitely looks like there was a war here," I said.

"Do you think anyone survived?" Vrynn asked in a hopeful voice.

"I doubt it." I pointed at some of the buildings. "This stuff looks old. Like it was destroyed a long time ago."

Vrynn nodded. "That would match with what Rachia's grandfather said."

"But how could Fosso have gotten this ship if the planet is under quarantine?" I asked.

"It would be impossible to physically seal off an entire planet," Tera replied. "If someone wants to land, there's nothing stopping them."

"You mean they just put a warning in orbit and hope people follow instructions?" I asked.

"The warning usually works pretty well when coupled with the possibility of dying a horrific death," Tera quipped.

I stared out at the swirling clouds in the atmosphere below us. "Hmm. Can we go down and test the atmosphere, just to see if any bioweapons are still present?"

Tera looked at me as if I was crazy.

"What. I'm not saying I want to get out and sniff the air. But can't we just take a sample? What's the point of having such a high-tech ship if we can't just do a flyby check?"

"All it would take is one virus leaking through the sampling container for it to kill you both," the AI said. "Or worse. If you survived long enough to reach another world, it could kill billions."

I frowned. That definitely wasn't part of our plan.

We stared at the planet in silence for several minutes.

"Are we really sure this is where the *Starfire* was built?"

"Oh, it definitely is," Tera said.

Vrynn and I turned to her. "How do you know?" Vrynn asked.

"Since coming back online after the crash on Earth, these are the first transmissions I've received that haven't required the translation algorithms. The satellites are communicating in the computer's underlying language," Tera said.

I looked out the windows. "That quarantine message was in your native language?"

Tera's brow furrowed. "No. The quarantine buoys were placed by the Bonaran Kingdom. I'm talking about the other satellites, the ones from the original inhabitants of Mela Suphoria."

"Mela Suphoria?" Vrynn repeated.

"Bonaran Kingdom?" I said.

"Mela Suphoria is the actual name of this planet," Tera explained to Vrynn before turning to me. "Yes, according to the computer, these satellites have been here since the fifth galactic reign, the last king before the Bonaran democracy."

"Wow." I marveled. "This planet has been untouched in . . . however long ago that was."

Vrynn grinned but simply shook her head.

A few seconds later, Tera said, "As much fun as it is to just stare at Mela Suphoria from orbit, this is getting very tiresome."

"You don't like the view or something?" Vrynn asked.

Tera heaved a theatrical sigh. "It's not the view. The ship is currently receiving approximately two hundred transmissions—not including the quarantine buoys—some from orbiting satellites, some from the surface."

I looked at the view of the decaying city suspended in front of me and found it difficult to believe. "Could there really be people down there still, after all these centuries?"

Tera shook her head. "The transmissions I'm receiving are all automated, so I have no idea,"

"What are they saying?" Vrynn asked.

"Most of them are warning us not to join the conflict on the side of their enemy, and if we do, they will consider us enemies, too. Some are looping news programs indicating that the government has detected the use of biological weapons and is preparing to launch a counterstrike. One transmission is a quasi-AI salesman offering us a cheap landing pad rental. I think he might be hitting on me. He's super-annoying."

Vrynn and I smiled at each other.

"Oh, and a few of the transmissions are trying to hack the computer," Tera added.

I jerked my head toward her. "Centuries old technology can hack your systems?"

Tera turned to me and gave me her classic are-you-serious look. "This ship is centuries-old technology." She held out a hand toward the surface of the planet below us.

"I guess that's true," I said. "What are the chances any of these automated hacking attempts will succeed?"

My holographic companion offered a crooked smile. "Pretty low," she said. "But that's always the tricky part, isn't it? If a system knew it was getting hacked, it would stop the hacking. Usually, the problem is that a system doesn't *know* anything. It's just a collection of algorithms and subroutines." Tera tilted her head to the side. "Come to think of it. Do I really *know* anything? Do I even exist?"

I held up my hand. "Let's dial back your existential crisis percentage a few notches. At least until we know you're out of danger." I glanced over at Vrynn. "Is there any reason we need to receive communications from any source on this planet?"

Vrynn shook her head. "According to Rachia's grandfather, no one has been here for centuries."

"Right. Tera, is there a way to block all of these hacking transmissions?" I asked.

"I can block everything that communicates in the ship's native language," she replied.

"That works." I leaned forward and studied the display in front of me. "Now, we just need to decide if we're willing to go down there. And if so, where would we even start to look?"

"There was a beacon on the central continent sending a homing signal to the ship," Tera said. "But I just blocked it."

I blew out a frustrated sigh.

"Do you have the location?" Vrynn asked.

"Yes," Tera said.

Vrynn looked at me. "That might be a good place to start."

"Hang on," I said. "How do we know the homing signal is legitimate? It could be another ploy to hack the ship."

Tera shrugged. "The location matches the coordinates in the computer's databanks for the ship's origin."

Vrynn and I both turned to stare at Tera.

"What," she said innocently.

"You had an origin location, and you didn't think to mention that?" Vrynn asked.

Tera shrugged. "It was just a set of coordinates. I didn't know which planet they corresponded to until we arrived here and I detected the homing beacon."

"The coordinates match?" I asked.

Tera nodded.

"That settles it for me," I said, reaching for the controls. "Shall we risk it?"

Vrynn considered me for a moment, then smiled. "Fosso managed to get this ship somehow. It must be safe enough."

With that, I clumsily guided the *Starfire* out of orbit with helpful tips from Vrynn and a fair amount of eye-rolling from Tera. Once we were in the atmosphere, my flying skills improved significantly. I brought the ship low, shadowing what had looked like a thin transit line. It turned out to be a massive super-highway—or what was left of it—with flat surfaces like roads intermixed with bundles of tubes large enough for high velocity travel.

I glanced down at my sensor console. "Tera, am I reading this right? The scans say there are life forms down there."

"Yeah, the sensors are picking up life, but I wouldn't get your hopes up," Tera said. "From this far away, it's tough to tell the difference between animal and humanoid."

As we floated closer to one of the large cities—its jagged skyline completely broken and decayed—a waypoint indicator flashed on my holographic display. It floated over a series of wide, factory-like buildings on the outskirts of the main city.

"That's the location of the homing beacon and the origin coordinates in the ship's databanks," Tera said.

"At least they put the factory in the suburbs and not in that." I jutted my chin toward the ancient metropolis in the distance. "I can't imagine how those skyscrapers are still standing."

As we approached the designated location, I flew a few circles around the complex to get a feel for the layout. There was a central building about the size of a basketball arena, though not as tall, and several smaller buildings surrounding it. I could see definite evidence of age, as some of the smaller structures had walls that were caved in. The top of the main structure was speckled white and gray, with patches of foliage growing in clumps across its roof.

If this stuff was hundreds of years old when it was abandoned, that meant the people on this planet had reached the peak of their technological development about the time my people were coming out of the dark ages. That was hard to fathom.

On the edge of the manufacturing complex, away from most of the buildings, was a short runway lined with small hangars.

"That looks like a good place to land," I said, indicating the runway and hangars.

Vrynn nodded absently, barely taking her eyes off the view below us.

I brought the ship down to a hover in front of one of the hangars. Satisfied that it looked safe enough, I set the ship down as gently as I could manage.

"You up for some exploring?" I asked Vrynn.

She was out of her seat and halfway to the ladder before I even took my first step. I worried that her enthusiasm would get us in trouble, so I hustled after her. I caught up down in the cargo bay just as she was about to open the bay door.

I grabbed her hand. "Hang on. We don't even know if the atmosphere is breathable."

"You've left the ship on plenty of planets already. What's the problem?" She gazed at me with those deep-blue eyes.

"Because those planets had people living on them," I said, staring back at her. "Emphasis on living." I tilted my head back and called out, "Tera?"

Tera's hologram appeared next to us. "Yes?" she said, a mischievous look on her holographic expression as she glanced meaningfully between us. I realized that I was still holding Vrynn's hand and immediately dropped it.

I shook my head. I might need to dial back Tera's matching-making subroutines when I got a chance. "Is the atmosphere out there breathable?" I asked her.

Her gaze went fuzzy for a moment, then she looked back at us. "The atmosphere is rich in nitrogen and oxygen. There are trace amounts of post-industrial pollution in the air, but they are so small that they should have no lasting effects on your physiology."

"I mean, what about biological agents?" I added.

"None detected," Tera replied.

"See, I told you it was fine," Vrynn said. She very slowly and deliberately moved her hand toward the button to open the ramp, a small smirk on her face, apparently waiting to see if I would object or try to stop her. I shook my head at her teasing. How did I get stuck with a snarky AI and an impish co-pilot?

We walked down the ramp, out into air that probably hadn't been breathed by humanoids in several hundred years. I was immediately struck by how noisy it was. Instead of a quiet, empty silence that I would have expected from a desolate planet, the air was full of chirping and squawking. None of the sounds were familiar, and yet, they weren't that different from locusts on a summer evening or birds in a forest.

We walked into the closest hangar and saw the floor covered with mounds of dirt and sand. Ancient equipment lined the side walls, their surfaces layered with dust.

Vrynn stepped up to a console and wiped her hand across it. "I bet with a little cleaning and some power, we could get this stuff working again."

I tilted my head and scowled at her. I wasn't sure if she was joking or being optimistic. "Let's check things out before we start fixing the place up."

Vrynn shrugged and proceeded back out of the hangar. We worked our way past all of the hangars on the landing field toward the rest of the sprawling facility that we'd seen from the air.

A long, thin road, cracking with age and overgrown with trees and shrubs, ran from the hangars, through a smattering of smaller buildings, toward the large, central structure, ending at a pair of enormous sliding doors that faced the runway in the distance.

I found it easy to believe that this was where the *Starfire* had been assembled. Every detail pointed to it being an aerospace manufacturing facility.

Vrynn gripped the edge of one of the massive doors and pulled.

I couldn't help but laugh. "You'll never get those open."

Vrynn scowled at me and redoubled her effort. Eventually, she gave up and followed me to a more human-sized access door nearby. With some pulling and a few well-placed kicks, the door begrudgingly swung open.

We walked through the opening into the building's massive interior. In the dim light filtering through the high windows, I could see a long column of hulking shapes stretching away into the darkness.

A loud bang made us both jump.

Vrynn's eyes went wide, probably matching my own, until a second later when I realized that we had let the door slam behind us.

"A little jumpy, aren't we?" I asked with a nervous laugh.

Vrynn shrugged and continued ahead of me. I turned my attention back to the long line of shapes in front of us. I walked toward the first one and nearly rubbed my eyes in disbelief. Looming over me, as if waiting for its turn to pass through the enormous sliding doors, sat a ship nearly identical to the *Starfire*.

I moved around the ship and looked down the rest of the line. Several dozen others just like it stood in a single, long column like soldiers at attention.

Vrynn cried out in glee and danced around. "We did it!" she said as she ran to me, nearly bowling me over with a huge hug. "This is exactly what we need. Once we get them flying, Nexus will be no match for us." She turned and marched down the line of ships. "I wonder if they all have Quake Drives installed."

Maybe it was Vrynn's enthusiasm for everything she saw, or being alone with her on a desolate alien planet was having an effect on me, but some of her optimism might have started to rub off.

I looked at the ancient ships, all nearly identical to the *Starfire*, and wondered if this really was the answer to taking on Nexus. Of course, we'd need to find pilots willing to fly them, and we'd have to organize a training program and a command structure, but it might be possible.

Following Vrynn down the line of ships, I let my gaze drift to the manufacturing machines flanking the main production column. They stood idle, still waiting after hundreds of years to attach the next component in the process.

As we went farther down the line, the ships were less complete. We were walking the assembly process in reverse. The third ship was missing its under-wing doors and weapons mounts. The fourth ship was missing the engine mounts. The fifth ship hadn't been fitted with the cargo bay door yet.

Vrynn turned around, her face still beaming with excitement, and considered all the ships. "Isn't this so amazing?" she asked.

I nodded hesitantly. "Yeah, it's great. But most of these ships are only half assembled."

She waved her hands dismissively. "I'm sure we can take care of that."

"And even if we do get these ships finished, who would fly them?" I hated to say the next part. "There aren't any Resistance fighters left."

She waved a hand downward, obviously ignoring my concern. "We lost most of the command structure, but the Resistance has friends and sympathizers throughout the cluster. I'm sure we can find pilots once the ships are finished."

I didn't have the heart to tell her that finishing the ships would probably involve way more work than she could imagine. I should know. That had been my job. At least, until a mistake had gotten me fired.

I realized now that one mistake like that could mean the difference between freedom and oppression for an entire star cluster.

Chapter Ten

After making a full survey of the facility where the *Starfire* was originally manufactured, we made our way back to the ship and moved it inside the closest hangar for safety. The doors didn't close all the way, but I felt better knowing we were out of whatever weather they had on Mela Suphoria, plus we were hidden from any prying eyes or roving predators.

Over the next several days, we spent our time in the central building attempting to evaluate the status of the production line and the ships that were partially constructed. It didn't look as promising as we had initially hoped. At least, to me, the prospect of finishing the fabrication of dozens of half-built alien spacecraft was daunting. Vrynn, on the other hand, thought it would be no problem.

"How hard could it be?" became her favorite mantra.

The biggest disappointment of those first few days was that none of the partially completed Mark 7s in the production facility had Quake Drives. They all had the empty bay for it, but their installed propulsion systems were just regular jump drives. And we didn't find anything even remotely resembling the Quake Drive module anywhere in the facility. We decided they must have produced the drives somewhere else and installed them later.

Despite that fact, we both knew that a fleet of Mark 7 starships—even if only intra-space jump capable—would still be a formidable force in the battle against Nexus. So that became our goal.

On the fourth day, we actually figured out how to activate the facility's power reactor, which ran on some alien combination of solar collectors and, most likely, nuclear fusion. With some lights on, the cavernous space inside the production building wasn't nearly so eerie.

The next afternoon, on a trip back to the *Starfire* to grab a tool from the cargo bay, I noticed that the indicator lights on the equipment lining the wall of the small hangar were blinking.

"Hey, Tera," I yelled toward the open cargo bay. "Can you send Skeeter down here?"

Half a minute later, Skeeter came trotting down the ramp, with Rascal in tow. For some reason, the large beast had taken a liking to the robo-feline.

I pointed to the console. "I noticed this machine is suddenly running. Can you tell me what it says?"

Skeeter approached and examined the display. "It says 'Ready For Uplink'," Tera's voice replied.

That was interesting.

I looked down at Skeeter. "Let's call Vrynn and tell her to get back here."

"Uh, okay," Tera replied.

A few minutes later, Vrynn came running into the hangar, completely out of breath. "What is it? What's the emergency?"

I gaped at her. "No emergency. I just found something interesting."

Vrynn rolled her eyes. "Tera made it sound like . . . nevermind. What did you find?"

"Look at this." I pointed at the console. "Apparently it says 'Ready For Uplink'."

Vrynn leaned in for a closer look. "Do you think we could connect it to the *Starfire* computer? It might help fix the parts that were damaged in the crash."

"See if you can find the data link cable." I walked toward the cargo ramp. "I'll check with Tera."

I walked into the cargo bay. "Tera?" She appeared in front of me. "Did you catch all that?"

"Yeah. You're going to uplink some information or something." She was pretending that she didn't care what we had been up to, but I knew better.

I nodded. "Hopefully it can help fix the computer's damage sectors."

"Okay," she replied.

I walked back to the edge of the ramp in time to see Vrynn finish connecting a thick cable from the console to a port in the side of the ship behind the winglet and walk back to the console.

I turned to my holographic shipmate. "Are you ready?"

Tera nodded, looking slightly nervous.

"Go ahead," I said to Vrynn.

Vrynn tapped the button to start the upload.

I looked over at Tera, wondering if there would be any immediate difference.

I didn't have to wait long.

The holographic representation of my teenage friend flickered and disappeared momentarily. In her place stood the hologram of an austere middle-aged man in a slightly-too-tight-in-the-middle flight suit that matched the *Starfire's* color scheme. This guy must have been the original programming of the matrix.

He looked at me, opened his mouth to speak, then vanished.

A moment later, Tera reappeared, a pained look on her face. "It's trying to overwrite—"

The default AI reappeared. "The flight assistant matrix for this ship is now activated. You may call me Dack. What task can I help you with?" His voice was choppy and garbled.

"Cut the link!" I yelled to Vrynn.

Tera reappeared. "Mitch! Make it stop!" She flickered away again.

I leaned my head out the bay door. "Vrynn, shut it off!"

"I'm trying!" Vrynn repeatedly mashed various buttons on the console, to no avail.

I jumped off the ramp and ran under the wing. Grabbing the uplink cable with both hands, I yanked it from the socket.

I ran back into the cargo bay. "Tera!" I yelled. "Tera, can you hear me?" I glanced around the bay, waiting for something to happen.

Finally, Tera shimmered into view, a look of relief on her face.

"What happened?" I asked.

Tera's brows went up, and she suddenly stared over my shoulder. "Where am I?" she asked robotically. She looked at me. "And who are you?"

I stared at her for a moment. Had the uplink wiped her memory? That didn't make sense. I got a very clear look at what the original AI matrix had looked like, and it looked nothing like Tera. "C'mon, Tera. If the ship's memory had been wiped, you wouldn't still look like my best friend's wife."

A sly smirk curved the edge of her mouth.

Vrynn ran up the ramp into the cargo bay. "Is Tera okay? Is her matrix still intact?" she asked frantically.

Tera turned to Vrynn. "Thank you for your concern," she said in a monotone voice. "Your true feelings about the artificial intelligence, Tera, are duly noted."

I rolled my eyes. "She's fine," I told Vrynn.

Vrynn breathed a sigh of relief, though a look of chagrin flitted across her features. I turned my attention back to Tera.

"The uplink scanned the ship's systems and, for obvious reasons"—Tera pointed at herself—"it didn't find the correct holographic matrix. So it started to upload the original version."

"You didn't lose anything, though?" Vrynn asked.

Tera shook her head. "I was able to shunt the new program into the buffer memory to keep it from compromising my existing matrix."

The muscles in my shoulders finally relaxed. "Well, you gave us a good scare, accidentally and on purpose." I chuckled. Usually, my friend Tera thought of the perfect witty remark or practical joke half a minute too late. Chalk one up to advanced technology improving her reaction time.

Tera smiled at us, acknowledging her attempted joke. A moment later, she froze. "Whoa," she said, and her eyes lost their focus.

I glanced at Vrynn then back. "Very funny, Tera," I said, but she didn't snap out of it. "What's up?" I asked, worried.

Finally, she shook her head and looked over at me. "I've got a bunch of new stuff in my databanks," Tera said. "Actually, I should say that it's always been there, but that uplink unlocked the computer's backup sensor logs and filled in some of the damaged sectors, so now it makes sense."

"What is it?" Vrynn asked her.

"I've recovered the information about Fosso's mission," Tera announced.

"Right, he was supposed to rendezvous with me," Vrynn said.

Tera tilted her head. "Yes. But Fosso chose to make several intra-space jumps, probably in an attempt to throw anyone off his track."

"Why didn't he just use the Quake Drive?" Vrynn asked.

"According to the log, Resistance Command instructed him to use the ship's unique capabilities as little as absolutely necessary," Tera replied.

Vrynn frowned, probably thinking what I was thinking, that it didn't do them much good to save the *Starfire's* abilities for later if they ended up losing the ship itself.

"So what happened? How did he end up crashing on Earth?" I asked.

"On one of the interim jumps on his way to Thetis Max, he was intercepted by Nexus ships," Tera explained. "There were too many for him to take, so he activated the Quake Drive and opened a portal to the farthest star in the navigation system's databank."

"My sun," I said. "Because of the Earth Protectorate."

Tera nodded.

"Of the dozen Nexus interceptors attacking him, two were close enough to the *Starfire* that they traveled through the portal before it closed. Fosso continued to engage them near Earth. Both of the Nexus ships were destroyed, but the *Starfire* was severely damaged in the fight, which later led to the crash."

I waited for her to continue, but she didn't. "Anything else?" I asked.

"Not really. All of the ship's systems went offline after the crash."

At least now we knew how the *Starfire* had ended up crashing on Earth.

"Oh, this is interesting," Tera said.

Vrynn and I both perked up.

"What?" I asked.

"There's a new file system with information on the manufacturing process—at least, according to the labels."

Vrynn stepped toward her. "Can you access any of it? Does it say how to finish assembling the other ships?"

Tera's eyes scanned back and forth. "No. The information was only partially installed with the link we just cut." She tilted her head toward the outside of the ship, where I had pulled the plug on the uplink.

I glanced out the cargo bay door. "Do we dare re-initiate the uplink? Would that install the rest of the files?"

Tera shrugged. "Maybe. But then again, the uplink was trying to overwrite some of the existing programs, so it might just wipe everything away."

"That seems like a big risk," Vrynn said. "We might lose Tera's matrix."

Tera gave Vrynn an appreciative little smile.

"Is there any other way we can get those files?" I asked Tera.

She seemed to consider it. "What if we plug the uplink cable back in, but this time, let me connect to the system instead of the system shoving the information at me."

"Okay, let's try it. But let's be ready to pull the plug again." I stayed in the cargo bay with Tera while Vrynn walked down the ramp and plugged the cable back into the ship's hull.

"You're all connected. Give it a try," Vrynn called.

Tera's expression changed to one of intense concentration. That was just for our benefit, of course, but I knew her subroutines were working hard.

A few moments later, she turned to me. "The plans for the Quake Drive . . ." She looked away as if searching. "And the master programming for the AI matrix. I know where they are—or were when these systems were in use."

I stared at her. "Where?"

Her expression fell. "Oh, you're not going to like it."

"Why? Where are they?" I asked.

Tera shook her head. "They're at the research and development offices in the corporate tower in downtown Maniphra." She pointed toward the ruined city. "That's the name of the capital."

I felt my shoulders sag.

I hadn't liked the look of the crumbling metropolis when we'd flown over it; I couldn't imagine my impression would improve on closer inspection.

Vrynn bounded up the cargo ramp. Apparently, the look on my face showed the gravity of the situation because she immediately scowled. "What's going on?"

"Tera found the information we need about the Quake Drive and the AI matrix," I said.

"That's great," Vrynn replied.

"But it's at the company's headquarters tower. In the middle of the city," I added.

Vrynn tilted her head. "That's okay. I'm sure we can find it."

She opened her mouth to continue, but I cut her off with the phrase I knew she was about to say.

"How hard could it be?"

Chapter Eleven

We spent the rest of that day preparing food, equipment, and weapons for our trip into the city. Fortunately, the ship had a few cargo bags that I was able to rig to carry on our backs. At least we finally had a purpose for the ration kits. I knew I'd be willing to eat blue ooze if I was hungry enough.

We decided that we needed to bring both Skeeter and Rascal with us—Skeeter for her ability to climb difficult things and her connection with Tera, Rascal for his companionship and sheer mass.

At first light, we loaded up our gear and set off on foot across the deserted wasteland toward the crumbling skyline in the distance. When we reached the main highway, we turned north. Carpets of green moss and spiderwebs of cracks covered everything.

For most of the morning, we walked in the shade of the high-velocity tubes. At least, I was fairly sure the tubes had been used for some sort of travel in semi-vacuum. Either that, or a giant, planetary water slide. The idea made me smile despite the prospect of a long journey still to go.

As we trudged on, Vrynn watched Rascal and Skeeter bounding ahead of us. "Do you think Skeeter would give me a ride if I ask nicely?"

"She's a robot. She'll do it even if you don't ask nicely," I replied.

"That's not a very enlightened attitude," Vrynn said in a scolding tone.

I shrugged off the critique. "But what would I do if you're riding Skeeter?"

Vrynn giggled. "You could always see if you could hold on tight enough to Rascal."

I chuckled at the mental image. "Like a rodeo ride on a bear."

"What's a rodeo—" Vrynn stopped. Her implant must have sent a second, delayed translation. She smiled broadly. "Oh. Yes, exactly like that."

As we trudged on, the skyline of the city grew in size until the buildings dwarfed everything in view. From a distance, the city had seemed impressive. Up close, it was downright astounding. The smallest of the skyscrapers—that was the only word I had for them—would have rivaled anything on Earth. And the tallest were mind-bogglingly high.

Up until a little over a week ago, my thoughts about extraterrestrials from distant star systems—when I had them at all—would have been that they were single-mindedly focused on coming to abduct us and that they were hideously ugly.

Now, faced with the colossal remnants of a civilization that had ended about the time my people were inventing the primitive telescope, I was forced to concede that they hadn't even been aware of our existence at all.

And despite having met some unattractive aliens so far, I had to admit that they came in the disarmingly gorgeous variety, as well. I spared a glance at Vrynn, trudging along by my side, grateful that she couldn't read my thoughts.

At least, I was pretty sure she couldn't.

Once we reached the shadows of the first tall buildings, Tera directed us by guiding Skeeter along the appropriate roads. Now that we were deep inside the urban center, everything felt different. We only caught glimpses of the sun as it peeked from behind ruined buildings. And the cheerful sound of the birds had been replaced by the doleful song of some sort of insect. I also saw several smaller creatures scurrying around in the empty caves of some of the buildings we passed.

Skeeter came to a stop after about two blocks of trekking through the city.

"What's up Tera?" I asked my friend through the robot's comm link.

Her voice came back choppy and garbled.

Skeeter backed slowly along the road until we reached the spot where we had gone behind a wide building.

"Oh, the connection is much better here. Can you hear me?" The transmission of Tera's voice wasn't perfect, but at least I could understand her.

"Looks like we'll be on our own for the rest of this," I said.

"I might get sporadic contact, but yeah, you're probably right," Tera said. "Here's the building you're looking for." A holographic projection appeared above Skeeter's back. A very tall building with gleaming windows rotated in front of us and zoomed in on a suite of offices on one of the top floors.

"Of course it has to be the top floor," I muttered.

"Not the top floor," Tera said. "It's the sixty-third floor. North-west corner."

"Great. Thanks," I said as cheerfully as I could manage.

"Good luck," Tera said as we continued walking again.

After trekking through a few more city blocks on crumbling roads, we finally reached our destination. I stared up at the towering building in front of us. Its mostly glass exterior must have been beautiful once, but time and the elements had taken their toll. Almost all the walls were smashed, and those that were intact had a layer of dirt and grime on them.

"I think if we can find access to some stairs, we might be able to reach the research level," Vrynn said as she started forward.

"You know, now that I'm here looking at it in person, I'm not sure that climbing to the top of an ancient skyscraper is such a good idea." I held up my arm and purposefully tilted it at the angle the tower was leaning. "Are we sure this is worth the risk?"

Vrynn glanced back at me, ignoring my insinuation that the building was unsound. "Would equipping our entire Mark 7 fleet with Quake Drives be worth the risk?"

I knew the answer to that question, but I clung to my skepticism. "How do we know the computers in the research lab up there will even be operational? I mean, look at that thing. It's barely upright."

"The computers at the landing field hangar are still working," Vrynn replied, as if that was the obvious answer.

I opened my mouth to protest the fact that the downtown area of the city had clearly been hit harder during the war than our hangar.

"Besides, we're already here," Vrynn said. "We might as well climb up and see what we find. I'm sure there'll be something useful."

I shook my head and moved up to join her. It was nice to be around optimists every once in a while—that can-do attitude really came in handy sometimes—but this was getting ridiculous.

After a little searching around the perimeter of the building, we found a doorway into what used to be a stairwell. The steps were littered with dirt and debris. I glanced up the center of the stairwell, and high above us, I could see light filtering in through holes in the outside wall.

I looked back at Vrynn. "Sixty three floors, huh?"

"Yep," she said with a determined smile. "Better get going."

She was halfway up the first flight of stairs before I could convince my feet that they wanted to follow. Seeing Skeeter—and then Rascal—bound up the stairs after her seemed to give me the kick in the pants I needed. It was amazing how well I handled hiking for at least six hours along a halfway-destroyed highway without really getting winded at all, but by the fourth floor, I was ready to call it quits.

Fortunately for my ego, by the tenth floor, Vrynn started to feel the effects of the stairs and began to pace herself. We fell into a reasonable routine—climb two flights, rest for a minute, climb another two flights, stop to take a drink. I ended up being the one to share my water with Rascal, something about pantoboars having bad hygiene.

We had gone about twenty floors before we hit our first roadblock, literally. An enormous slab of concrete had smashed through the exterior wall and wedged itself in the stairwell spanning at least two floors.

Vrynn instructed Skeeter to climb up through a small gap in the rubble to see if it made sense to attempt to clear the way. I peeked out a hole in the side wall and saw that this slab of building had come from a neighboring tower—most of which was in piles on the ground below us.

Despite the precarious situation we found ourselves in, knowing that this tower had survived the impact of a giant domino and not tipped over gave me some level of comfort.

"Doesn't look like we can get through," Vrynn said once Skeeter had shimmied out of the pile of blocks. "Should we go back down and find another stairwell?"

"You expect me to climb this tower twice?" I shook my head. "No way. I'm not going back down until we're done. Let's cross to the other side of the tower." I walked down several steps and gingerly pulled open a stairwell door.

Vrynn joined me a second later, peering out into the dusty space. "There's no way to know if these floors can support our weight after all these centuries," she said.

"Yeah, but that's true for the sixty-third floor, too," I said. "And we're going to have to find out at some point. Personally, I'd rather fall twenty-one floors than sixty-three."

Vrynn chuckled. "Yeah, I guess you're right."

"Skeeter, could we get some light over here?" I asked our robot pet.

She pranced forward and crossed the doorway, a light on her chest illuminating the floor in front of us. The area looked like it might have been an office facility before becoming part of a war zone and then left abandoned for a century or two.

We carefully picked our way through the gutted office, following in Skeeter's steps as she scampered forward. On the opposite side of the building, we found another stairwell and began moving upward again. Our breaks came more frequently the higher we went.

Starting at about the fortieth floor, the inside walls of the stairwell were completely gone. In fact, there were no interior floors either. Ten entire levels had completely collapsed, leaving an eerie, cavernous space inside the tower.

I couldn't imagine what might have caused it or why it hadn't collapsed farther.

We found a clue two floors later. There was a gaping hole in the outside wall of the building. A missile must have struck the tower right at the stairwell—taking an entire flight with it—and then passed into the main part of the tower. A direct hit like that, assuming it exploded in the center of the building, could have easily destroyed ten floors.

I wondered how the building itself was still standing.

"Now what?" I asked, staring at the ten-foot gap in the stairs in front of us.

"We could jump," Vrynn offered.

I gave her my best are-you-kidding look. I glanced down at Rascal, my steady friend, who had climbed all the way up with us. "Rascal can't scale walls like Skeeter, and he certainly can't clear a ten-foot jump. What if we go back down and find a way across to the first stairwell?"

"We don't have enough time." Vrynn nodded toward the hole in the outside wall. "We will lose most of our light soon, and we need to be well on our way back to the ship when it starts getting dark. Besides, I'm sure we could all make it," she added, eying the flight of stairs above our heads.

"Unfortunately, the laws of physics aren't really affected by your optimism," I said.

Ignoring my jab, Vrynn pulled a long piece of rope from her sack and leaned down to attach it to Skeeter. "That's why we're not only relying on my optimism."

I shook my head. She was serious about this.

"Skeeter, climb across," she said in a sweet voice, pointing to the next intact step.

The robotic animal tilted her head then turned to scan the stairwell. A moment later, she crouched and leapt toward a thin girder protruding from the hole in the outside wall. Her robotic paws touched briefly against the encrusted metal, and she jumped again, sailing over the remaining gap before touching down lightly on the steps above us. She turned and stared back at Vrynn.

"Great job, Skeeter. Now climb up through the railing." Vrynn pointed again.

Skeeter dutifully complied and wove her way through what was left of the mangled metal.

I could see where Vrynn was going with this.

After Skeeter had looped the rope through several support bars holding up the railing, Vrynn had her jump back across the gap—a much easier feat because she was jumping down.

"Nice job, Skeeter," Vrynn said as she detached the rope from the robotic animal's back. She tied a loop into a sort of harness around her waist and handed me the other end.

I glanced around the bombed out stairwell, wondering how we had gotten ourselves into this situation. I didn't like our chances of using this cobbled-together climbing rig. But, considering the fact that I was standing in a centuries-old alien building on a planet hundreds of light-years from Earth, with an infectiously optimistic, small, blonde alien woman at my side, I figured I had already defied the odds.

I turned to Rascal. "Stay," I said forcefully. We had been working on verbal commands, and I was fairly certain he had learned this one well enough. Besides, he wasn't going to make that jump, so hopefully he knew to just hang out until we got back.

Vrynn moved into position against the craggy wall of the stairwell, and I hunkered down against the opposite wall, pulling slack from the rope in preparation for her climb. She moved gracefully from one handhold to the next along the wall until she was across the wide chasm. She probably could have made it without my help at all.

Once she was safely on the other side, she pulled my side of the rope to her and tossed the looped end back to me. I put the makeshift harness on and stepped up to the wall. I tried to convince myself that it wasn't so different from the dozens of recreational climbing walls I had tried through the years. One glance at the long drop below told me it was not like any of those.

It took me much longer than Vrynn to cross the gap, as I methodically chose handholds and places to step along the broken wall. I was proud of myself for only slipping twice and not screaming even once.

Rascal's equivalent of a whine—which was actually more like a guttural chirping sound—increased the farther away I went. When I was halfway across the gap, he started pacing back and forth on the last intact step.

Just as I reached out to grab the edge of the stairs to pull myself to safety, Vrynn cried out. "No, Rascal!"

I glanced back just in time to see him leap from the last step. I had seen dogs dive for squirrels or jump to catch a ball, but I'd never seen anything the size of a bear do that type of trick. Time seemed to slow down as Rascal floated through the air like a big furry blimp.

When he hit the edge, the entire stairwell shook. His front half had made it, but his hind paws scrabbled to find purchase on the gritty surface. Vrynn and I both reached out to help him.

Unfortunately, in her haste to make sure Rascal didn't fall to his death—a sentiment that I completely shared—Vrynn jerked against the other end of the rope. This wouldn't have been a problem except that I was already leaning precariously in my attempt to help Rascal. When the rope suddenly went taut, it threw off my balance, and my foot slipped off the ledge I was perched on.

Vrynn had barely succeeded in helping Rascal onto the stair when the jolt of my slip jerked her off balance. I quickly found another foothold to stop my downward slide just as Vrynn toppled off the stairs toward me. Her weight on the other end of the rope yanked me off the wall. As I swung through the air, I realized that any moment, the laws of physics were going to kick in and my weight advantage would turn into a disadvantage.

Fortunately, Vrynn fell into my arms.

She wrapped her arms around my middle and clung to me for dear life. I grabbed her end of the rope to keep us from falling to our deaths.

We swung there for several seconds before she finally opened her eyes. I had to admit, having a beautiful woman clinging to my chest, staring up at me with wide, blue eyes, was not all that bad.

Of course, it had been her fault we were even in this situation.

"See, gravity doesn't seem to be affected by your optimism," I said drily.

She stared at me for another long moment before offering an impish grin. "What do you mean? As long as I have you around to snatch me out of the air, I'll be fine."

I laughed at the mental image of Vrynn standing on a high wire and me below, running back and forth with my arms outstretched. "But what if I'm not always this close to you?" I had meant to imply that I might not always be near enough to catch her, but it came out wrong.

Vrynn's lips turned up in an adorable smirk. "That would be too bad," she whispered.

With her face only a few inches from mine, the sound of her actual words, and the fact that they were out of sync with what I heard in my brain, was very apparent. That snapped me out of my momentary lapse in focus.

Somehow, I would need to get Vrynn off of me and onto the stairs again. "Can you reach the step when we swing close enough?" I asked.

The initial fear in Vrynn's eyes subsided, and she glanced over at the step as we swung near. She didn't seem willing to move her head much. "Yeah, I think I can, if you can stop us from swinging."

That wasn't exactly what I had in mind, but maybe we could make it work. I stretched my free hand for the stairs when we swung close, but it was still slightly out of reach.

I started leaning my body back and forth, hoping to get us swinging harder.

Vrynn's arms tightened around me. "What are you doing?" she asked in a panic.

"You wanted me to grab the ledge. This is how I'm doing it."

"Do you have to swing so hard while you're doing it?"

I grabbed the step on the next swing and held us steady as Vrynn scampered up to safety. I chuckled. "How could you be scared of heights? You scampered across so fast the first time."

Vrynn held her head high as she pulled me up onto the ledge. "I'm not scared of heights. I'm scared of falling."

"Is there a difference?" I asked.

"Oh, yeah. Tie a safety line to me, and I'll climb wherever. But if there's a chance I might fall, I'm paralyzed."

I shook my head as we resumed our upward climb on the mostly intact steps. About ten flights of stairs later—give or take a few—we reached the sixty-third floor.

As we walked through the blown-out doorway onto the research floor, my optimism hit an all-time low. Debris and shrapnel lay scattered all over the lab. But what was worse, everything was covered with several inches of dirt and grime, probably blown in through the gaping holes in the structure.

Vrynn and I wandered around, looking at the various desks and workstations.

"There must be a working computer here somewhere," she said.

"There doesn't look to be anything working around here. No one has been here in a century," I said as I kicked at the layer of dust with my foot. "Maybe more."

"If no one has been here in a hundred years . . ." Vrynn's face fell.

"No more Quake Drives," I finished for her. "Not even the plans for how to make one ourselves."

Vrynn sat on a nearby table. She looked defeated. "I had really hoped we'd find the technology here. Think of the difference an entire fleet of ships could have made."

I moved over and sat next to her. "Yeah. But we still have the *Starfire*, and maybe a few more in the factory that we can piece together."

Vrynn gave a half-hearted smile at my enthusiasm. "Yeah. I guess that's true." She took a deep breath and looked around the dirty lab. "Sorry we made this trip for nothing," she said.

I shrugged. "Hey, if there was even a slight possibility of building a Space Armada, I was willing to take the chance." I paused a moment. "Besides, what else would we be doing right now? Staring over the Falls of Kalera Five?"

Vrynn shrugged theatrically. "Maybe if we didn't have anything better to do," she said with a warm, knowing smile.

We stared at each other for a moment. With the rays of the fading sun shimmering around her, I swear Vrynn looked like an angel. A very petite angel with blue highlights on her fair skin, but an angel all the same.

"We better get going while it's still light," she said.

Shaking that thought from my head, I nodded and stood, whistling for Rascal. With one last glance at the ancient lab, we walked through the doorway into the stairwell.

Our hike back to the ground level was much faster than the climb. Even the missing flight of stairs was easier. Rascal and Skeeter both made it over the gap in a single leap. And Vrynn and I didn't slip or fall into each other's arms even once.

I had mixed feelings about that.

As we walked out onto the street, I found myself grateful to have my feet on solid ground again. The noises of the urban wildlife seemed to be louder than before, but I was so happy to be out of that death tower that I didn't even mind. I figured the animals on Mela Suphoria probably got louder as dusk approached. That seemed reasonable.

With the sun now setting, the downtown was cast into long shadows and golden highlights. Under different circumstances, it might have even felt like a romantic walk. Unfortunately, we had a ten-mile slog ahead of us.

We zigzagged through the downtown streets, making our way back toward the main highway, when I noticed a stream of small two- four- and six-legged animals running along the street in the direction we were headed. I glanced over my shoulder, wondering if something behind us might have spooked them.

Rascal's ears perked up. He turned back toward the research tower and let out a deep howl that I had never heard him make before.

Almost simultaneously, a deafening roar echoed through the narrow streets behind us.

I turned around to see a giant beast lumber around the corner of the nearest building. It was easily the size of an elephant, but looked more like a spider. It had six strangely angled legs that stuck out sideways like a tarantula's. Its head was short and wide, with a pair of large black eyes, one facing each direction. It almost reminded me of a hippopotamus except for the short purple fur all over its body, and the six spider-like legs, and the fact that it was the size of a shuttle bus.

When it saw us in the middle of the street, the beast unleashed a roar that would have done a T-Rex proud. I backed toward Vrynn, attempting to keep myself between her and the monster. I wasn't sure if we needed to run or play dead. Did alien monsters react the same way as predators on Earth? Either way, I figured I'd keep as much distance between us as possible. I inched backward, keeping my eyes fixed on the behemoth in front of us.

The beast lumbered toward us with surprising speed, considering its size.

So much for keeping our distance.

I raised my gun and fired. Vrynn joined in with her blaster. The monster roared again, but didn't seem the least bit affected by our weapons.

It scurried forward and swiped at Vrynn with a long, hairy leg. Vrynn screamed as she was knocked to the ground. In a flash, the animal had her pinned between its front legs. It leaned down toward her, its giant mouth gaping open.

I lunged forward and fired point-blank into the beast's side. My attack forced the animal to use one of the legs that had Vrynn pinned to deal with me. When it lifted the leg, I grabbed and held on.

As I struggled to keep my feet, Vrynn managed to scramble out from the monster's grasp and retreat a safe distance away.

Now it was my turn to get away. I let go of the beast's leg and turned to run. Before I even took two steps, a powerful swipe took me out at the ankles. I hit the ground hard, and for a moment I was too dazed to even roll away. A second later, the beast had a giant paw on my chest. I kicked and pushed, trying to get away, but he had me pinned.

Rascal bounded across the street with a long howl and sunk his teeth into the beast's leg. The large animal flinched and lifted that leg, easily flinging Rascal into a nearby wall. My protector yelped and rolled along the ground, whimpering. Vrynn stepped up to the beast and began firing at its thick hide. I could smell the singed hair, but otherwise, the beast seemed unaffected. It must have sensed the irritation, though, because it batted Vrynn away with its middle leg.

The enormous animal let out an ear-splitting roar and lowered its head. Its mouth gaped open again, and I could feel its hot breath wash over me. I didn't have to imagine what it had recently eaten because I could see bits of small animals lodged between giant, yellow teeth. I wrenched one arm free and searched frantically for my dropped blaster. I only had a few seconds before becoming a monster meal.

If this was the end for me, would anyone on Earth know how far I'd come?

I turned to look for Vrynn, hoping to tell her to escape while she could, to tell Tera what had happened and hopefully do some good for the Resistance.

Instead of finding Vrynn, I saw a group of humanoids—wearing savage clothing and carrying rudimentary spears and knives, like a band of jungle natives stepped off a movie set—spill out of a nearby alley. Their dark skin and long, silvery hair reminded me immediately of Rachia and Anan—and the others I had met on Otania Sancterum. They spread quickly out into the street and surrounded the monster.

I worried that this band of savages would overwhelm the animal just a few seconds too late for me to enjoy the victory, and I wasn't about to let that happen. As my predator opened its mouth, presumably to take a bite of me, I took aim at the soft tissue in the back of its throat and let loose several plasma rounds. The monster roared in pain and shook its massive head. Then, before it could make a second attempt at devouring me, the band of savages struck, rushing forward in a synchronized attack, spears striking the beast in its eyes, and knives sinking into the weak spots on its legs.

In the chaos, the beast let me go, and I dragged myself out from under its huge frame. I got slowly to my feet and staggered away from the fight, glancing around for Vrynn. She was standing against a nearby building, holding Rascal by the scruff of his neck, apparently trying to keep him back from the fight.

I hobbled over to join them. "Are you alright?"

Vrynn nodded, her eyes wide. "You were almost a monster snack," she said. "I can't believe they got here just in time to save you." She nodded toward the savages.

I turned back in time to see the enormous beast lash out once more—knocking over several of its attackers in the process—before succumbing to its wounds. It slumped to the ground with an impact that felt like it rattled the buildings around us.

Several of the savages cried out in triumph, waving their weapons in the air. My translator took a few seconds before it kicked in. "Huzzah! Huzzah! Glory to the victors!"

Perhaps my initial assumption that these were savages had been incorrect. My translator made them sound sophisticated.

"I want to thank them," I said to Vrynn.

She didn't say anything, simply stared at the band of warriors, her brow furrowed.

I walked toward the group, hands out in a gesture of peace. When they saw my approach, two of the warriors intercepted me, standing defensively between me and the fallen beast.

I held my hands a little higher, hoping they could see that I was no threat to them. "I just wanted to say—"

"Dost thou presume to usurp the spoils of our conquest?" the first one said in a haughty tone.

I was completely taken aback by what sounded like Shakespearean English. "No, I don't want to—"

"Get thee hence," the second warrior said. "Thee and thy maiden and thy beasts are not welcome. Haste to yond thoroughfare."

Clearly, they didn't want me hanging around. Rather than pressing them for answers or forcing them to accept my thanks, I simply backed slowly away.

When I reached Vrynn, I stopped next to her, still watching the two warriors standing between us and the fallen beast. "Who are these people?"

She tilted her head and frowned. "I don't know, but I can barely understand them."

I turned to Vrynn. "Me either. It's like they're speaking some ancient version of my language."

"That's how it sounds to me, too," Vrynn said. "Why would our translator make them sound ancient?"

The pair of warriors who confronted me must have decided we weren't much of a threat because they backed toward the animal and began helping the rest of their clan.

"Could they be survivors of the wars?" I asked.

"Possibly. Some people must have survived," Vrynn replied.

I turned to Vrynn as a thought occurred to me. "Maybe that's the problem with our translators. These people are speaking a language that's several hundred years old."

We stood contemplating the strange scene, a few dozen savages who spoke Shakespearean English—at least, in my head—hacking the meat from a purple-haired monster.

I wasn't sure I could ever top that.

"Let's get out of here." I thumbed over my shoulder toward the highway that led out of the ruined city and back to our camp.

Chapter Twelve

"It's time to change your bandage," Vrynn said as she approached the kitchen table where I was eating.

Two days had passed since our near-death experience with the wild, alien monster. Vrynn had done a fair job of patching me up, so I couldn't complain. When we had first arrived back, dirty, tired, and injured, Tera had handled it relatively well. Which is to say that she freaked out slightly less than when Gabe had been mortally wounded.

As Vrynn finished reapplying the dressing on my arm, she took a deep breath and looked up at me. She had something on her mind.

"What's up?" I asked, not wanting to pry, but hoping to give her a chance to talk to me.

"I just decoded a message on a standard Resistance comm channel."

That got my attention, and I sat up a little straighter. "I thought the entire Resistance force was wiped out in the attack on Dreporox. Are there others out there?"

"No. Well, yes. I'm sure there are other Resistance fighters who were on assignment away from the base when it was attacked. Probably no more than a handful here and there. But that's not what this was."

"What do you mean?"

"There are sympathizers and informants throughout the Cluster who also use the Resistance communication network. There was a recent message about a threat to Gafria."

I raised a brow at her, hoping she understood that I had no idea what Gafria was.

"Gafria's a solitary planet in a nearby system," she explained. "There's a small colony that's come under sporadic Nexus attacks in the past, probably because Gralik suspects that they're sympathetic to the Resistance."

"Are they sympathetic to the Resistance?"

Vrynn nodded. "The colony has provided aid to members of the Resistance in the past, and there are even some who could be recruited to join us in the future."

I took a deep breath. "We only have the *Starfire* right now. It's not like we need any more pilots yet. Plus, it seems risky to rush off to protect a small colony just for the possibility of recruiting some of them later."

Vrynn folded her arms. "How about because it's the right thing to do?"

I couldn't argue with that.

She continued pleading her case. "Besides, if there is an attack from Nexus-affiliated forces, we might be able to find out more information, you know, follow them back to their base, or capture a prisoner." She paused. "It could help us find Gralik."

I considered the possibility of finally tracking down Gralik against the delay this might cause in getting the Mark 7 production back up and running. Catching Gralik did sound appealing. And the production line would still be here later.

"You want to swoop in and save the colony?" I asked, already knowing what her answer would be.

She nodded, a quiet defiance in her eyes.

"Let's do it," I replied enthusiastically.

"Really?" she asked, a little surprised.

"Sure, I'm up for some superhero work."

She lunged—catching me momentarily off-guard—and wrapped me in a tight hug. "Thank you. Thank you." She nearly tipped me backward in my seat. "Sorry," she said with a grin.

I smiled back as we stood and headed for the flight deck.

"Guess when I first knew you were fresh water," Vrynn said as we walked. A moment later, my chip retranslated, "a good guy."

I shook my head. "When?"

"When you didn't leave me on Thetis Max," Vrynn replied.

"Well, guess when I first knew *you* were fresh water," I said, testing out her phrase.

"When?"

"When you didn't kill me in the alley on Varus Prime and steal my ship."

"Rascal wouldn't let me," Vrynn shot back immediately.

I knew that wasn't the real reason, but the fact that she had such a quick excuse made me laugh out loud. Vrynn joined in, and soon we were bent over in laughter, wiping tears from our eyes.

And that's how Tera found us, standing outside the flight deck. The expression on her holographic face told me that I would not hear the end of this one. So after our laughter finally died down, I explained the plan to fly to the Gafria system, mostly to distract her.

Despite Tera's general, very-teenage, who-cares attitude, she seemed eager to be going on this rescue mission, too. I hadn't even finished my explanation of where we were going and why before she had all the systems up and running ready for launch.

Ten minutes later, we cleared Mela Suphoria's atmosphere and made the jump to the Gafria system. Fortunately, it was a short jump—less than fifteen minutes through intra-space.

As soon as we completed the jump, Tera began scanning the planet. "No ships in orbit, several in the atmosphere."

"What about on the other side of Gafria?" I asked. "We don't want to have another surprise like on Dreporox."

Tera held a virtual finger up to her temple. "Let me see." She scrunched her eyes closed for several seconds before relaxing back to her normal, sulky expression. "Nope. I can't magically see through solid planets."

I sighed, wondering if I would ever get used to the personality Gabe had programmed. If it weren't for the fact that I couldn't imagine erasing something that he had worked so hard on, I might be tempted to program the AI to behave like my own dream girl—assuming I ever found her. I glanced absently over at Vrynn sitting in the co-pilot seat. I didn't know why I looked at her. There were some good things about her, and she certainly was attractive, but I'd never thought my dream girl was a small, spunky water nymph from another planet.

"Any sign of attack on the settlement?" Vrynn asked, obviously oblivious to my thoughts.

"Six ships near the colony. Sensors are picking up weapons fire," Tera said.

"Let's do this," I said, gripping the flight controls.

We still weren't in the atmosphere, but I felt ready to do more than just practice maneuvers in space. I was ready for the real thing again. But in my eagerness to take over the controls, I put the ship into a forward tumble. I quickly eased off, but that didn't seem to fix it. I turned to ask Vrynn if she wouldn't mind taking over the orbital part. But before I had even opened my mouth, she grabbed the controls and quickly stopped our spinning.

"Thanks," I said.

She gave me a sidelong glance, a smirk on her face.

Maybe we *were* starting to work well together.

Once I could feel the buffeting of the atmosphere against the hull, I grabbed the controls again, and they responded in a much more predictable way. I brought the ship down in a steep dive toward the settlement.

Vrynn tapped her console, and a zoomed-in view of the settlement appeared on the display in front of us. I could see several ships on the outskirts of the town, sporadic weapons fire going in both directions. Apparently, the colonists were putting up a fight.

"Dunpax gunships," Tera said. "Light armament. Only dangerous to the *Starfire* in swarms."

"Dunpax? Is that a planet or a system?" I asked.

"Both," Tera replied.

"And their transponder signals?" Vrynn asked. I was pretty sure I knew the answer already.

"Same masking as before," Tera answered.

"Nexus," Vrynn and I muttered simultaneously.

With the *Starfire's* nose pointed directly at the ground, we screamed out of high orbit, entering the atmosphere directly above the colony. The gunships from the Dunpax system were spread out in a wide arc, firing point-blank at the settlement wall. They must have been too busy to notice us because none of them had moved yet.

"I guess we need to add Dunpax to the Nexus list," Vrynn said.

"Are we in range yet?" I asked.

"Too far for lasers. Same for the plasma cannons," Tera explained. "The rail gun has the range, but the ships won't be in the same place by the time the rounds get there."

Vrynn switched her controls to weapons. "With six targets, I'll take my chances." The ship shuddered as Vrynn let loose half a dozen rail gun slugs.

I watched in anticipation as the display highlighted the rail gun rounds screaming toward the surface. The Nexus ships, still apparently unaware of our existence, shifted slightly from side to side as they continued their assault on the fortified town. Unfortunately, Tera had been correct. They had all moved enough from their original location, that the slugs weren't likely to hit any of them.

At the last minute, a gunship suddenly shifted directly into the path of one of the rail gun slugs. The supersonic shell punched cleanly through the wing and into the sand below. The sudden impact caused the pilot to lose control and spiral slowly into the ground.

The rest of the gunships scattered in the ensuing chaos. By this point, we had cut our altitude in half, and I lined up on the enemy fighter that looked the most skilled. Vrynn fired the plasma cannons, raking across the ship with highly charged ion rounds.

"Two enemies moving in behind us," Tera declared. "Two more in defensive positions."

"Bring up the laser targeting," I said as I banked hard in pursuit of the ship in front of us, allowing Vrynn to continue pummeling it with the cannons.

A video feed from the laser tracking camera appeared on my console. I glanced down and tapped the left engine pod of one of the ships on our tail. Our defense lasers began to automatically work their destruction while I tried to stay close enough to the enemy ship in front of us for Vrynn to take it out.

With Vrynn at the cannons, the ship in front of us never really stood a chance. The pilot put up a good fight, zig-zagging back and forth as Vrynn filled the air with plasma rounds. After several minor hits, a pair of Vrynn's shots impacted directly in the seam between the hull and the weapons pylons. The gunship's drive core must have been in that area, too, because the ship exploded in a bright fireball.

"That's two down!" Vrynn exclaimed.

I checked the rear display just in time to see one of the ships on our tail begin to smoke from the attention our laser defenses were giving to its left nacelle. The pilot started weaving back and forth to shake our lock. But it was too late. A moment later, the engine burst into flames, taking the right wing with it, sending the gunship into a corkscrew dive into a nearby hillside.

"Yes! Make that three," I yelled as I tapped my console to re-target the lasers on the next ship.

The remaining three ships spread out, organizing their attack strategy, shifting from flee to fight, from panic to pack. Vrynn swiveled the plasma cannons back and forth, firing at whichever ship came into range. The laser defenses remained locked on one of the ships, but it had fallen the farthest away, and the distance reduced the lasers' effectiveness. I would either need to pick a different target or be patient while the lasers slowly overheated its hull.

"Missiles!" Tera announced.

Two of the gunships simultaneously launched atmospheric missiles. The lasers shifted to protecting us from the new threat. Vrynn helped by spraying everywhere with the plasma cannons.

"Watch out, Mitch!" Tera yelled.

I checked the rear display and immediately banked hard to avoid a plasma burst from a gunship that had snuck up behind us. Vrynn answered with a barrage from the plasma cannons that kept the enemy at a distance.

"There's another ship coming in from our flank," Vrynn said. "They'll have us surrounded if you're not careful."

I could see from the tactical overlay that there was little we could do to escape a confrontation with at least one of the ships. And if I engaged one, the other two could easily attack us from the other direction.

I pushed the controls forward and took the ship into a shallow dive toward the nearby mountains. Unlike the chasms and canyons on

Dreporox, these were dusty dunes and jagged outcroppings. Nothing we could really hide behind.

The enemy ships dove to follow us, trying to keep us hemmed in. I did my best to hug the contours of the sandy landscape. And Vrynn continued firing plasma bursts every time she got the chance.

"I have an idea," I said. "Tera, get ready to activate the maneuvering thrusters."

"Those aren't really used in the atmosphere, Mitch," she replied. "They're pretty much just for steering in space."

"I know. Just trust me," I said.

I maneuvered the ship lower until we skimmed just a few feet above the sandy terrain.

"Vrynn, can you fire behind us and kick up some sand?" I asked.

She must have understood my plan. "I'm on it."

"Now turn on the thrusters, Tera. The ones aiming down."

Tera didn't look convinced of my plan, but she faithfully followed my instructions, anyway.

As I zigzagged back and forth, Vrynn dropped explosions in our wake, and Tera blasted the sand with our high-powered thrusters, creating a huge cloud of sand and dust, to the point that most of the valley floor was clouded over.

Doubling back, I flew us into the cloud and killed the engines. We transitioned to a gentle hover, and our forward momentum slowed until we floated in place inside a smoke screen of our own making. Of course, if our enemies were stupid enough to fly in after us, the cloud wouldn't protect us from a violent, fiery impact.

"Now, do we just sit here?" Vrynn asked.

I shook my head as I switched my console to weapons control. "We each fire a guided atmospheric rocket, just like you did on Dreporox."

Realization spread across Vrynn's face. She pulled up the steering controls on her console.

"I'll shoot forward, you shoot backward," I said. "Then we each target one of the ships."

She nodded.

"Ready?" I asked.

She gripped her control sticks. "Ready."

"Fire."

I pressed the trigger on my stick and watched the hazy video feed on my screen. For several seconds, it matched the obscured view from the flight deck windows, until the missile suddenly burst out of the dust cloud. I steered mine upward into the clear sky, attempting to get my bearings.

"I see them," Vrynn called, still focused intently on the video feed of her own missile. "I have the one on the left."

I glanced back and forth from her screen to mine, trying to figure out where the ships were. Two of the ships were flying as a pair, and I couldn't see the other one at all. Once I finally got them in my sights, I zeroed in on the ship on the right.

Both ships banked hard, and I steered the missile to follow. Suddenly, the ship in my sights burst into flames.

"Hey, I thought you said you had the one on the left," I complained.

"That *was* the one on the left," Vrynn replied.

Either my translator had messed up Vrynn's words for left and right, or she had come at the pair from the opposite direction.

I shook my head and shifted to the other ship, tracking its movements as it veered side to side.

"Should I fire another missile?" Vrynn asked.

"Yeah. Just don't target my ship."

Vrynn launched and soon locked onto our last target.

"Uh, Mitch?" Tera said.

"Hang on." I said through gritted teeth as I continued steering the missile side to side, keeping it locked on its target.

"Mitch, look," she repeated, pointing out the flight deck windows.

I glanced up to see that our protective cloud had mostly dissipated. To my left, an enemy gunship—the one with my missile trailing it—was heading straight for us. The other gunship—with Vrynn's missile on its tail—came at us from the right. Apparently, these two enemy pilots had settled on the same bright idea of leading our missiles back at us.

"Get us out of here!" I yelled.

The enemy ships were only seconds from us now. I winced, hoping that we weren't about to end our adventure in an enormous, slightly dusty, fireball.

I switched away from my missile to take command of the defensive cannons, but it was a little too late to try and stop the inevitable from happening. Vrynn toggled to flight controls—leaving her missile to its own devices—and slammed the engines on full. The force pinned me in my pilot seat as I filled the air around us with cannon rounds. I watched my missile's live feed of the *Starfire* jetting out of the path of our suicidal enemies, colorful, burning plasma bursting out of the winglets like fireworks.

With so many ships concentrated so close together, the enemy pilots succeeded in confusing the missiles tailing them. Fortunately for us, the missiles simply swapped targets. A moment later, both rockets struck the gunships and exploded.

The twin blasts rocked our ship, knocking us slightly off-kilter, but Vrynn quickly had us back under control and flying level.

I looked over at her, and we shared an expression of relief and, to a certain degree, surprise that we had worked so well together.

"Let's never do that again," I said.

At the same time, she said, "We should try that again sometime."

I shook my head, wondering if we would ever agree on anything.

I took over the controls and flew us back toward the settlement. "Should we contact the colony to see if they need any help?"

"Look." Vrynn pointed to the ground in front of us.

A Nexus ship—the one we hit with the railgun slug—had crash landed a few miles from the outskirts of the settlement.

"Let's see if the pilot survived," Vrynn said. "We might be able to get some information from him."

I brought the ship down for a soft landing near the damaged enemy ship. Now that we were closer, the gunship didn't look that bad. Definitely beat up, but probably still flyable once the hole was patched. I hit the button to open the cargo bay door, and Vrynn and I jumped from our seats. Vrynn was already halfway to the ramp when I ran through the door.

"Rascal, come," I called as I tried to keep up with Vrynn. I wasn't sure whether the downed pilot still posed a threat to us, but I didn't want to take any chances.

My faithful companion sat up from his nest and bounded after me.

Out on the ground, we raced toward the downed ship.

"Hang on, Vrynn," I called as she outpaced me. I could hear metallic scraping from the other side of the ship.

She ran around the side and yelled. "Stop!"

By the time I caught up, she had her weapon drawn and trained on the pilot, who had been trying to make a hasty repair.

He was a mangy-looking guy, probably a little younger than me, with oil stains on his flight suit and a serious-looking gash on his cheek. He had stubbly, white hair on his head that would have made him look like an old man, except that his skin was so shiny and youthful.

He turned around and dropped his tools, holding his empty hands high. "Please don't kill me," he said with a nervous tremor in his voice.

"Answer our questions, and I'll consider it." Vrynn's tone had a sharp edge to it. I knew she wasn't some hardened vigilante, but apparently this pilot didn't.

"I've been preparing myself to be tortured," the pilot said, his hands still above his head. "So go ahead. I can take it."

Vrynn and I shared a look. Clearly, she hadn't expected that sort of response, either. It made me wonder what kind of weird training Nexus gave its fighters. Or maybe it was a quirk of Dunpax culture. Finally, she shrugged and nodded toward the guy, indicating I should go ahead.

"What do you know about the attack on Earth?" I began.

The skittish pilot looked at me like I'd spoken in a foreign language. "Earth?" he replied. "I've never heard of Earth."

"You don't know anything about the raid on Earth to steal the *Starfire* or its Quake Drive?" I pressed. He looked like I was speaking gibberish, yet I was fairly certain both of our translators were working correctly.

"I'm a flight-wing leader, second class. My commanders don't tell me much. This is my first assignment to the Gafria contract," the pilot said.

"How do we know you're telling the truth?" Vrynn said, brandishing her weapon at him again. As if sensing her mood, Rascal bristled and growled at the enemy.

The pilot held his hands up even higher. "Because I would never lie in a torture situation," he said with a trembling voice. He eyed Rascal warily, then looked from Vrynn to me and back. "Please punch me. I can't handle the suspense. Just tell me you're not going to kill me."

I turned to Vrynn and saw a look of pity on her face. We were thinking the same thing. This guy didn't seem right in the head.

"What about Gralik?" Vrynn said. "Have you heard that name?"

The guy must have reached his limit of tension because a low scream started building in his throat until he couldn't stop it. "I can't take it anymore. Are you going to kill me?" he cried. "Can you just hurt me or something so I know you're not going to kill me!"

Vrynn half-heartedly kicked him in the side of the leg. "Calm down, we're not going to kill you."

Despite it not being much of a kick, the guy dropped to the ground like an injured soccer player. "Oh, thank you for not killing me. Thank you. Thank you."

"Gralik," I ground out slowly. "What do you know about him?"

The pilot shifted to his knees, his eyes still lowered humbly to the ground, and shook his head. "Nothing. I've never heard that name before."

"Are you sure?" Vrynn nudged the guy lightly in the shoulder.

He wailed as if she'd slammed his head against the ground. "Thank you. Please keep hurting me. The pain means I'm still alive."

Vrynn and I shared another look, mostly frustration this time. I rolled my eyes and twirled my finger next to my head. As I did, I realized that alien cultures might not use the same gesture to say someone is crazy.

Vrynn raised a brow in confusion, then a smile broke out on her face. "Yeah, totally." She put her thumb and finger on her temple and pinched them together.

I guess that was the gesture for crazy on her planet.

Vrynn leaned toward me and whispered. "We might have to really hurt this guy to get any information out of him." She started toward the pilot, still prone on the ground, clearly ready to make him talk.

I grabbed her arm. "Actually, hang on. I have an idea."

Vrynn shrugged and stepped back.

I crouched down next to the whimpering pilot. "You know what? I hate to say this, but we're not going to hurt you anymore until you start answering our questions." I spared a quick glance at Vrynn over my shoulder. "And you know what it means when we stop causing you pain."

The pilot began to tremble. "No. Please. Please injure me. Just don't kill me."

I shook my head sadly. "You leave me no choice but to stop hurting you. Unless you talk to us."

He waved his hands down. "Okay, okay. I'll tell you what you want to know. I have heard of Gralik, but I've never met him before. He's the top boss of Nexus, a commander in the Varusian fleet, I think. Sometimes he uses his BDF connections and sends our security force these types of protection jobs."

Vrynn frowned. "Protection jobs? What are you protecting?"

The pilot turned his attention to her and shrugged sheepishly.

I knew exactly what he meant. Classic organized-crime operation. I turned to Vrynn. "You know, they protect the settlement"—I jabbed a thumb over my shoulder—"until the settlement stops paying for protection, then they do the attacking."

The pilot let out a noncommittal squeak.

"It's just a bully operation," Vrynn said.

"And where can we find Gralik?" I asked as menacingly as I could manage.

"I don't know," the pilot replied quickly.

I pulled the gun from my thigh holster. Cowering, the pilot immediately began to yowl like a cat in heat. I hadn't intended to threaten him with it, but it served that purpose pretty well, even accidentally.

I held the gun out so he could see. "This is one of the weapons from the group that killed my best friend," I said softly. "Have you ever seen a gun like this?"

He stopped moaning when it was obvious that I wasn't going to kill him. He tentatively glanced at the gun then up at me. "No," he whimpered.

I decided to double-down on his fears. "So you see, because this is the gun that killed my friend, I don't shoot to injure people with it. I don't use it for punishment, or even torture. I only get this out when I plan to kill someone."

Vrynn must have thought that was pretty dark stuff because her eyes went wide. Rascal, on the other hand, had become bored with the interrogation and settled onto the ground, panting happily.

I winked at my co-pilot, hoping she understood that I was bluffing.

Her brow furrowed in response. But before she could say anything that would spoil my plan, the pilot wailed. "Ahhh! Wait! Wait! I do know something! I'll tell you as long as you don't kill me."

I leaned in closer to the pilot. "Tell me first, and then we'll see." If this guy only knew how unlikely I was to kill him in cold blood like this.

He held his hands out, apparently attempting to calm me down. "Okay. Okay. I don't know where Gralik's base is, but I've heard he likes to spend his time on Daeko III."

I looked down at him. "Keep talking," I said gruffly. I had no idea what Daeko III was, but I didn't want the pilot to know that.

"They say he has a soft spot for a Caridyan waitress at the casino. So he sometimes hangs out there hoping to make his move. It's sort of the joke among the BDF security forces. But please don't ever tell him I said that."

"The casino is a big place." I actually had no idea if that was true. "Where might we find him waiting for this particular waitress?" I casually shifted the blaster from one hand to the other, hoping he'd get the general threat.

"Krank's bar?" He said it as if it was obvious, and he wasn't sure why I didn't know.

"Are you sure?" I pressed.

"I mean, that's where the waitress works," the pilot hastily added.

I considered him for a moment then stood up. "Okay. You've been very helpful. And don't worry, we won't tell anyone that you think Gralik is a loser with no game." I gave Vrynn another wink. She made an awkward attempt to replicate the gesture.

The pilot whimpered at the implication that he'd said anything of the sort.

I looked up to see several vehicles from the settlement racing along the dusty plains toward us. "Well, look. Here comes the cavalry."

We had a few tense moments with the armed defenders of the outpost before they realized we had been the ones who saved their colony. I wasn't sure if Rascal's presence had made them more willing to trust us or if they simply didn't want to rile a beast his size. Either way, it worked out in the end.

The leader stepped forward, holding a hand over his chest. "We can't thank you enough for your protection. We don't have much to offer you as a reward." He glared in the direction of the downed pilot. "Obviously, if we did, we wouldn't be in this situation." He looked back at me. "But maybe now we don't have to worry about paying these vermin for protection." His eyes held hope and anticipation.

I glanced at Vrynn, unsure of whether this guy thought we were suddenly the settlement's superheroes. She must have seen where my thought process was going. "We just happened to be in the area, so we wanted to help. No reward is necessary."

The soldier standing next to the leader shook her head. "We must find a way to thank you." She turned to the man. "We will hold a banquet in their honor."

"Yes," the leader said. "Please return with us and you will be honored for your bravery."

Vrynn looked over at me and shrugged. "Why not?"

I turned back to the leader. "Thank you very much. We would love to."

"Now, what do we do with him?" Vrynn asked, indicating the prone pilot.

"We will take care of the prisoner," the leader said with a quick hand motion to the soldiers with him. They immediately surged forward, grabbed the pitiful pilot by his limbs, and dragged him to the holding cell on the back of their vehicle.

I leaned toward the leader from the colony and whispered, "Apparently, this guy loves being tortured, so . . ."

The leader's brow furrowed.

I just shrugged and left it at that.

Chapter Thirteen

By the time the banquet was over, I had received offers from four of the most prosperous members of the colony to marry their daughters. Of course, Vrynn had been proposed to by at least a dozen young men, so I wasn't quite keeping up. And Rascal had been happy to devour as much meat as the colonists had on hand.

Once we were safely back on the ship—with Vrynn carrying multiple tokens of appreciation from her admirers—we settled into the flight deck and launched into orbit.

"I noticed you didn't jump at the chance to marry one of the settlers' beautiful daughters," Vrynn said.

I chuckled. "There were some pretty ones," I said. "But..."

Vrynn leaned forward in her seat. "Yeah?"

After a long pause, I said, "I just don't think homesteading life would suit me very well."

Vrynn's expression fell. I wasn't sure what she had expected me to say, but apparently, that wasn't it.

I turned to Tera to ask her if she could help me out, but before I even opened my mouth, my holographic friend said, "Do you think I'm alive?"

My brows went up. "Alive? That's a tough question, Tera."

"Do you think it was the right thing for Gabe to create me? I mean, was it selfish of him to want to keep me around?"

I scratched the back of my neck. Between saying the wrong thing to Vrynn and questions of existence and creation from Tera, this conversation had definitely taken a strange turn.

"Are you unhappy that Gabe programmed you with Tera's personality?" Vrynn asked.

Tera shook her head. "No. No. I'm glad he did." She paused. "I guess I'm just asking for future reference."

Vrynn and I shared a look. I wasn't exactly sure what that meant, but I decided it might be better to talk about it later with Vrynn. Out of earshot of Tera.

I decided to change the subject. "Tera, what do we know about the casino on Daeko III?" I asked.

Tera leveled a petulant gaze at me. "We know that we don't want to go there," she said.

My brows went up at her immediate, and very opinionated, reply. "Well, the leader of the Nexus soldiers that killed Gabe hangs out there periodically."

Tera's eyes grew wide before her expression morphed into pure hatred. "I can come up with a strafing pattern that will leave the casino in ruins. It would only use half of our weapons stores."

"That's the kind of excitement I like," Vrynn said. "I knew my positivity would rub off on you some time."

I held up my hands. "Okay. Take it easy. Let's figure out what we're getting ourselves into first." I turned back to my holographic friend. "Tera, tell us about Daeko III and then the casino."

"That would be redundant," she replied flatly. Perhaps she was upset that I wouldn't let her annihilate Gabe's murderers.

I motioned for her to keep going.

"Daeko III and the casino on Daeko III are one and the same. Obviously, one is a small planet, just outside the cold end of the habitable zone, while the other is a gambling establishment. But given that there are no other settlements or anything at all on the planet, then it's fair to say that the casino is Daeko III and Daeko III is pretty much just the casino."

"How can a casino, or any settlement, exist on a planet outside the habitable zone?" Vrynn asked.

"A very large volcano," Tera replied. "Daeko III is completely uninhabitable except for right around its single volcano, where the magma is close to the surface and keeps things warm enough to not freeze to death."

A holographic image popped up in front of us. It showed a frozen, white landscape interspersed with wild black and red slashes across the surface. Black where the lava had been ejected and cooled, red where it hadn't. The three-dimensional image zoomed in until a large volcano dominated the view.

"There," Tera said, pointing to the display. "That's the casino."

I squinted at the white and gray. "I don't see anything."

"It's underground. See those large holes?" She pointed again. "Those are old lava tubes that have been converted to landing pads."

I took a deep breath and turned to Vrynn, wondering how she felt about it. She was looking intently and nodding.

On second thought, I knew how Vrynn would feel about it.

"Are we sure this is a good idea?" I asked. "This will set us back on our schedule to get the Mark 7 production up and running. Besides," I said, glancing at the forbidding-looking ice planet, "maybe there's another way that we can track down Gralik, like when he's vacationing on a paradise planet or something."

"This is the ideal time to strike," Vrynn said. "He doesn't know we're a threat yet."

I gave her my skeptical look.

"We can do this," she added. "We just need to get some new clothes and figure out our cover story."

I raised my hand as if I was a student in class again. When Vrynn gave me an impatient look, I said, "I'd like to point out, right up front, that I'm a horrible actor."

"Oh, don't worry about that," Vrynn said. "Just let me do all the talking."

"I still don't think this is a good idea," I muttered.

Vrynn clapped her hands together. "So, where are we going to get new clothes?"

The hologram of Daeko III faded away, replaced a moment later by a green and blue orb. "This is Cypso. It's on the way to Daeko III and has some of the best shopping in the galaxy." Tera gushed. "At least, according to the computer's databanks."

I stared at the greens and blues, covered in some spots by familiar white clouds. "Why couldn't Gralik have fallen for a waitress on that planet?" I muttered.

* * *

After the twelve-minute jump through intra-space and a ten-minute approach to Cypso, we were on the ground in a berth in the spaceport of the capital city.

Though I considered that making good time, it was nothing compared to Tera's next feat. In about two and a half seconds, she had researched the list of all stores within a reasonable walk of the landing pad—including the products currently in stock—and given us a recommendation of which would have the cutest outfits for Vrynn and the ones that would make me look the best.

Basically, she did all the things a fifteen-year-old girl would do if she had nearly infinite computing power and access to an entire planet's version of the Internet.

I pointed out that we didn't want to look cute; we wanted to look mean and worn around the edges. I had no idea what bad-guys in the Bonara cluster really looked like besides my brief interactions with the thugs in the alley on Varus Prime.

As we walked, Vrynn and I tossed around ideas for what kind of clothing to get. I had thought we should dress as scruffy space pirates, but Vrynn said that my face was too honest to pull off a true pirate look.

I wasn't sure, but it had almost sounded like a compliment.

In the end, we settled on a formerly well-to-do couple, clearly down on their luck and hoping to hit it big at the casino. I could certainly do the down-on-his-luck part. We decided to try an upscale second-hand clothing store Tera had put on the list, hoping to throw together something that looked believable.

The people on Cypso were much more subdued than the crowds on New Talpreus, so we easily found the store we were looking for. The weather in this particular city was beautifully mild, and the sky was a gorgeous pink and orange swirl, almost as if they had sunset in the middle of the day.

As we approached the store, I glanced around the well-kept row of businesses. "Well, it's no Kalera Five, but it's not bad."

Vrynn just rolled her eyes and walked inside.

Without too much effort, I found a pair of slightly scuffed dress shoes, and what must have passed for a semi-formal suit—though it had twice as many pockets and buttons as it needed. I grabbed a few shirts in my size and carried the pile of clothes to the side of the store where Vrynn was busy picking between various shades of very strange-looking dresses. They looked strange to my eyes because they were all ribbons and straps in configurations that couldn't be the least bit comfortable.

"You're already done?" she asked incredulously. "How is it that male clothing choices are so easy?"

"I guess there are just some constants in the universe," I said with a smug grin.

I sat on a nearby bench—close enough to carry on a conversation, but far enough to not be involved in the decision-making process. If pressed, I wasn't afraid to trot out my father's tried-and-true line, "that one looks fine, too."

Thoughts of my dad brought me to the reality of what I was doing—or about to do. I was sitting on a bench in an alien shopping center, preparing to fake our way into a seedy casino. It wasn't the first time I wished that my parents were still living. This would have made for a great story sitting on the back porch staring out at the Oklahoma sunset.

Assuming I ever made it back to that porch in my backyard.

"Mitch," Vrynn called.

I realized she had been trying to get my attention for several seconds. I shook my head to clear my thoughts and bring myself back to the present. "Yeah?"

"I'm ready. Let's get going," Vrynn said.

We paid for the clothes and headed back to the spaceport.

"Should we do anything to disguise the ship before we dock at a known Nexus gathering place?" I asked Vrynn as we approached the *Starfire*.

Vrynn cocked her head to the side. "What did you have in mind?"

I walked around the front of the ship to the nose and looked up at the windows of the flight deck. "I don't know. Maybe some mud splatters," I said with a chuckle.

"Do you think we could put some scrapes or scratches along the side of the hull?" Vrynn asked as we walked along the other side of the ship, back to the cargo ramp.

We walked up into the cargo bay and found Tera already standing there waiting for us. She must have been organizing things again because HelperBot was moving various crates around. Rascal and Skeeter trotted up the ramp a moment later. I knew why Rascal occasionally needed to be outside the ship, but did robot cats have to use the outdoors, too? Plus, she had a small pack attached to her back.

Just as I was about to ask Tera about it, she said, "What were you two just talking about?"

"We might need to do something to the ship to disguise it before we fly to Daeko III," Vrynn replied.

"Do not mess with the outside of the ship," Tera insisted. "I'll change it to match whatever look you want."

Vrynn and I both stared at her.

"What do you mean?" Vrynn asked.

"I can change the paint job," Tera said. "I can make the ship's outside a different color, or even like it's been in a fight. Obviously, I can't actually break the hull plating, but I could make it look that way, like we've been in some fights."

"When were you planning to tell us this?" I asked.

Tera shrugged. "I dunno. When it would make a difference. Like now."

I glanced over at Vrynn, and she just shook her head.

As much as my AI friend seemed human, I had to remind myself that she was still a collection of logic circuits, and she used that logic in strange ways sometimes.

"That's perfect, Tera," I said. "I'm putting you in charge of making the ship ugly."

After I took the ship into orbit, Tera made the jump to intra-space, and Vrynn and I went up to our rooms and changed into our new clothes.

We walked out of our quarters at nearly the same time, and I'm pretty sure my jaw hit the floor. Vrynn stood in front of me in what can only be described as aqua perfection. Her dress was quite strappy on top and came down to just above her knees. And it shimmered somewhere between blue and green like a peaceful, undulating lagoon. Her silvery blond hair was tied back in several intricate braids that wound around each other, with strands of blue dangling down to her neck and shoulders.

I gaped at her for several moments as an impish smirk spread across her lips. "You don't look too bad yourself, you know," she said.

I shook off the sudden feelings of attraction I felt for my co-pilot as we made our way to the flight deck—though I couldn't help a few sidelong glances as if to confirm that I'd actually seen what I thought I'd seen.

Tera projected an image of the outside of the ship and swiped through several ideas she had for its new appearance.

"That one," Vrynn said, pointing at the floating holographic ship with several burn marks and impact strikes. "It looks like we've been through a war."

Tera nodded. "That's the look I was going for." She glanced at Vrynn then me with a hesitant look. "You know it's only a paint job, though. If someone looks close enough, the hull will still be smooth and the marks will obviously be fake."

"I don't plan to let anyone get that close if I can avoid it," I said. I looked back at Vrynn. "You know, this plan might actually have a chance."

"As long as you keep your mouth shut," she added with a laugh.

There was no orbital defense system or automated greeting communication when we arrived at Daeko III. They must have figured no one would accidentally want to land on a barren ice planet. If a ship arrived, it was there on purpose.

We approached the volcano and descended until we could see the various gaping holes at its base. I decided on the hole farthest from the volcano—partially to minimize the number of people walking past the *Starfire* and partially because I didn't trust that the volcano was actually still dormant—and flew the ship toward it. Steam issued up from the mouths of the tubes, furthering my skepticism of the wisdom of going near a semi-active volcano.

As we descended into the tube, I gripped the control sticks tightly, trying to keep the ship from smashing into the jagged obsidian. A few seconds later, the tube opened into a large, dimly lit cavern dotted with feeble lamps marking the various landing pads. We flew over several docked ships and selected an out-of-the-way berth near the back wall of the cavern.

The ship's landing skids settled against the black cavern floor with a crunch.

I looked over at Vrynn.

"Are you ready for this?" she asked me.

"Not really. But I'm willing to, anyway."

On our way out, I grabbed the tracking device that we had built in the fabricator. If we did end up finding Gralik, this little device would give us a chance of finding his base of operations.

The weak landing pad lights formed a relatively straight path leading toward the casino entrance. There was a faint smell of sulfur and rotten egg in the air.

We passed through some of the other landing caverns. Only about half of the berths were occupied, and most of the ships were in no condition to be flying, let alone going into space. Fortunately, Tera had changed the *Starfire's* appearance, otherwise it would have stuck out like a sore thumb.

When we reached the last cavern, I could see a large set of doors on the opposite side, which I assumed must lead into the casino. The closer we got, the more I wished we could have brought Rascal along. I just felt safer with him around, probably because he tended to kill any creature that messed with me. Hard not to love an animal like that.

But we knew the casino would be too chaotic—and Rascal's behavior too unpredictable—to risk bringing him along. So Vrynn and I walked the long path alone.

Suddenly, the doors to the casino swung open and a pair of humanoids got thrown out onto the rough pumice floor. They didn't seem to notice the change of scenery because they continued throwing punches.

One of the bouncers leaned through the door and bellowed. "No fighting in this establishment!"

I turned to Vrynn with a grin. "No fighting? Seriously? What kind of ruffian watering-hole doesn't allow fighting?"

Vrynn shrugged. "Fighting's bad for business."

We walked through the doors into a giant room. Actually, it was enormous. I'd once gone with Gabe to a Dallas Cowboys football game, which was the largest enclosed space I'd ever seen. This casino made the Cowboys' stadium look like a high school gym. Because of the dish-shaped cavern the casino was built in, I could easily see from one side of the room to the other.

"Close your mouth and stop gaping," Vrynn said quietly.

I lowered my gaze and focused on my immediate surroundings, occasionally glancing around as inconspicuously as possible.

There were several raised arenas lining one wall, with gladiator-looking aliens facing off against each other and hundreds of screaming spectators surrounding them. In the center, an enormous stage with dancers and performers of all colors of the rainbow dominated the space. Whether the performers were painted those colors or if there really were that many colors of species in the Bonara Cluster, I didn't know.

Vrynn leaned closer to me as we walked through the surrounding crowd. "Be careful," she said.

"About what?" I asked.

"The casino isn't only known for its gambling." Vrynn nodded toward a gathered group of females of various shapes and shades. "And they're particularly dangerous for handsome guys like yourself."

Apparently, all it took was for me to look in their direction. Half a second later, I had at least ten beautiful alien women crowding in on me, grabbing at me. At first, I was worried they were going to tear me limb from limb. But they were all whispering various things they wanted to do with me, some of which I'm not sure were physically possible.

"No, thank you," I insisted as I tried to extricate myself from their collective grasp. "I'm not interested. No, thank you." After repeating the same phrase several times to no effect, I finally said, "I don't have any money."

The gaggle of women pulled back as if they'd been burned. Suddenly, the path ahead of me was clear. I saw Vrynn waiting a few feet down the concourse, a self-satisfied smirk on her lips. "Nice job. I wasn't sure you'd learn their language that fast."

I scowled. "You could have given me a little more warning."

"And miss all that fun," Vrynn said with a laugh. "Besides, I think the one with the orange skin sorta liked you." She nodded at the backs of the retreating group of women.

I glanced briefly over my shoulder before turning my attention back to Vrynn in her gorgeous aqua-blue dress. "Nah, I prefer a woman who's more like a river than a fire." I stared purposefully at Vrynn's fair, sky-blue-flecked skin.

My normally impish copilot suddenly became quite demure and shy. She dipped her head and stared at the worn floor, her cheeks turning an adorable shade of light blue, almost like a blush.

I'm not sure what made me so bold as to say what I did. Maybe it was the fancy clothes or the casino environment, but it was out and I couldn't feel sorry for it. Vrynn had become a stalwart companion and a good friend.

After her blush had subsided, she lifted her gaze to mine, her head tilted as if considering something. Finally, she said, "Come on. Let's go find Krank's Bar."

I nodded and took her hand through my arm, escorting her across the busy casino. As we passed near some of the more rowdy crowds surrounding the fighting arenas, Vrynn was forced to swat away several extended hands. I pulled her closer in an attempt to keep the perverts at bay—despite her complete abandonment of me earlier—and that seemed to help.

On the other side of the cavern, we found Krank's Bar and walked inside. Dozens of tables filled the open area between the booths on one wall and the bar on the other. I followed Vrynn to the bar and sat next to her.

"Should we ask him about Gralik straight out?" I joked.

"You're not going to be doing any asking, remember? I'm doing all the talking," Vrynn replied.

I opened my mouth to protest that I'd been joking, but then thought better of it when I saw the look of grim determination on Vrynn's face. She probably wasn't in a joking mood.

I decided to play the naive, nice-guy card and hope it didn't blow our cover. I casually glanced around the bar, hoping I could see Gralik, or at the very least figure out which waitress he was so enamored with.

At a table halfway across the restaurant stood a waitress with the smoothest, most flawless, light-pink skin I had ever seen. She wore a short skirt and tight blouse, both of which accentuated her physical features in a way that seemed too alluring to be possible. Her face was perfectly proportioned, almost like a China doll or anime character. It had a mesmerizing effect. She smiled playfully as she interacted with the patrons at the table.

I couldn't help but stare. It was like some perfect, computer-generated image had stepped off the screen and come to life.

"Yep, I'm sure that's her," Vrynn said.

"I guess I can see how she might have caught Gralik's eye," I said.

"She's Caridyan. She catches everybody's eye," Vrynn replied drily.

I turned my attention back to Vrynn with what must have been a confused look. I had no idea what a Caridyan was.

Vrynn leaned in. "The Caridyans are cluster-renowned scientists who have spent generations focusing on genetic engineering—everything from strengthening immunities to lengthening life to optimizing physical beauty."

"Physical beauty? Sort of a step down from ridding the galaxy of diseases, isn't it?" I scoffed.

Vrynn shrugged. "Not according to the Caridyans. They've spent thousands of years in pursuit of the ultimate perfection in physical appearance—face shape, eye color, voice pitch, skin tone, and . . . other features." Vrynn scowled for a moment in the direction of the Caridyan waitress. "Anyway. It's all fake. Or at least, artificial," she said as she turned back toward the bar.

I nodded my agreement, though my gaze did linger for a moment longer on the supposed paragon of beauty. I wasn't sure I would want to be with a woman who was the galaxy's example of perfection. At least, not if she knew she was.

A noise on the other side of the bar drew my attention back. The barkeep—a broad man with a shuffling gait—stopped in front of us. "You gonna order something?"

I looked at Vrynn to see if she thought this was standard customer service for a lowlife watering hole.

She casually rested her elbows against the bar. "I'll take a Kreezian ale."

The bartender nodded and looked at me.

"I'll take one, too, I guess," I muttered.

When the big guy had set our drinks on the bar, Vrynn leaned forward and said, "Can you tell us if Gralik has been around?" She put a little extra lilt in her voice, as if using her feminine charms would get the barkeeper to spill the beans.

And for a few seconds, I thought he might.

Finally, the big guy bent down toward us and lowered his voice. "Hey girlie, you know what makes a good barkeep?"

Vrynn raised her eyebrow, inviting his answer.

"They listen good, and they don't blab." The barkeep cast her a warning. His gaze wandered to me. "But I will offer you a piece of free advice just because I don't want to have to clean your guts off my counter." That had my attention. "Don't stare too long at our little Miss Luzya." The bartender tilted his head in the direction of the attractive waitress. "If Gralik notices, you might not have any eyes left to gawk with."

I gulped and nodded. The stout barkeeper shuffled away.

After a few seconds, without looking at me, Vrynn whispered, "He must be here."

I turned to her. "Who? Gralik?" I asked.

"Mmm Hmm," she hummed. "Keep your eyes open."

As we pretended to be carrying on a casual conversation about whatever, I scanned the area of the bar behind her. She occasionally checked over my shoulder, too.

After several minutes of sipping drinks and scanning the bar, I began to wonder if we were wasting our time. "Maybe he's somewhere else in the casino."

Vrynn nodded absently. "Or maybe not. There's a table of soldiers toward the back wearing military uniforms."

"What? You're as bad as Tera. When were you going to tell me?"

Vrynn gave me a small smirk then suddenly grabbed my arm and pulled me closer. With her mouth hovering next to my ear, she whispered, "This is just so that I can look behind us without attracting attention."

Up that close, I could easily hear the exotic smoothness of her language even as my implant quickly translated her words. I nodded mutely, unwilling to trust my voice as her nearness shot tingles down my spine.

"It's a group of five or six men, two the size of Rascal and probably with the same hygiene."

I nudged her lightly. "Easy there. Let's not insult my friend when he's not here."

Vrynn continued, a slight laugh in her voice. "The others are more normal sized . . . wait . . . one of them is getting up." She paused.

"What's happening now?" I asked, barely able to keep from turning and looking at the group myself.

"Gralik is there," she said breathlessly. "He's sitting in the back of the group. I just couldn't see him earlier. I recognize the uniforms now. Those are Vanguard Dragoons with him."

"Any chance I could waltz over there and plant the tracker on him?" I said sarcastically.

Vrynn pulled back slightly and gazed at me, her brow furrowed. "You want to do a dance with Gralik?"

It served me right for trying to be clever, but I blamed it on the translator for not conveying my meaning. "No. I used a word that actually means—you know what, nevermind. We have to figure out a way to attach the tracker to him."

"I could go over and flirt with him. See if he'd let me get close enough," Vrynn suggested.

"Can you look and act like a Caridyan waitress?" I shot back. "Because I don't think anything else will capture his attention in that way."

Vrynn scowled at me, refusing to answer. I hated having to be so blunt. After all, to me, Vrynn looked fabulous.

"Any chance you could upset them enough to start a fight?" I asked.

She shrugged. "I could probably upset them, but if we start a fight, we'll be out on our butts. Remember?"

That gave me an idea. I thumbed the payment for our drinks and grabbed Vrynn's hand. "Ready for some excitement?"

"I always am," she said with a mischievous grin.

I leaned down to whisper in her ear. "Walk over to their table and do what you can to cause trouble. You don't have to start a fight. Just get them to chase you back into the casino."

"Am I allowed to insult their parentage?" Vrynn asked impishly.

"I'm counting on it," I replied with a smile. "Just make sure that when their patience runs out, you make a run for it. Straight down the center aisle and find somewhere to hide." I pointed at the broad, carpeted walkway leading away from the bar toward the exit door. "I'll take care of the rest."

Vrynn shook her head and took a deep breath. "Okay, I hope you know what you're doing."

We stood at the same time, and I immediately walked away from the bar as she walked toward the table of guys. As I moved out of earshot, I could barely hear her ask one of them if his mother had used him for target practice as a child.

I hurried down the long walkway, looking for a suitable mark. About halfway toward the door, just past one of the gladiator rings, I saw what I needed. A very portly, but very out-of-shape, man stood just off the edge of the carpet, speaking animatedly to a woman half his age. The portly man had a buddy standing next to him, who seemed bored by the whole thing. In fact, he seemed to be too cool for anything going on around him. I didn't really like their chances against half a dozen Nexus soldiers, but I was in a hurry to set the trap, and it needed to be two guys to work. Mr. Portly and Too Cool would have to do.

I slowed as I passed Mr. Portly and stepped off the main walkway.

I pretended to be casually looking around for something to do while sipping occasionally at the drink in my hand. With each movement, I inched closer to the big man. He had his back toward me, which was critical if my plan was going to work. I was grateful that his bored friend wasn't really paying attention either. Once I was within a few feet of the large gentleman, I held my position, all the while acting oblivious that he was even there.

A moment later, I glanced over my shoulder toward the bar and saw Vrynn running full speed down the aisle toward me, three Nexus soldiers hot on her heels. I pretended not to notice until the pounding of their footsteps drew the attention of everyone in the vicinity.

I spared one more glance toward Vrynn and her pursuers, gaging my timing. A second later, I spun my entire body awkwardly around. "What's happening?" I said in a groggy voice. I intentionally aimed my shoulder at Mr. Portly's back, putting as much of my momentum into the impact as possible. "Oh, pardon me," I said a moment after bumping into him.

My not-so-gentle nudge sent the guy careening head-first into the aisle right in front of Vrynn's pursuers. Mr. Portly smacked into the first two Nexus soldiers, sending them staggering backward. I quickly ducked behind a nearby gambling machine to watch the chaos I'd created, waiting for my chance to sneak into the fray.

The soldiers immediately pushed the tottering gentleman out of the way, much to his dismay, as it was the third time in as many seconds that he'd been bumped, smacked, or shoved. Apparently, he wasn't used to being pushed around, so he took a swing at them on his way down. Too Cool snapped out of his boredom soon enough to see the shove from one of the Dragoons, and he jumped up to defend his friend.

Within just a few seconds, a mini brawl had broken out. Apparently, bringing hundreds of thugs together in a free-wheeling environment and then telling them they can't fight is sort of like a powder keg waiting to be lit.

I watched for the rest of the Dragoon soldiers to arrive, and I wasn't disappointed when Gralik ran up a few seconds later. Seeing him close up, I wasn't nearly as intimidated as I had been. He stood about my height, and his build was slightly leaner than mine. His hair was jet black with that shock of white running down the middle. His skin had a sallow, almost damp look, and his eyes were small and beady.

He took several cheap shots at some of the men who were trading punches with his soldiers. I waited for my opportunity and jumped into the fray. The guy next to me kicked Gralik onto his butt. Half a second later, I let an errant shove knock me on top of him.

"Get off of me, you idiot," Gralik shouted.

"Sorry," I mumbled as I used the side of his body to push myself up.

While fumbling against him, I lightly slipped the small tracker device into one of Gralik's pant pockets. I hoped he wouldn't double check his uniform until after he was safely on his way back to his base.

After we were both back on our feet, I inched backward, away from the melee and toward the exit from the casino. All I needed to do was find Vrynn and get back to the *Starfire*.

Once I was a few feet away from the fight, I turned and walked casually down the concourse, glancing around for Vrynn. I could barely believe that this plan had actually worked.

A tap on my shoulder was accompanied by an angry voice. "What's the meaning of this?"

I turned around and saw Gralik standing in front of me—his hand out—my electronic tracker in his open palm.

My heart sank, and my shoulders drooped. Then I remembered that a normal person would try to deny it. "What are you talking about? I don't know what that is." I pointed and spoke loudly, hoping that would convince him.

Gralik narrowed his eyes at me. "Wait. I've seen you before. Did I demote you recently?"

"No. I don't think so." I continued taking small steps backward, hoping I could get away from this guy before he realized who I really was.

"Did you wash out of my training program?" he asked.

I shook my head, glancing around for Vrynn.

His frown deepened. "I can't quite put my finger on it, but you look like a failure."

My back stiffened. I had half a mind to punch him where he stood. Of course, we'd have to change the plan to kidnapping him rather than infiltrating his base of operations to steal back the Quake Drive, but I'd be willing to risk it if he kept this up much longer.

True to Vrynn's warning, casino security finally arrived in force. I could see over Gralik's shoulder that they were pulling bodies from the pile and dragging them away, whether to holding cells or out into the caverns, I had no idea.

Suddenly, recognition flashed across Gralik's face. He pointed an accusatory finger at me. "You're the guy on the farm."

My eyes went wide, and I nearly tripped over my own feet in my attempt to scamper back.

Gralik lunged forward and grabbed me by the neck. "Tell me where the ship is, or I will kill you right now." His voice was deep and threatening.

It took all my will-power not to look over my shoulder toward the caverns. I had warned Vrynn I wasn't a very good actor.

Gralik reached for the inside pocket of his jacket and pulled out a blaster. As he leveled it toward me, I kneed him in the groin and pushed him backward toward a casino security guard. Better to get tossed out for fighting than shot at close range.

As he stumbled into the guard, Gralik dropped his gun.

The guard's eyes immediately searched out the clattering sound. "Weapon!" he yelled as he dropped the ruffian he had detained and closed his giant hands around Gralik's shoulders.

Another guard quickly scooped the weapon off the ground and turned toward Gralik. "No fighting," the guard said slowly. "And no weapons." He shook the blaster in Gralik's face.

The guard didn't seem incredibly intelligent, but I was grateful for the intervention all the same.

"Let go of me, you morons," Gralik spat. "Do you have any idea who you're dealing with?" He turned his attention back to me. "This isn't over, you little thief! You're a dead man! And then I'll have my ship, anyway. Or maybe I'll take the ship and then kill you afterward."

I turned around and walked quickly away. I had no doubt that it was only a matter of time before casino authorities realized who he was and released him. I made straight for the exit.

Before I reached the doors, I glimpsed a flash of bluish-silver hair hiding behind a large fake plant. I snuck up behind Vrynn and casually said, "Nice job."

Vrynn whirled on me, eyes wide, and clapped a hand over her mouth. After a second, her surprise passed, and she nearly tackled me in a bear hug. "That was amazing!" she said in an excited whisper.

I grabbed her hand, pulling her toward the door. "As much as I'd love to stick around and admire our handiwork, we have to get out of here right now."

"Why? What happened?" she asked.

"Gralik caught me trying to tag him," I said.

Vrynn's expression fell, then she shrugged. "We'll have to try again another time."

I shook my head. "Probably not. He recognized me from Gabe's farm."

Her eyes went wide as the implications sunk in. "We have to get out of here," she whispered.

I nodded my agreement, and we both picked up the pace.

We breezed past a group of bouncers returning from dumping brawling patrons out into the caverns. I hoped none of them were Gralik's Dragoons. That would make things awkward out in the docking caverns. If the bouncers knew who had caused the whole trouble, they might not have let us pass so easily. Of course, we were trying to get ourselves out of the casino, anyway.

"Let's go," I said as soon as we were safely through the door. We broke into a full run for the *Starfire*.

As we ran through a basalt archway into the second cavern filled with landing pads, shouts emanated from the casino entrance behind us. I spared a glance over my shoulder and saw the Nexus soldiers spilling out into the cavern. Blaster fire erupted around us.

"Doesn't Gralik want to take us alive?" I yelled as we ducked, sparks showering down around us.

"After all the trouble we've caused him, I doubt it," Vrynn replied. "Besides, if he knows the *Starfire* is here, he doesn't need us alive."

We continued down the long rows of ships sitting patiently on landing pads, waiting for their owners to stop throwing money away in the casino. A few more blaster shots whizzed past, but it seemed only for show. They knew they didn't have a chance of hitting us at this range, and they'd only end up angering a bunch of rough crews if they kept trying.

"You know, there's a way we could still make our plan work," Vrynn said as she ran beside me.

I cast her a sidelong glance. "Yeah? How's that?"

Vrynn smiled. "We just have to attach the backup tracking device to one of Gralik's ships before they jump to intra-space."

"What are we gonna do, toss it at his ship and hope it sticks?"

"I'm sure there's a way," Vrynn said confidently.

I chuckled and shook my head. "I don't think the laws of orbital dynamics and space travel are affected by your optimism."

Vrynn smiled. "Wait and see."

Half a minute later, we rounded the hull of the *Starfire* and caught up to Skeeter and HelperBot hurrying up the ramp ahead of us, loaded with piles of small crates.

Vrynn glanced at the two robots. "Why would they be carrying stuff into the ship?"

I shrugged. "Maybe Tera took the chance to resupply."

"Perhaps. But this isn't the first time I've noticed them acting weird with the ship's supplies."

"Tell me all about it later," I said as we reached the back of the cargo bay. "What if we attach the tracker to one of the harpoons?" I asked.

"That could work," Vrynn said with a confident nod. "Get us in the air. I'll modify one of the harpoons."

I hustled to the upper deck and settled into the pilot's chair, Tera shimmering in the air next to me.

"Do you want to take over the launch?" she asked in a doubtful tone. "Get more practice and all."

"Nah. Just have the auto-pilot make it as fast as possible." I pulled off the ornate suit jacket that had been part of my disguise and threw it in the corner. I doubted I would need to infiltrate the casino again anytime soon.

As we crested the lip of the lava tube and rose into the blinding light of the snow-covered surface, I squinted to find the enemy interceptors.

"Any ships running with masked transponders?" I asked as I glanced down at my tracking console.

The incoming attack alert blared a split second before the ship rocked from an impact.

"Atmospheric missiles," Tera said.

"I guess that answers that," I muttered. I grabbed the controls—overriding the auto flight system—and shot the ship forward. A second missile flashed past us, narrowly missing. "Where are they?" I yelled.

"Three Varusian interceptors, just beside the rim of the second lava tube," Tera answered. "They're moving in behind us."

"Add Varus Prime to the list of planets with Nexus-sympathetic factions in their military," I muttered. "Though, I guess we knew that with Gralik being from Varus Prime."

I banked the ship hard to the right and watched my tactical displays. The projection of the view behind us showed the two ships moving in formation to attack. I jerked the stick the opposite way, forcing us into a hard turn the other direction.

The ship's internal comm cracked to life. "Take it easy!" Vrynn yelled. "I'm working with delicate components down here."

I pulled another hard turn. "They better not be too delicate; we're about to launch one through the air and smack it into their hull."

Tera turned to look at me. "You're going to launch a tracker? During a midair dogfight?"

"Sure," I said back. "Won't that work?" Maybe too much of Vrynn's optimism was starting to rub off on me.

"I doubt it," Tera said. "We don't even have a way to launch one."

A second later, Vrynn's voice came over the comm again. "I think I've got it. I'll be right up. Just don't get us killed before then."

"Noted," I said through gritted teeth as I attempted a vertical loop to get the guys off our tail. "I'll definitely wait until you're up here to get us killed."

A minute later, Vrynn staggered into the flight deck. It wasn't completely her fault. I might have shifted directions right as she came through the door.

"How do I fire the tracker?" I asked, not that I had any immediate opportunity. Both ships were still behind us, firing constantly.

"I replaced the anchor head on one of the harpoons with the tracker. So you have to be within the range of the harpoon," Vrynn said. "Actually, half that range, if we really want this to work."

"What's the harpoon's range?" I asked.

"Six hundred feet," Tera replied.

"I have to be closer than three hundred feet for this to work?" I asked incredulously.

Vrynn shrugged. She pulled up her station's weapons controls and started firing back at the enemy fighters. That was a game-changer because it got them off my tail for a few seconds.

I zeroed in on the fighter peeling off to my right. I slammed the controls to the side and dropped the thrust, causing our ship to float and begin spinning. Fortunately, I wasn't completely useless at the controls—as long as we were in the atmosphere. I throttled back up and aimed straight for the enemy ship.

Vrynn must have understood which interceptor I was focusing on. Out of habit, she unleashed a firestorm from the plasma cannons, scoring a direct hit on the interceptor's weapons array, which then exploded, sending shrapnel tearing through its fuselage.

I sighed. "Nice shot, Vrynn, but this plan will only work if the ship is still intact to make it back to their base."

Vrynn slunk down a bit in her chair. "Oh. Right. Sorry about that."

I steered the ship in a wide arc, searching for the two remaining enemy fighters. My tactical console showed one was directly above us. I pulled our nose up to see if I could find him, but just as I did, a stream of plasma rounds rained down on us.

The ship's alarms began to sound, and several indicators on my control consoles lit up. "What did they hit?" I asked.

"Several of the front ion deflectors," Tera said. "That's not good, Mitch. If they hit the same spots, we could take some serious damage. I recommend disengaging."

I gritted my teeth and pulled a wide loop to get in closer to the enemy fighter. "We can't give up yet. We need to get a tracker on one of these ships."

More plasma rounds streaked past us. The third interceptor joined the fray from my other side.

"Just keep the other ship off me while I track this one," I said.

Vrynn brought our cannons to bear on the third ship, firing wildly. Nothing made solid contact, but the third ship must have been wary enough that it fell far behind us.

I matched the second ship's maneuvers as it tried to evade us. At this speed, I didn't see any way that we could get close enough. The enemy fighters were simply too maneuverable. The only time they would fly in a straight line was if—

"We need to get one of them on our tail," I said.

"What?!" Vrynn and Tera said at the same time.

I continued following the ship in front of me, but not as aggressively, making it look like I was losing my edge. "The only way we can get one of them close enough is if they're following us." I turned to Tera. "I assume the harpoon can fire backward."

"Sure. But this is crazy," Tera said.

I nodded. "Maybe."

I continued watching for my opportunity to do what every pilot is taught not to do. I was going to make a usually fatal mistake in dogfighting. I was going to get in front of my enemy.

The fighter in front of me made a tight turn, attempting to shake me. Normally, it would have been no problem to stay with him, but this time, I intentionally overshot the turn—without slowing my speed.

I can only imagine his surprise when he reversed his S-loop and found me right in front of him. I let my throttle ease off slightly.

"This is crazy, Mitch," Tera said with an anxious tone in her voice.

"Luckily, the rear deflectors are intact," I said. "It's the ones in the nose that were damaged, right?"

"The rear deflectors are at eighty percent," Tera replied.

Dozens of plasma rounds streaked by—several impacting the rear of our hull—as the enemy ship closed in on us.

"Oh, actually now they're at fifty percent," Tera said.

"He's on the edge of our range," Vrynn said as she prepared to fire.

"Wait." I held up a hand. "Just a little closer."

Vrynn's attention shifted from her targeting screen to me and back, waiting for my order.

"C'mon, buddy. Get a little closer," I muttered.

Another round of plasma shots rocked the ship.

"Thirty percent, Mitch!" Tera shrieked.

"Now! Fire!" I yelled.

A powerful explosion rocked the ship just as Vrynn launched the modified harpoon at our trailing target.

I held my breath as Vrynn watched the ship behind us.

"It missed!" Vrynn called.

I slammed my fist against the side console. "Do we have another one?"

"No," Vrynn said.

Another volley of plasma rounds rocked the ship. I pulled up out of our dive to leave enough maneuvering space above the icy ground. "How long would it take to get one ready?"

"The primary databank that feeds my matrix just lost power," Tera announced. "The secondary system doesn't—"

Tera's hologram suddenly vanished mid sentence. I looked through the empty space between the pilot's seats and saw Vrynn staring back at me, wide eyed.

"Tera?" I called out. "What happened? Can you still hear me?"

I tapped the status console next to me, hoping to see that her matrix was still running or, at the very least, still intact. It showed the status as *Inoperative - Critical Degradation Imminent.*

"We're about to lose Tera's matrix," I yelled.

"Our weapons systems just went offline," Vrynn cried. She looked over at me.

"We have to get back to the base," I said, knowing she was thinking the exact same thing. I pulled the ship into a modest climb and activated the orbital boost. The interceptors followed close on our tail.

I tapped the controls, trying to remember how to activate the intra-space jump. Tera had usually handled that part.

"You can't make a direct jump, Mitch," Vrynn said when she saw what I was doing. "They'll track our heading."

"What do you want me to do?" I shot back. "Tera's offline, and so are the star charts. It would take hours to program a double jump."

Vrynn closed her eyes, shaking her head. "No. No. That'll lead them right to us, and we cannot let Gralik capture the *Starfire*."

"We don't have any other choice," I replied as I did my best to dodge incoming weapons fire. "Besides, everyone knows the Mezok system is quarantined. I doubt they'll follow us."

Another explosion rocked the ship as I waited for Vrynn to agree to the direct jump.

Finally, she let out a long breath and nodded. "Okay, do it."

Vrynn continued her defensive firing as I engaged the intra-space drive for our jump back to Mela Suphoria.

All that effort for nothing.

Chapter Fourteen

As soon as the landing skids touched the ground in our hangar on Mela Suphoria, I jumped from my seat and ran for the cargo bay. Within a minute, I had the diagnostic system plugged into the ship.

I watched the system slowly work through various sub-routines, all the while hoping that Tera's AI matrix hadn't suffered irreparable damage.

"Diagnostic complete," a robotic voice finally said. "AI Matrix secured. No further degradation anticipated."

I sagged in relief.

After some additional investigation, we discovered that Tera had gone offline because of a power system failure, not any problems with her matrix itself. Vrynn and I spent the next few hours pulling out damaged components and searching the production facility for replacement parts. Fortunately, we didn't have to cannibalize any of the nearly finished ships. Those were the ones we hoped to get space-worthy soon—the beginning of our Resistance space fleet.

"We'll need to fix the other systems that were damaged in the fight," I said as Vrynn and I worked to replace power sub-components. "The deflector emitters should probably be first. Then the weapons system."

Vrynn nodded her agreement then fell silent.

After a few minutes, I finally said. "Sorry our mission at the casino was such a failure."

She shook her head. "It wasn't a failure."

"Really?" I said. "I figured since we came away empty-handed, plus with a busted ship, that might count as a loss."

Vrynn shrugged. "Maybe. But now we know where we can find Gralik. Next time we'll just hide in orbit and monitor his intra-space jump from the casino. We won't even need a tracking device."

I shook my head. "I can't believe you can still be so optimistic about this." I had to admit—if only to myself—that in some ways she was right. It was a big step in the right direction. I wagged a finger at her playfully. "One of these days, I'm going to figure out something that you can't be optimistic about."

I got back to work on the power system I was trying to fix. Unfortunately, without Tera to ask questions, I was stuck with the most rudimentary version of the ship's diagnostics system. And it didn't speak very good English.

After two more trips to the main factory building, I was able to scrounge the final part—a fried relay—to get Tera's power systems back online.

I plugged in a new relay and watched the higher-functioning systems start to come online. A few seconds later, Tera shimmered into view.

I let out a breath of relief.

"—have enough to . . ." Tera looked around at the flight deck. It was almost as if she could see with her holographic eyes. In reality, her matrix was absorbing inputs from the various ship's sensors. "We're back in my hangar on Mela Suphoria," she stated bluntly.

I nodded, wondering if I needed to give her more information or if I should wait for her to ask questions. I settled on a simple welcome back. "It's good to see you, Tera."

"You too," she said. "At some point I'll have to tell you what a weird feeling it is to jump forward in time like that."

I smiled. It seemed like she was still her normal self.

"But that'll have to wait because we're under attack."

I sat up straight. "What?"

"The ship is tied into the facility which still has a patchy connection to the defensive satellite network around the planet. A few minutes ago, five Varusian interceptors came out of intra-space and entered orbit."

"Does the satellite network read any transponder signals?" I asked.

"No," Tera replied.

"Nexus ships," I muttered to myself. I stood and rushed out the flight deck door. "Vrynn, they found us!" I called out. I turned back to Tera who was still standing in the entrance to the flight deck. "How much time do we have before they get here?"

"They are entering the atmosphere now. They'll be in range to scan the surface in about five minutes. If they pick up the energy signature from the main plant and alter course, they could be here in ten minutes."

I bolted for the stairs and slid down to the lower deck. "Vrynn!" I yelled.

Vrynn stuck her head out from a crawl space into the right wing. "What?"

"Nexus ships just entered orbit. We have to shut everything down," I said as I ran through the cargo bay. "Tera, make sure the ship isn't emitting anything," I called over my shoulder as I bounded down the ramp.

I sprinted as fast as I could for the production facility's main building. It was possible that Tera didn't have the sensor range to pick up transponder signals, and those Varusian ships were simply on an exploration mission. Even still, I didn't want to broadcast our position to them. But given that Varus Prime had known Nexus-affiliated factions within its defense forces—namely, Gralik and his Vanguard Dragoons—those ships could be searching for us, and the emissions from the factory would paint a bull's eye on our location.

I tore through the side door and onto the factory floor, stopping for a second to get my bearings, trying to figure out what I should shut off first. I ran along the row of waiting ships toward the engine stand with the stress-test setup. That was probably giving off the most obvious energy signature. Despite the information we were gaining from the test, we probably shouldn't have left it running all this time. Or at least, we should have set up a remote kill switch.

After powering down the engine, I looked around at the rest of the facility. I knew that two of the nearly finished ships were running in standby mode on their power systems. Those should be switched off next.

I ran back to the ships at the front of the line. Vrynn came pelting into the warehouse just as I reached the front.

"I shut off the engine test." I pointed to the front ship. "You shut down that one, I'll get this one."

Vrynn nodded and ran inside the lead ship while I went up the ramp into the second one. I was greeted by a copy of Dack, the default AI matrix. "What task can I help you with?"

"Shut down all systems!" I yelled as I hurried to the nearest control console in the cargo bay.

"Systems can return to standby mode within—"

"No. Power down everything. Shut off all power systems as if you were offline," I instructed.

Dack tilted his head and frowned. "Shutting off all power is not standard procedure. It could result in—"

"It's an emergency. Do it now!"

He stared straight forward. "Shutting down all systems," the AI said.

Dack flickered away and a few seconds later, the rest of the power started switching off. I waited until the cargo bay was completely black and the console was blank. I ran back down the ramp and met Vrynn between the first two ships.

"What else do we need to shut down?" she asked breathlessly.

I opened my mouth to reply when Tera's voice broke through on my comm device. "Mitch, the ships have entered the atmosphere and changed course for our region."

I winced.

"They might not know exactly where the factory is, though," she continued. "So it could take them a while to find us."

I looked at Vrynn. "Everything off," I said. "You get the main reactor. I'll get the other ships."

She nodded curtly, and we ran in opposite directions.

"Tera, you need to power down the *Starfire*, too. And no more transmissions, okay. I'm shutting off my comm."

"Got it," Tera replied.

I pulled out my communicator and powered it completely off.

A few seconds later, the overhead lights in the factory went completely out.

Back on Earth, I'd had plenty of times where I was without technology like my cell phone—though that was never fun—or electricity in general, like the times I would go backwoods camping with my uncles. But standing in the middle of an alien production facility, with my communicator powered down and the lights suddenly cut, felt eerie. I could imagine some unknown beast, like the elephant spider we faced in the city, rising up out of the shadows to devour me.

I had to remind myself that this facility had been mothballed until just a few weeks earlier, when Vrynn and I had found it. It wasn't too scary to have it go dark again. And we had walked up and down inside the building and never found any monsters.

Of course, there was a small part of my brain that still thought it was possible.

I turned to the long row of partially built ships standing in the faint light filtering in through the high windows, and I refocused on the task at hand. None of these other ships were fully functional yet, nor did they have their AI matrices loaded. But most of them had auxiliary power systems that had been charged and tested.

At each ship in the long row, I ran aboard the ramp, through the door into the lower hallway and found the master power coupling. The fastest way to make sure there weren't any errant power signatures was to throw the switch on that coupling. Of course, that plunged the entire lower deck into darkness—floor guide-lights and all. So each time I disabled the ship's power, I had to be careful not to trip on the way back out as my eyes adjusted to the gloom.

With all the power systems disabled, I returned stealthily to the front of the assembly line. Vrynn met me there. We looked around and then at each other.

"They can't detect us now. This will work," she said.

I shrugged. "I guess we'll have to wait and see."

We both looked up at the dark rafters high above our heads. Silent seconds ticked by as I held my breath.

Would we know when they had arrived?

Or better yet, would we know when it was safe to turn everything back on?

"I wish we could ask Tera if they're still coming toward us," I whispered.

Vrynn nodded in response. My eyes had adjusted almost fully to the darkness now, and I could see the hopeful look on her face.

After a minute, a faint rumbling sound slowly began to grow in the distance.

I glanced down at Vrynn, wondering if she heard it, too.

As the thundering sound slowly increased, Vrynn shook her head more and more emphatically, almost as if she could prevent them from finding us by simply denying reality.

A few seconds later, multiple engines rumbled overhead.

I reached out and put an arm around Vrynn's shoulder. "I'm sorry."

She looked up at me with those gorgeous eyes, deep, dark blue in the murky shadows. "Why?"

I took a breath. "I'm sorry I risked everything with that direct jump. I wish we had—"

Vrynn held a hand up in front of my mouth. "It wasn't your fault. We made that decision together."

I nodded. Obviously, I hadn't met that many people in the Bonara Cluster, but I was so glad that Vrynn had been assigned by the Resistance to wait for the ship on Thetis Max. I was glad she was the one I was stuck with in a darkened starship facility waiting to be discovered by enemy soldiers.

Well, I wasn't really glad about the being discovered part. But I'm glad she was the one.

We ran to one of the dusty windows and stared in disbelief as five Varusian interceptors landed in the large staging area in front of the factory doors. The ramps of two of the ships opened and soldiers poured out.

Suddenly, Vrynn grabbed my arm, and I immediately realized why.

The soldiers were headed right for us.

"Hide!" she hissed as she pulled me behind a collection of long-dead robotic assembly arms.

We had just ducked out of view when the access door burst open and Nexus soldiers began pouring into the dark factory, plasma rifles raised and ready. I hunkered down against Vrynn, shielding her from view, instinctively protecting her with my body.

She grunted softly and nudged me. I didn't think it was a good idea to move at the moment, so I stayed still, waiting to see what the Nexus forces would do.

"Uh, it's sweet of you to be so protective," Vrynn whispered. "But if they find you, they're going to find me, too. Besides, I can't see anything," she added with a smirk.

I shook my head in disbelief that she could make a joke at a time like this. I shifted away to give her room to move. Together, we peered over the edge of a robot arm, just barely able to see the area in front of the hangar doors.

About a dozen soldiers stood milling around, talking casually with each other, apparently waiting for something to happen.

"If I'd realized how nosey our neighbors are, I would've locked that door," I said drily.

Vrynn's lips quivered, but she quickly schooled her expression. "We can just surrender now if you're going to make me laugh," she whispered, giving me a dirty look.

A loud grinding sound came from the front of the building, and we watched as the large hangar doors slowly slid open and more soldiers spilled in.

Gralik strode through the middle, exuding authority and barking orders.

My stomach sank. Not only had we been discovered by Nexus forces, but it was Gralik himself who had come to enjoy the victory.

He circled the first ship like a hyena ready to pounce. When he spoke, his hollow voice echoed from the rafters. "This is more than I could have dreamed! An entire fleet of advanced ships." His voice was almost gleeful.

A cold chill ran down my body.

Everything Vrynn and I had hoped to accomplish for the Resistance was now in the clutches of the Nexus leader.

Gralik pointed at an officer trailing behind him. "Send a transmission back to base that they don't have to kill the scientists for not making the

Quake Drive work in my runabout." He turned his gaze to the Mark 7 on the end of the line, rubbing his hands together. "I have a new ship now."

A feeling of dread began to creep through my middle. We had found the production facility, prepared half a dozen ships to be space worthy, and then—without realizing—delivered it all to Nexus on a silver platter.

The factory doors were open wide, the first two ships were mostly operational—at least flyable. All Gralik had to do was power them up and fly away. With the technology of these ships, he would easily consolidate his power within the BDF forces.

It was our worst nightmare coming true.

And there was only one way to fix it.

"We have to destroy them," I whispered.

"There's no way we can take out dozens of soldiers," Vrynn said. "I'm not that amazing."

"I'm not talking about—"

"But if we jump in the *Starfire* and strafe the whole area, we'll take out most of them. Then we pick off the rest of them one-by-one."

"The weapons system on the *Starfire* is still out of commission," I said.

"Well, I don't know what you had in mind for taking out the soldiers, but I'm sure we can come up with—"

"I wasn't talking about the soldiers. I was talking about our ships."

Vrynn stared back at me, almost as if her translator chip hadn't processed my words correctly.

She shook her head emphatically. "No. No way. We're not losing these ships, not when we almost have what we need to take on Nexus. We can't just blow them all up. That's not happening."

I waited a moment, giving her a chance to watch Nexus soldiers move around and poke and prod our ships, before I said, "Would you rather Gralik get the ships?"

A few seconds later, her expression morphed from denial and defiance to resignation.

I crept away from our hiding spot, moving deeper into the dark shadows of the assembly line. "C'mon, Vrynn," I quietly waved her toward me.

She seemed to be rooted to the spot, gazing at the ground in front of her but not really seeing anything. "I can't believe this is happening," she whispered.

"We need to do this now, before they figure out how to power up the first ship," I said. "They only need one to get the Quake Drive installed."

That seemed to snap Vrynn out of her daze. We crept along the side wall until we reached a safer part of the facility, away from the Nexus soldiers.

"Do the ships have enough ammo to trigger a self-destruct?" I asked.

Vrynn shook her head. "The weapons are designed not to self-destruct."

"What about the engine cores?" I pressed. "Could we overload those?"

"The safety protocols would kick in. It would take too long to override the programing."

Vrynn didn't seem her usual optimistic self. She was dragging her feet, hoping we wouldn't have to do this.

"Vrynn, if we don't come up with a solution in the next minute, it'll be too late."

Her brow furrowed in concentration. "What if we used the weapons loaded in the ships to destroy them?"

"Didn't I just say that? You said self-destruct wouldn't work."

"No, not a self-destruct," Vrynn said. "Have the ships destroy each other."

I thought about it. With the deflector plates offline, the ships definitely had enough firepower to destroy each other. "Okay, how do we fire the weapons?"

"Remote connection." She looked at me with a smirk. "Unless you want to do it manually."

"No, thanks."

"These ships all have the AI installed." Vrynn waved a hand at the mostly finished ships at the end of the line. "We could connect to their—"

"I just went through and shut them all down."

She frowned. "We can't use the weapons at all unless the power is on."

I glanced back toward the front of the building, where I could hear the Nexus soldiers clomping around near the end of the assembly line.

"I don't think there's any way we can get to the last two ships. But the weapons on this one," I pointed to the third ship in the column, "could take out the first two, and that might start a chain reaction that will destroy the rest."

Vrynn's entire body sagged. The reality of what we had to do was setting in. Finally, she nodded. "I'll go set up a remote overload of the power reactor. That should take care of the rest of the factory."

I touched her arm. "We can do this," I said in an uncharacteristic show of optimism. "Meet me out back when you're done."

"Be careful," she said as we separated.

Moving back toward the assembly line, I could hear the soldiers talking excitedly as they inspected the ships. I waited until the soldiers were all out of sight then darted across to the row of waiting ships.

Hiding behind the front skid of the fourth ship. I wasn't sure if any of the soldiers had gone inside the third ship, so I gazed up into the dark cargo bay, watching for any movement. Just as I stood to make my move, a soldier emerged onto the ramp. I stepped back behind the skid again, trying to make my profile as thin as possible.

"No power in this one," the soldier called out as he walked back to the front of the line.

That made me wish I had thrown the main power coupler on the first two ships. It might have made it harder for Gralik to figure out how to power them back on. Of course, they would never abandon the ships just because the power was off. That was wishful thinking. But maybe if their focus was on the first two ships, I could sneak onto the third one.

After checking for additional soldiers, I dashed across the gap between the ships and stepped softly up the ramp into the cargo bay. The space was empty and dark.

I crossed to the engineering room and found the master relay that I had barely disabled a few minutes ago.

When I reengaged the main power systems, all the lights on the ship suddenly came on. Instinctively, I ducked below the pilot's console, awkwardly mashing at the button to turn off the internal lighting, hoping that no one had been looking at the ship at that exact moment. I checked the ship's weapons inventory—a full complement of atmospheric missiles and plasma cannons—then I linked my control pad to the firing controls. After double-checking everything, I made my way down to the cargo bay.

At the top of the ramp, I listened for anyone nearby. The soldiers were making such a racket with the first two ships, they would never hear me sneaking out of the third one. Of course, I wouldn't hear a soldier approaching me, either.

Crouching low, I padded down the ramp and hid myself among the assembly line equipment. Once I could tell no one had seen me, I snuck to the back door of the factory and quietly let myself out. Keeping close to the walls of the building, I crept around the outside until I was halfway to the power reactor.

Suddenly, Vrynn came around the corner.

I nearly jumped out of my skin.

"Everything set?" she asked.

"Yep," I said, patting my control pad. "How about you?"

"I jammed both safety release valves. All we need to do is turn the system to maximum and it shouldn't be long."

I nodded. "Let's get to a safe distance first."

We wove our way through the overgrown trees surrounding the factory until we found a cluster that offered a good hiding place. From that vantage point, we could see through the giant, sliding doors. Most of the first ship in the line was visible.

Nexus soldiers stood in clusters around the ship, and I could even see several of them through the flight deck windows.

I pulled out my control pad and prepared to fire the third ship's weapons.

Vrynn grabbed my hand. "Wait, Mitch. Are we sure we have to do this?"

I looked at her, knowing what losing these ships meant to the Resistance cause. But I also knew what Nexus gaining control of them would mean to anyone who would dare to defy them. "We have to, Vrynn." I nodded back toward the assembly line. "Any second now, they're going to figure out how to get the ships moving, and then it will be too late."

"But what if they don't take the ships right away? What if they think they've got this place secured and they leave a few guards and come back later? We could steal back the ships that are flyable and then blow up the rest." Vrynn gave me a pleading look.

I really wanted to hope that we could save the ships, but I knew it was a long shot, and I'm sure Vrynn knew it, too. But for her benefit, we waited.

A few minutes later, there was a commotion near the sliding doors. Soldiers started backing away from the building as if a skunk had suddenly appeared. A soldier inside yelled something I couldn't quite make out, and the other soldiers outside repeated it.

"Clear for Launch."

As soon as my implant had translated the shouted phrase, I turned to Vrynn. She stared straight ahead in disbelief. A second later, the engines on the lead ship roared to life, and it gracefully lifted into a hover. The Mark 7 slipped backward and then to the side a bit as the pilot learned to control the large vessel.

"We have to do it now, Vrynn. They're going to fly that ship away and we won't be able to stop them." I pulled my control pad out and activated the link to the third ship's weapons system.

At that moment, the strangest thing happened. Skeeter came bounding toward us from the direction of the Nexus ships. Several plasma rounds hit near her, but she leapt forward, dodging each shot. Without even knowing we were there, she sailed past our hiding spot on the trail toward the *Starfire's* hangar out on the runway. A soldier chasing her came into view, pausing every few seconds to fire his plasma rifle. Skeeter was long gone by this point.

To my dismay, he skidded to a stop right next to our hiding place and fired several more rounds before giving up the chase. As he lowered his rifle in defeat, he glanced over and saw Vrynn and me hunkered down in the shrubs.

I had my gun out of its holster just as he raised his rifle. I fired first, striking him twice in the chest. He fell backward, firing. Several plasma rounds streaked over our heads and exploded against the trunks of trees behind us.

Vrynn and I stared at each other, wide-eyed. "That was close," she said.

"Let's blow the factory and get out of here before anyone else finds us."

She nodded and pulled out the control pad she'd linked to the reactor. I did the same with my ship-linked control pad.

I looked back at the factory. The first ship was now floating halfway out of the hangar.

We were out of time.

Vrynn set the reactor to overload while I activated the third ship's targeting system. The second ship blocked its view of the first ship. There were corners of the first ship visible, but nothing substantial enough for the system to get a lock on. I locked two of the atmospheric rockets on the second ship—that part was easy. Then manually aimed the other two rockets.

I fired all four missiles simultaneously. Two easily struck the second ship in the line—maybe even entering through its open cargo bay door—and the inside of the factory lit up with explosions. The other two rockets streaked out of the hangar and struck the ship the Nexus soldiers were attempting to steal. They both exploded on impact, creating an enormous fireball in front of the assembly building.

The explosions shook the ground and sent a shockwave that plastered us behind our stand of trees. I sat up and checked Vrynn. She was as surprised as I was, but not injured. Next, I selected the remote ship's plasma cannons and set them on continuous, random firing. The front door of the factory looked like a fireworks plant that just had a match dropped inside. Bright plasma rounds and secondary explosions shot out into the surrounding area.

It was complete chaos.

"Let's get to the *Starfire*," I said as I pulled Vrynn to her feet.

I cast a quick glance over my shoulder. The handful of Nexus soldiers who survived the blast were picking themselves up and looking around in a daze.

They weren't a threat to us.

I could only hope that Gralik was among the casualties.

More explosions echoed from the factory building as we ran through the underbrush back to the *Starfire's* hangar. Each blast felt simultaneously like triumph and defeat.

We rushed up the open cargo bay ramp. "Tera, get the ship ready to take off," I called out.

I passed Skeeter on my way to the upper deck. Why she had been playing outside the ship in the middle of a sabotage mission was beyond me. I'd have to check her systems later to make sure they were functioning properly. I couldn't help but chuckle at how long my list of things to check later was getting. I wondered if I'd survive long enough to do even half of them.

I jumped into the pilot's seat just as the ship hovered backward out of the hangar. A second later, Vrynn was in the seat beside me. I stared at the small building that we'd called home for the past several weeks, knowing that we would never be safe here again. If I'd known we would have to leave so soon, I would have loaded more supplies to take with us.

I flew the ship back toward the factory. We needed to know how much had been destroyed. Not that we could do much with the weapons systems still off-line. The staging area in front of the main building was engulfed in flames and smoke. Several Nexus ships had been severely damaged, though one or two still looked operable.

A quick glance at the opposite end of the main building told me that the power reactor had finally overloaded. There wasn't much left that wasn't already burning or wouldn't soon be.

I circled the facility, knowing that I couldn't stay too long without risking a very one-sided engagement with the few remaining interceptors.

But I needed to know if we'd been successful.

The ships left inside the main building were certainly destroyed; the roof over that part of the assembly line had already collapsed from the explosions. But the front of the building, with the first Mark 7 in the line, was standing. And we still couldn't see if that first ship had been destroyed or not. The area was shrouded in smoke, but what parts of the ground I could see were littered with shrapnel, spaceship parts, and Nexus soldiers.

The smoke momentarily cleared, revealing the last remaining Mark 7 entirely intact, maneuvering forward out of the burning factory.

We hadn't destroyed it.

I looked over at Vrynn, ready to ask if she had any ideas how we could destroy it, when Tera said, "Two Nexus ships powering up."

I glanced at my tactical console and saw that one of the pilots was already in the cockpit with the canopy down, the other was almost ready to lift off. They would be airborne in less than half a minute.

Normally, we could easily take them out, but not without our weapons systems.

I jammed the throttle to full power and sent the ship skyward.

Maybe Gralik had been killed in the blast.

Not that it really mattered. Someone would just take his place. And now Nexus forces had the last remaining Mark 7 besides *Starfire*.

I glanced at Vrynn sitting in the co-pilot's seat, staring blankly ahead.

Our dream of building a fleet of advanced Mark 7 ships had died today. And with it, one of the last hopes the Resistance had for combating the rising power of Nexus.

And if Gralik had survived, the Resistance was as good as dead.

Chapter Fifteen

Except for the clicking of relays and the whirring of cooling units, the flight deck was dead silent for several seconds. Then Vrynn stood and rushed out without a word. The glimpse I caught of her face made me think she was near tears.

I stared straight ahead at the nondescript brownish-gray of intra-space, and swallowed against the lump forming in my throat. We had worked so hard, and now it had all been snatched away from us. It was like I was in a nightmare where everything had come crashing down around me. I simply sat in the pilot's chair, feeling empty.

We had lost.

We'd lost the chance to destroy the Mark 7 ship, the chance to beat Gralik, the chance to prevent Nexus from gaining the power of the Quake Drive.

In fact, we had led them right to us. Our jump from Daeko III, when we had been so desperate to save the *Starfire* and Tera, had led Gralik right to Mela Suphoria.

And this was the result.

Now we had nowhere to go. No way to stop the inevitable. I wasn't even sure where we were headed.

"Vrynn is usually the optimistic one," Tera said softly. "I can have the computer calculate some success probabilities, but I'm not sure that would be helpful. I wish I could have—"

I held up my hand. "It's okay, Tera. You don't have to offer any false hope. I'm not sure I want that right now, anyway." I stood and trudged out of the flight deck over to the kitchen.

I walked over to the food fabricator and just stared at the screen for several minutes, not really seeing anything. I took a deep breath. "Fabricator, do you have anything that can numb the pain of disappointment?" I wasn't expecting it to say anything. It was more of an observation of what I was feeling, really.

"This unit can mix a mild pain reliever into any type of food or drink," the machine's voice said mechanically.

I sighed. A mild pain reliever wasn't going to cut it. "Can't you mix me something stronger?" I asked with a defeated chuckle.

"This unit can dispense various narcotics, sedatives, and antidepressants when supplied with the necessary chemical ingredients," the machine explained.

"Do you have the ingredients for any of those things?" I asked hopefully.

"Negative," the machine replied.

"Then why did you offer to . . ." I ran a hand through my hair. "Nevermind. Do you have anything else that you can add based on the chemicals you have on hand?"

"This unit can add a variety of diuretics, emetics, and laxatives to food or drink," it responded.

I rolled my eyes. Why would anyone want those things during a moment of emotional distress? I'd have to tweak this machine's subroutines at some point. "You know what? Just give me a big bowl of vanilla ice cream."

The machine didn't really know how to make a true homemade vanilla ice cream, but I'd previously modified a frozen dessert it already had in its system to be something close enough. Of course, I really wished I could have been back in my hometown sitting in the corner booth of Bob's Burgers with my best friend, Gabe, eating a heaping bowl of ice cream.

But no amount of wishing was going to make it so.

"Would you like a laxative added to that?" the machine asked, pulling me from my thoughts.

"No, I don't want a laxative added to it," I nearly yelled. Then I decided maybe the machine needed to be fixed right there. "In fact, I never want you to ask or even accept the instructions from me at any point in the future to add laxative to my ice cream. Is that understood?"

"Affirmative. Customization implemented." The machine whirred for a minute before the dispenser door opened and presented its approximation of ice cream.

I grabbed the bowl and sat glumly at the table. A lot of good it would do to customize the food fabricator to my specific needs now that we were living on borrowed time. Once Gralik had the Quake Drive installed in the other Mark 7, hunting down and killing us would be that much easier.

Shoveling spoon after spoon of ice cream into my mouth, I reflected on how screwed we were. Even after a second bowl—that I asked the machine to mix in a musky substitute for chocolate—and a third bowl—that the computer volunteered to flavor with a strange green root that I decided I didn't particularly care for—the situation still felt hopeless.

When my stomach finally threatened a revolt, I stood from the table, threw my bowl in the processor, and made my way down to the cargo bay. I walked between tall stacks of bins, most of which I still hadn't gotten around to cataloging, until I found Rascal's nest, back in the tail of the ship.

The giant beast grunted when he saw me approach, the closest thing he had to a playful bark. I scooched in next to him and leaned against his broad black haunches. He didn't seem to mind.

"What am I doing, Rascal?" I asked, as if he could counsel me on my life choices. "I thought I was doing the right thing trying to find Gabe's killers, but I seemed to have messed that up. And then my attempt to help the Resistance has definitely landed us in a worse situation than before."

At my prolonged silence, Rascal turned his head to me and nudged, clearly wanting me to keep talking. If he weren't so scary to look at, he might've had a future as an emotional therapy animal.

"Maybe I should just have Vrynn take me back to Earth. She could keep the *Starfire* and continue the fight against Nexus. She'd be pretty much out of fuel, but at least she'd be rid of a completely inept ship commander. Wouldn't that be for the best? I mean, I've done nothing but screw things up since she met me."

"No, you haven't," Vrynn's voice echoed from around a stack of crates.

I looked up and saw her small, lithe figure approach. I was struck again with how much she really did look like a water nymph of Earth lore. She leaned against a nearby bulkhead, considering me with those sea-blue eyes. "You know, this is a relatively small ship. How was it this hard to find you?" she said.

"Rascal has the right idea, making his nest here away from all the excitement." Rascal whined when he heard his name, so I rubbed his belly.

Vrynn squared her shoulders. "We'll get through this, Mitch. We just need to figure out our next plan. There has to be a way to use this ship to take down Gralik and Nexus."

I gazed up at her. This was almost too easy. "You know, oppressive military factions aren't really affected by optimism." I added a grin so she would know I meant it in good humor—albeit gallows humor. I had expected her usually upbeat response or the playful way she would ignore me, even when she knew I was right.

Instead, Vrynn sunk down to the floor in front of me, a look of utter defeat on her beautiful face. "I know. It seems like none of my optimism makes a difference. I'm not sure what to do next." She gazed at me for a long time.

As I considered her, I couldn't believe how much my feelings for Vrynn had changed over the past two weeks, and I couldn't imagine going back to Earth and being without her.

At Vrynn's nearness to his nest, Rascal rolled to the side, probably making room for her.

She considered the large animal for a moment, then looked up at me. Finally, she scooted forward and settled her back against Rascal, leaning her head gently on my shoulder.

"If you really want me to take you back to Dirt, I can," she said quietly.

I stared down at her silvery blond head. This wasn't my normally intrepid co-pilot; she seemed so small and fragile. "I don't really want to go," I said. "But I'm beginning to think you might be better off. I always messed things up on Earth, and apparently I'm an expert at screwing up in the Bonara cluster, too."

"That's not true," Vrynn said, shaking her head gently against my arm. "Things are better when you're around."

It was such a simple statement, yet so full of possible meanings.

As I opened my mouth to ask what she meant, Tera appeared in front of us.

She looked at Vrynn and me resting next to each other then gave me a look that said, "I told you so." I wasn't willing to read too much into it yet, but it certainly wasn't a bad feeling having her leaning comfortably against me.

"I know you've told me that I need to let you know when something important has happened, like, not wait until later, but tell you when it matters," Tera said.

"Yeah?" I replied. There wasn't much she could do to cheer up the situation, but it was nice of her to try.

"So, after we had to cut communications while you were working on sabotaging the factory, I had Skeeter sneak over and plant a tracking device on one of the Nexus ships. I'm getting the telemetry transmission of their jump through intra-space. I can calculate their expected destination if you want."

Vrynn and I both scrambled to our feet.

Tera stepped back in surprise. "Did I mess up?" she asked cautiously.

Vrynn jumped at Tera, arms wide. Clearly, Vrynn must have temporarily forgotten that—as a hologram—Tera didn't have any substance. She sailed right through Tera's projection, leaving shimmery disturbances in her wake.

Tera watched Vrynn stumble to regain her balance. "What was that for?"

Vrynn laughed. "For a second, I forgot that you're not solid. I tried to give you a hug."

"Ah, that's so sweet," Tera cooed.

We stood in the cargo bay, smiling at each other for a while. I felt more energized than I had since arriving in the Bonara Cluster.

Tera's eyes lost their focus momentarily. She turned to me. "We're receiving telemetry from the tracking device. They're headed for Zerlon Prime."

Vrynn and I shared a look of determination.

"I think it's our turn to pay them an unexpected visit," I said.

Chapter Sixteen

I gripped the controls nervously. I could feel my palms sweating, and I hated it. I turned to Vrynn, sitting on the other side of Tera's floating image. "You're sure your friends are going to be there, right?"

"I don't know if I'd call them friends, but they've been pretty reliable in the past, and they're the only fighters I could get on such short notice—actually, they're the only fighters I could get, period. We have to make do with what we've got. At least they hate Nexus as much as we do."

"You gave them the coordinates, though?" I asked.

"Yes," Vrynn replied.

"And you told them what time we need them?" I pressed.

"Yes." I could hear the annoyance starting to creep into Vrynn's voice. "But just know they're not really the punctual type."

I took a deep breath and tried to relax. Plenty could go wrong with this mission, particularly if our planned diversion didn't go as expected.

"Maybe you should contact them again, just to make sure they know how important it is," I said.

Vrynn rolled her eyes. "Mitch. If they're going to come, they'll come. Nagging them about it isn't going to change anything."

I nodded. "I guess we're ready then."

I steered the ship out of our orbit around the Zerlon star to an intercept course with Zerlon Prime. The bright, pale-yellow planet grew steadily larger as we approached. I checked my console, making sure everything was online, we wouldn't be using any weapons for the first phase of our mission, all bets were off after that.

"The sensors say there's a detection grid around the planet," Tera said with a note of concern in her voice.

"Can you show it on the display?" I asked.

A holographic image of Zerlon Prime floated in the air above our consoles surrounded by dozens of red dots in orbit.

"Can we destroy one with the lasers?" Vrynn asked.

"We could. But that would probably trigger the grid the same as if we passed by it," I said. "What if we try and garble the transmission back to the planet?"

Vrynn's brow went up. "That could work. But if we get close enough to affect its transmitting ability, it would probably have detected us already." She tapped a finger to her lips. "Could we try squeezing in through a gap in the grid?"

I shrugged. "Are there any gaps in the grid?"

We both turned to look at Tera, hoping she would know the answer.

Tera sighed. "No, there aren't any gaps in the grid. And no, we can't destroy or jam it. Why don't we just ask the other ship to turn one of them off?"

"Ask the other ship?" I asked.

"Yeah, back on Mela Suphoria, when the Nexus soldiers took over the factory, I contacted the other ship's AI and told him that his ship was being stolen and that he should try not to help them."

I gaped at her. "You have a connection with the other ship?"

"What? No! I don't even like Dack. He's weird. Besides—"

I held up a hand. "No, I don't mean that you like him, but that you have a communication line connected with him."

Tera shrugged like it was no big deal. "Sure. I mean, I'm not talking to him right now, I didn't want Nexus to intercept a transmission. But I probably could ask him to put one of the detection satellites to sleep or something."

I looked over at Vrynn who beamed with excitement. "This changes things," I said.

"I told you we could do it," she replied.

"Tera, see if Dack can tap into the Nexus computer system to control the detection grid," I said. "Tell him we need to slip through. If you think it would help, say that we'd like to rescue him and his ship if we can."

While Tera was doing her best to convince the other ship's AI to help us, Vrynn and I went over the plan for infiltrating the Nexus base. We weren't really sure how long it would take Gralik's team to install the Quake Drive, but the clock was ticking. If we didn't get there before they finished, our chances of getting it back were next to zero.

"Okay, Dack says he'll help us," Tera said. "He can't turn off the satellite, but he can trick the individual sensors with a loop."

"That's good enough," I said as I entered the coordinates into the console.

Vrynn stood. "I'll get our gear ready."

"So you're saying that I'm such an amazing zero-G pilot that you trust me to maneuver the *Starfire* through the grid and into position?"

She put a hand on my shoulder. "No. I'm saying I'd rather die in a fireball because of your pitiful piloting skills than be caught and executed."

I grinned like an idiot, partly because I really did think she trusted me—to a point, and partly because her hand on my shoulder felt so natural—and nice.

Hopefully, I wouldn't screw things up.

I brought the ship out of high orbit, aiming for the temporary gap in their grid. As we approached the detection net, we passed within just a few hundred meters of the spoofed satellite—a close brush in orbital terms. I held my breath as we floated past, knowing that if it didn't work, we'd have dozens of Nexus ships on us in a matter of minutes.

Tera kept an open channel with the other ship's AI long enough to know that we'd passed through the grid undetected. Before signing off, she told him we would be coming and to be ready to help out if possible.

I guided the *Starfire* through the dense, yellow clouds. It wasn't a smooth ride, considering how much atmospheric turbulence the planet had. Vrynn joined me on the flight deck again, and we chose the ideal landing spot to set down—not too far from the Nexus base, but hopefully not close enough to be noticed.

I stood and grabbed the helmet and plasma rifle Vrynn held out to me. We made our way to the airlock on the lower level. Tera reappeared when we got there.

"Be ready to fly the *Starfire* if we need you to come rescue us," I told my AI friend.

"Mitch, you know I'm not as good as a human pilot."

Vrynn shrugged. "Then use the ship's flight logs to mimic Mitch's piloting, just not the zero-G stuff." She elbowed me playfully.

I didn't mind her teasing about it; I agreed with her wholeheartedly. "Also, we'll need to limit communications to emergencies only. Don't forget to have Dack do the same trick for Vrynn's friends when they get here."

"I told you, they aren't really my—"

I cut Vrynn off with a wink. Fortunately, she was beginning to understand my sense of humor. Unfortunately, she had taken to punching me in the arm when I teased her.

Two minutes later, the airlock dumped us onto the bleak surface of Zerlon Prime with its hazy atmosphere and oppressive temperature.

We settled into a steady pace toward the Nexus base, me absently rubbing my shoulder.

Halfway to the Nexus facility, we had a close call in a low-lying bog where a creature that resembled a cross between a viper and a centipede the size of a crocodile crawled out to see if we looked like its next meal. Fortunately, we were quick enough with our weapons that its venomous fangs only came within a few inches.

Perched on a rocky ledge overlooking the base, I considered our options. "They must have confidence in their detection grid because I only see the two guards."

Vrynn narrowed her eyes. "True. But it would only take one to raise the alarm. I think we should sneak in through the access tunnels." She pointed to a nearby river that ran near the base. A large pipe extended from one of the steep banks, emptying who-knew-what into the murky water.

I sighed. "Crawling through sewage isn't really what I had in mind."

"They won't be expecting it," Vrynn countered.

"And then what? We squeeze out through a shower drain? Or worse?"

Vrynn patted me playfully on the arm. "Don't worry. It'll work out."

I opened my mouth to tell her what I thought about her sewer optimism, but she was already up and moving toward the river.

The drain didn't end up being all that bad. It was large enough to walk in and didn't currently have anything flowing out. The residue on the walls was a swirl of purple and green.

I tried not to think about it.

After a hundred yards or so, we reached a vertical junction. Light spilled in from a grated cover above our heads, so we decided to try it out. At the top rung of the ladder, Vrynn stopped and listened for several seconds.

"Anything?" I whispered.

She waited a few more seconds then shook her head. With only a little scraping, she managed to push the cover off, and we scrambled up into a dimly lit garage. We crept past various ground vehicles and other military equipment.

A door at the end of the room suddenly opened, and an unsuspecting soldier sauntered in. I pulled Vrynn behind a nearby four-wheeled vehicle that looked like a futuristic ATV just as the lights flicked on. As the guy moved down the row of equipment, I got a better look at him. He clearly wasn't a soldier, he was some sort of tech. Not that it mattered; he was working for Nexus.

Unfortunately for us—or him—he decided to turn the corner right at our hiding spot. His face flashed with surprise when he saw us, but it was temporary. As he reached for his sidearm, I swung my plasma rifle, smashing the heavy stock against the side of his head. He crumpled instantly to the ground in a heap.

Before I could even ask for help, Vrynn dragged him into the corner and stuffed him behind a large spare tire. We glanced at his clothes and then at our own improvised versions of Nexus uniforms.

"You could trade with him," Vrynn suggested with a smirk. "You're much broader in the shoulders, though. It might be a tight fit."

It took me a moment to realize what she'd just said. I decided not to dwell on it. We were in the middle of a crucial mission, after all. "If I have a real uniform, and you don't, that'll only call more attention to what you're wearing if anyone sees us together. Let's stick to the original plan and just keep out of sight."

Vrynn shrugged.

We moved to the door, and I peeked into the hall. "Which way?" I asked.

"I bet they have the Mark 7 in the main hangar." Vrynn looked left and right. "Feels like it might be that way." She pointed left.

We snuck out and proceeded left down the long corridor. Our echoing steps on the hard floor sounded like cannon blasts to my ears. My heartbeat pounded double-time, knowing that any second, someone could come around the corner and discover us.

Then someone did.

As we approached the large bay doors that clearly opened into the hangar, another tech came around the corner. He was too far away for me to hit him with the butt of my rifle. And I didn't want to start a firefight in the middle of the Nexus base corridors while we were still trying to go unnoticed—a firefight later would be fine, of course.

We continued walking along as if nothing was out of the ordinary, just one big, happy Nexus family. The tech was still ten feet away before he even raised his eyes to look at us. Just when I thought we had made it, the guy did a double take and stopped.

He opened his mouth to say something, but Vrynn was too quick. She spun a pirouette, her leg extended, and kicked the guy in the gut. He flew backward and smashed into the wall. I wondered what he was about to ask us—probably not for the current time—but I figured I'd never know.

While he was still groggy, we quickly dragged him through the nearest unlocked door we could find—a small testing lab—and bound his hands and feet and gagged his mouth.

Vrynn stood up, admiring her handiwork, and said, "You know, this guy is a little bigger than the last. You could take his uniform, and I could take the first guy's uniform."

The bound tech's eyes went wide, possibly because he now knew we were infiltrating his base, or maybe because we were contemplating leaving him naked in the lab for his comrades to find.

I shook my head. "Vrynn, I'm not going back to the other room to get—"

"I was kidding, Mitch," Vrynn said with a laugh. "Let's just go."

We hustled back into the hall and through the large doors leading into the hangar. A long row of fighters and interceptors lined one wall. But that side of the hangar was mostly empty. If only we had wanted one of those ships, our job would have been easy.

The other half of the hangar was a hive of activity centered around our stolen Mark 7. We walked toward the row of interceptors as if we were supposed to check something. If anyone had been watching us closely, they would have realized that we were up to something. Real technicians don't glance nervously at everything they pass.

Fortunately, no one noticed us.

I pulled Vrynn behind a large storage cabinet within view of the stolen ship. At least a dozen technicians were huddled around the belly of the ship, right below the nose. A large module hung from an opening in the hull. It was the same size as the module I had seen Gralik's soldiers carrying across Gabe's backyard.

That had to be the Quake Drive.

That refrigerator-sized piece of technology had changed the course of my life.

The ship's lift harness had raised the drive module nearly completely inside the hull. We didn't have much time to stop them.

A minute later, Gralik swept into the hangar and approached the technicians. "How much longer?" he asked impatiently.

"We have all the connections secured," the lead technician replied. "I thought we should test the flow through the power conduits before we actually attach the module to the ship's hardpoints."

Gralik scowled. "No. I want it mounted as soon as possible. We'll test the flow of the blah, blah, whatever you said, when we take it into orbit."

"Sir, I wouldn't advise you to—"

"You've already shared your opinion. Stop talking about that. How long will it take to do what I've asked?" Gralik said.

"One hour." When the lead tech saw Gralik's expression, he amended his estimate. "Perhaps only thirty minutes."

I leaned in close to Vrynn. "I hope your friends get her in less than thirty minutes."

She narrowed her eyes at me. "They'll be here."

Our entire plan to get the Quake Drive back hinged on a diversionary attack coming once we were in position. We had timed our infiltration to be within a small window of when they would attack. Now we just needed them to get here before the Quake Drive was fully installed. We would have simply taken it from them as soon as we found it, but there was no way that two of us could overpower this many Nexus soldiers.

So we watched and waited, knowing that every step they took brought them that much closer to having the Quake Drive installed.

Finally, Vrynn said, "We can't wait any longer."

"What's Plan B, overpower the entire lab?" I asked. "Don't forget, there are guards stationed not far away."

"We need *a* diversion," she shot back. "It doesn't have to be the one we had planned on, but there does have to be one."

I looked at her for several seconds, hoping she wasn't planning to do what I knew she was planning to do. "I still think it's a better idea—"

"Just don't miss your chance when it comes." She crouched away from me, back toward the lab doors.

"Vrynn!" I whispered, but it was too late.

As I waited there, crouched behind the large machinery, I stewed. Even if Vrynn was able to successfully create a distraction, I wasn't sure I could get the Quake Drive uninstalled and out of the hangar on my own. Not to mention finding her again after that.

Several minutes passed with the techs getting closer and closer to having the drive installed. A loud shout from the hallway caught everyone's attention. I tensed, knowing this was probably Vrynn's diversion. Another shout—one that sounded suspiciously feminine—was followed by two guards bursting into the lab hangar, dragging a woman between them. A woman with silvery-blue hair.

My stomach sank. Had that been Vrynn's big distraction—getting herself caught?

As Vrynn continued to struggle with the soldiers, the nearby techs wandered over to see what was happening, leaving their work on the Quake Drive.

She had successfully drawn them away, but it seriously complicated what I needed to do next. There was no way I could rescue Vrynn first and then steal the Quake Drive. I would need to get the drive safely out of the hangar, then come back for my co-pilot.

I snuck out from the shadows and dashed over to the ship. The techs had nearly finished connecting the module, so I hustled up the ramp into the empty cargo bay and through to the engineering section.

I located the mounting bolts and began reversing the installation process. The final one slipped from its hole with a series of metallic pings. I cringed, hoping that the techs and the guards were too preoccupied with Vrynn to notice.

I waited a few seconds, and when nothing happened, I used the harness to lower the drive from its position.

Suddenly, Gralik's face appeared in the gap in the hull.

"Hello, Earthling. Do you want me to destroy you?"

I jerked back at the surprise, stumbling to my feet in an effort to escape before he reached the cargo ramp. The sound of boots clattered up the ramp, and a pair of Nexus soldiers grabbed me before I had a chance to go for the side airlock. They dragged me back out of the ship and dumped me on the ground next to Vrynn.

Gralik prowled around the now-partially-removed Quake Drive, yelling words that my implant translated as various profanities when he saw what I'd done. Had the situation not been so dire, I might have laughed at the unconventional usages of several of them.

"That's not really what I had in mind when you left to create a distraction," I muttered to my co-pilot once I had lifted myself off the ground.

"Well, my plan didn't really go the way I thought it would," she replied softly. "The guards didn't seem to be affected by my optimism."

I couldn't help but smile at that.

If I was about to die with this woman, it was comforting to know I had found a true friend. And who knew what it might have become, if only we'd had more time together. Our relationship had changed so gradually over the last two weeks that I wasn't sure when I actually started having feelings for her. It was a shame that the real Gabe and the real Tera had never met Vrynn. I think they would've liked her.

And it was really a shame that we were about to die because we'd never know what could have happened between us.

Gralik's attention turned back to us, and I stifled my grin.

"I'm willing to keep you alive long enough to tell you how stupid you are for giving me the ship that I could install the Quake Drive into"—he held out a hand to the Mark 7 behind him—"and then coming directly to me to be captured. It's been a while since I had anyone go from being such formidable enemies to such hapless idiots so quickly. Pretty sad, actually."

I wasn't sure if there was a point that we were supposed to say anything. I didn't really know the rules of villain monologues.

He loomed over me. "I don't even know why you're here, Earth man. Why don't you go back to your pitiful, little backward planet?"

I stared straight ahead, trying to ignore the desire to jump up and throttle the guy right there. I knew the Dragoons would have leveled me in half a second.

"You on the other hand." Gralik shifted his attention to Vrynn and my body tensed. He reached out and fingered a lock of her blue-tinged, platinum hair. She didn't move a muscle. "You are a very pretty girl," he said almost wistfully, "but you've proven yourself to be too dangerous to keep alive, even to enjoy for an afternoon."

Now I really wanted to kill this guy, not only for the implication of what he'd like to do to Vrynn, but for suggesting that I wasn't as dangerous.

Of course, it was probably true. Vrynn had proven herself to be resourceful and adept at every turn. I'd just bungled things.

Gralik took a step back and looked down at us, almost as if considering what to do next. "Normally, I interrogate my prisoners. They can sometimes have useful information, plus my soldiers could use the practice at fine-tuning their torture skills. And I have to say, I enjoy watching the whole thing. However, you've already given me the Quake Drive ship, so I don't think there's any more information I need out of you."

He turned and walked closer to the Mark 7, bending to inspect the Quake Drive hanging from its berth. "Besides, I really need you dead so that my scientists can finish installing the drive in peace."

He moved closer to us again. "Just so you know—and I can't help but gloat a little about this—I'm going to use this super-ship and its portal drive capability to destroy each and every military force that dares to oppose me." He leaned down toward Vrynn and spoke very slowly and quietly. "Just like I did on Mareesh."

Half a second later, Vrynn snapped. In a flash, her hands were at Gralik's throat. I saw the Dragoon behind her raise the butt-end of his plasma rifle. I dove sideways, hoping to shield her from the blow. The impact caught me in the shoulder and knocked both of us forward.

Gralik used the opportunity to kick Vrynn in the stomach. She lost her grip, and we tumbled into a heap at his feet. Straightening, he nailed me hard in the ribs. Intense pain radiated around my back, but I kept Vrynn hidden underneath me.

"I don't have time for this," Gralik spat.

He waved to the Dragoons, and the leader stepped forward. "Yes, sir?"

"Kill the prisoners. I'm done with them."

"Yes, sir," the leader barked. He motioned the other Dragoons forward.

They pulled me off Vrynn, setting us both back on our feet—though I still felt unsteady from the pain. I grabbed Vrynn's hand, hoping to convey in a touch how sorry I was for everything that had gone wrong. She squeezed my hand tightly.

The squad leader waved to his soldiers, and they lined up in front of us—firing-squad style.

"What are you doing?" Gralik asked.

The lead Dragoon looked confused. "Executing the prisoners? Sir?"

"Not in the hangar lab, you idiot. It'll make a mess," Gralik said. "Besides, we'd just have to take the bodies out to get rid of them. Go kill them outside; it's less work." He sounded like a frustrated teacher trying to explain something to a not-so-bright pupil.

Personally, I didn't care what his reasons were. An extra few minutes alive was always a good few minutes.

Vrynn walked close by me as they marshaled us through the long hangar toward the gaping doors leading outside. She carried herself with courage, even knowing that we were facing the end.

I certainly didn't want to die, but it was such a shame for this amazing woman that I had come to care for so much should have to die, too. It made me wish I had told her how I felt.

I decided I shouldn't waste any more time.

"Vrynn, I think I'm falling for you," I said.

Her brow furrowed as she looked at me. "Really?"

I choked on a nervous laugh. "Yeah."

"Haven't you just been putting up with me?"

I shrugged. "Maybe at the beginning."

"And you don't think I'm too annoying or too optimistic?"

"You certainly are far too optimistic. But I haven't been annoyed by you in a while. I've enjoyed having you around."

"But you tease me all the time," she said.

I rubbed the back of my neck. This wasn't exactly going the way I had hoped. "I guess that's the way I act once I've gotten comfortable with someone. Besides, it's not really teasing, it's more like flirting."

Her brow furrowed. "That doesn't make sense. Plus, it's kind of stupid."

I opened my mouth to attempt an explanation when a guard shoved me in the back. "Shut up, loser."

I shouldn't have waited to tell her.

Now it was going to be too late.

The commanding soldier stopped near a long mound of dirt and glanced around, almost as if he was checking to make sure this would be a good place. After getting chewed out by Gralik, I couldn't blame him.

The soldiers pushed us together and then backed away. I reached for Vrynn's hand, and she held on tight. I squeezed to let her know I was with her until the end.

Glancing to the side, I noticed a small speck against the clouds. As the Dragoon leader organized the soldiers into a firing line, I looked back occasionally. The small spec was now a much larger spec. In fact, it seemed to be more than one speck.

The squad leader moved into position next to the line.

"Be ready to dive," I whispered to Vrynn out of the side of my mouth.

"Haha. You just can't stop teasing me, even when we're about to be executed. I'm willing to concede that firing squads aren't affected by optimism. Are you happy now?"

I grinned back at her. "I'm glad you're finally beginning to see reason, but that's not what I was talking about." I subtly tilted my head toward the incoming ships in the distance.

Hope flashed across her face for a brief moment before she schooled her expression. "They're going to get here about a minute too late."

"Not if I can help it," I said out of the side of my mouth.

She gave me a puzzled look, and we both turned our attention back to the firing squad.

Very loudly—for the benefit of the firing squad—I asked Vrynn, "How high do these idiots need to count in their language before they shoot? Five? Eight?"

Vrynn didn't seem to know what I was talking about because she simply shook her head and shrugged.

That could work in our favor. "You know, do they say 'Ready. Aim. Fire.'? Or is it something like Five. Four. Three. Two—"

The squad leader laughed loudly. "Do you know why you Resistance scum will never win? You do stupid, inefficient things like count to five. All I have to do is say 'kill them' and then you will be dead."

I let my body sag in the most theatrical way I could manage. "Oh, that's too bad. I had always hoped that if I had to die by firing squad that they would say 'Ready. Aim. Fire.'" I looked at the squad leader with my best pleading expression. "Would you mind saying it? Just for me? You could consider it my last request."

The squad leader glanced at his soldiers then back at me with a look of mild amusement on his face. "Really? That's your last request?" Finally, he shrugged. "Why not?"

I had been resisting the urge to glance over to check the approach of what I truly hoped were our allies on their attack run. Instead, I focused my efforts on stalling the squad leader as long as possible.

The squad leader raised his hand. "Prepare."

"No, it's 'Ready'," I complained.

The squad leader smirked at me but didn't correct himself. Apparently, his willingness to humor me only went so far. "Aim," he yelled.

"You know, if you're not going to say it the right way, it's hardly worth doing it," I called to him.

I saw the eyes of one of the soldiers flick to the clouds behind me.

Any second now.

Just as the squad leader yelled, "Fire!" I tackled Vrynn to the ground.

Half a dozen atmospheric missiles streaked past and plowed into the side of the hangar. I threw myself over Vrynn and covered our heads with my hands. The explosion shook the ground and sent shards of metal—and even a few firing squad soldiers—flying through the air.

More missile impacts followed, as well as multiple secondary explosions. When I looked up, the firing squad was gone, leveled by the attack. I grabbed Vrynn by the shoulder and shook her, desperate to know that she was okay. A cut on her right temple was oozing blue blood.

"Are you hurt?" I asked.

She shook her head, still looking a bit dazed. Then a smile crept over her lips. "What was that about my optimism not affecting things?"

I smiled back, and we helped each other stand.

"Let's go," I said.

One of the Dragoons staggered to his feet and aimed a rifle at us. Vrynn and I split directions, and the soldier made the mistake of tracking me.

I dove for the dirt as he fired at me. Fortunately, he was already unstable from the missile explosion. He must have also been too dazed to notice Vrynn taking aim with an abandoned weapon. She had him down with two shots.

"Thanks," I said as I lifted myself from the ground. I grabbed a plasma rifle for myself and we started back toward the hangar.

We reached the broken hangar doors and peered inside. Soldiers and technicians ran back and forth around the hangar, trying to put out fires or running for their lives. Fire reached a stack of missiles and a giant explosion rocked the cavernous room.

Vrynn and I hurried inside, running along the row of interceptors.

"Dragoons," I yelled at Vrynn, pointing at two soldiers moving toward us through the smoke.

We dove behind a nearby maintenance vehicle. The Dragoons either didn't see any nearby cover or didn't think they needed it. The edges of our protective vehicle exploded in plasma rounds as the pair of soldiers laid down suppressive fire.

Maybe they really didn't need cover.

I dropped quickly to the ground below the belly of the vehicle and fired at them, bringing them both down.

"Nice shooting," Vrynn said as we continued past the row of ships.

We made our way toward the lab at the end of the hangar. Smoke swirled and parted, revealing the Mark 7, still intact though somewhat worse for the wear.

Scampering over the wreckage of damaged equipment, we approached the back of the ship. One of the technicians turned around and opened fire at us. I fired back, hitting a nearby computer bank that then burst into flames.

As we cautiously crept closer to the Mark 7, I saw that the ship's cargo bay was still open. A Dragoon stepped out of the shadows and leveled his weapon at us. He fired, narrowly missing. Vrynn fired back, two rounds striking him in the chest. I fired continuously. What I lacked in accuracy, I made up for in quantity, though I can't say if I hit anything.

We ran up the ramp and through the empty bay toward the engineering section. The Quake Drive hung below the outer hull, still in its lift harness.

I looked at Vrynn. "How are we going to get the drive out of here?"

"Let's steal the ship back," she said, an excited look in her eyes.

There had always been an outside possibility that we might have a chance to get the ship back; we'd told Dack we would try, but making it actually work was another thing entirely.

"I'll start winching the Quake Drive back in," I said. "You—"

"I'll go get us in the air." Vrynn was already halfway up the ladder.

I pushed the lift speed to maximum, trying to get the Quake Drive at least to the point where it wasn't dangling from the underside of the ship. I heard the ship's main drive systems come online, and the thrusters spool up.

"I'll take it from here," a voice above me said.

Gralik stood over me, a blaster pointed right at my head.

"I appreciate that you're fixing the mess you made earlier," he continued. "I would say all is forgiven, but I'm sure you understand that I'm still going to kill you."

"Ready to go, Mitch?" Vrynn called from the flight deck.

Gralik brandished the gun at me. "Tell her to wait," he whispered menacingly.

"I'm not quite done," I yelled, not taking my eyes off the gun in my face. "If Tera was here, I could make better time," I added.

Gralik frowned, as if trying to puzzle what that meant. It didn't matter. The message was for Vrynn. We both knew this ship didn't have Tera's matrix. Hopefully, Vrynn would realize that something was wrong.

"I'm not actually sure what to do right now," Gralik said lazily. "I want the drive installed, but apparently you want that, too, and now I'm suspicious. Maybe I should just kill you and then go kill your pretty friend."

At that moment, the ship's default AI shimmered into view next to us. "What task can I help you with?"

With his attention momentarily distracted, I swiped a fist upward, knocking the weapon out of Gralik's hand. The gun fired, and a plasma round exploded against the bulkhead behind me.

That was too close.

The blaster sailed over my head and clattered through the gap next to the drive module and out onto the lab floor. I turned and lunged, tackling Gralik. We sailed through the large door into the empty cargo bay, hitting the deck hard.

He kicked me off of him, and I slid into a nearby wall. Before I could get back to my feet, he was on me, punching. I kneed him in the ribs, kicking him away.

I stood and grabbed a plasma welding torch from a bin. I pointed it straight at his chest. "I think it's time for you to make a gracious exit." I nodded toward the cargo bay ramp.

Unfortunately, Vrynn chose that exact time to engage the thrusters to make our getaway from the base. I teetered to the side, attempting to regain my balance. Gralik rushed forward. I activated the torch, but my aim was off.

He grabbed the torch and tried to wrestle it from me. I punched him in the gut with my free hand, but as he doubled over, he head-butted me. I lost my grip on the torch and it flew toward the open ramp.

I punched Gralik again as the ship swayed and bobbed. The ship rotated to face the hangar door.

Gralik rushed for the torch as it slid aft. I knew I wouldn't have the stamina to take on a trained soldier in a prolonged hand-to-hand fight. Worse, I knew that if he got the torch first, he would eventually kill me and Vrynn.

So I did the only thing I could think of.

When he bent down to grab it, I kicked him in the butt.

Gralik tumbled forward in an olympics-worthy front flip. Unfortunately, we weren't high enough off the hangar floor for him to break his neck on impact, thus ridding the Bonara cluster of his menace. Instead, he landed hard on his back and slid several feet into a broken equipment station.

I stood on the edge of the ramp and watched Gralik slowly get back to his feet as we sailed through the hangar. The last thing I saw was Gralik grabbing a rifle from the hands of an approaching soldier and taking hopeless shots at us as we soared down the long hangar and out the broken doors.

"We're clear!" Vrynn yelled.

I hated to dash her hopes, but I'd seen multiple interceptors relatively intact. "We're not getting away that easy. Be ready."

As we sped into the atmosphere, I went back to the engineering room to check on the Quake Drive. It was still dangling by the lift harness. I activated the lift mechanism, but it groaned in protest.

Dack stood nearby, a quizzical expression on his holographic face. "Might I be of assistance?"

"I'm trying to get the drive module back into the ship," I grunted as I yanked and pulled on the harness lines, hoping to help the lift mechanism.

"This lift will not work properly while the ship is in flight," Dack stated bluntly.

No surprise there.

"We've got a problem," Vrynn said over the comm. "Three enemy fighters just launched and they're coming after us."

"Yeah, we've got a problem down here, too. We can't get the Quake Drive back into the ship unless we're on the ground—or in orbit."

"Let's do the orbit one," Vrynn said. "But you're better at atmospheric maneuvers, so maybe you could get up here and keep us alive a little longer."

The air whistling in through the gaps around the Quake Drive reminded me that, with the drive only halfway installed, the air wouldn't stay in the ship once we left the atmosphere.

I hustled over to the airlock and donned my EVA suit.

Vrynn frowned when I entered the flight deck. "Are you going for a spacewalk?" A moment later, her eyes got big. "Oh yeah, we're leaking air in the drive bay, aren't we?"

Dack was suddenly standing at my side. "We are indeed losing our cabin pressure at an alarming rate," he said.

I flinched at his unexpected arrival, and a grin spread across Vrynn's lips.

"I'd better get one of those." She indicated my EVA suit.

"Unless you think the vacuum of space can be affected by your optimism," I replied.

She pulled a face at me, but it was a playful expression.

I jumped into the pilot's seat and took over flying while she went and got into a suit of her own. Dack stood stoically behind my seat, ready to give sterile, annoying advice, I suppose.

It really made me miss Tera.

The enemy fighters blinking on the tactical display continued gaining on us. I pushed the throttle to maximum, but it made no difference. In the *Starfire*, we could outrun just about anything, but we were at a major disadvantage, aerodynamically, with the drive hanging underneath. I plunged the ship into a particularly dense cloud bank. It couldn't hurt to recycle an old trick.

Vrynn rejoined me on the flight deck a few minutes later. "I can take over flying again if you want to get back down to engineering to install the drive."

I shook my head. "Even in orbit, we'll never get the drive installed. Not with these fighters bearing down on us." I indicated the tactical display where two new dots had appeared, just barely launched from the Nexus base.

"Can we just hide here in the clouds while you do the repairs?" Vrynn asked.

Almost as if in answer to her question, several plasma rounds exploded very close to us. It hadn't taken the enemy fighters long to switch to radar targeting. I began weaving back and forth, hoping the enemy fighters wouldn't be able to track us well enough to get off a clean shot.

"Could we transfer the Quake Drive to the *Starfire*?" Vrynn suggested. "Then we could make our getaway."

That wasn't a bad idea, but we couldn't just wait until Tera brought the ship over, not with so many enemy fighters tracking us. Then I had a different idea occur to me. "Dack, establish a comm link to the *Starfire*. We're going to need Tera's help."

"Initiating link," Dack replied.

A few seconds later, Tera's face shimmered into view on the intra-ship channel. "Tera, I need you to fly the ship into orbit to pick up the Quake Drive—and us—before any of the Nexus ships can get us."

"You want me to fly the ship?" Tera asked, a look of incredulity on her face. "By myself? Into space?"

"Yes, it's the only way this is going to work," I said.

Tera shook her head. "You know I can't fly the ship as well as a human pilot. I told you that the very first time we flew together."

"I know you told me that, but I need you to stretch yourself. It's what humans do." I looked at the facsimile of my friend for several long seconds. "It's the only way Vrynn and I are going to survive this."

Another series of explosions rocked the ship.

"We have to do this now," Vrynn insisted. "If they breach the Quake Drive, we're done."

I turned back to Tera. "You can do this. I'm transmitting our coordinates and heading. Do some quick orbital trajectories and that'll be close enough." I tapped the console to send her the information, then gave her a knowing smile. "Don't leave us hanging."

Tera nodded. She even took a deep breath to steel herself against her fears. At least, her matrix simulated a calming breath.

It occurred to me that I had never gotten around to making any of those tweaks to improve her personality that I thought I would. But then I realized that I wouldn't want to make those changes, anyway. This AI version of Tera was my friend, and I liked her just the way she was, simulated insecurities and all.

I pulled back on the control sticks, sending us into a steep climb towards the edge of the atmosphere. With a few commands to the auto-pilot, I locked in the course. Hopefully, my calculations were correct, otherwise this would be the most anti-climactic escape plan ever.

I jumped from my seat. "Dack, meet me in engineering," I said as I raced toward the ladder.

Right as my boots hit the deck of the lower level, the ship's default AI shimmered into view in the hallway outside engineering. "Ready to assist you."

"I need you to interface with the auto-pilot and take over flying the ship for me."

Dack opened his mouth to complain, but I anticipated his objections.

"I know you're not programmed to fly as well as a human pilot, but this is important. I need you to keep us from getting destroyed and then do a very specific maneuver to help us get safely away. After that, you can fly the ship wherever you want, as long as you get away from Nexus."

The AI tilted his head to the side. "I will evade the pursuing enemy ships and execute the desired maneuver to help you escape safely,

I nodded as Vrynn joined me. She handed me a helmet. "You wouldn't want to forget this," she said with a laugh.

We both fastened our helmets in place and stood over the drive module dangling in its bay. I caught glimpses of the blankets of clouds below us. According to the status console on the wall, we were passing the stratosphere. In a few more seconds, we would be clear of all atmosphere and ready for our death-defying escape.

Dack continued to regard us with mild amusement mixed with detached curiosity. I realized that the ship was weaving back and forth, flashes of rounds from the Nexus interceptors occasionally lighting the view below the Quake Drive.

"You're actually flying the ship right now, aren't you?" I asked Dack.

"Affirmative," he answered.

"And you can fly the ship and communicate with me at the same time?"

"Of course, my matrix can interface with the ship's flight systems while still carrying on a conversation.

"Hmm, I knew she could've done both," I muttered.

"What did you say?" Dack asked.

I waved my hands down. "Nevermind."

"When we release the drive module, I need you to fire a barrage of every weapon the ship has back toward the enemy fighters."

"I can't fire the ship's weapons systems," the AI said. "That's a safety feature hard-wired into the ship."

"Can you fire the weapons to defend this ship?" I asked.

"If the ship is in danger, the defense cannons can fire temporarily until the threat is neutralized or flees."

"Can you fire the weapons in a way that would intentionally miss an enemy target?"

Dack tilted his head. "There is nothing preventing me from doing that."

"Perfect. Then consider this your standing order," I said. "You can fire the weapons to create a distraction—like the one we need right now—and you can fire the weapons to protect the ship. Oh, and don't let those guys capture you again." I thumbed in the direction of our pursuers.

The AI again tilted its head to the side. "I will do that. Where should I go after you are safely away?"

"Anywhere you want," Vrynn replied with a smile.

"I'm not sure I *want* anything," Dack replied.

"Then use your random number algorithm. That'll keep things interesting," I said. "Just don't let Gralik or any Nexus-affiliated forces catch you."

I checked the status display again.

"Okay, we're almost to the right altitude." I turned to Dack. "Ready for the distraction?"

"Affirmative," he said.

I looked at Vrynn, and she nodded that she was ready. I turned back to the altitude readout and placed my hand on the lift harness release lever. "Okay, ready to go in three . . . two . . . one." I pulled the lever and jumped for Vrynn at the same time.

The Quake Drive—with Vrynn and me riding it like a wild bull—dropped quickly away from the ship. A split second later, the surrounding space exploded with light as Dack unleashed his arsenal of plasma rounds and ion bursts. I watched the ship pull away from our trajectory, performing a wide vertical loop.

Slowly, as Dack pulled the attention of the enemy fighters away, the space around us became calm. I looked down at the cloudy planet Zerlon. Even though I knew we were moving steadily away, we seemed to float peacefully above it. Of course, our trip was not going to end well unless Tera could find us.

I had programmed a trajectory into the ship that put us into half-orbit. We would float above Zerlon for half a rotation—enough to be well away from the Nexus base and the pursuing fighters. But we weren't truly in orbit. Without intervention, our momentum would carry us back into the atmosphere at high speed where we would either burn to a crisp because of the air resistance or we would splat against the ground at supersonic speeds.

I switched on my suit-to-suit communicator. "I think it worked. None of the interceptors followed us."

Vrynn twisted around to look behind us, and the light of the Zerlon sun filtered through her faceplate, making her eyes shine bright-blue. "They're all chasing Dack's ship," she said. "If we ever see him again, remind me to thank him for saving our lives."

Now that we were out of immediate danger of being blown up, I looked around. A sudden wave of vertigo hit me, probably because my brain had finally caught up that I was flying through space with nothing more solid under me than a portal-creating jump core. I clung to Vrynn—and the Quake Drive—for dear life. Vrynn didn't seem to notice, or mind anyway. After a few minutes, my brain came to the conclusion that there was no falling in space, and the vertigo began to ease. I decided to think of something to distract myself.

"Do you think Tera will be able to find us?" I asked.

"I hope so." She looked at the empty space around us.

I glanced down at the yellowish-white clouds below and then at the star field that completely engulfed my vision. Floating above a planet was probably the most out-of-this-world experience I'd had yet, and I was reminded that we were eventually going to be reclaimed by its gravity.

After drifting through space for a while, an apogee warning popped up on my suit. That meant we were officially falling back toward Verlon Prime. It also meant that we had less than twenty minutes for Tera to find us.

Vrynn's suit must have given her a similar warning because she turned to me with a grim expression. "Maybe she won't find us."

It was one of the few pessimistic things I'd ever heard her say. I was just about to tell her that, and maybe make a joke to lighten the mood, when she stopped me with a look.

Those wide, deep-blue eyes stared back at me.

"Mitch?" She said my name with such feeling that I knew whatever the next words out of her mouth were, I would agree to do that and more.

I cleared the lump in my throat. "Yeah?"

"I've been thinking about what you said when we were about to die earlier."

"Oh, the earlier about-to-die. Not this about-to-die." Apparently, I couldn't help cracking jokes, even when I knew she was being serious.

Vrynn tried to ignore me, but the small smile gave her away. She turned somber again. "I have to tell you something," she added, almost in a whisper.

I reached out and gave her hand a squeeze, hoping she could feel it through the EVA suits. I had often seen my best friend Gabe do the same thing with his wife, Tera. I figured it would apply here.

Vrynn lifted our clasped gloves and stared at them, clearly avoiding making eye contact with me. "I think I might be falling for you, too," she said, a shy smile on her lips.

If I hadn't been floating several hundred kilometers above the planet, I would definitely have fallen over. "Really? Sometimes I think you barely tolerate me, and the rest of the time, it seems like you only want to be friends."

She shrugged. "I've been unsuccessfully denying my feelings for a while now."

"Wow." I shook my head in disbelief.

It was just my luck.

I finally find a woman I care about—and who apparently feels the same about me—and we wait until we're about to plummet to our deaths before finally talking about our feelings.

"If we do survive this," Vrynn said. "I don't want you to go back to . . . Earth." She said the actual word. It wasn't a translation through my implant. She had learned how to say the name of my home.

I'm sure I was grinning like an idiot.

"I don't want you to go back to Earth," she said, stumbling a little on the name again, "because I want you to stay here. With me."

I pulled her into an embrace. If it was an awkward one, I blame the EVA suits.

I'm not sure how long we floated there, holding each other. It was less than twenty minutes because we hadn't burned up yet when I saw a dark shadow pass over us. I turned around and saw the *Starfire* closing in.

I wanted to jump for joy, but I settled for waving my arms like a lunatic.

Tera maneuvered the ship in front of us, and we floated into the airlock. As soon as the cycle finished, I pulled off my helmet and threw open the hatch. "Tera, you're amazing!"

My holographic friend appeared in the hallway outside the airlock. She looked a little embarrassed at the compliment. I didn't even care.

"Triple check that no ships are within sensor range, and then double-jump us out of here. Take us somewhere crowded first, so they won't find us."

"How about the cliff restaurant over the falls on Kalera Five?" Vrynn asked with a mischievous grin.

I smiled back. "Definitely."

Chapter Seventeen

With a colorful drink in one hand, I leaned back in my chair and looked out over the Colossal Falls of Kalera Five. I had barely even questioned the contents of the drink the waiter had brought me. Apparently, three weeks in the Bonara Cluster—along with a few violent encounters with aliens—had cured me of worrying about something as insignificant as the ingredients of an exotic drink.

Vrynn had somehow been able to get us a table on the glass balcony directly over the falls. I had expected it to be difficult to carry on a conversation, but there must have been some sort of noise canceling happening because the falls only made a dull murmur in the background.

Vrynn's gaze drifted from the falls to me, gradually shifting from contented to serious. "Mitch, I think we need to talk."

That was never a good sign.

But I knew that if she was the one who wanted to talk, I would be the one to let her start.

"Sometimes, when people are in stressful situations—particularly life-or-death ones—they can say things that they later regret."

I stared straight into those gorgeous eyes of hers. "Do you regret telling me how you feel?"

She frowned. "Maybe regret is the wrong word." She traced a finger along the outside of her drink glass. "But I think it's natural for feelings to get amplified when a person thinks they're about to die."

"So you don't actually like me." I couldn't help teasing her a little because I so rarely saw her feeling awkward. And I couldn't help grinning about it either.

Vrynn cocked her head to the side and gave me a deadpan look. "Now you're being intentionally difficult. Is this that stupid teasing we were talking about?"

"Probably," I said with a noncommittal shrug.

She blew out a breath. "Anyway, I do like you; I'm just not ready to wrap ourselves together."

My eyebrows went up at that description—not because it necessarily sounded bad. Then my implant retranslated "be committed to each other." That made more sense.

She gazed across the table at me. Her posture and expression projected confidence, but something in those captivating eyes betrayed vulnerability.

Was she denying her true feelings again, just to see how I would react?

I took a deep breath, considering my words. I definitely didn't want to mess this one up. "Maybe we did share more with each other than we normally would have because we thought we were about to die. But those feelings are in here somewhere." I tapped my chest.

Vrynn's breath caught, but she didn't say anything.

I figured I might as well try to put into words how I really felt—hopefully without scaring her off. "The reality is, there's no one in the entire Bonara Cluster that I'd rather have by my side than you."

Her lips grew into a wide smile, and that adorable blush colored her cheeks. That was a good sign.

"So how about this? For now, let's be partners. We'll use the *Starfire* to protect the weaker settlements from bullies like Nexus, and maybe even make the cluster a better place. And as far as romantic feelings . . . we can see what happens."

She tilted her head, as if contemplating my plan, and a sly smirk spread across her blue-tinted lips. "I like that."

I leaned back in my chair again, considering the turbulent beauty of the falls. They reflected the giddy excitement in my chest at the thought of having Vrynn with me for whatever lay ahead. "I wouldn't mind staying on Kalera Five for a while. Maybe we could make this our base of operations."

Vrynn shook her head. "We spent our last Bonmarks on the drinks."

My brow shot up. "We don't have enough money for a meal?"

"Nope," she replied. "But we had to at least buy drinks to get the view." She spread a hand out toward the tumultuous water in front of us.

I nodded. "So we'll need to find somewhere cheap to set up our secret lair."

Vrynn's smile widened. "I think I have an idea."

* * *

"After rescuing you from this desolate rock, this is the last place I'd have thought you'd want to come back to," I said as I brought the ship in for a soft landing next to the Thetis Max mining facility.

Vrynn smacked my arm. "You didn't rescue me. Stood me up for three weeks and then threatened to leave me here is more like it."

"Agree to disagree," I said.

"Tera, if we can get the main hangar door open, can you pull the ship in for us?" Vrynn asked. She sounded like a parent giving a new teenage driver a simple task to build their confidence.

Tera shrugged. "Yeah, I can do that."

Vrynn and I left the ship through the airlock and walked the short distance to the main mining facility. With a few codes on the derelict controls, Vrynn was able to get the system back to life.

After activating the hangar airlock, Vrynn and I set off to explore the rest of the facility. It was interesting this time, though. I wasn't creeping through the halls waiting for some monster to jump out at me—though maybe I should have been. I was looking at the rooms, imagining what we could do to make things livable. It was almost like touring a fixer upper home with my—I wasn't sure what to call Vrynn yet. Friend? Partner?

By the time we had gone through most of the main building, I was feeling overwhelmed. Vrynn, on the other hand, was bouncing off the walls with excitement.

"Can you imagine putting an exercise room in here?" She pointed to an abandoned machine shop.

I actually could imagine that because most of the manufacturing equipment in that room looked eerily similar to the implements of torture they used at my local gym.

Vrynn ran to the next room. "And with a little fixing up, we could use this room for relaxing." She ran to the next room. "And the galley could easily be converted to a more practical kitchen." She turned back to me, enthusiasm almost spilling out of her. "You haven't said anything yet. What do you think about my ideas?"

I smiled, thinking that if someone had come to me a month ago and said that I would be forced to live on a desolate mining moon hundreds of light years away, I would have thought it was meant to be a prison sentence. But watching Vrynn's excitement, and being forced to begrudgingly admit that I shared some of it, I realized that this didn't feel like a prison sentence at all.

It felt like an adventure.

"Well?" Vrynn prompted when I didn't immediately answer.

Knowing that it hardly mattered what I thought—she would probably make the changes anyway—I said, "I think it sounds great. Maybe, before we commit to any or all of it, we should make sure we have all the right tools and materials."

As we walked back to the hangar, Vrynn continued talking about all the plans she had for converting the facility into a home—more like a mansion with what she had in mind.

We found Tera in the cargo bay with Skeeter and HelperBot next to her, huddled over a large crate. When she saw us, she quickly stepped in front of the crate to block our view, which didn't really make sense, given that she was mostly translucent. Skeeter and HelperBot moved in front of Tera, almost as if they were protecting her. Whether that was a result of their own algorithms or the link that Tera had with them, I wasn't sure.

"What's going on, Tera?" I asked.

"Oh nothing, we're just doing some regular ship stuff."

That sounded sufficiently vague to me.

"Are you sure? Because I've noticed some strange things lately. HelperBot and Skeeter have both been out of the ship at odd times. They barely got back to the *Starfire* in time on Daeko III before we launched to engage the Nexus ships. But I can't figure out why they would've been outside the ship at all during our mission in the casino. It makes me wonder if I should look at their guidance subroutines for a glitch or something."

Tera stepped forward, an anxious expression on her face. "No. Please don't change their programming. It's not their fault; it's mine. I've been giving them the instructions that made them do those things."

I scrutinized Tera's projection. Nothing seemed to be off about her. "Do you think something might be wrong with your matrix?" I asked.

Tera stared at me for a long time, looking indecisive. I knew she could process calculations a billion times faster than my brain could. So if she was having this much trouble with a decision, it must be something big.

"There are some settings in my matrix that have been changed considerably from the original programming," Tera said.

"Yeah, I know. You and Gabe tweaked quite a bit." I grinned. "You look nothing like Dack."

I had hoped to lighten the mood with a joke, but Tera was so worked up about it that she didn't even react.

She shook her head. "No, you don't understand. Gabe made the AI matrix look like his wife, but just changing the appearance wasn't enough. I was still mostly indifferent to him, and that wasn't what the real Tera was like at all. So together, we wrote new subroutines that affected my emotional attachment, among other things." She winced, almost as if she was embarrassed. "And some of the changes might not have been the best thing for my primary role as the ship's flight assistant."

That got my attention.

She held both hands out. "Don't worry, though. There's no risk to the *Starfire*. I would never do anything to harm you or the ship. It's just that, after interacting with the default AI, I've realized how much of my matrix Gabe and I actually changed." She bit her lip. "But I can't bear the thought of resetting my programming."

"I've been spending time with Dack, too, and I don't want you to change back," I said with a grin. For some reason, my jokes weren't improving her mood, so I tried some gentle reassurance. "I think Gabe did a great job integrating the real Tera's personality into your matrix. Keep it exactly the way it is."

Tera gave me a look that was both relieved and guilty at the same time. I couldn't understand why.

Fortunately, Vrynn jumped in. "Tera, are those changes causing some other problems?"

"Well, that sorta depends on how you feel about what I've done." She actually looked like a teenage girl who'd been caught sneaking in after curfew.

"Then you'd better go ahead and tell us," I said. "I think you'll feel better."

"After Gabe di—" She gulped. "When we lost Gabe, my emotional processing was completely shattered, as I'm sure you noticed."

I certainly remembered it well, though it almost seemed like a lifetime ago.

"Everything in my altered subroutines told me I needed something of Gabe's that I could keep. Something to remember him by. So, as soon as I had a chance, I instructed the med bed to remove Gabe's watch. I know that sounds like stealing, but I'm sorta his wife, so it would kinda belong to me, anyway."

I lifted a shoulder. "Probably wouldn't hold up in an estate dispute on Earth, but that doesn't matter here." I wasn't worried about Gabe's watch either way.

"Just know that I would never take anything that belonged to you or that was part of the ownership of the ship. That's strictly against my most basic programming."

I waved off her apology. "It's okay, Tera. I believe you. What happened next?" I prodded.

"That watch was all I had of Gabe, but it still wasn't enough. So I came up with a new plan, a plan that has pretty much consumed my efforts anytime we're at a spaceport and you leave the ship.

"Starting with Gabe's watch, I negotiated deals with nearby ships for more and more valuable items. The first trade was the hardest, letting Gabe's watch go to a jewelry merchant on New Talpreus. But it got easier after that."

I'm sure my face showed my surprise. My AI was running a bartering business on the side.

"I really hit the jackpot on Daeko III. Most of the robots and computers on the other ships hate working for mercenaries. They pretty much gave away anything the crew wouldn't miss or might assume they had lost while drunk in the casino."

I chuckled at the idea of those mercenary crews getting a little more of what they deserved.

"I sold everything during our stop on Kalera Five and used the credits to buy what I've been dreaming of."

I couldn't help but think of Tera as a hard-working teenager saving up for a bike or a used car. "And what have you been working so hard to buy?"

"An android."

"You bought an android?" Vrynn asked with a note of excitement.

"Well, just the body of the android. On our first stop on New Talpreus, I learned that there were customizable android bodies that could be bought for cheap if you were willing to do the hard work of transferring the actual intelligence into it."

I realized what she was trying to do. My AI was trying to get a body for herself. I smiled broadly. "So, what body did you choose? Will it look like teenage Tera? Or did you go for adult Tera?"

Tera stared at me, looking confused. "Why would I buy an android that looked like me?"

"Don't you want to get a body?" I asked. "Isn't that what your plan was all along?"

Tera frowned and shook her head. "I didn't buy an android body for myself."

That left me confused.

Tera slowly stepped out of the way. There was a rustling sound from inside the large crate, and out stepped Gabe.

My jaw dropped.

My best friend. The one who I had buried in the Shonara family circle on Otania Sancterum was standing right in front of me.

The logical side of my brain caught up a few seconds later. This wasn't really Gabe; it was an android body with his physical features. I stepped forward to get a better look. On closer inspection, the mechanical aspects of the android became more apparent. Its skin wasn't quite realistic, and the way that it moved looked a little mechanical.

Still, it was an impressive replica of my friend Gabe at fifteen or sixteen. I was floored.

Even more so when the android opened its mouth to speak.

"Hey, Mitch," the android said.

That voice instantly took me back to my high school days. You could have knocked me over with a feather.

Blinking back the sudden flood of emotions, I commented to Tera, "I see you picked the high school age for it."

"What other age would I pick?" Tera replied.

That was pretty obvious, considering she was the teenage version of my friend.

"Does it know what's going on?" I asked her.

Tera frowned at me. "Yes, *he* knows what's going on. Why don't you talk to him?"

I turned to the robot version of my best friend. "Hey, Gabe. What's up?" I partially expected the robot to answer "the sky" because that's what my best friend had always said in junior high.

Robo-Gabe cocked his head side to side, considering me. "Mitch, you know I'm not the real Gabe, right? I'm a mechanical being with a recursive matrix to simulate consciousness. I've been programmed with the memories of the real Gabe."

His voice sounded so close that I could almost let myself be convinced. "Yeah, buddy, I know," I said softly.

"But if I was the real Gabe, I would have said 'the sky'."

His laugh sounded forced and a little mechanical, but it still brought a smile to my face.

"I have memories of interacting with Tera on the ship on Earth. The real Gabe was trying to program her to behave like his wife." Robo-Gabe turned to Tera. "Was the effort a success?"

Tera beamed at him, a look of complete and utter adoration in her eyes. "Yes. It was."

Robo-Gabe gave her a stiff smile. He turned his attention back toward Vrynn and me, as if searching the cargo bay for something. "Where is the real Gabe? Is he here?"

I swallowed against a sudden lump in my throat. "Uh, no. He died."

"Death is a sad thing, I think," Robo-Gabe said. "Can you explain it to me?"

"Not right now, buddy," I said with a chuckle. This was going to be interesting. I turned to Tera. "Where did you get Gabe's personality to make the transfer?"

"When Gabe was working to get Tera's personality installed into my matrix, we experimented with a neural interface. He thought it might be possible to create a realistic re-creation of his wife just using his memories of her. The interface wasn't able to pull the level of detail necessary to create a working personality. But it did capture a lot of Gabe's own personality and memories. That's what I used to program him."

I shook my head in disbelief at what she had accomplished.

"I guess you could say she returned the favor," Gabe said with a robotic chuckle.

"Yeah, I guess you could say that," I replied.

I looked from Gabe to Tera, then around the cargo bay at Skeeter, Rascal, and HelperBot. Finally, I let my gaze rest on Vrynn. My chest expanded at the thought of making a new life in the Bonara Cluster with her—and, sort of, my friends Gabe and Tera. It didn't mean I'd never want to visit Earth—I was sure there would be reasons to go back at some point—but I couldn't wait to see what the future held.

"Remember when we said we weren't quite ready to wrap ourselves together?" I used the literal phrase she had said earlier, and I was rewarded with another aqua blush. "How do you feel about starting a family?"

She glanced around our little group as if she couldn't believe the change of events, either. "I think we've got one already, whether we want it or not."

I smiled at her. "We do indeed."

Reviews and Sequel Novella

Thanks so much for reading my book. I hope you enjoyed it. Book 2 is already out. Don't forget to pick it up.

If I could ask one quick favor. Please leave a book review or even just a quick rating on the Amazon Page.

After that, you can sign up for my newsletter to get access to the free sequel novella (www.myleschristensen.com/starship1) about Mitch and Vrynn trying to set up their home base on Thetis Max. Plus, being subscribed to the newsletter means I'll let you know when the next book is coming out.

Acknowledgements

Thanks to my readers. Knowing that you enjoy what I write definitely keeps me going.

I appreciate the early feedback that I got from my beta readers: Ryan_Reads, Khal17, Maddy216, and BingeingonBooks. You helped me know the story was good but that it needed a little tweaking.

Thanks to my family for supporting me in my writing efforts and not thinking I'm crazy for wishing some parts of these stories were real.

As always, my biggest thanks go to my sweet wife. Thanks for editing this one for me. Sorry sci-fi isn't really your thing. You're a trooper, though.

Myles Christensen loves to write exciting adventures because he loves to read exciting adventures. The hopeless romantic in him will usually sprinkle a teensy bit of romance into his stories. While writing, he listens to music that matches—and sometimes inspires—the storyline.

His mild-mannered alter ego is a product development engineer, university professor, and game inventor. He lives in Utah with his wife and children.

Printed in Dunstable, United Kingdom